NIGHT OF THE TARANTA

Christoph John

Also Available

The Steel Wolf
Gilgamesh
Back to the Devil

About the author

Christoph John lives, works and writes in south London. After a long career in retail management, he took a step back to fulfil his ambition of publishing a novel. The result was the first Jon Drago novel, *Steel Wolf*. A follow up, *Gilgamesh*, promptly followed. Both titles were available through Troubadour. Subsequently Chris won a Koestler Award for a poetry pamphlet *The Silence of Butterflies*. Chris is currently an Arts and Humanities student with The Open University. He enjoys the cinema, literature, music, history, European culture, wine and gastronomy – but not necessarily in that order. *Night of the Taranta* is the fourth Jon Drago thriller.

http://www.facebook.com/christophjohnauthor

Acknowledgements

Many thanks must go to Claire Selishta at Quill and Scroll, who took the time to edit and proof this novel. Her attention and assistance has proved invaluable. A quick word of thanks to my beta-reader from r22aug who picked up what we missed. I am forever grateful for the encouragement and patience of all my family and friends, far and wide without whom *Night of the Taranta* would never have made it into print.

Copyright *Night of the Taranta* © 2023 Christoph John

Self-published through KDP by Christoph John

ISBN 9798864221334

The characters and situations in this book are entirely fictional. and bear no relation to actual persons or happenings. Several genuine locations have been mentioned and sometimes elaborated on, but all actions remain imaginary.

Front cover image: Adobe Stock #399112006 *Pick the red ruby diamond in to the sun at Patong beach, Phuket* by Narong Nemham, licenced to the author.

NIGHT OF THE TARANTA

One 7
Two 18
Three 29
Four 37
Five 48
Six 64
Seven 83
Eight 101
Nine 118
Ten 134
Eleven 151
Twelve 165
Thirteen 183
Fourteen 201
Fifteen 214
Sixteen 229
Seventeen 239
Eighteen 251
Nineteen 263
Twenty 275
Twenty One 287
Twenty Two 300
Twenty Three 319
Twenty Four 332
Twenty Five 350

One

The Heel of Italy

When Jon Drago first saw her, he sucked in a breath. She was spectacularly beautiful. The most splendid thing in the marina. She was perched on the outskirts away from the ferry routes and fishing boats. She had anchored four days ago and was loitering, lapping up the envious glances of lesser ships.

Drago studied the big yacht. The white edifice, almost seventy metres of her, looked impressive even at distance. Through the binoculars, she became a sleek powerful looking craft, sitting low in the water on a broad monohull and composed of only three staggered tiers, including the bridge deck. The cabins were all below decks, identified by two lines of squashed oval portholes, a row of eyes staring at the sea. The differing sizes hinted at the importance of each room. Drago noted the flat bow. It would create a lot of drag, unusual for a cruiser. He would have expected to see a slimmer, knife-edge design. Emblazoned in broad black italics on both the prow and on the aft section was her name: *Diamantin*.

Two power boats were circling from the stern of the yacht. A pair of water skiers trailed behind, both clad in black body suits including a head covering. They carved wide white curves through the wash, the two foaming ridges crashing against one another. They raced until one of the men lost balance and tumbled into the water. After a swift recovery and much laughter, they raced again. They skied like this for about half an hour, then the boats trundled up to the shore, heading for one of the few genuine spots of yellow sand. The few remaining swimmers avoided the moving obstacles with some discomfort. The skiers and drivers chatted and drank Coca Cola. It might have been laced with rum such was the men's dreadful ability to ski. After a time, they pushed the boats off the shingle and dipped the outboards back into the water. The two skiers waded into the sea, bent down to fix their skis and held the plastic handle, waiting for the tow line to tense. As the throttles extended, the lines flicked out of the water snapping like angry serpents. For a moment the men absorbed the strain, bending slightly forward, then they rose out of a crouch and took off, soaring across Neptune's lair.

It was 8pm. The night waves licked at the tips of Drago's plimsoles. He sat, perched on the very edge of a rocky promontory. A few hundred yards up the coast was the Atlantis Club, a playground for the Milanese who travelled from their northern homes to the sweltering south every summer and decamped every day to the beach bar with its varnished wooden pontoons.

Drago didn't wear a watch. He used his mobile to tell the time. But there was no need even for that today. The time was written on the faces and in the actions of the people who spent their days at the Atlantis. The day was drawing in for the tourists who soaked up the sun and drank the beer.

Otranto sprawled south. Early shadows extended over the colourful rooftops, swamped by the looming Castello Aragonese. The town's historic citadel was about to be bathed in warm ruby light. The harbour would be filling with returning tourist launches, those small affairs that still plied a trade along the heel of Italy. Hungry foreigners would be disembarking, lilting after a day visiting coves and grottos. Fishermen would be landing baby octopus and swordfish, ready to be delivered to restaurants like Dal Baffo, Zia Fernanda and Vicino's, ready to be served to those same ravenous stomachs. Meanwhile, along the wooden decks of the Atlantis Club, the sunbeds began to empty and the parasols came down as the sky turned from a bright summer blur to indigo ink and everything was tinted in shades of crimson.

Drago wasn't there for the sunset. He wasn't there to admire the yacht either. He was there to watch the water skiers who, it transpired, had learnt nothing from the lessons of yesterday: it was too late an hour to be water skiing.

One of the motorboats towed its charge around the far side of the yacht. As the skier rounded the prow of *Diamantin*, there was a flurry of white and the black figure tumbled and disappeared. He'd come off yet again. The motor launch sidled back to pick him up and affix any loose blades. It was just like yesterday.

The man stayed under. Even encumbered by skis, Drago had

expected him to float quickly or swim to the surface, but he stayed down. Was the line caught? Drago couldn't see the driver untangling anything. He lost count of the seconds.

As soon as the first launch cleared the way, the other attempted a pass with the same sharp-angled manoeuvre. It was obvious they wouldn't make it. Unceremoniously, the second skier fell. Drago put aside the binoculars and thoughtfully lit a cigarette. Yesterday, he hadn't taken in what the men were doing, not until the accident.

It had happened suddenly. Early evening had been slipping across the bay. He recalled the sun was low and there was a slight salty chill in the air. Cohorts of bathers were packing up as if a whistle had been blown at a school playground. A young couple-in-love were making one final turn of the shore in a yellow pedalo. Boys cheered as they competed at foot volleyball. Girls laughed. The juice and gelato sellers had congregated to discuss the day's trade and which women wore the tightest bikinis. Sunglasses were lifted.

The same scene would be enacted up and down the Otranto coast. Holidaymakers retreating, preparing for the promenade walk along Lungomare and then pizza or risotto and a glass of earthy primitivo.

Drago had been reclining on a deck chair, laid flat, thinking vaguely about the cookery course, how Signora di Pace had blended salts and spices to flavour the anchovies, mussels and clams and how many days old asparagus had to be before it was considered too old for omelettes. And he was also thinking about the forthcoming evening meal, where they would eat and drink and afterwards the romantic walk back to the little room in the Hotel San Pietro and another evening of guilty passion.

He saw it happen on the rim of his sightline. The speedboat, its engine purring, crossed the path of a bobbing head. He saw the chestnut hair muzzled by the bright green snorkel and mask. Madeleine been underwater and had just resurfaced. Her head spun. Drago thought he saw the body pitch out of the water attempting to avoid the inevitable. He thought the skis struck her shoulder. He heard the scream even over the sound of the gunning engines.

For a moment the scene on the beach was a photograph. Everything paused. Only the motorboats and the waves moved. The head and its green mask disappeared, then resurfaced, rocking gently on the evening tide.

***

There was a girl who lived in the flat below Jon Drago. She was called Madeleine and she was an arty bespectacled sort who bought her clothes second hand, didn't wear bras and like to smoke a little 24/7. He liked her freckly complexion and constant laughter. Occasionally they fucked. It had happened the first time a few years back and every so often when they both found themselves single and bored they would arrange to spend time together. She'd taken to posting little love notes through his door when she wanted him. Drago was usually more direct.

    That afternoon, he appeared at her door with a bottle of prosecco and two glasses. Madeleine only had cheap tumblers, not crystal flutes like these, the sort that echo when you chink the rim.

    "What's the occasion?" she asked quizzically, dropping her spectacles sexily onto the tip of her dainty nose.

    "Does there need to be one?" he replied. "Can't a man simply want to share time with a beautiful woman?"

    "Flatterer."

    She opened the door wide and retreated from him, unbuttoning her blouse as she did so. "Open it and take off your clothes. I've been waiting for you to visit for a week."

    He did as he was told and joined her on the bean bags she used for fun and games and watching telly. A pale head and shoulders, thin long legs and two perky breasts poked out of the cushions that swaddled her. Drago kissed her lightly and waved the bottle.

    "What do you want first?"

    "Better give me a drink," she said. "I can tell you want something from me. What is it this time: tickets to a show?"

    He poured.

    "Does it have to be about anything?"

    "You already answered that and yes, it does."

"Alright. I'm horny and I want to fuck you."
"You're lying."
"I'm not."
"You think I can't tell?"
"Am I as bad a liar as that?"
"Yes. Anyway, you're not horny, I can see from here."
Drago looked. It was half true.
"Well, you're usually more co-operative, Maddie."
"Are you flattering me again?"
She giggled. She never laughed, always a childish giggle.
"Probably."
Drago kissed her hard on the mouth, exploring her teeth with his tongue. She breathed a long sigh.
"Hmm, that's good. Why don't you come by more often?"
His hand move under the folds of the cushion, found her belly and pinched the flesh. She gave a startled yelp.
"You need more meat on your bones. I prefer my girl's well-fed."
"You never said."
"You never asked."
"I should be annoyed, but you're here now." She gently pushed him away. "Open the doors, babe. It's hot in here."
Drago propped open the big French windows so the afternoon air could waft lazily into the apartment. Someone close by had open windows too and was playing old Marvin Gaye tracks.
"Won't the neighbours hear?" he asked.
"You are my neighbour."
"Touché. Your last note said you had a surprise for me."
When he turned back, she was stretched across the cushions dipping a hand seductively down to her pubis. At the tip of her sex sat a fat diamond stud.
"Do you like it?"
He knelt beside her and ran his forefinger over the stone. The piercing waggled and she giggled again.
"That tickles."
"I'll bet." Drago's fingers ran lower. "Take off your glasses, Maddie, you're in for a ticklish afternoon."

At about eight o'clock, they ordered pizza and had it delivered. He raided her fridge for more wine and they ate from the pizza box, the mozzarella forming long strings as they lifted each piece to their mouths. Her phone kept buzzing. She didn't answer it. Eventually, once the meal was finished, she picked up the mobile and stared long and hard at the screen, flicking a few pages of text. She pulled a face and tossed the offending gadget aside.

"Who is it?" he asked.

"My boyfriend."

"Oh."

"Sorry."

"No. It's alright." Drago felt a tiny pang. "You never said."

She shrugged.

"You never asked. He says he loves me."

"That's good, isn't it?"

"I don't know. What do you think?"

"I'm not best qualified. I'm not sure I realise I'm in love until it's all over. Then I mourn. Most of my relationships end in a terrible anti-climax."

"Like the French girl?"

Drago fought back the urge to wince.

"Sylvia? Yes. And Amy."

"Who's Amy?"

"You never met her. I was with her last summer, in Crete."

"When you researched your book?"

"Yes."

Drago didn't think dealing with old-school gangsters, double crossing daughters and incestuous invalid millionaires necessarily constituted research, but he didn't want to shatter her illusions. Explaining his scars had taken too long once before.

"What about that haughty blonde woman who comes around for dinner?"

"Abbey's an old friend. We go way, way back. There's nothing romantic there."

"But you like her."

"She's my agent. I have to. Anyway, you like me too. Now I discover you've got a boyfriend, I feel betrayed."

"Hey!" She gave him a playful slap on the arm. "Fair's fair. We've just been discussing all your girlfriend's. Not jealous, are you?"

"No. More curious. Do you love him?"

She paused.

"No. I don't think so. I wouldn't be doing this otherwise, would I?"

"Probably not." Drago took a swig of the over fragrant sancerre. "So, there's still hope for me yet?"

She giggled and slapped him again.

"No, seriously," he said. "I was hoping, well, I wondered if perhaps you might want to go on holiday with me."

There was a short frightening pause.

After it, Madeleine held out her glass.

"Wow. You'd better top me up. Where did that come from?"

"I was already going. I have a trip booked to Puglia, a sort of wine and food week. You know the kind of thing, indulge yourself in the local cuisine, eat, drink and make merry. I was going with Abbey, but she cried off at the eleventh hour."

"She likes letting you down."

Maddie squeezed his arm affectionately. Her touch sent a little shock along his torso. It wasn't the sort of movement someone made just for effect. This was genuine sentiment. It had never been there before. They had a playful, amoral relationship. Now, the invitation scared him.

"Well?" Drago asked.

"Well what?"

"What about Italy?"

"What about it?"

"The flight leaves in a week."

The girl scrabbled about on the floor and found her spectacles. She put them and puckered her lips as she considered.

"My boyfriend won't like it."

"I'm not asking him."

"He'll be dreadfully sad."

"You don't love him. You just told me that."

"But I'm not sure I love you either, Jonathon."

"I didn't ask you because I love you, Maddie. I asked you because you're fun and because I think you're too pale and need a decent tan and because, honestly, I'm frightened to go alone and look like a spare prick."

"You just don't want your prick to be spare."

"That too."

Drago gently touched her hand. The motion had the same effect on Madeleine. He sensed it. they were crossing an unexpected, unwritten line. She played with her fingers a while.

"I do love Italy," she murmured.

Drago said nothing.

They made love long into the night. Crane flies and moths started to gather in the room and disturb the paper lampshades. Finally, as she lay cuddled against him, hair a mess, mouth bitten raw by kisses, the delicate insect shadows fluttering over her face, she said: "Alright."

***

They landed in Brindisi at midmorning and, having gathered their cases, they headed for the car hire. Drago fussed at the Avis counter. Maddie said he ought to have organised a car sooner. Drago shrugged off the protest. They ended up with a Fiat Panda, as good as new with only a few thousand on the clock. It suited their purpose and more importantly it had air conditioning. There was no air outside. The atmosphere was jammed with hot scalding sweat. Everything shimmered. It was sun cream and glasses weather, make no mistake.

Brindisi wasn't a grand airport. Functional described it well. Drago hated it. Maddie was equally eager to escape.

"The Avis man kept looking at my legs."

"Your legs are very nice," he replied. "Especially in that skirt and with those boots. You look like a girl out of the sixties. All you need is some wicked eyeshadow and a bubble blower."

"Don't be cheeky."

He turned the engine. Avis provided a Tom-Tom navigator and she punched in the hotel's address. The screen scrolled rapidly to their destination.

"Two hours," she said.

"In this heat?" muttered Drago. He took off his jacket and turned the air con to maximum. They'd talked a lot at Gatwick and on the plane, but now they drifted into silence, not because they'd run out of conversation, but because Drago generally didn't talk when he drove. He was too busy concentrating on the engine, the suspension, the torque on the axles, the constant whirr of wheels, listening for the one fault which might later deliver a breakdown. He mastered the Fiat quickly, chose not to drive excessively fast and generally behaved himself on the motorways, letting others do the overtaking, which perhaps uniquely in Italy required darting racing-style from the slipstream a metre or so from your bumper. The two-door Fiat certainly wasn't his idea of a stylish automobile. It wasn't powerful enough for flashy acceleration, but it drove handsomely well.

Away from the dusty airport, they passed through flat green meadows which might have been another Eden, peppered as they were by rich orchards and groves segregated by walls of ancient stone. The modern world only revealed itself in blank strips of tarmac and armies of wind turbines, sails rotating slowly. The cars seemed to transgress the landscape, zipping through it on black heathen asphalt. The Apian Way finished at Brindisi, but it still felt as if they travelled on a straight Roman road, as if time had hardly touched the land and the past was as interwoven with the present, shaking each other's hand every second. They could have detoured to Lecce, its baroque colours creeping out of the fields, but they passed its basilicas and piazzas and ornate corbels and carvings, saving them for another day, another world.

The SS16 emptied after Lecce and the driving became easier. The landscape seemed to descend into a wide plateau, the Salentine Peninsula, not a peninsula at all but an enclave buried in Puglia's countryside, where they still shared influences from both Roman and Greek cultures. The gold and emerald world seemed even brighter here and the whitewashed houses could have been marble. Occasionally among small villages and isolated farms, a crumbled villa or castle sat obdurate and abandoned, stones stolen for other projects, now guarded by bleating goats and a host of flies. The pastel stone of Sternatia's bell tower rose out of the earth as spectacularly as the great steel pillars which held the wind turbines. World's shaking hands indeed.

They exited the plateau and turned east, descending to the coast, down the throat of the Idro valley, opening wider and wider until Otranto spread out before them along both sides of the bone dry river and the flat blue horizon of the Adriatic lapped at their eyes.

Maddie grabbed his arm.

"The sea!"

"You act like you've never seen it before."

"I haven't. Not from here."

Drago couldn't argue with that. She wanted to see it close up, but the sat-nav would need redirecting and he didn't want to bother. As it was, the damn thing – which had worked so well on the open road – misdirected them in town because it wasn't programmed to understand one-way systems. The San Pietro was on such a street, Via 800 Martiri, cars parked along one side, many gaps for access to underground garages and hardly enough room for cyclists let alone vehicles. Drago took it very slow. The hotel was on the right. He turned under a gated archway and entered a small esplanade lined with miniature palms and blushing geraniums. A uniformed steward was already walking towards the car. Drago activated the window.

"Buongiorno."

"Buongiorno, Signor."

"Jon Drago," he said. "The Gusto dell' Italia Tour."

"Ah. Si. Si. Yes." The man switched effortlessly to English. "You wish the garage?"

"Yes, please."

"Prego, prego."

The steward led them to the back of the driveway where the hotel building came to an end. Drago eased the Fiat gently after him. The man turned down a steep curving access ramp to the lower level car park. Drago thought both the slope and the spaces a tight fit even for a small Fiat. He took great care not to damage the bodywork. They left the steward to deal with the baggage and strolled to the elevator.

"Seems a bit swish," Maddie said as the lift doors slid noiselessly shut. "I'm not used to this sort of treatment."

"You'll get used to it."

"Like you have?"

"I can't deny it. Luxury has obvious perks."

"Costs a fortune too."

"Don't worry. I'm not asking you to pay for it."

"All the same, you are paying for two."

"My credit card can cope."

"Would you have done this for Abbey?"

The doors hissed open. Before they stepped into the lobby, Drago slid his hand under her too-short skirt and gave her backside a surreptitious smack. She made a little jump of surprise.

"What was that for?"

"Abbey isn't here."

She turned around and placed a single restricting finger on his chest.

"Neither is Brandon."

"Is that his name?"

"Yes." Maddie smiled coquettishly. "And we're not to mention them again, Jonathon, you promise?"

"Alright. And you mustn't fret about money."

"Fine." She stretched up and kissed him quickly. "Let's check in. The sooner we do that, the sooner you can get me out of these knickers. You've been aching to all day, I can tell."

Two

Vicino's

For the first time Drago sat alone in Vicino's. It was late and he had just returned from the hospital in Lecce. Maddie was sleeping, sedated, suffering shock as well as injury. The doctors advised him to get some rest. That old saying 'there's nothing you can do here' rang true and hollow. He could have stayed in Lecce, but finding a bed at short notice didn't appeal. He drove at breakneck speed back down the SS16, a road which had revealed such beautiful promise days before but now only sung of despair. Sternatia's sulphureous tower darkened as he sped past, a dusky, dirty, diseased finger raised to his soul. Fuck it.

"Fuck it."

Drago pulled on the last dregs of a Marlboro. His lungs ached. He was rarely tearful, but the effort made him weep. He angrily wiped it clear.

***

The idiots in the speedboats were very quick to respond. They understood what had happened immediately. One of the skiers loosened off his boards and swam to Maddie's rolling figure, keeping her afloat with his own body. Drago watched the rescue in stunned silence. Someone was making a call to the ambulance service. Two lifeguards swam from the pontoon. The other speedboat came to a slithering halt and the second skier also went to aid the rescue. Drago's eyes switched to the yacht. A small group had been on deck the whole afternoon. They now congregated along the rail. The captain had come down from the bridge. With a couple of deckhands in ubiquitous striped t-shirts, he stood next to a big brutal man swaddled in a white towelling robe. Beside them, clutching dramatically at her neck, was a darkhaired woman in a navy blue bikini.

Drago tore his eyes away. The life guards had made rapid progress. They had floats with them and slid the supports under Maddie's helpless form. For a moment, Drago thought one lifeguard was administering CPR. There was a lot of gesticulating as the speedsters were charged with hooking up the makeshift raft so Maddie could be towed to the beach. A line was thrown out. One lifeguard took hold and wrapped it around an arm and shoulder. The other held onto the float beneath Maddie's back. With his colleague also helping to keep her head and torso above water, the helmsman inched his way back towards Atlantis.

Drago lifted his sunglasses and stared at the big yacht. The girl had taken hold of the big man's arm. He brushed her off and made a huge dismissive gesture. He puffed at a fat cigar and bellowed instructions down to the three remaining men. Drago couldn't catch the words. The manner was authoritative. The phrases precise. The men obeyed immediately.

"Signor?"

It was one of the gelato sellers. Every day he tried to sell Drago and Maddie a cornet and every day they said 'no' at least three times until relenting. He was agitated. The owner of the bar was with him.

"We have an ambulance. It is coming."

"Thank you."

Drago didn't know what else to say. All the guilt and deception suddenly snapped at him. He'd not been conducting an illicit affair, not really, but it bloody felt like it now. Everyone would know of it. Visible and invisible damage. He grimaced. What about Maddie? He pushed his way through the crowd. The sirens were audible already. It would only be the municipal service, but at least it was here. The speedboat was still some way from the shore. They were sensibly taking it very slowly. People were clearing a space on the beach. Drago stepped off the pontoon deck onto the rocky ground, skirted the first jumble of boulders and went to the sliver of sand which was the only proper beach at the Atlantis Club.

They pulled her gently onto the shingle. Maddie was breathing, thank God, but in sharp, short, panicked breaths. The left side of her face bulged with a fearsome black bruise. Below it, her shoulder was ripped open. She was losing blood. The arm hung useless. He thought a bone jarred out of the mangled flesh. Her feet twitched. Drago was close enough to grab her other hand. He said something, but didn't know what the hell it was. The fingers squeezed. The lifeguards cleared the crowd to a respectful distance. Shouts from the rear announced the arrival of the emergency crew. They abruptly pushed Drago aside, unwrapping a stretcher, opening green plastic cases emblazoned with red crosses on white circles. Italian was exchanged between everybody. Drago didn't understand what was happening. They pumped her full of something, slapped on an oxygen mask. They strapped up the gutted shoulder and transferred her to the stretcher.

"Where's she going?" asked Drago.
"Il Citta Hospital."
"Where's that?"
"Lecce. We take all internationals there."

Drago watched as Maddie was taken away, the crowd parting like bow waves. He took a deep breath and returned to their seats. Her summer dress was there. Her shoes too. He picked them up and stuffed them into the canvas shoulder bag she'd bought on Corso Garibaldi. He put his own things in it too, pulled on his shirt and decks and went to the car.

"Are you okay, signor?"
It was the gelato seller again.
"Yes. Si. Grazie. Will the police be called? Should I wait?"
"What is your hotel?"
"The San Pietro," he said and dug in his wallet for a business card. "That's me."

The man looked impressed. A fine time to be, thought Drago bitterly. He got in the car and slammed the door so hard the opposite window shook.

Drago didn't like hospitals. He had good reason. He'd recently suffered several extended stays in those tombs of agony. He rubbed the puncture wound where the khanjar blade had pierced. Occasionally his foot complained as if it was still broken. There was nasty scar by his thumb, another by his belly, his back and chest was a litany of stories not to be told, of chains and claws, whips and rocks and fallen masonry. Hospitals were only temporary asylums. The doctors sewed you up in their sanitised world and thrust you like a newborn back into the cesspool of existence to suffer Fate's slings and arrows and torments. Sometimes Drago hated the whole fucked up world and its sanctimonious masters.

He caught up with the ambulance near Maglie and followed it along the SS16 and onto the 225, where it finally pulled into the silent grounds of the Citta di Lecce Hospital, a blueish-white building which wouldn't have looked out of place on a 1960s university campus.

There really was nothing he could do except wait. Wait and think. All those little incidents one considered immaterial suddenly loomed large. He thought of when he first saw Maddie, reading a romantic novel in the garden; of their first kiss; the silly emails she sent him; what she did with the stray cat which had invaded her apartment and kept delivering dead pigeons; her impish smile; the freckles he stroked with his fingers after love; the boyfriend he had never met; the family who would be devastated. And then there was the last few days, days of something which might be called love but really wasn't. The intimacies, watching her eat, sleep, beautify, bore easily, quick to chide, slow to rise, how she smoked, drank, coughed loudly, delicately took a piss, all the domestic intricacies of a relationship.

A nurse found him sitting in the bleak antiseptic corridor several hours later. She placed a cold hand on his shoulder.

"You can visit now, signor. Please. Stay only a short time."

Drago gazed up at the nurse and shook his head, trying to clear the cobwebs of memory. "Yes. Of course."

He stayed for ten minutes. He held her hand. He stared at her drug-addled eyes. He whispered God only knows what reassurances, wishing he'd never uprooted her from London, never been such a prick, just how she said it.

Fucking hell, Jon.

**

Paulo Vicino was an ageing restaurateur who wore a pair of reading spectacles high on his forehead, pushing back what might once have been a fine head of hair, but was now reduced to strands of curly grey and white and black slicked with gel. His belly spoke of fine food and lots of it. His eyes spoke of fine wine. His voice of a fine life and bad cigarettes and many broken promises.

They'd found the eponymous establishment on the first night. They'd walked from the old town and along the promenade. The bars and restaurants were still open. Everyone ate as late as possible in the south. It was the tradition and as the resort was so busy, people ate even later than tradition. Vicino's was crushed among a row of a dozen similar trattoria, each one advertising its own brand of specific sea food. There wasn't a steak in sight. They chose Vicino's because it looked homely. The twin set of double doors stood open. The yellow and white lights glimmered with mysterious opacity. One wanted to know what was on offer within its walls. Unlike most venues there was no advertising board, no bill of fare. Here, like in life, you took your chances. They needn't have feared. They were greeted as if they'd always eaten at Vicino's and that night a friendship was formed over good conversation, delicious frittini and succulent negromarro.

Now, Drago lit another cigarette and stared out at the blackness. There was a tremendously large scotch sitting on the table, ice melting, diluting the bitterness. It was only Johnny Red, so that didn't matter. The nuances of fine drinking were not uppermost in Drago's mind. He shook the tumbler and the cubes rattled. Drago sank half the contents in one gulp.

Paulo Vicino appeared at his shoulder and patted it. He took a seat and a long sigh passed through his lips. They'd not really spoken of the accident. The news had swept through the town. Paulo had received Drago with a sudden hug which spoke more than words. Paulo knew that now was the time for those words.

"How is she?" he asked.

"Sleeping when I left."

"It is a good hospital. Top level. One of our best."

Drago had gathered that from the starched uniforms and the clipped accents. It didn't make him less apprehensive.

"Fucking hell, Paulo. It's a mess."

"I know it. It is not good. Will she be injured," he paused, searching for the term, "forever?"

"I don't know. I guess she'll have a terrible scar. Thank Christ it wasn't her head."

Paulo crossed himself.

"What will you do?"

"I'm going back to the hospital tomorrow. What else can I do?"

"You love her much?"

"Yes. No. Not like that."

"Then, like what?"

"It's not a traditional friendship, Paulo."

Paulo said nothing. He shifted his small feet back and forth below the chair. Eventually one of the staff brought two more tumblers of whisky. The waiter knew it was never good for a man to drink alone, so he encouraged Paulo to join his friend. The proprietor took a sip, pushing the second glass towards Drago.

"I had a woman once, one of many," he declared. "She too was not a traditional lady. My mother forbade it. I didn't think mothers could still do such a thing. I learn the hardest of ways. I think sometimes it drove me to madness. It is easy to find love. It is hard to keep it. If you do not love Madeleine, really love her, you would do best to surrender her or you will be in a constant struggle with her, her family, yours and yourself. The self, you understand, is always where the madness starts and ends."

"Love isn't madness." Drago finished one drink and took the next. "Everything that surrounds it is."

"Or makes it so."

"You can't say that unless you've really been in love."

"And I have. Have you?"

"Yes. I think once. Perhaps twice."

"But not with Maddie?"

"No."

"The madness is the difference between love and infatuation. When you cannot live without the bliss of insanity, that is when love is deepest, when it has bitten your soul and conquered your heart."

"You should have been a poet."

"I should have been a husband and father. I am merely my mother's son. A good trade, but not an eternal one."

"You have all this."

"And in time so will someone else."

"There is always time for love, Paolo. Even in dotage."

Paulo Vicino raised his glass and stared long and hard at Drago. "Are you making fun of me, Jon?"

"No, but I could. I'm not so young myself." Drago lit a cigarette, watched the smoke twirl and die. "Maddie, well, perhaps I didn't realise what I wanted. It happens an awful lot when you get older, don't you think? You get cautious. Then you make sudden decisions, those mad ones you talk of, and they invariably get you into trouble."

"You are talking of the accident?"

"Yes."

But he wasn't. Drago's mind drifted to a different scene, a different day and a conversation he'd overheard at the Hotel San Pietro.

***

He was sitting on the terrace outside their room, drinking a glass of red wine left over from the bottles provided for the Gusto dell' Italia. He could hear Maddie's voice from below. Drago peered over the parapet. Maddie stood on the esplanade outside the hotel lobby. As usual she had thrown on her long flowery all-in-one summer dress, complemented by a wide brimmed fake-straw sunhat. She was talking to a tall, slender, dark haired woman. The woman was deeply tanned and wore sophisticated fashions: hot white jeans which stopped shy of her ankles and a bashful hoop-necked top. A patterned scarf covered her fringe, the ends clasped in a big bow beneath a mane of long black hair which fell between her shoulder blades. Her voice was a pitch lower than Maddie's. They were talking restaurants and Maddie was persuading the woman to come to Vicino's.

"It's the very best. The seafood is to die for."

"I must watch my figure."

"I don't see why. You've got a lovely figure. One bowl of risotto won't hurt."

The woman was reluctant.

"We usually eat on board."

"Persuade him. It'll be fun. He can stretch his ego with Jonathon. There's nothing men like more than a good argument."

The metallic chime of a pop-song ringtone interrupted the conversation. The woman took a mobile from her bag, saw whose number was calling and declined to answer; yet it seemed to help her reach a decision.

"No. I will try, but it will be no. I am sorry."

She didn't say goodbye, turned on her heel and walked towards the gate. Drago thought she moved gracefully, like a dancer.

He'd seen her twice already. The first time they'd passed in a corridor. She'd been wearing a silk blouse and a knee-length skirt which looked as if they had been manufactured in Milan or Paris, Jimmy Choo shoes – he saw the logo – and a bag which could only be from Fendi. The second time she had been visiting the spa. He'd been waiting for Maddie and was checking his phone's playlist. Drago had been singing badly to Bixio's *Mamma*. A brief puzzled smile crossed the beautiful face, a tiny frown accompanied by little twin jitters at the corners of her mouth.

Maddie crossed to the outside stairwell and Drago quickly resat, taking up the glass, surprised by an unexpected sudden pang of guilt. She looked pink and refreshed from the spa. Her tan was gently starting to build. Maddie plonked herself down opposite him and arranged the cushions on the cane settee for maximum comfort.

"What are you doing?" she asked.

"Writing recipe tips."

"Again?"

"I'll forget. The Signora packs in a lot of detail."

"And drinking too. You should come to the spa. It's probably better for you than sitting in the sun."

"This way I'm getting a tan."

"So am I."

Drago continued to write the last details for the alici arracanate.

Across the alley in the next door block of flats, a husband and wife started an argument. Something broke. A window closed with a bang and the noise vanished.

"Who was that?" Drago asked mildly.

"Who?"

"The woman you were talking too."

"She's called Ariana."

"Is she nice?"

"Why?"

"I've seen her around," said Drago. "She comes to the spa."

"That's right. The hotel has the best facilities in Otranto, so she tells me. Make that the only facilities. She comes ashore to use them."

"Ashore?"

"From the yacht. The big one you've been admiring since it turned up."

"Is she coming to dinner then?"

"I doubt it."

"Pity."

There was a pause in her patter. Drago squiggled the final words and signed with a flourish. Old habits die hard. He put down his pen. Maddie leaned forward, took the notebook and inspected his handiwork. She flicked back a page, tutted and handed it back.

"It was 200g of breadcrumbs."

"Was it? Are you sure?"

"Certain because she came over and told me off for using too much."

He made the correction.

"She's very beautiful, isn't she?" said Maddie.

"Who?"

"You know who."

"Yes. I suppose she is."

"Well, she's with a man, so you can forget it."

"You have a man too."

"That's different."

"Is it?"

Maddie bunched her dress and hitched up her legs, crossing them into the lotus position.

"Yes," she declared. "I'm quite happy being unfaithful. I don't think she would be. She seems more dependent."

"She doesn't look it."

"So, you have been looking."

"Like you said: she's very beautiful."

"Stop it," snorted Maddie. "No. Scrub that. Just tell me. Go on. You fancy her, don't you?"

"Is it that obvious?"

She shrugged.

"Don't worry, Maddie. I'm not going to run off with her."

She pretended to be in a huff, but was putting it on for his benefit. Drago had seen a lot of these games recently and he was tired of playing them. He knew where they led and he wanted a change of seduction.

"Of course, if you did go off with her, I'd be tremendously upset."

"Why's that?" he said sharply. "After all, when we get home, you'll go back to your boyfriend and I'll get my bottles of wine. We'll end up in the same ménages as before, only this time with a little more knowledge. I mean honestly, Maddie, who's eating whose cake?"

She breathed deeply. Her eyes were closed. She opened them and peeked at him. "Sometimes your ambivalence is charming, Jonathon. Other times, you just sound mean."

"Yes," he agreed after a moment's reflection, a moment during which he weighed up every word of his outburst and regretted each one. "I'm a bit of a shit, aren't I?"

"Sometimes."

"Alright." Drago winked. It was the best he could do. "I promise I won't run away with her, at least not while you're around."

"Oh dear," she sighed. "I'm not sure whether that's endearing or still being mean."

Drago's words haunted him. He hadn't wished the accident. It had been a remark thrown out in jest, designed to bring an itchy subject to a prompt close before it gestated into a full blown row, like the one which had continued across the alley behind closed windows.

Now, long after all the arguments had been resolved, after the sun had settled on another day and it should be the time to make better the hurt, Drago sat without her outside Vicino's and lit another cigarette. The restaurant was a good place to think, a good place to make sudden decisions, mad ones that inevitably got you into trouble. He watched the smoke drift lazily into the night air, caught on a breeze, sucked out to sea, the sea which led everywhere and left behind so much. The sea where she slept.

"Are you talking of the accident?" asked Paulo.

"Yes."

Drago was lying. He was thinking of the dark haired slender woman in the blue bikini anxiously craning over the starboard side of the yacht, the woman with the poise of a dancer and a beautiful enigmatic smile.

Three

Sabatini

Marcelo Sabatini lit a cigar. It was starting to rain; a rare occurrence at this time of year, but a welcome one. It would distract the coastguard. One less authority to concern himself with. Sabatini only trusted two authorities, God and Satan. Even then, he laughed at their arrogance. When you are a man capable of great sin, he considered, deities no longer deserved a prayer.

Sabatini stepped away from the guardrail and retreated to the lounge. The raindrops, once a few seconds of sprinkles, became a sudden tumult, peppering the deck of his yacht, juddering the hot steamy air and forming a dull curtain which cut off his view to the coastline. He glanced at his watch. It was past one. The evening had been a success. He didn't like the old villa, but if you were someone of merit in the Salentine, if you wanted to meet anyone who was someone in the Salentine, you had to take an audience with the Comte d'Orsi.

There had been a fine feast: consommé, seafood risotto and bowls of pasta drenched in basil and pine nut pesto. Prosecco fizzed on the tongue. Limoncello bit at the throat. The coffee was hot and sweet. An eight piece orchestra played on the terrace beneath the overhanging arms of a huge hibiscus. There had been a little dancing, mostly for show and by request. The old Comte listened to the music, his fingers tapping to the rhythm of the dancers' shoes.

Everyone on the small guestlist had dressed in their finery. No button or shoe went unpolished, no hair was out of place or nail unvarnished. Tuxedos and dinner dresses were the accepted fashion. Occasionally, dark rimless sunglasses blotched a face, white gloves were slipped over ladies' hands, smiles were as false as teeth. Sabatini enjoyed the evening and gained new acquaintances. It was unusual for an outsider to be accepted into such regal society. The reception and his welcome to it had been as elegant and as the beautiful ancient surroundings.

It would not always have been so, he reflected, blowing a cloud of cold smoke between his teeth. Everyone knew the public story. Sabatini was a mighty champion, a campaigner for the trade unions, the dock workers, the cargo and the transport men, the lower castes of industry. He'd sought nothing but recognition for his workforces, indemnities for their families and money from the government. It had been difficult at first. The men who ruled the unions in Albania and treated the young outsider with contempt and it was his duty to fight them, to gain respect and influence. He earned it the hard way. His reputation was made from those battles, from the deals he brokered, the politicians he unseated and the police he fought. Now, they said, he had reached an epiphany. His past life appeared to mean nothing. They said it was his woman. The beautiful, slim dark haired beauty had appeared at his side almost seven years ago. They liked how she soothed his rough edges. They always assumed it was the woman's doing, that only love could change a man's heart.

They forgot about power.

Sabatini fiddled with the elaborate gold signet ring on his left index finger, the first recognition of his authority. He remembered how he had torn it from Lorenz's hand. He went to the bar and poured a large brandy from a crystal decanter and swilled the amber liquid around the bowl until it coated the sides. He sipped it. The warm sharp tang licked at his throat. He stared for a full minute at the painting which hung on the wall behind the bar. There was a man who understood power. Skanderbeg, Albanian hero, scourge of the Ottomans, victor and dictator.

Power, Sabatini wondered. What had power cost him? His left eye certainly. Sabatini momentarily touched the opal, a jewel ingot inlaid in the glass surround which fitted snugly in the socket. Only a few carat weight but worth almost half a million euros. Years ago, he wore a black velvet eye patch. When the anger swelled, he would tear it aside to reveal the empty ugly hole and show the world what power had cost him. The loss of his sight was a constant precious reminder of his rise in status, the glimmering opal a portent of his future, its riches and its power. Despite its beauty, he detested how it came about. The old anger surged. He remembered the day he physically fought Lorenz, how the bastard had beaten him, gouged him with a letter opener, abused him and threw him out of the N.M.T. Union. He remembered too the sweetness of revenge: how he slipped into Lorenz's house and kidnapped his daughter, how he humiliated Lorenz for three months with the sickening ransom notes and how he declined each new offer of conciliation.

Sabatini grinned as the salacious memory swept over him. His fingers gripped the glass tight. The sad misguided girl had been a good pupil. How could he ever forget the soft, plump flesh, how she fought him and then at last surrendered to his will? After he'd taken what he wanted and finally received what he demanded, Sabatini returned the daughter to Lorenz as a broken doll of flesh, minus the fingers on her left hand to prevent her marriage, plus an unborn child. Lorenz was livid with rage, but the Union boss had already sworn to give Sabatini the position he wanted. The feud simmered. Sabatini allowed what he had done to be an open secret around the dockyards. He ensured his supporters made it so. Lorenz went to the police. They did nothing. This was an affair they wanted no part of.

The daughter died giving premature birth to Sabatini's son. Lorenz's grandchild breathed only a few hours longer. Had he lived the boy might have become a solution to an escalating quarrel, by dying he became the catalyst for war. It lasted almost five years and at the end of it Marcelo Sabatini ran the Union and Lorenz was dead. They said it was suicide. They all knew the truth. Sabatini had laughed as his men administered the fatal dose of heroin. He'd smoked his first ever cigar as his adversary's eyes finally glazed over and stared uselessly into nothing. When the dust settled on the years of violence, Sabatini took the big gold ring with the fat glowing diamond. It was a symbol of triumph. Like the Pope, he made Lorenz's lieutenants kiss the ring as he offered them roles in the new 'Union' – his Union. It was always best to assimilate your enemies. It was easy to watch them when they remained close. It was when people drifted, they became a danger.

Two years later, the men from Berat came to see him, men with expensive suits and neat moustaches who smelled of rough cologne. They had a proposition for him, if he was interested. There was a wealthy businessman in Durres who had maliciously insulted a Krye, the head of one of the great families. Could Sabatini help them right this wrong? Sabatini was greatly respected for the manner in which he disposed of Agron Lorenz, the troublesome arrogant upstart unloved by the traditional families. Sabatini was deeply respected for his background, for his Italian father who left the colonists and fought with Shehu's partisans and later formed the Saranda Shipyard Union and fought the government. And he was profoundly respected for his mother, the daughter of Bogdani, the priest who died protecting Onufër's icons during the war. They knew also that the Nautical, Merchant and Transport Union was more than a political force, that they had the means if they chose to mobilise men of violence and strength to ensure their grievances were aired and acted on. If anyone could, they knew Marcelo Sabatini could provide a swift and adequate solution.

The men explained at length the wrong that had been committed. Sabatini watched their eyes as they told him of the slur, some insignificant thing which a fist and a handshake could resolve. These were not the eyes of insulted men. He saw greed. He saw money. He saw power.

Sabatini was cutting slices of garlic sausage with a large carving knife. The slices got thinner and thinner as the story continued. The blade shaved the top layer of skin from a knuckle and then he stopped carving and stopped the men from talking.

"I will tell you what I will do," he announced. "I will rid you of this businessman even though he has done me no wrong. I will seize his assets. That is what you want. I know you can do it. You have done it before. I know you have a man on the board of the Joint Stock Company, an accountant, and another at the Ministry of Public Economy. I know it is so, gentlemen, because I too have such a spy. Because of this, I already know what you want and if you wish it, you shall have it. I will give it to you as a gift."

The men were eminently pleased. They nodded with surprise and enthusiasm. The leader was about to utter his thanks, when Sabatini stopped him with a raised hand, the one which still contained the carving knife.

"Now listen closely," he said. "This is what I want."

When Luca Rovíc drowned, it was assumed to be a tragic accident. The founder of Lundrim Luksoze had fallen from his luxury yacht, the first of a dozen exclusive private cruisers built at his new shipyards. It was always moored just outside the confines of Durres and its harbour. Sabatini could often see it from his window. They said Rovíc was drunk. Marcelo Sabatini laughed as he watched his men pour the rakia down the squealing man's throat. Sabatini laughed again when he took up his position in the boardroom for the First Annual General Meeting of the shareholders of Lundrim Luksoze. Sabatini was the only man present. He renamed the company International Luxury Sails and granted himself a pay rise.

He laughed a final time when, several years later, the insulted Krye died and, as requested and without opposition, Marcelo Sabatini became the head of the Banda Family. He was already a rich and prosperous man. International Luxury Sails had allowed him to escape the shackles of the dockyard, the politicians and the unions. Although he remained President of the N.M.T., he allowed his more qualified lieutenants to conduct its business the way the unions always had, with blackmail, corruption and murder. He had to be respectable now he was the Krye of a Family. Those old men came to him once more, kissed the ring and presented their own jewels of fealty.

The men in expensive suits would visit Sabatini regularly to ask for his wisdom. He became judge and jury. He hid like a king behind mansion gates and bullet proof windows, dispensing justice like Solomon. Beneath him, a team of executives ensured his private wealth grew, not only from building yachts, but from the Banda Family's other more substantial interests: the flow of illegal goods and services into and out of the country: guns to Serbia, girls to Greece, cocaine to Italy. So it was not love which changed him. It was something far more potent. He realised it one day in his comfortable office, which still overlooked Durres. He sat on cream leather cushions, a secretary handed him balance sheets, a P.A. the brandy and anyone who entered his realm acted subdued, eyes downcast, feet together, like children. He realised, slowly, surely, compellingly, how power annihilated everything and everyone. He tasted power and he gorged on it. His whole life up to that point began to feel empty, his achievements insignificant, his soul unfulfilled. What was life without real power, real control? What was life without the knowledge that presidents and popes, kings and princes, the hierarchy of the world, men of commerce and invention, men of the land, the oligarchs and exploiters, would look at you and know that you held sway over their realm?

The thought excited him. Once more, he felt the waves of onrushing instinctive violence. He had not forgotten the feeling. It had lain dormant, like a volcano. Now it erupted. That night, he raped, twice, and he enjoyed it. Yes. Power allowed you to maim and hurt and soil. Power allowed you to control. And it was control he wanted, control over everyone.

Sabatini swallowed the cognac and went to refill his glass. He caught a reflection in the mirror. The silica in his false eye flashed rainbow-coloured freckles against its ebony sheen. Wherever I go, whoever I meet, they always know I am a man of capital, that I earned my prosperity in blood and that is why I am powerful, Sabatini thought as he swallowed the cognac. He walked to the intercom and flicked the switch.

"Blaku, I'm going below. Don't disturb me."

Sabatini took the glass and the decanter, went down the wide spiral staircase and along the passage to the state bedroom. He thrust open the door, the cigar chomped between his lips.

The room was sumptuous. It backed towards the prow of the ship, tapering gently to a flat apex. The walls were lined with porphyry columns buttressing four big oval windows, a pair on each side. Thick nets blocked the rain-swept night. The doors and panels were beech wood, varnished to the skin of an ant's kneecap. They glistened in the golden glow of the bedside lamps. The carpet was a deep plush wine red angora. The room's centrepiece was a huge crystal chandelier, made to order by Swarovski. Sabatini closed the door and walked past the couches and coffee tables towards the enormous oval bed, which seemed to occupy the whole far end of the room. It was big enough, he boasted, to sleep five people. The rain still cannoned against the windows.

The girl was sleeping. He licked his lips lasciviously, reached over and yanked away the sheet. She was in the foetal position, naked, curled like a baby, her slim shoulders turned away from him, the slender buttocks tucked next to her feet.

Sabatini put down the glass and decanter. He placed the cigar in the ash tray and removed his clothes, leaving them in untidy pile on the floor. He knelt beside the girl. She looked small and defenceless. His bulk dwarfed her as he loomed over the sleeping figure.

"My darling," he whispered, but it came out hoarse and growly.

"Hmm," she murmured, stirring. "What do you want?"

"You know what I want."

"Hmm."

Sabatini didn't wait. He reached down, turned the half-roused girl onto her belly and spread her legs. The heart-shaped backside rose to meet him. He positioned himself. The girl whimpered as he drove forward. There was always a tiny resistance when he entered her. Sabatini enjoyed the thrill of conquest she gave him. It was always the same, from the very first time he had taken her. She had shrunk from him at first. Now, she accepted the punishment and after each initial fight, she became pliant and submitted to the ravishing. An animal creature, she even seemed to enjoy the bestial act and encouraged him in his lusts. He didn't know if she loved him or not. He didn't care. She fulfilled his needs. As the moment arrived, he reached under the girl, grabbed at her nipples and pinched them hard. She wailed for him to stop. He didn't, screwing his fingers tighter as his thrusts matched hers, becoming more forceful and urgent. When it was over, he tossed the girl aside and relit the cigar.

After a minute or two, when she wanted caresses and sweetness, but he wasn't going to offer it, the girl rolled off the bed and went to use the shower. Sabatini poured himself another measure and reclined against the pillows, smoking and sated. On her return, the girl draped herself carefully across him.

"Must we always do it this way?"

"I like it this way. So do you."

"Sometimes it would be nice to be gentle."

Sabatini scoffed and took a swig of brandy and placed the glass on the mattress. The cigar smoke haloed around him.

"Please, Marcelo, maybe just once."

"For what?" he scolded and pushed the girl away. "You forget what I want you for."

"Sometimes I wonder."

The one good eye scanned her face. The lips formed a sneer. The left hand shot out and snapped across her cheek with a loud crack.

"Don't be insolent, Ariana. You like the good life. I can take it from you in a second." Sabatini clicked his fingers, the harsh movement an inch from the girl's shocked face. "Don't forget it."

Four

Witness Statements

When Drago dragged himself back to the Hotel San Pietro, he found a bored looking officer from the state police waiting for him. The night receptionist wasn't the most cheerful of people at the best of times, but he'd got used to Drago and Maddie appearing at two o'clock every morning, so this interruption barely raised an eyebrow. He mumbled something and put on his apologetic face.

Drago ran a hand through his hair. His head hurt. The sun, the driving, the stress, the whisky. The combination screamed 'migraine'.

"Signor," the officer began, "I am sorry. The Inspector would like to speak with you."

"I'm exhausted. Can't he see me tomorrow?"

"The Inspector has also been awake all day." It wasn't meant as any kind of apology or an excuse; it was simply a fact. "The station is near."

He was quite a young man and seemed efficient and bright eyed. His navy coloured uniform had perfect creases. Drago didn't see the point in arguing.

"Let's go then," he sighed.

The officer wasn't joking. The station really was close by, three doors away in fact, tucked between two low apartment blocks. Drago had noted the 'Polizia Questura' signs but assumed it was a subsidiary office. Lights shone at the windows, but the sign bore no illumination at all. It could have been anything but a police station.

Drago was shown into a small, spartan room, undecorated with a bald sticky table and two chairs. The young policeman brought lukewarm coffee. It tasted foul. Drago slumped half on the chair, his back to the wall, side on to the table. There was one window, high up near the ceiling. It was propped open. Hardly a breath of wind entered.

The Inspector was closer to Drago's age. He opened the door carefully and stood on the threshold studying his interviewee. Drago stared back. The Inspector was dressed in a plain grey crumpled assortment that was missing a necktie. He carried a sheaf of papers stuffed badly into a flat green document file and two mobile phones. He placed everything haphazardly on the table and sat down.

"Signor Drago?"

"Yes."

"Inspector Gigli."

The Inspector rifled through the papers and produced Drago's business card, which had been clipped to the top of a sheet of A4.

"Author and journalist," he read blandly. "I hope you are not searching for stories."

"That's rather callous, Inspector." Drago raised a curious eyebrow. "My friend's just been bashed to shit by some idiot in a speedboat. I have other things to worry about right now."

"Nonetheless, disaster and danger does chase you, does it not?"

"Tends to."

"I looked at your website. Very interesting. 'Based on personal experience', it says."

"That's partly a lie. My agent thinks it helps sell my books. She's probably right."

The Inspector reattached the card. Niceties were done.

"I don't need much from you, Signor, a few questions answered and a written statement. It's a mere formality."

"If it's a formality, why the sudden rush?"

The Inspector looked sorrowful. "We have certain standards, Signor. I wouldn't want it suggested I can't do my job."

"I saw your people at the hospital. They have Maddie's next of kin, passport number and all that."

The Inspector didn't say a word. He was reading one of the documents. He flicked the plunger on his elaborately patterned ball point pen. The noise made Drago jittery. He suddenly realised he didn't know any personal details about Maddie at all, not her age, her birthday, medical issues, nothing. Those sorts of intimacies never mattered before.

"I'm planning to speak to Mr and Mrs Forrest tomorrow," Drago added defensively. "Their number's on the booking form."

"You don't know it?"

"No."

The Inspector's mouth twitched as if he suddenly realised the sort of relationship he was dealing with. Drago shrugged. Inspector Gigli could think whatever he wanted. Drago wasn't about to justify himself, although the uncomfortable statement did make him consider how he ought to be behaving.

"Si. Good."

The brief inflection gone, the Inspector no longer seemed to care. He was staring at a blank form. "I've been asked to take statements, Signor."

"Are you going to prosecute those idiots?"

Gigli flicked the pen several times and closed his eyes. Only the clicking echoed in the chamber. When he opened his eyes, Drago was still there, immobile, immoveable. He looked disappointed, even though he must have expected it.

"It was an accident. The speedboats ought to have been more careful, but Signorina Forrest too has some responsibility. Was she a good swimmer, an experienced diver with the snorkel?"

"Are you blaming her?"

"I am trying to ascertain why she was so far from the shore."

"She bought the snorkel the day we arrived, from a shop on Corso Garibaldi. I expect she was a good swimmer, yes."

"Did she say anything to you before she went into the water?"

"No. 'See you later' perhaps."

The Inspector didn't appreciate flippancy. He got it all the time from the truants and petty thieves, who clogged up his day. He offered a long sigh and asked: "Did she say anything unusual?"

Drago noted the emphasis on the word 'anything'. He thought for a few seconds. "She took a string bag with her," he said tentatively. "She was going to collect shells or rocks, I think."

The Inspector raised his chin an inch. Drago expected Gigli to ask a question. He waited, but nothing came. Instead, the pen clicked.

"I will need a statement from you, Signor Drago, about what you saw. If we finish soon, you will be in bed and rested and so will I."

The Inspector uncovered two sheets of headed and lined paper among the debris on the table and proceeded to fill out the formal details in big careful block capitals. He asked his assistant for coffee and the youthful policeman disappeared outside the room.

Drago declined the offer. He told the story exactly as he remembered it and slowly, so the Inspector could keep up. The process took much longer than he expected. A slight breeze eked through the window and ruffled his neck. Towards the end of Drago's story, the coffee arrived and Gigli paused, giving his writing hand a breather.

"Have you spoken to the other witnesses?" asked Drago.

"We have statements from the life guards, the drivers and skiers."

"No. The people on the yacht. The big man. He was issuing instructions to the men driving the speedboats."

"Of course he was." The Inspector sat back in his seat and clicked the pen once. "They are his crew."

"But he didn't seem remotely concerned about Maddie. He was asking them about something else."

"How could you tell? You were a long way from the yacht."

"Something in his manner."

"Perhaps he was annoyed with them. The skiers did keep falling in the water. You said so yourself. They obviously need more practice."

"Have you questioned him?"

"No."

"Don't you think you should?"

"Not yet."

The statement was made with certain, deliberate finality. Drago refused to react to it. The two men watched each other's faces. The assistant watched them. The Inspector broke the stalemate, leaned forward, read out the last dictated sentence and asked Drago to continue. When the work was over, Gigli signed and dated the bottom of the page. He turned the papers around and pushed them across the table.

"Read it, please, and sign below. I hope my English spelling is correct."

Drago read the statement carefully. Satisfied, he took up the plain biro offered to him, but paused before putting pen to paper.

"What did the driver say," he asked, "the one who hit Miss Forrest?"

"He said it was an accident. He didn't see her."

"Naturally."

"Don't be bitter, Signor," said the Inspector. "Accidents happen in all places in the world. It is sad, yes. We will of course speak to the victim. Did the hospital indicate when she might be well?"

"No. I'm going there tomorrow. I can find out."

"That would be kind. Grazie."

"I have lots to organise. Insurance, flights home, that sort of thing."

"Si. That is good. It is good to remain occupied at a time such as this."

"Yes."

Unexpectedly, one of the mobile phones rang with a jarring sound. The Inspector picked it up and talked in rapid Italian for several seconds. He shut it off and smiled.

"My wife. She wishes me home." The Inspector tapped a long tapered finger on the papers. "Please, Signor."

Drago signed off the statement. The Inspector took it, gathered all the documents together and parcelled them back in the green wallet. "Thank you, Signor. We should not need to speak again, but if you do need to, you know we are here."

Drago wondered if he should be grateful. He nodded. No hands were shaken. He was escorted outside. Another summer's day was about to break. He lit a cigarette, took the short return walk to his hotel suite and slept for two hours, if restlessness could be called sleep. On waking, he showered hot until his skin hurt. Afterwards, he sat at the small dressing table, still cluttered with Maddie's beauty products, and made a list of who to contact and what he needed to say.

At exactly seven, he went down to the breakfast hall where the waiter offered polite concern. It was a big open plan room, with a large kitchen to one side. This was where Signora di Pace conducted her Italian cookery classes. By ten o'clock, the staff would have cleared the hall and the kitchen and prepared the way for the Signora's daily feasts. The dozen novice amateur chefs would join the bustling, cheerful Signora at half-past and cook non-stop until two thirty when they would eat what they had prepared and retire, just like the rest of Otranto's catatonic populace.

There were still two days of the course to run, but Drago wasn't going. To be honest, he'd taken all he could stand of the jolly woman's incessant banter and her ever demanding meals. Food ought to be simple. She made it too damn complicated, all those fish to bone, the pesto to mash and endless garlic shaving. Fantastic, but damn fussy.

After breakfast, Drago started on those important phone calls. The first was to the hospital. The second to England and an at-first panic stricken then confused conversation with Maddie's parents. They had not known she was in Italy. They had no idea who Jon Drago was. He didn't enlighten them either. A friend is a friend if the suit fits. The cuffs and collars could come later. He left his contact details. It did not surprise him to learn they planned to fly to Brindisi on EasyJet. Drago insisted on meeting them at the airport. Then he spoke to the insurance people and spent a long time discussing the details of the accident and the possibility of potential compensation. Drago rarely took his laptop abroad with him, certainly not for a holiday. It proved too much of a distraction. He had the Personal Injury claim forms emailed to the hotel for his attention. He was certain the management would oblige him some private time at a workstation.

Lastly, Drago returned to the breakfast room and apologised to Signora di Pace. Having escaped her clutches, he made his way to the garage to collect the Fiat. It was a long dispiriting journey to Lecce. The hospital looked no more pleasant in the sunlight.

He found Maddie drowsy but awake. She almost smiled, although one side of her face was horribly purple. She'd been immobilised using a cross-sling strapped to her chest which kept her injured shoulder and arm upright. The doctor's prognosis was like a medical dictionary. In layman's terms, her shoulder was fucked. The head of the humerus was broken in two places and had been set, but the injury was compounded by a dislocated shoulder. The collarbone was shattered in two places and had broken through the skin at an angle. They'd cut her open and reset it with pins and screws. The scapula was merely fractured, which the doctor attributed to the blow coming from the front. If she'd been hit from behind they didn't think it would have survived in any shape at all.

"You look dreadful," he said after a long moment of silence during which he just stared at her.

"Thanks," she mumbled. "Is this what you look like after your scrapes?"

It was good that she has retained her good humour.

"I don't need you to talk, Maddie, just rest. Listen. I've got some news for you. I contacted your parents. They're flying out today. I'm going to pick them up from Brindisi this afternoon."

Her eyes widened. He couldn't tell if this was from surprise, fright or pleasure.

"And the insurance company says you're fully covered. You won't have to pay for anything."

She nodded.

"I made a statement to the police."

Another nod.

"I expect they'll be paying you another visit."

She nodded a third time.

"A tall man," she croaked. "A bit scruffy."

"Yes. Inspector Gigli. He didn't wait for my call then. What did you tell him?"

"Not much. I was tired. He didn't believe me."

"What about?"

"About why I was swimming so far out in the bay."

It was painful for her to speak. Tears began to well up in the corners of her eyes. Drago tried to make her stay silent, but she wouldn't.

"I'm a good swimmer, Jonathon, ever since I was a little girl. It helps with my asthma, the doctor told me. Well, I've got so much better now I'm older and I can swim easily even in the sea. The water in the bay is so clear you can almost make out the seabed. You know; you've seen it too. And using the snorkel I was diving for short periods and looking at the sea life, the rocks, the aquatic plants. It really was beautiful and undisturbed down there, especially further out where the tourists don't play. I saw starfish the size of plates locked onto rocks and boulders, mackerel schools and loping grey mullet patrolling the sea grass. And then, I got far out and the speedboats started to mess everything about. I had no idea why they were skiing so late in the day. I should have known because we'd seen them do it for the last few days."

"Yes. I remembered that too."

"Shh. Don't interrupt." Her voice was small and he could tell she feared she might not make it to the end of the tale before one of the nurses returned and admonished her. "I mean, they have miles of open sea on the other side of the yacht, why were they skiing close to the shore? The sea life got scared. Those foaming arrows frightened the fish. The vibrations made them squirrel in circles, seeking an escape. Even I could feel it: the steady thump of the motor. Crabs were retreating under rocks or burying themselves in the sand. I was coming to the end of the air in the sump when one of the skiers toppled into the water. I'd half expected it. We'd seen if before, right? Well, the man wasn't down for very long. I could see his black suit hanging in the water while I made for the surface. The motorboat had come back, I assumed to help him fix the skis and the man was clinging to the rear of the hull, his hand scrambling over the fibreglass. Something dropped from the stern and fell to the seabed."

"What do you mean 'something'?"

It was a struggle for her now, but Maddie kept at it, the words coming in little gasps.

"I kept looking, Jonathon. Kept diving. Further and further out. There was a whole chain of them. Little canvas packages scattered all over the seabed. Some of them were black, some of them were brown. You remember the skiers stopped for a bit?"

"Yes."

"That's when I touched one. It was wrapped tight, sealed with wax and tape. I couldn't open it."

"Did you tell the police?"

"I told you I did. The Inspector, he said nothing about it, made a little note in his book, that's all."

"Fuck."

"That's not all I saw." Maddie continued to whisper through half a mouth. "When the men restarted the skiing, the messing about, this time they dived right down and retrieved the black bags."

"Only the black bags?"

A nod. Drago gave her some water which she drank through a straw. Maddie kept talking a while longer, explaining exactly what she saw, how she got hurt and why. She'd run out of air and surfaced too quickly directly in the speedboat's path. Drago soothed her perspiring forehead with a cool towel.

"Do you think the bags are still down there?" he asked.

"How should I know?"

"Do you want me to find out?"

Maddie took a shallow breath.

"No," she said. "Not if it means you're going to end up like this as well. You've got enough scars already."

"Yours are way worse than any of mine. Christ, Maddie, I thought you'd died."

He wiped her face once more. She winced as the cloth passed over her swollen cheek. "Will I be pretty again?"

"Of course you will. Brandon will shower you with flowers. He's got good taste."

"So have you. Sometimes." She paused and stared straight at him, recognition suddenly clicking on. "Oh, no! Is he coming too?"

"No, no, nothing like that. I just thought –"

It'd be better for you, was what Drago intended to say, but the words wouldn't come out. He was saved by a nurse who appeared with a small plastic tray of drugs. While they were administered, he checked his phone for flight arrivals.

"I need to get a hotel sorted for your Mum and Dad," he said. "Give me a moment."

There was a Cittadilecce bed and breakfast very close to the hospital and after trying to speak over the phone, he walked there instead and arranged matters in person, paying for three nights. Back at the hospital, Maddie was dozing again. The drugs had worked almost instant magic. She looked dreamy from one side, aghast on the other. He sat on the dreamy side and took her good hand and played with the fingers, just how she liked it. Maddie stirred and smiled weakly.

"That's nice," she murmured.

"I have to pick up your folks soon."
She didn't seem to hear.
"Hmm, come closer, I want to tell you something."
Drago leaned in and she whispered in his ear.

***

8pm. Drago sat on the rocky shelf, flippers next to him, mask and snorkel in hand. The water skiers had finally retreated. The Atlantis Club was in transformation. The night lights were switched on and the music began to pump its obnoxious beat. To the south, several yards to his right, the harbour light was winking.

Drago picked up his binoculars. While waiting for Maddie's parents, he'd looked up online to discover which shops in Lecce sold 'binocolo'. There was one close to the hospital. First, he ensured her relatives were settled in. Drago was polite and pleasant. They were suspicious and slightly intrigued. He took them to the hospital first, then showed Maddie's father the hotel's location. It was within walking distance, so they wheeled the cases there and Drago arranged for everything to be charged to his card.

"You don't have to," said Mr Forrest.

"It's the least I can do." He needed an excuse. "I'm not good with this medical stuff. Gives me the shits."

A pair of sixty-year old eyebrows raised to the obscenity.

"You're doing fine."

"No, not really," Drago said. "I was wondering – I don't know how you'd feel about it – shouldn't Maddie be moved? Back home, I mean. She'd be better cared for in England, surely?"

"I hadn't thought about it."

"Well, the insurance company will pay for it and at least she'd be home."

"We'll see."

They walked back to the hospital in virtual silence. Drago made an excuse to exit as quick as he could. He blew a kiss to the dreamy half of Maddie's face and left her to the smothering attentions of Mum and Dad. He noted her eyes pleaded for him to stay.

Drago went straight to the address stored in his phone. It was an outdoor specialist selling hunting equipment, mostly fishing tackle and bait, but he saw boxes of ammunition behind the counter and through an archway was a gunsmith's shop. Drago was only interested in the field glasses. He inspected three types and chose the Cavalry 10x50, designed for hunters, boaters and the military. The binoculars were lightweight and came with rubber armour for an easy grip and multi-coated optics for increased resolution. The 50mm aperture allowed better light efficiency in poor visibility.

Once more, Drago raised them to his eyes. The pilots were tucking the two motor launches onto the rear landing deck of the yacht. There was a sea level access door which allowed the boats to be winched into a holding pen. When both craft were inside the belly of the yacht, the landing deck was raised and the doors closed and sealed.

Drago scoured the deck side. He saw no one. He returned his focus to the open stretch of water between the two craggy arms of land which shaded the bay. He noted the position of the boat and the marker Maddie had told him about. The rear anchor chain was flexing. There was a slight breeze. He measured distances, calculated times. Quickly, he stripped off his shirt, trousers and plimsoles and wrapped them around the binoculars, placing the bundle in a dry crevasse among the rocks. He pulled on the flippers, wetted the mask and delicately trod down the stone reef until he was up to his waist in the cool Adriatic Sea. He strapped on the mask, fixed the snorkel and slowly thrust out into the darkening tide.

Five

Brief Encounters

Drago moved slowly through the lapping waters, conscious the sun had not fully set and he could be observed by anyone from the yacht if they chose to glance his way. The twilight swim would be better achieved by scuba diving, but Drago hadn't the time to hire the gear. He didn't know how long the yacht would be staying in Otranto or how long Maddie's bag could stay undetected. The water skiers might have already seen it. They might, out of curiosity, have recovered it. So, he'd watched the skiers carefully as they repeated the same tomfoolery of yesterday and the days before. Underwater, they were no doubt repeating the same operation Maddie had witnessed. Drago hadn't seen anything resembling her string bag being slung on the deck of a speeder, but it was hard to tell in that hazy late-day glow, even with the binoculars.

It was getting noticeably darker the further he padded from the shore. Drago carried with him a waterproof pencil torch, bought from the same outlet as the field glasses and stored in the zip pocket of his swimming shorts. He didn't want to use it unless an occasion demanded more light. The flash might attract attention. Even in the gathering gloom, his tan-pink skin was beacon enough. From above, he must look like a gigantic red mullet. Below him, Drago could see nothing. Neptune's world, which by day was always active, wriggling with life, was a heartless indigo blue, the colour of the stygian deep, turning the watery mass into nothing more than a dead sailor's grave.

He counted to one hundred as he swam, then broke through the beating tides, twisting his head to stare through the visor and adjust his route. He took a deep breath, filled his lungs and the sump to capacity, and dived a few feet below the surface to continue his journey hidden by the blurred refraction. The current wasn't strong today. There was hardly a breath of wind. He was thankful for that. Despite the darkness, Drago had the impression the seabed was shelving away from him. Occasionally an outcrop of submerged boulders hedged into his peripheral vision. As he stuck to his navigable route, they became fewer and further away until only the tips poked at his sightlines. Drago swam lazily, arms by his sides, ankles flapping, letting the broad rubber flippers propel him forward like a slow torpedo. He controlled his breathing, taking long delicate breaths for optimum air efficiency. Years of snorkelling had attuned him to recognise when the sump was draining. His lungs had a high capacity; he'd once had them measured at almost seven-and-a-half litres. The sump's air pocket was his back up. He felt the tweak in his lungs now, pushed upward and broke the surface with a tiny splash.

The sea was sparkling. The lights were on in the yacht's staterooms, throwing glimmering white shadows across the near vicinity. The stern of the yacht remained in semidarkness. A small yellow half-halo illuminated *Diamantin*'s name plate. The last glimpse of amber sun was disappearing below the horizon. Drago grimaced. He'd left it too late. His caution had delayed him and the swim had taken longer than he expected. Now, having to use the torch might make this a tricky little trip after all.

Air refilled, Drago dived again and swam on. He gave it another hundred counts. The windswept current was stronger now he was fully exposed from the shelter of the bay. It rippled off the ragged coastline and dragged his body towards open water. Drago felt the pull and push as the undertow forced him back and forth into and out of the cove. He kept himself as flat as he could, a thinner target for the slow, sucking flux. It was hard, lethargic work. He was using more oxygen than he wanted. He began to feel lightheaded through lack of decent air and had to surface much earlier than he intended. He trod water a moment. The final rise revealed the long black slanting chain vanishing into the water about twenty metres to his right, some five or ten shy of the yacht. It was loose, allowing the boat to move with the motion of the waves. From this angle, the deck appeared empty. Drago refilled his lungs and the sump, bit down hard on the mouthpiece and headed straight for the anchor chain.

Twenty counts later, his right hand grasped the slick interconnected links. Using the chain as a guide, he descended through the mystic blue. Initially Drago fought his body's urge to float. He didn't have any weights and his body was full of lightness because of the air he'd swallowed. After about fifteen metres the volume of water pressing on him made the descent unexpectedly fast. He landed on his knees, narrowly avoiding a fat ridge of bare rock. Drago dug out his pocket torch and rotated the barrel a notch. The thin light winked on, penetrating into what had been nothing but gloom. The panorama wasn't sandy. Seagrasses pulsated with the current, a soft fur in a breeze. Limpet covered rocky crests blighted the harmony. Amphibians spiralled away from him, frightened by the lance of light. He couldn't make out what species they were, but they were small, silvery fish, like the whitebait or anchovies served in every restaurant along Lungomare. The big iron hook clung into the matted grass and sand, half buried under its weight.

Now, where was it? Drago panned the torch in a wide arc. Maddie said she'd left it down here, close to the anchor, a good and thorough sign post. He couldn't see it. Holding the chain with one hand, Drago swept the ocean floor again. Wait: there it was, virtually hidden by a rocky winding crevasse which jutted out of the vibrating meadow in a jagged disorientated jigsaw. He could just make out the tatty rope bag buried in the sloth. Maddie told him she'd been collecting shells since she was a teen. It was the colours, the ridges and curls that interested her, appealing to her artistic nature. Sometimes she painted them. Drago had seen one of her efforts: a collection of conch shells reflected in Poseidon's eyes. She'd entitled it *Mythology Ecology*. He'd told her it was startling. It was certainly better than her usual portraiture, all those representations of people's children or pets. As he made his way towards the bag, he noticed the air was beginning to dissipate. Damn. He was almost out.

Drago stretched out a hand and grabbed the fake fishbone handle. Immediately, sand ballooned around him. Something rose out of the crevasse. It was lumpen, glossy, red and grey and honed its big eyes on Drago's torso. Muscular ugly limbs suddenly swirled angrily around him. One of the tentacles seized a wrist. Octopus! It was a big one. A strong one. Not the sort they served in those damn restaurants. The body wasn't huge, they never were, perhaps the size of Drago's own chest, but the legs were enormous, long twisting ropes, almost two metres long. It must be a grass octopus, usually camouflaged, but now flushed crimson with rage.

The creature was clearly alarmed. What the hell was it doing so close to the shore? Was it a female nursing its eggs? Had he disturbed its sleep? The questions came as fast as Drago's reactions. Instinctively, he pulled away. Big mistake. The suckers clamped down on his skin. Another long snakelike limb whirled through the water. It clasped the same arm, higher up, near the elbow, yanking at him. Confused, Drago found himself wrenched towards the beast. This wasn't right. They didn't attack humans, not usually. This one must be agitated, disturbed by the constant fooling of the water skiers, the constant diving, the dropping of packages. It had lost patience and Drago was the metaphorical last straw.

They wrestled. The tentacles encircled him. A tug of war for his arm. He was losing. The bastard thing was too strong, all out of proportion to its size. Through a misty sandstorm Drago could see the body, misshapen like a half-full rucksack, the waving tendrils as thick as a man's wrist and covered in an army of vicious suckers. The two on Drago's arm were cutting into his skin, a lethal unforgiving grip. He was stunned by the violence. He had no hands free to fight. His eyes widened as he was pulled inexorably forward. He couldn't understand it. Octopus ate crabs and molluscs, not big fleshy humans. That was why it had a tough nose, a beak shaped like a parrot's, designed to smash shells. Beneath the hooked stub the creature had a mouth. It had one tooth, a radula, rucked on its tongue. He saw the blubbery orifice open, waiting to crush his arm and deliver its venom. That was it! Octopus poisons didn't kill. They disabled. The venom was a bacteria, stored in the mouth's saliva, and the bacteria had no respect for size. If the tooth bit, Drago would be paralysed. The tentacle pulled him closer.

Everything seemed to happen in slow motion. The weight of water made his movements cripplingly sluggish. He took what had to be the last breath of air from the snorkel. Keeping a tight grip on the bag with one hand, he fought the tentacles and raised the torch with his other. Clumsily, he rotated the barrel full on and thrust forward. The piercing light arrowed onto the monstrous twin eyes. The thing took fright. It spun away with a sudden brutal movement. The tentacles heaved over like a bullwhip. Drago was flung upside down and swept over the dense carpet before a cloud of black oily soot enveloped him. Drago panicked. His arm was free. He still held the bag, but he'd lost the snorkel and he'd taken on salt water. Instinct made him claw his way upward. It was like swimming through treacle. He forced his legs and arms to push harder, fuller strokes. How far to the surface? Not far, surely. Twenty metres, thirty. Panic gave way to something resembling terror. His lungs and throat burned. Saturated with water, there was barely any oxygen left in them. His insides curdled as he struggled to escape the rapacious deep. He might yet pass out, as good as dead. He gagged. His body gave up. His throat opened and he was swallowing putrid salt water. His feet made one final urgent effort, kicking rapidly.

Drago burst through the surface and heaved an enormous gulp of air. He spewed the crap from his gullet, coughed, spluttered. A thousand thorns lanced at his throat. His head pounded. His eyes glazed. His hearing sang. He'd come up too fast. He was going to faint. Don't do it! Don't pass out! Drago sought the safety of the anchor chain. It was there, close by, thank God. He stretched a weakened arm. His free hand clasped the metal links. The torch had been dropped during the struggle. Just as well. His coughs had been heard. Through the whistling in his ears, he heard voices. His eyes were unfocussed, but it was dark, night time, as dark above as it had been below. All of a sudden Hades was everywhere, his mythological presence some portent of disaster. Fleetingly, by chance, Drago's vision cleared enough to make out the yacht's stern rail. Two men stared out at the sea. Had he been spotted? The men were gabbling. He couldn't pick the words. A foreign language. One of them disappeared. He was going for a searchlight. Had to be. It was too much of a risk to stay put.

Drago took a deep, agonised breath and sunk himself underwater once again. He headed vaguely for land. The pain was immediate and immeasurable. His skull wanted to explode. He was confused, uncertain which way he was headed. The weight on his arm didn't help. The bag contained more than bloody shells, just how Maddie said it would. Madeleine. Thinking of her spurred him. Concentrate, Jon. Forget the pain. It's only temporary. Think! Think clearly. Look for the light. Look for the lighthouse. That's why you picked the south promontory. It was close to the beacon. The light will guide you – use it!

He swam in a dreamworld. Some sort of nightmare. Swimming. Tentacles. Black seas. Rolling waves and sprinkles of stars. Shouts. The ever present clap of his blood coursing life back to his brain, of oxygen filling the void in his blood, of his soul fighting. Pump your legs. Roll your arms. Kick your ankles. Surface. Dive. Surface. Keep moving. Keep fighting the waves and the exhaustion. A huge beam of light shot from the stern of the ship and swept across the cruel sea. Had they seen him? Why did they want to find him? Gasping, he paused, eyes open, salt stinging. The white arc retreated. He swam on, a robotic, jerking sideways stroke, half beneath the surface, half above, watching for the returning span of light. When it came, he vanished to a shallow depth. He almost expected a suckered limb to curl itself around a leg and pull him back down into the deadly dark coffin. And then his flippers slapped at sharp rocks and his fingers latched onto solid ground. There was the lighthouse. Here, somewhere, was his bundle of clothes. Drago hauled himself onto the spiteful shore and collapsed into a heap on the wet stones, sheltered from the roaming light by a cluster of boulders.

He didn't know how long he lay there. He probably passed out. Sometime, something woke him. He could hear the familiar putt of a speedboat, one of the launches from *Diamantin*. The engine was rumbling closer, then fading. Drago peered into the night. One of the boats was slowly patrolling in widening circles, its passengers spreading powerful torch beams over the impenetrable sea. Soon they would turn their attention to the shore.

Drago decided to move. He kept low, located the bundle of hidden clothes and headed for the shale plateau, where he'd left the car. He ached all over. His right arm was particularly sore. There were fat red blotches where the octopus had snared him. He winced. Worst of all, his lungs felt bruised. Breathing was awkward. They must have been under tremendous pressure to collapse. He'd been damn lucky. Miracles and nine lives sprang to mind. Gingerly, Drago pulled on his trousers and shirt. As he crouched to fix his plimsoles, he heard another vehicle pull into the makeshift carpark. Quickly, Drago shifted behind the nearest boulder. The new vehicle's front lamps flashed by.

The precaution had been instinctive, yet it also felt strangely necessary. The car was a Ford Escort. Two men got out. One walked over to Drago's Fiat Panda. He gave it a brief inspection and returned to his colleague who had opened the Escort's rear boot. Both men were already dressed in black scuba diving suits. In the trunk were stored tanks, flippers and masks. The men also took out a rope net the size of a pillow case. Unseen, Drago watched as the divers took the gear down to the very same promontory he'd just abandoned. Intrigued, he skirted the field, edging towards them. His ears were still shot, but this time he deciphered Italian accents. One of the men pointed to the circling speedboat. They sat down, waiting for the bay to calm. Drago sat too, hidden by the scrub and the dark. The evening breeze chilled him a little. He had the binoculars with him and popped off the cap. Looking through the lens he saw the two men talking. The nearest one constantly scratched at a boil on his face. Drago, and the men, had to wait almost a whole hour before the speedboat ended its search. When it was over, the scuba divers pulled on their gear and marched into the lapping sea.

So, they were searching too. They might find their treasure one parcel short. Drago returned to his car, sat in and pulled the package from Madeleine's string bag. It was hefty, solid and wrapped and sealed with black stitched canvas. Drago picked at the ties, eventually split one and started to untangle the knots. There were more packages inside, these ones clear and heat sealed.

"Shit!"

Drago couldn't help the exclamation. Each package contained an enormous stack of bright, clean twenty Euro notes split into wraps of a thousand. He counted the wedges and stopped counting when he reached fifty.

Urgently, Drago shoved the money back inside the canvas sacking. He drove apprehensively back to the Hotel San Pietro. In the hotel car park, he transferred the money into his own rucksack before returning to the suite and throwing the haul on the bed. He stared at it. There was way, way more than fifty thousand Euros.

It was almost midnight when he phoned Maddie, but he found her parents still fussing. Now he understood why the poor girl had looked so startled when he'd informed her they were flying out. He couldn't tell her much over the phone. Deciding against a blow-by-blow account, he casually said: "I've got it."

"So, you might have a story, Jonathon," she whispered down the phone line.

"I might have evidence. I don't know about a story."

"Are you going to the police?" There was a pause followed by an agitated: "No, Mum, it's Jonathon. He's thinking of talking to the police again about the accident."

"I'd better not tell you what's in the damn thing."

"Let me guess." He could tell she was trying to make the conversation sound two-sided and innocent. "Is it about money?"

"Yes. Lots of it. You think I should go to the police?"

"That's up to you."

"There's more than enough here to get you away from Italy."

She didn't reply. He sensed Madeleine frowning. No. She was better off out of it. Better off not knowing everything. Drago told her she was beautiful and hung up. He repacked all the money in the rucksack, placed it in the wardrobe and took a long revitalising shower. He dabbed moisturiser on the burns, drank water and then headed to Vicino's.

Drago sat outside reflecting on his sunset swim. He was accompanied by moths. He nursed a beer and stabbed thoughtfully at olives with a cocktail stick.

Otranto was finally giving in to sleep. The buttery walls of the old town still shone under the night lights and occasionally he'd notice someone making their way beneath Porta Alfosina. The sound of lightweight end-of-the-night disco music hung in the air, whistling from one of the bars along Via Idro, begging the punters to go home. Eventually the last of the diners also departed and Paulo came and sat with his best English friend.

"Who owns that bloody yacht, Paulo?" Drago asked.

"I don't know. Why do you want to know?"

"The police didn't seem especially bothered. I thought perhaps they were famous."

"I doubt it. Someone in oil, maybe."

"Maybe."

"Try the harbourmaster."

This turned out to be a pernickety man who'd seen better days. His English was fair to middling. Drago knocked on the door to his office the next morning. Positioned beside the Lega Navalle Italiana building, the thin faced man could stare all day across the lines of small pleasure boats which now formed the brunt of Otranto's portside space. Drago noted he couldn't actually see the big white yacht from such a vantage point.

The harbourmaster only half listened as Drago made up an excuse for calling unexpectedly and unexpectedly early.

"I wanted to ask about the *Diamantin*," he ended. "My friend was injured the other day."

"The accident?" confirmed the thin man. "It is a police matter."

"I was surprised you haven't asked the yacht to move back from the shore. It is rather close."

The man glanced at Drago suspiciously.

"Don't tell me my job, Signor. It is not close to the harbour. The Captain, me, we have a good relationship. There has never been any problem before. Your friend, she got too close."

"Who is the captain?"

"Belzac. He knows the shallows well."

"Is he a local man?"

"Local? No. he comes every few weeks. Signor Sabatini is conducting some business here. He always stays on the yacht, never ashore. When he visits, you understand. He has many houses, so I hear."

Drago opened a fresh pack of Marlboros. He offered first pick to the harbourmaster. The crab hand swept out and seized a smoke. They went outside and talked a little more. The curve of the big yacht's rear deck was just visible beyond the north arm of the bay.

"She is a beautiful ship," said Drago.

"Si, Signor. Bella. Bella. When I first saw her, I was almost in love."

Drago smiled. Only Italian's could talk about love to inanimate objects with such sincerity. It sounded laughable in other accents.

"When did you first see her?"

"Two, perhaps three years ago. She comes several times a year, for a few weeks each stay."

"So Signor Sabatini can attend to business?"

"Si. They come and go. Today, for instance, the Captain informs me they will be heading down the coast this evening. Just to the peninsula. They'll stay a few days and then return."

"Perhaps the water skiing is safer there."

The harbourmaster caught the bitter tone. He exhaled long and hard and a plume of grey mist encompassed his head. Drago thought the thin man was going to say something profound, but no; his insight manifested itself through silence.

"Sabatini," he ventured. "That's an Italian name."

"Si."

"So he's Italian."

"I cannot say. The yacht is registered in Albania."

Drago offered another cigarette and was about to depart when the harbourmaster said: "Of course, the woman, the beautiful girl, she is not Italian."

"How do you know?"

"She doesn't siesta. She comes with the motor launch every afternoon and goes into town. I don't know where. Maybe she shops. Maybe she has a lover." He smirked at the thought. "I don't ask. I merely watch. But if she was an Italian, certainly a woman from Puglia, she would rest in the heat."

"I see."

Drago nodded his thanks. He was glad he'd gone swimming last night because *Diamantin* was departing for a few days. That gave him just enough time to arrange Maddie's medical care and journey home, perhaps to arrange some other things too. Maybe Maddie was right. There might be a story in the yacht after all. His instincts were exercising their muscles once more.

It was only a short walk back to the hotel. He camped out on the terrace, drank coffee and used the local stationery to write a long letter to Maddie, apologising for being a bastard and explaining how he was going to pay for her medical care. He would be staying on a few days in case anything came of this potential story. As an afterthought, he added that she not disclose the contents of the letter to anyone. He sealed and addressed it. Later on that day, he would drive to Lecce and deliver it, but only to the nurses' station. He didn't want to say goodbye. It might hurt too much.

Next, Drago called the hospital and after much confusion he managed to speak with Madeleine's father and assured him, if the doctors agreed, the finance was available to transfer his daughter to London via a private jet and with complete medical care. He was astounded. Drago insisted, without explaining.

He left the letter on the empty dresser. Only his Samsung, wallet and the binoculars remained. Everything else of Madeleine's was now at the hospital or with her parents. It looked desolate. He picked up the wallet and phone and went to visit Paulo.

"I need a place to stay," he said quickly before Paulo had the opportunity to quiz him about all manner of unimportant subjects, like he did every time they met before condescending to real business.

"I thought you would go home with Madeleine," Paulo said diplomatically.

"Her parents are better qualified for that. No. There's something I need to take care of here. I was hoping you might know somewhere with a spare room."

"At this season?"

"Yes."

They were standing in the kitchen. The restaurant wasn't open yet. Pasta was being prepared, fish boned, pesto ingredients smashed. Drago felt as if he was back in the theatre of Signora di Pace. Paulo gave a tiny shake of the head. Behind him, his mother poked the restaurateur with a serving spoon and muttered in rapid Italian.

"No, Mama, I can't."

She continued talking until her son's objections subsided.

"Alright, alright."

"What?"

"A family friend," explained Paulo. "An architect. Francesco Lombardo. He is on holiday in Morocco. Why he would wish to go somewhere hotter, I have no idea. He has a villa in the new town. It's on the hillside. It looks over the harbour."

Drago said nothing. He knew better than to make a suggestion. The offer had to come from his friend or it would not be made at all.

"I have the key." Paulo saw Drago's face crease into the makings of a smile and started to backtrack. "I can't let you run amok.

It is a nice house. Very clean. I shouldn't let you there. I am only to answer the post, you understand."

"I can do that for you."

"How? You don't know Italian."

"I'll bring it to you." Drago continued to smile. "Every morning. I promise."

"I once had a woman who promised me that."

"I'm not her."

"True enough."

"I'm very clean, very tidy. I won't break a thing. Hell, I won't move a thing." Drago paused. "Is it about money?"

"No, no. no. Trust. A greater thing than money."

"Talk to your friend. You have his contact details, right? Tell him I'll pay a hundred Euros a day."

It took a while to get the architect on the phone. The conversation didn't seem to be going well. Drago didn't think Paulo was being direct enough.

"Tell him I'm writing my book," he suggested. "I need peace and quiet. And I'll pay him. Tell him I'll pay one hundred a day."

The architect must have overheard because Drago detected a change in the tone of the conversation.

"Two hundred," said Paulo.

"Done."

Afterwards, for some inexplicable reason, they shook hands. Paulo held the hand longer than expected. His eyes latched onto the nasty red blotches on Drago's forearm.

"What happened to you?"

"It's nothing."

"Doesn't look like it."

"It's fine. Mosquito bites. I had a window open last night."

Paulo knew it was a lie, but didn't ask. You never asked those questions in the south. You waited for your friend to tell you. But even if Drago never told him, he would understand, like he'd always understood about Madeleine.

***

Drago woke early and headed for the balcony of the Villa Camprese. The name amused him; an Italian salad. Paulo's architect friend either had a sense of humour or he was from Capri. The villa was spacious, light and clean, constructed on two floors above a car port and service bay and with a small driveway and ornamental garden, itself surrounded by fragrant pines. He breathed in the fresh welcoming scent of morning. Drago stared at the red streaked sky and the shimmering bay of Otranto and the big white yacht that had moored in it last night. Once more *Diamantin* sat astride the flat silver sea.

The last three days had been a hectic round of phone calls and goodbyes. Madeleine had read the letter and immediately inundated him with phone calls and messages. Drago spent most of his time organising her return home. He found the steadying influence of Maddie's father best for this. Neither daughter nor mother seemed capable of these big decisions, being too nervous or too irate. Drago had never seen Maddie so angry. By taking control for her, and by being complicit with her parents, he had overstepped the boundary of friendship. He'd cost her independence and he saw the bitterness in her eyes. But what did she expect? he told himself. Everyone's actions, not just his but the nurses and insurers, the cabin crew on the plane, the holiday representative who belatedly arrived, were all taken with her best of health at heart. Her peace of mind though didn't come into it. Maddie knew that, of course, but she fought the inevitable until they strapped her onto the stretcher for the journey to the airport and the private flight home.

Drago shoved the cash required into a separate section of his suitcase so it was ready to deposit into his British bank account and pay the multiplying credit card. He felt no compunction to report to the police his discovery of €200,000 wrapped in a canvas bag. The telling might create more problems. Nor did he tell Paulo, although he was tempted. It was the sort of windfall any man would desire. Drago had counted the remains several times and wondered to himself exactly how it might benefit him.

He took a revitalising shower. As he prepared breakfast of fruit and yoghurt, the earliest hot pangs of the day were tickling the air. He took a cursory glance through the long windows, stopped chopping bananas and squinted.

There was movement on the yacht. A figure was walking along the port gangway to the forward deck.

Quickly, Drago was outside. He grabbed the cavalry binoculars from the table, raised them to his eyes and sucked in a breath.

She was naked. The girl walked confidently, either because she knew she was alone or because she knew she didn't care. Drago blinked and rescanned the remainder of the boat. It was empty. Not a single crew member in evidence. Nor could he see any obvious security cameras. He dismissed the latter thought as an irrelevancy. If the girl wanted to expose herself, that was her choice. He manipulated the lenses to full zoom.

She was flawless. Her skin was like melted butter, in the moment just before it burns in the pan, when it is dark, caramel and mysterious. She wore a slim bracelet on her right ankle and a larger one on her left wrist. They were identically patterned, weaved white and yellow gold. Nothing else adorned her. She walked with a gentle sway, as if she wore heels, the hips gyrating with her footfalls, the shoulders in time with the hips so the breasts, proud, upright and beautifully sculpted, moved with them. The taut backside showed not an ounce of fat and dovetailed to long athletic legs. She had lustrous black hair, shiny in the sun. The ebony mane fluttered with the breeze. She made no attempt to brush it away.

The girl carried a large beach towel over her shoulder which partially obscured her. She dropped it beside the pool and for a brief tantalising few seconds Drago saw her revealed. The neat chocolate brown nipples atop their peaks, the slender waist and capacious hips, the buttery skin descending over a smooth swallow belly to a plump hairless sex. Drago exhaled long and hard. The girl stepped into the pool and the moment was gone. She swam for ten minutes using big lazy strokes.

Drago could only make out glimpses of her, yet he sensed the first unmistakeable twinge of lust. His breathing became heavy. His heart beat faster. A single bead of sweat formed under his fringe and slowly, gently trickled its way down his cheek to his freshly shaved chin. Her natural behaviour, simple yet exotic, was profoundly arousing. The exercise soon bored her. She sat on the edge of the pool, her back to the coast and her face to the sun. Drago frowned. What was that on her right shoulder? He'd not seen it as that side of her had been hidden from view. It looked like a tattoo. Drago peered closer. No. It was a bruise, a large one or a cluster of them, just below her shoulder blade. It was the sort of hidden location abusers would focus on, a place where a bruise could be explained: she fell out of bed, she knocked it on the cupboard door standing up, she carried too heavy a rucksack. Drago's mouth set hard. His teeth gripped.

After fifteen minutes, the girl picked up the towel and wrapped it around her body, tucking it into her cleavage. She made for the interior of the yacht where he couldn't follow her. Drago sat down, almost shaking with excitement. He remembered those few brief encounters at the San Pietro, the semi-shy eyes, the instant intrigue of a half-smile on her graceful lips, how he'd resisted the urge to pause and stare. She was probably used to that. Women so spectacular generally expected it. So, any approach had to be carefully considered. Being cheeky wouldn't cut it. He needed a moment of serendipity and an interest to share, common ground like swimming, or perhaps food or people. Drago stroked his lower lip with a thumb. They did have an acquaintance of sorts: Madeleine.

He ought, he knew, to feel guilty. Not only had he recently been bedding Maddie and committing close to adultery for it, but now the poor injured girl was back in hospital in England wondering why Jonathon Drago wasn't there to comfort her. If he felt like a bastard, and probably deserved the title, Drago consoled himself by ensuring Brandon, the mysterious boyfriend, had been contacted. The young man turned out to be an aspiring musician. His appearance might confuse the parents, but Drago sincerely believed Maddie was getting better comfort and attention from proper friends and family, not his dressed up, see-through, part-time efforts. That was his all-round problem with love affairs. Domesticity didn't suit him. He knew it. It was why he never saw the end coming, because he never prepared for the future, so a relationship simply hovered in cuckoo land, a fine madness while it lasted, but it would never last, it'd all come hurtling down.

And here was a new madness. He couldn't tell exactly when it had started, but it had something to do with a beautiful girl, a yacht, bundles of money and the man who held sway over them. It intrigued him. She intrigued him. He itched to talk to her, to find out exactly who she was, who he was and what they were doing in Otranto.

Yes. An itch. It was as if he'd been bitten.

Six

The Translucence of Pears

The first time Marcelo Sabatini had been invited to Tarantella was two summers back. The party had been a big affair. He'd visited once before, out of courtesy, an introduction by the request of the local Mayor.

"It will smooth your operations, Signor," said Mandriano. "Take your companion. The Comte enjoys the company of women."

This time the party was a big affair. Sabatini had received a printed invite, delivered from a small slow-moving catamaran, the letter handled with tremendous reverence.

From outside Tarantella resembled a Moorish palace, bathed only in moonlight and the haze of a hundred flickering candles. Inside, the Arab furnishings and drapes suggested an obsession with a long deposed era. The crusty, faded, thick wallpaper peeled at the tips. There was a faint whiff of decay to the atmosphere, one which the assembled, beautifully presented guests could not erase. Everything, even the food, tasted of decline and fall. Only the small orchestra appeared unaware of the sickly nature of the estate. Sitting outside on a terrace overrun by hibiscus, they played Italian interpretations of American jazz standards, the vibrant music at odds to the overarching gloom. The party was at its best outside. The guests preferred it there, away from the deathly pall. They could relax in the breeze, a hint of cooling sea salt interwoven with the fragrance of fresh flowers and scented candles, an aroma enough to bury the animal lick of the surrounding woodland. Night lamps provided shimmering flames of yellow. When guests danced, shaking shadows formed on the patio. Someone had told him the terrace had been re-laid especially for the birthday party. So there, among the battered pink walls, under the gleaming glow of those one hundred candles, the villa finally revealed its charm.

The Comte d'Orsi found large gatherings difficult. The sound of so many voices and so much movement echoed off the walls and around the room. It disturbed his concentration. Sabatini half understood the old man's struggle. He wondered if it also explained the garishness of the mansion.

Sabatini chomped his jaw tight over the cigar and sucked the acrid scent deep into his lungs. He exhaled slowly and surrounded himself with smoke. Someone was watching him with distaste. Let them watch, he told himself, his neck twisting left to observe the offending woman in the little group. It was Madriano's wife; a shrewish looking thing with ideas far above her station. Sabatini's one good eye craned to take in the conspicuous jewels she wore on her neck, wrists and fingers. Sabatini closed the lid slowly over the false left eye, opened it and turned away just as the woman clasped a horrified hand to her throat. He let out a single dismissive snort. Later he would speak to the Mayor. Clearly his wife did not understand how Madriano achieved his wealth and position. The Mayor had recently been reelected. Sabatini would remind him that a Mayor's power was finite.

The girl was dancing with someone, a younger man. For a few minutes, Sabatini watched them. The girl made no suggestion of impropriety. She knew never too. The young man gazed at her as if she was the most beautiful thing in the world. Well, she was, Sabatini told himself; almost. He reserved that moniker for the great gemstones of the world, one of which he wore constantly, set in a glass surround in his empty eye socket.

Black opals were the world's rarest gemstones, more expensive than white diamonds, a jewel only the truly wealthy, the truly powerful could afford. There was only one location in the world where they mined black opals: Lightning Ridge in Australia, a mere speck of land on that vast continent. He'd visited the site once, fascinated by the idea that wealth could be discovered by nothing more than luck. Black opals didn't form in veins, like precious metals and carbon based stones; they came from layer upon layer of spherical sand deposits, trapped for centuries under the earth as the surrounding water evaporated. Now, compacted and clear and crammed on a surface of black potch, an opal under light revealed a prism of gaudy colour. Ostentatious and ugly, some said. Beautiful, Sabatini thought. There was something undefinable about the richness of a gemstone, be it a diamond, a sapphire, a slice of blue quartz or the dark ebony resin of an opal. He had many such treasures in a huge collection purchased through the illegal proceeds of material gain. There were many fine pieces of jewellery in the Comte's personal collection too, but only one fascinated him and he went to seek it out.

Sabatini turned into the dusk of the interior. He passed from one reception room to another. They were empty of people. The rooms were musty. There were no carpets. Tiny dunes of dust and grit settled in corners. Cobwebs clung to the high ceilings. Sabatini scratched his face. All this dirt made him uncomfortable. It reminded him of his days as a poor man, the hovel he lived in before the riches.

He paused by the entrance to the final room. The sound of the orchestra stopped with him and melodramatically started again as he took a pace inside. The room was decorated with Persian fashions. Heavy curtains were pulled back from the windows, allowing twilight to penetrate the sadness. Sabatini stared at the walls. He was surrounded by oil paintings and display cases. There had been none in the other rooms. No mirrors either. The Comte d'Orsi had no use for them. Most of the pictures were faded portraits of family members. No great artists created these works, even though they stretched back to the early 1700s to the beginnings of a long lineage. The most recent pictures were as dark as their predecessors. Comte Umberto, 1880 – 1951, resplendent in a Navy uniform. Umberto Felipe 1921 – 1959, also a military man, but wounded, missing an arm and horribly scarred. Ferdinand, the thirteenth Comte d'Orsi, the current incumbent, depicted at an age when he ought to be young and sprightly.

Sabatini stretched out a hand to the canvas until, an inch from the dark, blemished oils, his fingers could trace the thin figure with its twisted face. What a lonely child he must have been. Born premature, better off dead. Sabatini sucked hard on the cigar. The tobacco of the Cohiba was rough and spiky. Another memory his youth, when he rolled cigarettes in cheap paper from the leftovers of others. A hard smoke. A hard life. What did this man, this Comte, know of hard worlds? Had he ever fought? Had he ever loved? Sabatini stared at the portrait. Beyond the obvious there was nothing. The eyes were blank. The expression bland. The artist had been unable to capture the essence of his adolescent subject. Instead, he portrayed blossoming life through the deep surrounding colours, the dense green of the fields outside the windows and the blood red poppies in the vase. And there, fixed to the chest of the young Comte, alongside the medals he could never have earned, was a beautiful stone. It was painted the same shade of red as the poppies. Blood red: Il Papavero.

Slowly he circled the room, studying the other portraits, his steps keeping time with the orchestra's muffled rhumba. There was no sign of any such spectacular stone in those works, not even in the days when opulence was commonplace. A family as important as the d'Orsi's would surely have wanted everyone to admire their riches. So where was the blood red stone? Sabatini inspected the display cases, expecting the search to reveal nothing. The exhibits held rings, brooches, tiaras, coronets, clasps, necklaces, timepieces, plates, medallions, earrings, chokers, eggs, statuettes, pins and stones set in fixings, extravagance for display only, jewellery produced by the great houses of Europe: Zolatas, Bulgari, Chopard, Van Cleef and Arples, Faberge and Boucheron. There was no blood red diamond.

Sabatini paused again in front of Ferdinand's portrait. Twists of tobacco smoke slid through his lips and hung about his head before the lightest of draughts cleared them, exactly as his mind cleared. Sabatini had seen the Conte's portrait before of course, when he made that introductory visit. He'd sat in this same room, shared mannered conversation and politely drank morning coffee. His one good eye had been drawn inexorably to it, over and over, until impatience and curiosity made him ask. The Comte waved a dismissive hand. Sabatini pressed on.

"I've seen this image, Comte, this diamond, thousands of times on a completely separate portrait. The same shape, the dimensions, even the same claw handed brooch. I tell you it is the same stone. I've been fascinated with it since I was a boy."

The Comte merely smiled.

"Let me tell you the story," said Sabatini. "My mother told it to me first when I was a boy. Then I'd read it, seen pictures in books, in museums and galleries, seen representations, fakes, all of this fabled treasure. We call it Il Papavero, the blood stone poppy. It was wrested from the Ottomans by Skanderbeg, the great Albanian hero. He installed it in the nation's coronation mace, so they said. The Pashaliks held it for centuries, so they said, and after them Mehmet Ali the Kingmaker acquired it, so they said. Ali had been born in Albania to a shipping merchant and he rose to prominence as governor in Egypt at a time when the Mamluks were struggling to maintain power across the empire. His rule as governor ended in senility. It was said that after the ruby disappeared, the French painter Couder was ordered to remove it from all the governor's portraits. Depending on which legend you read, the mace and the jewel were stolen by usurpers to the Mamluk dynasty or returned to Albania and lost on the shores of Lake Ohrid or sold to raise funds for Ali's impoverished family. There is documented evidence that Mehmet Ali visited Italy during his illness, to take the spa waters near Naples."

Sabatini paused. "Tell me, Comte, was the jewel lost then, or sold perhaps, and ended, miraculously, secretively, in the hands of the d'Orsi family?"

The Comte had only blinked. He drank his coffee.

"What does your companion think of my portrait?"

"I think it is a wonderful likeness," said the girl.

The Comte chuckled, thanked her and the moment was lost. Sabatini had cursed her frivolousness. It wasn't the first time she had failed to grasp his intentions. How could she not see the similarities? It was as if she hadn't even noticed the painting on *Diamantin* and the blood red diamond represented in it. Or perhaps she simply didn't care.

Sabatini cared. The story of the diamond had lingered through his youth. Now, it's image clung to his person. Sabatini stared until his one real eye hurt. He blinked, felt a twinge of wetness and brushed it away with a finger.

"May I help you?"

The voice came like a thunderbolt. Sabatini didn't let his surprise show. He turned swiftly on one heel and lowered the Cohiba.

"Some prosecco perhaps," he said to the interloper. He carried a tray, a bottle and two glasses freshly poured. The man had anticipated the request.

Sabatini took a glass and tasted. It was dry, sharp. He nodded approval while his good eye inspected the newcomer. The man was in his mid-forties and neatly presented in a formal coat and tails, but he did not look comfortable in the occupation. The suit hung badly, as if he'd been pressganged into wearing it. The stranger had a wild, rugged face. He had shaved, but hairs already crept through his pores. His eyes were dark, almost black and hooded. He was thick set and not especially tall. He'd be happier in slacks and a t-shirt working in the fields or the dockyards or stabbing a stiletto blade in a back alley for a leather wallet. He had arrived in near silence, quiet on his feet, like an assassin. Instinctively, Sabatini knew this man was someone to watch.

"I've seen you here," Sabatini declared. "The Comte d'Orsi relies on you. You give him his food. His wine." Sabatini drank again. "How long have you worked for the family?"

"Many years."

The man took the other glass without waiting for an invitation. He sipped it, twitched his nose with distaste and then downed the alcohol in one dramatic gulp. He placed the glass back on the tray and stood with the glass and bottle on the salver, exactly like any well-trained manservant.

"Years enough to learn all their secrets."

"All families share secrets," said Sabatini, "small and great."

"That is true, Signor; and the more powerful the family, the greater the secret and the greater the damage that secret will cause if the world discovers it."

"Oh, yes?" Sabatini finished the prosecco, placed it on the tray and indicated he wanted it refilled. "And who are you who knows so much?"

"My name is Atilla Ferrara," said the man, pouring from the bottle while still holding the tray aloft. "I am the Comte's valet."

Sabatini almost scoffed.

"Why should I listen to a servant?"

"I told you, Signor. I know many secrets." The valet was not perturbed by Sabatini's disdain. He held out the tray and the refilled glass. "For instance, are you aware the Comte d'Orsi is associated with the Unione Sacre Croce?"

"Many people know this."

"I have access to the current Capo."

"Do you?"

Sabatini flipped the long stub of ash from his cigar. It fell onto the floor where it smouldered until Atilla Ferrara stepped forward and stamped on it.

"The Comte is not from a respected family. The d'Orsi's have owned land and titles in the Salentine for centuries. But you notice from the portraits on the wall the Comte is not descended from a direct line. He has none of the features of the other portraits. A generation ago, the d'Orsi family could not provide a male heir. The line died out in the late 1950s. It was then, that the Unione Sacre Croce came to prominence and the Sada family built its reputation of ruthlessness through a series of bloody coups, eliminating each of its rivals. But Andrea Sada, Il Padrino, had a problem. He had three children. Two daughters and a son. But the son, Ferdinand, was blind. He was considered a liability, a man to be exploited, to be deposed. Yet, Andrea couldn't remove his son completely from influence, that would be disrespectful of the family tradition. It would make Andrea appear a bad father, a man who not only sired a disabled heir but could not, or would not trust him to manage the affairs of the Unione. So, Andrea Sada bought his son the title Comte d'Orsi from the last descendant, Umberto."

Ferrara waved his free arm at the two portraits, Umberto and Ferdinand. Sabatini followed the arm. It was true. There was no similarity between the two men. Perhaps that was why Ferdinand's portrait stuck out so much, for it lacked a true aristocratic mark. The blankness he'd spied, the unusually stiff manner, the inelegance, none of it marked him as a member of the d'Orsi family.

"It is ironic how the Sada family, who always tended to the poor, the peasants and the underclasses, suddenly became members of the elite," continued the valet. "It enabled Ferdinand to do local philanthropic work. He became the friendly face of the Unione and he garnered much sympathy. He played the role perfectly. He was honest and unprepossessing –until it came to the moment of his inheritance, for when Il Padrino died, he transferred the running of the Unione to his grandchild. Almost overnight my employer became an old and bitter man. Rejection can do that. Failure too. Ferdinand was weak in spirit. If you hurt a weak man, he bleeds easily. Perhaps now we see the result of that hurt, of the madness it caused. Even blind, a strong leader would have protested, reasoned and argued his case. The Comte did none of this. It was easy for power to be snatched from his failing grasp."

The lecture had not interested Sabatini much. One word made him take notice. "What do you know about power, Ferrara?"

"I know it is blessed. I know it is a curse. It is something to be prized."

"And why is a valet interested in power?"

"The Unione Sacre Croce is the largest mafia in the Salentine. I have worked for the Sada family since I was a boy, running errands for my father who also worked for them. My father was very close to old Andrea Sada, a caporegime who sat at his right hand. You see him in photographs. Look."

The valet pointed with his free hand. Sabatini looked at the black and white print in an exquisite gold frame. Three men were sitting at a dinner table. The signatures, scribbled left to right, read: *Il Padrino, Ferdinand Sada, Victor Ferrara.*

"How did your family lose such a position?"

"My father was murdered. He seduced another man's sister. Had my mother been alive he would have suffered in many worse ways. Murder was not necessary. The sister appreciated my father's doting. I was young and mad with revenge. I did not wait for the Capo's approval. After I took my revenge, I was caught. My deed was not supported by the Unione. Instead my revenge was used as an example by the police force who proved they could be tough on criminals. I was an example for the Unione who demonstrated that if you disobey them, you suffer by the law of the land, not the law of the Sacre Croce. I suffered in prison for twenty years. On release, the new Capo was not disposed towards me. I was offered a lowly position, serving the Comte."

"The families in Albania would not look so badly on your revenge."

The valet bristled.

"The Unione is not what it was. I told Sada this."

"What did you say?"

"The truth. The Unione is too respectable. It has abandoned the roots of its class, its people, concentrating on business in the cities, investments, banking, while the people in the fields still needed rescue from exploitation, from intimidation, protection from other lesser unions. Sada refused to listen."

"So, you wish to return to the past."

"I wish to restore order."

"And to attain power?"

"Who would not wish it?"

Sabatini admired the blatant admission. Ferrara was a straightforward, unimaginative man. Sabatini knew many like this in his entourage. They had uses. Occasionally they flashed with brilliance. Most of them died in some reckless endeavour, shot by a rival, knifed by a whore, an overdose of something lethal. Ferrara wouldn't be one of those. He was a strong looking man with a steady gaze and a dark, mysterious expression. He wasn't remotely intrigued by who stood in front of him, only by how Sabatini could assist him. It was a hungry expression. Sabatini recalled his own lean youth. The pain of want. The desire, how it drove him, kept him alert in moments of crisis and fear, helped him to sleep in times of respite, made him think carefully, callously, urgently. This valet, this Ferrara, had considered this moment, carefully and callously, for a good number of years. Sabatini could see it in those dark incessant eyes. Interestingly, he noticed the valet did not look at his false eye, his gaze stayed fixed on a point almost in mid-air, not quite on his face, almost disinterested.

"So, Ferrara," Sabatini sucked long and deep on the almost extinguished cigar, "it is revenge you seek, not power."

"It is both."

"Many people come to me seeking to avenge another. I turn all requests down. There is little benefit for me. If you come to me, Ferrara, and I help you attain this position, I must know what you intend to do to help me."

"I have been watching you, Signor," said the valet carefully. "Your boat is very hard to ignore. Everyone talks of it. I know who you are, Signor. You are Marcelo Sabatini, the famous ship builder, director of International Luxury Sails. I also know of your other life. This was harder to discover. I am afraid a single small slip from one person to another revealed it to me."

The valet paused. He shuffled, as if anticipating the next revelation would cause some embarrassment. Sabatini enjoyed the display. It showed manners. Of course, this man Ferrara had no idea Sabatini's heart was hardened to almost everything, but it was a king gesture nonetheless.

"Your woman," said the valet. "She is very beautiful. The Comte enjoyed talking to her. He found her voice soothing and her choice of words amusing. Occasionally, you understand, he relates to me what people have told him in confidence. I had to reassure him you were not the great Albanian gangster she claimed. Luckily, the Comte trusts my ear more than a woman's tongue."

"Then I shall thank you and punish her."

"I also know of the heroin you import."

"Ah."

Sabatini showed no surprise. He took a last sip of prosecco and moved closer to the valet until they stood almost toe to toe. His good eye swept over the interloper in seconds. He raised the cigar to his mouth and took a cautious drag on the fading stub. The tip flared white hot, flecked with burning yellow and orange, the blazing colours of an imperial opal. Instantly, Sabatini jerked his hand down. The blazing cigar hissed as it collided with the valet's wrist. The man's hand shook and the tray it held wobbled. Nothing fell and the man didn't utter a sound.

"You want power very badly," said Sabatini. "We must see if there is some way both of us can attain what we want."

***

Two weeks later, Attila Ferrara had made the long dusty journey through the Salentine and into Basilicata, the poorest of the poor southern regions. He made the journey often because he had a small sassi dwelling in Matera. He went there to relax, to forget about his burden and to plan the demise of his employer. Those plans usually took the form of fantasy. A hopeless assassination. A quiet murder. A coup from within the Sada court. An uprising. He would stare at the stone ceiling, trace the cracks, watch how the condensation dripped from the crevasses and formed pools on the bare floor, wonder when he could live in real luxury, not this inherited hovel from an era of sorrow.

Ferrara had been born in Matera, but in the new town above the gorge-side sassi. His father and mother had been forcibly removed from the ancient town as children. It was only in their dotage, when Victor Ferrara had done his duty with the Sada Family that they had returned to the place of their birth. His mother had died almost as soon as she returned. It was like the days of old: from the womb to the stone coffin.

The rock cut home had all the amenities a modern house might. It also had a spectacular view of the gorge and the city from the roof terrace. The terrace itself was a rock shelf bordered by other houses and rooftops, cut out of the surrounding cliffs. It was a suntrap and on summer days and evenings, Ferrara sat and watched the sun die, his heart full of hate, his fingers toying with his favourite gun, playing with it like a circus act, loading, unloading and reloading, timing himself, aiming, practising, imagining the moment when he pulled the trigger and Sada's face would erupt in gore and blood. Ferrara felt a chill run down his spine during those fleeting moments of madness. He came to Matera almost always alone, private and undisturbed. There was no landline phone in the sassi. He could turn off his mobile and revel in the anger of his thoughts and dreams.

Ferrara was doing that that now on the terrace, sitting at a small wooden table beneath a parasol. He polished the barrel of the Tanfaglio T95 semiautomatic pistol. He slipped it into the chamois leather holster that he wore under his shoulder. It was reassuring to feel it there. Below him, below the maze of rooftops, he could make out the single road and the black tinted Mercedes Benz V-Class which had pulled to a stop beside the stone staircase. Three people got out of the car. Ferrara checked his Swatch, one of the few extravagances he allowed himself, although he would never be seen wearing it while at work. It would take a few minutes for them to climb the distance to his house. He went downstairs into the cool of the interior, picked up his leather jacket from the back of a chair and slipped it on. He opened the front door and watched the three men make their way up the last few steps. They were looking uncomfortable after the climb. One of them was perspiring and carefully mopped his brow with a handkerchief, squinting into the sun.

"Ferrara," said the tallest. "The Capo wants to talk."

"I know. It was me who asked for an invite."

"You look as if you were expecting us."

"I saw you coming."

"You could have phoned. Saved us the climb."

Ferrara grinned. The tall man didn't like it.

"Come on, Ferrara. We don't want to be late."

"It's a good thing I was here. What would you tell the Capo then?"

"We knew you were here."

Of course they did. The Unione Sacre Croce liked to claim you couldn't move anywhere without them knowing of it, but there were ways. Ferrara knew several, mostly through his own more extreme contacts, a faction within the Unione who wished to restore its grip over the population, something which had slipped as the threat of violence diminished.

Ferrara stepped into the sunlight, closed and locked the door behind him. The three men escorted him down the steps and into the car. He took the descent slowly and carefully, not wanting to break sweat despite the heavy jacket on his back. The Mercedes was airconditioned and cool. He sat in the middle seat, sore and uncomfortable, with a man either side. The perspiring one was the driver.

"Will you bring me back?"

"Yes," said the tall one.

No one said anything more. The driver set a sedate pace. The fields and low hills of Basilicata vibrated with the midday heat. The wheat was turning gold in the fields. The fruit was hanging heavy on the trees. Ferrara concentrated on the back of the driver's head. The world outside could wait. It took just over an hour to reach their destination.

I Campo de Mielle was ring fenced with stone pines and a low wall criss-crossed by an electric fence. Acres of orchards stretched away to a broad hillock where a slate grey Coronado stone mansion was perched, the big windows overlooking its domain. The gatekeeper recognised the car. Immediately the gates swung open for admittance. The driver proceeded at a snail's pace along the drive. Every turn of the wheels was accompanied by images from ancient history, as if to remind a visitor that here was a place and a family whose world was as old as the earth. Every statue was the ghost of a long abandoned deity, benevolence staring from half expressive faces, Jupiter, Mercury, Ceres bringer of the harvest, Fortuna for luck and Fides for loyalty, marble silent effigies, tinted blue as if they'd really fallen from the sky. The silent guard of honour was designed to keep a visitor in place, beneath the Gods, beneath the Family, who watched your approach, watched your retreat and cast judgement upon your soul.

The road included several turn offs and dead ends which the driver ignored, a deliberate security measure. Only a trained chauffeur knew the correct route through the playground of history. The Mercedes came to a gentle stop outside the main portico. Ferrara and his escort dismounted. He stared at the ornate Italian gardens, spotlessly clean, weedless, colourful, the sun touching everything as if the grey worlds of death and taxes had never condescended to visit. Ferrara chuckled at the analogy. When did the great families ever pay taxes?

The villa doors were being opened by a neatly attired butler, white gloves on brawny hands, the jacket stretched. He didn't offer any welcome. Ferrara recognised in the man his own position under the Comte d'Orsi. He followed the butler up the steps and inside. The ceiling was two stories high. The windows almost as lofty. Sun rays flooded the big open spaces and seemed to dance to the echo of his steps on the tan varnished floor. The villa was built on a single level facing the beautiful gardens and endless orchards that surrounded it, the mazes and sunken fountains, the summer house and the lake.

The butler led him down a central passage and stopped outside a plain pine door, probably cut from the forest outside. A guard stood outside. Without speaking, he reached into Ferrara's jacket and removed the pistol before gesturing to the door. The butler opened it and they were shown into a small salon lined with beech wood. The room was sparse to the point of absurdity. Against one wall stood a glass cabinet full of trinkets, eighteenth century antiques such as cameos and engraved silver spoons. There was one very old Bible, binding peeled, laid open. In the centre of the room was a square table and two chairs. On the table stood a crystal fruit bowl laden with produce, a jug of iced water and two tumblers. Sitting in one of the chairs was Sada.

"Buongiorno, Attila. Welcome."

The formality didn't surprised him. The Capo was older than Ferrara and demanded respect. Ferrara wasn't about to give it.

"I know I'm not welcome."

Sada's dark eyes squinted. A long time had passed since Attila Ferrara last stood in this room. He was still an angry, rangy, dangerous looking individual with an uncouth slouch to his shoulder, a roughness born not from a wild upbringing, but from restlessness. He had none of the subtlety of his father, none of the grace. He had, though, the same suspicious, obnoxious, all-seeing nature, just like there had always been with Victor. It rested in the man's expression, how his eyes flickered about the room, over people and places and objects, gauging their benefit or weakness. It was the reason Andrea Sada had sacrificed a young man and his sister to remove Victor Ferrara as a caporegime. Sada remembered the conspiracy. Victor Ferrara had become too popular, too knowledgeable, too dangerous. Elimination had become a necessity. Sada wondered how many of the family's secrets Victor had passed onto his son. The hope had always been that Ferrara would die in prison, in some fight or an accident. He was either too wily or too lucky. And he was always prepared. The Capo noted the gun which the bodyguard placed on the table. The minder stood, fixed and solid, blocking the door.

"And I know you need something from me," continued Sada.

"Your mind is made up then. You are going to humiliate me and my family once more. Perhaps I should leave now and avoid the embarrassment."

"That would be impolite, Attila. You know the history of our families. You know our fathers loved each other as comrades."

Ferrara cackled. The butler was busy pouring water, the ice chinking as it slopped. The dismissive sound resonated. He glanced at the Capo, saw no reaction and continued to pour, the movements effortless despite the constrains of his uniform. Task completed, he also went and stood beside the door.

"Sit down, Atilla." Sada gestured to the other chair. "Have some fruit."

"I know how these meetings go, Capo," said Ferrara. "I tell you how much of a debt my family owes you. I tell you I am enjoying my position in the house of the Comte d'Orsi, your uncle, that he is a generous employer, even in his failing health and old age. I tell you I am pleased to still be associated with the Unione Sacre Croce, that the organisation protects me and the community. I tell you I am grateful. You know I won't say any of these things with a single honest word. The Sada family and the Unione could have freed me from prison without a moment's hesitation. You did not. I suffered in those cells for twenty years. I never betrayed the Unione even though I had many opportunities. You repay me with nothing. A worthless job for a worthless man, someone you don't even care for. So, let us not reminisce. Let us talk business straight away before we are both angry at the sight of each other."

Sada didn't react.

"Very well. Business it is. But please, drink, eat, tell me."

The Capo opened a palm towards the empty chair.

Ferrara finally sat down, his hands clasped together on the table top. He didn't take any food, but moved a glass of water closer to him. Sada waited. One tapered hand reached out, took a plump conference pear from the fruit bowl and placed it side down on the table. Ferrara sipped the water. The coolness tickled his parched throat.

"I have a proposition for you, Capo. A small one which I hope will be to both our advantages."

"Big or small, Atilla, I will be the judge of its advantage."

Ferrara ignored the deliberate slight.

"I bring you an avenue of development," he said. "There is an Albanian, a rich man, who comes to the coast every few weeks in his yacht. Rich men often waste time in the marina, but this is a different rich man. He moors in the bay and comes ashore to complete various social engagements. You may have heard of him. He calls himself Sabatini."

"That isn't an Albanian name."

"The man's father was Italian."

"The name is familiar. He builds yachts."

"He does."

"You say that as if it is a lie."

Ferrara paused dramatically. Sada allowed the moment of pantomime.

"He is indeed the director of a ship building company, but it is a useful legal front. Marcelo Sabatini is the Krye of the Banda Family."

Sada showed no emotion. That would be expedient.

"How did you find this out?"

"He has a woman. She comes ashore with him for the functions, charity events and parties. She is a very beautiful dancer. She also has a loose tongue."

Sada breathed in slowly. For a moment, Ferrara thought it turned cold in the room, then the breath was released and the warmth returned. A slim sharp peeling knife rested beside the fruit bowl. The Capo picked it up and carefully sliced off the stem of the pear.

"I know there have been problems with the Albanians in Puglia," continued Ferrara. "Nothing out of hand. I wouldn't dare suggest the Capo is incapable of conducting affairs for the Unione. Nonetheless, everyone knows the Albanians are fast becoming a force throughout Europe. They have infiltrated every criminal activity, often with startling success. It is an inevitable tide, Capo. Now might be an opportune moment to engage them in a parley."

"What are you suggesting?"

"A business arrangement. The Albanians are already selling their contraband on your doorstep. They've been doing so ever since Sabatini's yacht first appeared off the coast. You know there is a new grade of Afghan heroin being sold in Puglia and Basilicata. It is his. But he is struggling to find reliable outlets because those are all in your hands. Now, if you bought and distributed his heroin yourself, it would be advantageous to all parties."

Sada watched Ferrara closely as he spoke. Something was hidden. Something was being plotted, perhaps for a long time. Ferrara had a quick agile mind. It hadn't been dulled by years of waiting in prison or working in service for the ageing Comte. Sada remembered old Victor Ferrara. That grizzled war veteran had been one of Andrea Sada's very best caporegime, a tough almost fanatical leader of a men. They said he ran with the devil. He'd managed the smuggling operations along the coast, fought in the streets when there was dissent, paid off the police. Victor Ferrara set up the organisation so well he began to see it as his and when changes had to be made, when the legitimate business interests became fundamental to the growth plan of the Unione, he objected. Andrea Sada couldn't allow such disagreement; to do so would be a display of weakness. But to execute a loyal accomplice might spark unrest, so a zecchinetta was arranged, a little piece of business which would benefit the Unione as well as a poor girl from a poor family. Victor Ferrara would be seduced, he would shame the girl and suffer a fast death. Victor's son would avenge him. Blood would be spilt. The Unione's face would be saved and Atilla Ferrara would never inherit his father's post as caporegime.

When Ferrara was released from prison, Sada had a moment of weakness. Guilt is a powerful emotion. Ferrara should have been ignored. Instead, he was banished to work in the employ of the ageing Comte d'Orsi. He was efficient, thorough and rebellious. An unruly flicker existed in his eye. He was ambitious, like his father. He had thirst and hunger. Sada saw it in those eyes, eyes looking three or four steps ahead to a deal which hadn't yet been struck. It was the type of subtle, sudden fury that occurred when a person gained money, notoriety or power, or a combination of all three. It would be difficult to quench this devil's appetite once he began to feast. Ferrara was steady and still, his wiliness uncurbed, his anger unfrozen, a heart hard as marble, dark as death. Yes, a devil was sitting at the Capo's table. A strong hand and a short leash would be needed to control this one. Perhaps the weakness had not been a mistake. Sada preferred to let ambitious fiends stay inside the Unione. In business, as in life, there was always time to hold the hand of a devil.

Sada sliced into the pear and dug out the core. It had been picked from the orchards that morning. The virgin flesh was almost transparent, like river water, flashing as the sun caught it, bright and alive, soon to dull. Hadn't the devil killed Roman emperors like this, the poison taster cutting the fruit, the venom spread on one side of the blade, the deadly segment passed to the king, his crown soon to fall.

Was this the moment? The pear tasted sweet. It snapped welcomingly under the Capo's teeth.

"All parties?" declared Sada. "You want to be an intermediary."

"Yes."

"Why should I suddenly trust you?"

"Because I met Sabatini."

Sada chewed thoughtfully.

"I need to know more about him, Atilla. I need to know his ambitions, his battle plans. He has outsmarted the Unione already. We pay money to the coastguard to ensure only our goods arrive in Puglia. Sabatini must be paying an increased rate."

"Or nothing at all," hinted Ferrara. "There are many empty coves along the coastline. Recently the Albanians were caught moving the heroin inland. You may have read about it."

"I did. It was a tiny haul. Sabatini can't be selling much heroin."

"He doesn't have the distribution network which you do, but it won't take him long. His product is excellent. Given the expanding status of Albanian gangs, can you afford not to supply the new grade?"

Sada nodded. It was true the Afghan Heights were producing rich fields once again and the Afghan farmers didn't charge as much as those in South America. The poppies grew on the cheap. It skewed the market. Maybe Ferrara was right. This infringement of territory could lead to something more dangerous for the Unione. A market flooded with high grade cheap heroin could ruin a business they'd spent the best part of thirty years developing.

"And what do you wish to gain from this?"

Ferrara allowed himself a little smile.

"I want to be released from my penance. I have served the Comte for almost ten years I would like to work for the Uninoe again."

Sada's eyebrows raised. This time the pear snapped between the strong, thin fingers. "The Comte relies on you, Atilla. You know change disturbs him."

"I don't intend to leave the Comte. He would be lost without me. I wish merely to expand my portfolio from valet to executive pharmaceutical distributor."

"Dealing in death," said Sada.

"If you like." Ferrara paused. "Just like you."

Ferrara returned the stern, proud gaze. The expression had barely flinched once throughout the entire meeting, only that slim raised eyebrow, the sudden small mouthfuls of fruit. It was like being in the presence of an inscrutable judge. The bile rose in his throat. He tensed. He wanted to attack the face, despoil it, cut out the vanity like the arms of the Gods outside, shorn short, useless relics.

Sada saw the glint in Ferrara's eye and bit down on a slice of pear. So, it would be like the old days of Andrea and Victor. The grasping, clawing anger was back. One devil, two devils, three if you included the heroin. The Unione would be shaking all their hands in a moment.

"I will consider the proposal when you bring me the details I want," replied Sada. "Don't forget, the Unione will require a substantial cut."

Ferrara almost hissed an answer, but stopped himself in case his inner serpent spoke. He waited and listened while Sada outlined the terms of a prospective arrangement. He wrote nothing down. That would suggest incompetence. Sada spoke for six minutes, sat back and picked up another quarter of pear. The interview was finished. Ferrara nodded and stood up. He refused to extend a hand and instead picked up the Tanfaglio pistol.

The bodyguard audibly tensed.

Ferrara grinned, twirled the gun into its holster and headed for the door. The butler was already opening it.

Sada watched the bastard back visibly straighten as it retreated. The door closed and the Capo sat alone, slowly digging at another sliver of pear. The translucent flesh was already stained, as if poison was seeping into the world.

Seven

Itch

Drago stared at *Diamantin* for a long time, wishing the naked girl would reappear. His pulse thumped. She was stunningly beautiful. He'd known it, of course, ever since he'd seen her at the hotel. This fresh encounter made him quiver. He took a final hopeful glance through the binoculars before discarding them with a grimace. He was acting like an infatuated schoolboy. Drago went inside the villa, slipped into shorts and a shirt and pulled on his plimsoles. In the kitchen he finished preparing breakfast. Ten days of the San Pietro's continental fare had formed a habit. Bananas sat in a fruit bowl. In the fridge he had orange juice, plain yoghurt, eggs to boil, Parma ham and salami, cheese, pate, grapes and olive bread, all purchased from the independent grocers which lined the back streets of Otranto. He spooned yoghurt over the banana he'd already sliced, poured out the juice and prepared a breakfast platter. He made black coffee, not espresso how the Italian's liked it, but a long Americano, freeze dried for convenience. The supermarket cashier had grunted disapprovingly. Drago ignored the inference. He didn't have the time to grind his own beans. He ate on the balcony, gazing across the bay where the big yacht was resplendent.

Diamantin had appeared the evening before, slowly edging into position halfway between the entrance to the harbour and the curve of the Atlantis Club. The interior lights had blinked on as the sun set. Drago had spied figures in the state rooms. No one appeared on deck, save for an increasingly bored crew member who slowly patrolled the gangways. Drago observed the boat for an hour or so from the balcony of the Villa Camprese, pondering what the harbourmaster had told him.

He resolved to play a waiting game and spent the morning listening to local radio stations while reading a trashy paperback he bought at Gatwick duty-free. He watched the sea and he watched the boat. At nine o'clock a steward appeared from inside and began to prepare the table on the rear deck. A white cloth came out, blue cushions, cutlery, glassware, a little bowl of bread rolls. Chairs were set neatly at tangents to corners and faced the open sea. Lastly, the steward unwound the awning until the table sat in semi-shadow.

The big man appeared first. He wore a towelling robe which fell to his knees yet still didn't look big enough to contain him. He was already smoking a fat cigar, although Drago thought it more for show as the man didn't inhale much. He placed it on a heavy glass ash tray and called out instructions. Drago lowered the field glasses and rubbed his eyes. The sunlight was reflecting off the water and occasionally, when his hands dropped, the sparkling surface blinded him. The steward reappeared with a pitcher of orange juice and two tumblers dripping with condensation from the crushed ice they contained. The big man reeled off another order before sitting at the table.

Presently, he was joined by the girl. She'd put on a wrap-around dress tied tight at the waist. She carried a small handbag. Expensive looking shades were pinned in her hair. Seated, she crossed her legs and the two halves fell either side to reveal the long exquisite calves and thighs. The couple exchanged pleasantries. There was no physical communication. She poured juice for them both, sat back and pulled her sunglasses down from her fringe. With her apparel and accessories, she looked less a carefree, gorgeous young goddess and more a sumptuous, sophisticated woman. The steward returned with breakfast: meats and cheeses, fruits and cake. After they'd eaten a little, he returned with coffee. The man and woman barely said a word. It was a frosty morning, even in the heat.

Once breakfast was completed, the big man used an intercom to relay orders. A few minutes later a slight, bearded middle-aged man appeared on the rear deck. His starched white uniform with epaulettes marked him out as the captain. Drago remembered he was called Belzac. There was a brief discussion between captain and master, before the big man stood, picked up the long extinguished cigar, relit and disappeared into the state rooms. The woman dutifully followed him.

After another hour, when the sun was warm but not yet biting the skin, the man and woman reappeared, kitted in swimwear, and took up positions on the forward sun deck, near the pool. Drinks were provided. They lay still and silent on the sun loungers. The woman regularly rubbed sun lotion onto the man's hair covered skin. She didn't seem to need it herself. Drago kept his lookout, marking the times when a crew member appeared to patrol the deck. It seemed only a rudimentary exercise. They carried no weapons. At exactly half past midday, the steward re-entered the scene and again laid the table on the rear deck. Lunch was a cold salad accompanied by a bottle of white wine. The couple ate it in their swimwear. Once finished, puffing on another cigar, the man barked an order and the steward trotted forward, pushing a trolley on which was fixed an LCD screen and keyboard. The woman took this as an invitation to leave the fray and she returned to the sun deck where she loosened her bikini top and reclined on her front, sunning her back, the bruises obvious.

Meanwhile, the big man conducted his daily business. Through the glasses, Drago could make out the screen flickering over spreadsheets, reports and forecasts. There was a live conference call, the screen splitting into a dozen squares each with a tiny face on it. The parching heat didn't appear to bother him, being deeply tanned also. It was as if the play with the sun lotion was done for reassurance and routine not necessity.

Unlike the owner of the yacht, Drago didn't have a laptop with him. He found them to be an encumbrance on a vacation, a too easy distraction. He did however have Google access on his Samsung mobile. Bored with the dull activity on the boat, he switched on the app and typed in 'Diamantin.' As always, despite typing 'yacht' and 'Albania' into the search box, he drew a laborious blank. The majority of entries concerned jewellers, gemstones, a plush marina and an exclusive, expensive, shifty looking nightclub. He flicked through the data with hardly any interest, keeping one eye targeted on the yacht. Halfway down the third page he came across something about an Albanian blood diamond. Intrigued, Drago clicked on it, read the article, expanded the black and white photographs, shrugged and clicked back. Lastly, he conducted an image search and was confronted with pictures of dazzling yachts. Many were not even called *Diamantin* or anything close to it. The search brought up any yacht made in Albania. Three words kept recurring amid the descriptions: International Luxury Sails.

He searched again. There it was. A small entry on Wikipedia. International Luxury sails, I.L.S. for short, was an Albanian ship building firm formerly known as Lundrim Luksoze. Based out of Durres, it manufactured spectacularly appointed private yachts for multimillionaires. Founded by Luca Rovíc, the company was saved after his untimely death by the intervention of the union executive Marcelo Sabatini, who lodged a takeover bid utilising union funds. He declared the company a national industrial icon, one which Albania could not afford to allow to collapse and offered dividends to the union as reward for investment. Its renowned yachts continued to be among the most exclusive and luxurious in the world. Sabatini's name featured as a respected donor for a long list of charities. He had also commissioned a museum to rehouse many of Albania's artefacts, as well as pieces contained in his private collection.

Drago explored further. He was rewarded with a picture of Marcelo Sabatini. Initially he thought it was a different man. The big hands still clutched a cigar, but the hawk-like face with its jutting almost Roman nose was appended with a black velvet eye patch. He must have lost it, an accident, perhaps. Further photos, taken more recently, showed him with a spectacular rainbow coloured glass eye. Drago clicked through some more articles. One photo was from Reuters, taken at a union meeting in Albania. Sabatini resembled a tub thumping Trotskyite, the sort of politician which ought to have gone out of fashion, but still occasionally held audiences and party members in thrall. The biographical details when he found any were sketchy. Drago read them with little excitement. Place and date of birth – check. Formal education – check. Union activity – check. Marital status – check. He could have guessed most of it simply from the man's appearance and performance on the yacht today. Controversy – hello.

'There is some suggestion Sabatini is involved in organised crime. Most unions in Albania have at one time or other been associated with criminal activity. Since 1991, when the Albanian Party of Labour was defeated in a general election, the trade union movement has been split between two factions and Sabatini's organisation, the Nautical, Merchant and Transport Union has switched sides depending on which faction has the most political momentum. It is rumoured Sabatini exacts influence over the Banda Family, one of the country's leading Mafia organisations. This allows him to flex his political muscles. It has been noted that twice his close political rivals have met untimely deaths. The police however have not brought or sought to bring any charges. This would not be unusual in Albania, where police and political corruption is systemic.'

Drago studied again the images of Sabatini. Anger. That was what hit hardest. The man was in a rage. His muscles were contorted. His one good eye was bulging. Whatever had upset him, he was allowing his fury to take over. It simmered below the sublime surface and occasionally broke free. The picture of the rally was one such time. Whatever had happened with the girl, whatever made the bruise, was a second. And Drago had witnessed a third, when Sabatini shouted at those idiot water skiers. The short fuse could be easily lit and relit like his cigars, untampered, untethered, impatient. He didn't look like such a man today, reclining in the sun on his luxury yacht, but you could hide many lives beneath the exterior of plush respectability.

Drago knew that of himself. An author of three bestselling novels, he still battled the demons of his misspent youth, still found the torment rise in his own psyche, when moments of violence and terror had to be fought with ferocity in equal measure. Those times appalled him. His own behaviour sickened him. He dreamt about it. Even during the daytime he had flashbacks. Guns, knives, dead bodies, mutilated limbs, the screams of the dying, obscene vicious animals trained to kill, fights to the death, endless destruction, all that death. He blinked. The app had lost its connection and he was staring at a remote customer service message. Drago put down the phone. He was sweating and not from the heat. The memories turned on him like this.

He scanned *Diamantin*. There was as little activity as before. The deck hand still wandered. The woman lay in the sun. The big man sat at his portable desk. After an hour, his work was done and he joined the woman on the sundeck.

Drago made his own sandwich lunch. He was drinking coffee when the villa's telephone rang. He let it. No one knew he was here and that was how he wanted it. After ten rings the answerphone kicked in and an Italian voice chimed on for a minute or so.

There wasn't much to the afternoon either. The steward cleared away the lunch debris. Another member of the crew started polishing handrails. Eventually it got too hot even for the sunbathers and they took shelter indoors. Drago could make out the big man mixing cocktails in the lounge.

The doorbell sounded.

Annoyed, Drago swore. It would be harder to ignore a personal caller. The Fiat Panda was on the drive, demonstrating someone was at home. The visitor rang again. Persistent, they rang a third time before Drago decided he had to answer. It was a slightly stooped middle-aged man, older than Drago, with a neat black moustache and greying hair. He started to speak immediately. When he realised Drago didn't understand a word, his speech tailed off into an exasperated series of shrugs.

"I'm sorry," said Drago. "Signor Lombardo is not here. Holiday. Vacation."

The man started to repeat whatever he was trying to say. Drago played the charade for a minute before lifting a hand to stop him.

"Wait."

Drago pushed the door to. The villa had an architect's studio in one of the lower rooms. It wasn't large, housing only a couple of angled drawing desks and a few cupboards. The plans for one of Lombardo's successful building projects illuminated one wall. The other provided natural light through the bay windows. There had to be paper and pens in here. Drago found a loose leaf A4 pad, took a Bic biro from a pot and returned to the lobby to find the visitor had taken it upon himself to enter the property and was admiring the furnishings. Drago offered the man the writing materials, miming for him to compose a note for Signor Lombardo.

"Ah, si, si."

While Drago waited, the visitor spent several minutes writing and rewriting his message. The man would not be rushed. Drago propped himself against the wall, bored. The man finished with a sudden flourish, seemed pleased and handed back the pad. Drago made out numbers and Euro signs. He started to usher the visitor away, but the man spouted more Italian. Impatient now, Drago manhandled his unwanted visitor through the doorway and issued a staunch "Ciao" as he finally closed the door on the intruder.

Not for the first time, Drago wished he was better at languages. The odd phrase was all well and good, but hand gestures and pigeon speak only took you so far. He made a mental note to enrol in a class when he got back to London. He left the pad near the front door, so he wouldn't forget to drop it at Vicino's. On reflection, it would have been easier to get the man to phone the restaurant in the first place. Drago decided he'd pilfer some business cards tonight, just in case.

He returned to the cane chair on the balcony, casting a glance at *Diamantin*. He picked up his glass of water, took a sip and sat up startled. He snatched for the binoculars. A motor launch was exiting the rear of the yacht. At its helm was the woman.

Damn! It was mid-afternoon. Siesta. The yacht was quiet, as it had been all day, but no one was on deck any longer. It was too hot. The town below him was weary. Everyone was retreating from the sun. Everyone except the beautiful woman, Jon Drago and an annoying Italian with debts to settle.

Quickly, he grabbed his wallet, keys, phone and Persol sunglasses and headed for the car port. He knew exactly where the woman was going: the same place she went every day, the same place he'd originally seen her, where she'd heard him singing. His stupidity almost made him chuckle. With luck he'd arrive just after her.

***

As the Fiat Panda swung out of the driveway and the little motor launch jostled its way towards Otranto's marina, a second pair of eyes was watching *Diamantin*. Slowly, Bergamo lowered the binoculars and sighed with boredom. It was the same routine every day. Three-thirty sharp, the woman would come into town, walk up the lanes from the quayside and visit the spa at the Hotel San Pietro. He didn't know why he was assigned to watch over her. He did as he was instructed and he was paid well. That was all that mattered.

Bergamo tossed a few cent coins on the café table, as he did every day, and walked swiftly from his vantage point on the Bestione Pelasgi to the Porta a Mare which linked the castle's two eastern towers. Here there was a cut-through to Via del Porto across the dried bed of an old sea moat. Most tourists, and even the locals, preferred the longer route to the militarily scenic. The woman had already docked by the time he reached his regular spot. She was walking confidently along the quayside, chatting to the harbourmaster. That was unusual: she rarely spoke to anyone.

Bergamo took up his position near the entrance. If she'd ever seen him, he wasn't aware of it and wouldn't have cared anyway. He waited until she was well past, the long legs taking her elegantly up Via Madonna del Pesso. Still bored, Bergamo followed at distance. He was unsurprised when she turned into 800 Martiri and entered the hotel. He made his usual foray into the car park where he met his ally, the same doorman who a minute earlier had welcomed the woman with the expression he reserved for all beautiful female guests.

The doorman led Bergamo to the staff entrance and into the CCTV monitoring room. No one at the hotel watched the screens. They didn't even have proper security. They only used the cameras if a client reported an incident or made a complaint, or if the police asked for a copy. Bergamo thrust the payment directly into the doorman's sweaty palm. The man asked for too much for such a tiny favour. The money would be wasted, probably on wine or the football scores.

Bergamo closed the door and flicked through the monitors until he found the camera showing the woman entering the changing cubicle. She was alone. He yawned. It would be another afternoon of boredom. Despite his orders and the money, Bergamo yearned for a siesta.

***

The beautician sat at a glass-topped desk and looked up as Drago entered. Her mild curiosity was only half-hid behind a gorgeous wide smile.

"Buongiorno, Signor Drago. I was not expecting you."

Drago was surprised she knew who he was, for he had no recollection of her at all. The name tag on the clean ironed shirt read 'Lore'. She was small and young with immaculate skin. Her domain was a room hewn from the rock below the hotel car park accessed by the elevator. Several glass doors branched off from the little lobby. It was bright but cool. The rocks were real, he reckoned, but whitewashed.

"I wanted to use the spa," he said. "Madeleine told me it was wonderful. You remember Madeleine?"

"Oh! I forget!" She almost blushed. "Scusi. The accident. How is the signorina?"

Drago could forgive anyone with such delightful well-toned cheekbones. "She's back at home in England. She's not in a good way, but she'll recover."

The beautician's brow creased and she flustered over a piece of paper she held in her hands. Drago detected an unasked question, so he answered it.

"She's better off being looked after by her parents. I'm terrible at that sort of thing. Like an Italian man, yes?"

"Yes." It was all the reassurance Lore needed. "I remember when my father was ill. My brothers, well…" She motioned with her hand then realised she had a customer to deal with. "So, Signor, how can we help?"

"Well, Lore, what do you recommend?"

"We don't have so many male guests. There is no gymnasium."

"That's okay. Do you have a swimming pool?"

He knew they didn't. He wanted to put Lore at ease. Behind the broad reception desk in the cave-like foyer was a full length mottled glass door. Printed on it in Italian and English were the words: massage, beauty, manicure, pedicure, wax, hair salon. He could make out a body moving down the passageway beyond. It was wrapped in a white bathrobe, the dark hair swaddled in a towel. The shoulders swayed.

"I'm sorry, Signor. We have a jacuzzi and a sauna and a relaxation room."

"I suppose that might do. You see, I'm not really interested in all this healthy living. I really wanted your help."

"Help?"

He wasn't sure about her emphasis. The eyes, big, round and hazel, seemed intrigued. The lips, beautifully painted, parted a tad and the point of a little pink tongue stuck out between tiny white teeth.

"Yes. Madeleine made friends with someone here. A woman, a very beautiful woman, long dark hair, striking, elegant, always dressed in Milan fashions, sunglasses from Dior. I think she's from the boat, the big yacht in the bay."

The eyes fell.

"I cannot say, Signor."

"Yes, you can. I know she's just entered your salon. I followed her."

"Oh!"

"Exactly."

There was one large chair opposite the desk and Drago sat on the plush, plumped, white-as-snow cushions. He rested his right ankle on his left knee. His left hand strummed the sole of his deck shoe, the plastic making little echoes in the chamber.

"What's her name?"

"I cannot tell."

"Go on."

"I am sorry."

"I won't get you into any trouble, Lore. I promise."

"The hotel refuses to give the personal information of any guest."

"No one will know. I could always phone Madeleine and ask, but I don't want to disturb her and I'd probably have to negotiate with her parents." He paused. "They're not very happy with me at the moment."

Lore stared at the paper.

"I could ask the lady myself," said Drago. "But that would involve having my legs waxed and I don't much fancy that." He said it with the half-cocked grin most women liked. He stroked the hair on his shin. Lore stifled a chuckle behind a dainty palm.

92

"Is that what she's here for today?" asked Drago.

"I should not tell."

"It'll be our secret."

"The signorina is very private, Signor."

"Jon," he corrected. "She hardly looks as if she needs any beauty treatment."

"Beauty is not cheap, Sig – Jon."

"I'm sure she'd be very expensive. Does Signor Sabatini ever come here?"

"Who is that?"

"Oh, no one important." Drago put his feet on the floor and sat forward, lowering his voice. "Listen, Lore, I really don't want to get you in trouble. Please, give the signorina a message from me. Tell her Jonathon Drago would like to buy her coffee. Tell her I am Madeleine's friend. She'll understand."

Lore considered his proposal for a moment, then she smiled sweetly, the tongue poking out again.

"Si. Okay. I like her. I like your friend and you also. I will tell her. The signorina will be an hour and a half. Perhaps you would like to use the jacuzzi and the sauna after all?"

"What does it cost me?"

"For you, Jon, Signor, today the spa is free." Lore said it with another lovely smile. "It is a gesture from the hotel to you. Please, let me help you."

An hour later, Drago wrapped himself tightly in the warm towelling robe and considered his image in the mirror. Not too shabby, Jon. His eyes were a shade too hollow. You need more sleep, matey. Hair not turning grey, just a few stray hairs by the ears. He hadn't shaved that morning and the pin pricks of shadow were starting to seep through the pores of his freshly beaming skin. His light tan had almost vanished beneath the pinky hue brought on by the sauna and the steam bath. He did feel fresh and invigorated. All he needed now was coffee and a cigarette.

The spa was certainly luxurious. The attendants very circumspect. He'd been alone and spent an hour dreaming about better times. When the other, bad memories invaded he immersed himself in the bubbles or poured more water on the stones, anything to distract himself back to the here and now. Inactivity was always the problem. That was why he chose the gym, the karate classes, the shooting range or the golf course, why he drove his cars too fast, drank hard and ate too well. Activity helped take his mind away from the memories. Zapping his energy made him sleep soundly. No more nightmares. He sat on a leather upholstered reclining chair, adjusted it flat and within a few minutes was dozing. He didn't miss the sweat of the gym. This was a selfish deception, a way to make himself feel fit, even if he wasn't.

He woke with a start. Lore was shaking his shoulder. She had a finger raised to her lips in unspoken conspiracy. Drago dressed quickly, smoothed his hair, wished there was some gel to wet it, wished he wore trousers and a decent shirt, and made his way out. He ordered coffee for two and asked Lore to have it delivered to the terrace.

The sun was high. He felt the moisture gather on his forehead and down his spine. At least it was clean sweat. Drago took one of the comfy seats beneath the striped canopy. After a few minutes a waiter appeared with a tray full with cups, glasses and coffee in a percolator, with complimentary bottled water and ice. They still remembered how Drago preferred to take his coffee.

He didn't have to wait long. The woman appeared cautiously at the step to the terrace. She was wearing a cotton trouser suit of blueberry white, the neck open, its décolletage distinctly revealing. She watched him for a moment.

Drago smiled. Finally meeting her face to face made something click in his memory: a name.

"Ariana," he said. "Won't you join me?"

She didn't move.

"Who are you?"

The voice cut through the air. She had a thick gorgeous accent. The vowels seemed to roll over the tongue. She was slightly angry, he thought, but even angry there was a hint of seduction in the resonance. He started to rise.

"My name's Jon Drago."

"Why are you following me?"

"I'm not."

"The harbourmaster says so."

Gotcha.

Drago visibly winced. "Alright," he said, "maybe I've been asking about you, but I don't mean to pry. This all feels rather embarrassing."

Her eyes dragged themselves across his face, down his torso, to the creased open necked shirt, buttons almost all undone, yesterday's shorts and the scuffed plimsoles. Lastly, they latched onto the coffee for two.

"You are not the type to be embarrassed," she announced. "How did you know my name?"

"I've spent most of the day trying to remember it," said Drago confidently. "you know a friend of mine: the woman in the accident with the motor boats: Madeleine."

"Aha."

She cocked her head to one side. A hand was on her hip and in it was clutched her sunglasses, the Christian Dior logo prominent on the lens. Over her shoulder rested a patterned Fendi bag. Her hair, which would surely be blown about by the wind when she drove the motor launch, was washed clean and neatly tied with a coloured zebra-patterned scarf. Her eyebrows were dense, but scrupulously plucked. So too were the lashes around the big deep walnut eyes. Similarly, her nose and mouth looked almost too large. Thankfully, high cheek bones allowed her face to straighten rather than grow wide at the jaw. He thought she looked like a young Sophia Loren. She had the temper for it.

"I'm sorry to intrude," Drago said. "I wanted to tell you about Maddie. I thought you might be worried."

She said nothing. The glasses tapped against her thigh.

"Are you worried?" he asked.

Her head made a tiny shake, right to left and up and down at the same time. "Maybe, probably."

"She's not well. She has multiple fractures. I've sent her home."

There was a longish pause. She looked uncertain and lowered her gaze a second, frowning.

"I take it this is about money," she said plainly.

Serendipity, considered Drago. Just comes along by chance and without knowing it, Ariana, you've just given us an excuse to continue talking. Compensation had never crossed his mind, but he wasn't about to tell her that.

"Or maybe just an apology," he said.

"I am sorry," she said, heavy emphasis landing on each syllable, "but I cannot speak for others."

"Alright, perhaps I shouldn't have asked."

Once more, she frowned. It reminded Drago of Maddie when she had decisions to make. Ariana was in a moment of minor crisis. Instinctively, Drago made to leave, feigning disappointment. Finally he detected the tiny sigh of a pricked conscience. They were inches apart. He could smell her scent, orange blossom and fresh cedar. Kiko Milano for sure. He stared directly at her. Ariana's brown eyes inspected his face with equal care.

"She is nice. I would not wish her harm."

"Maddie liked you a lot," Drago said quietly. "She wanted you to have dinner with us, but you didn't seem keen."

"I remember."

"Then you know I'm genuine. Please, stay. Let's have coffee."

Ariana gently bit her lower lip, before taking the opposite sofa. She sat forward on the cushion, one leg wrapping itself over the other, foot tapping, encased in a thousand Euro sandal. As Drago poured coffee, he caught a glimpse of a gorgeous breast beneath the blouse. She seemed not to notice where his gaze strayed. Drago sat down again.

"I think Maddie was right about you."

"What right?"

"She said you were an intelligent, perceptive woman and quite a challenge."

"I am a challenge?"

"You make quite an impression. Most men would never cope with the pressure of keeping up with you."

"You make that sound like a compliment." Ariana brushed a loose lock of hair from her sultry cheek. "I am not sure it is."

Drago's mouth twitched half a smile. Ariana's lips flickered in response.

"I'm sorry if this intrusion upsets you," he said. "I feel I ought to make it up to you. Perhaps I could buy us lunch?"

"I see you don't feel the pressure, Mr Drago," she answered. "No. It is too late for lunch. The coffee will suffice."

The sun had peeked beneath the awning and lit her face. Ariana replaced her sunglasses. From her shoulder bag she produced a packet of Camel Light cigarettes, shook one out and dug for her lighter. Drago offered his Ronson.

"There's an irony," he said, "smoking at a health spa."

"I come here for the sauna and the skin treatments."

"Probably wise; sunlight and nicotine prematurely age the skin." Drago lit his own smoke and sat back on the cushions. "Your friend, Mr Sabatini, does he ever come to the spa?"

"No. We don't do everything together."

"Really?"

"He doesn't mind what I do in the afternoons. He has business to attend to."

"But you are his partner?"

"That question is unnecessary," she said. "You are a very rude man, Mr Drago. Marcelo looks after me. He has done so for some years. That is enough."

"And what would Marcelo think if he saw you now, taking coffee with a strange Englishman?"

"He would think his woman is a nicotine addict who drinks too much coffee."

"His woman," repeated Drago. "Are you married?"

Ariana continued to smoke as she leant forward, picked up the spoon and stirred the coffee. She stirred for a whole minute until attempting a reply.

"I am not married. Marcelo cares for me."

"You chose those words very daintily."

"I am lucky," she continued firmly. "He is a very rich man. Marcelo Sabatini. You may have heard of him."

"Not exactly. He's some sort of industrialist. Quite important in Albania, isn't he?"

"Very good. You are of hidden intelligence, Mr Drago."

"I probably read his name in the papers."

"I doubt that."

"And you live on his yacht."

"Yes, mostly."

She breathed out her last lungful of tobacco, lifted the coffee cup and took the espresso in one gulp. The movement suggested finality, but she didn't move.

"That must be a fantasy come true," said Drago. "The yacht looks tremendous. I can see her from my villa. Are you staying in Otranto long?"

"A few days."

"Business or pleasure?"

"You tease too much, Mr Drago."

"I didn't mean it. Honestly. Is Mr Sabatini here on business?"

"Marcelo has Italian heritage. His father was born in Puglia. He wants to give something back to the land of his father's birth."

"Very admirable. How does he do that?"

"Charitable trusts. Donations. Small business investments. I help him sometimes. It is perhaps the only time we work together."

"How long did you say you'd known him?"

"I didn't say."

"But you're bored, aren't you?"

Ariana flicked her head. The manicured fingers lifted the specs high enough so she could peer at him. Her nose twitched.

"You really are a very rude man, Mr Drago."

"I get that a lot."

Drago thought she bit a lip, but she answered him anyway.

"Seven years."

"Sounds like you have an itch."

"Itch?"

"Something to scratch, like a mosquito bite."

Ariana inadvertently rubbed her left forearm with a long freshly manicured finger, realised she was doing it and stopped.

"I see you are persistent as well as rude," she said. "What would Madeleine think of our meeting?"

"Maddie and I are not like that. We're more like you and Mr Sabatini."

"I think not."

"Why?"

She took a deep breath as if contemplating something. "Has Madeleine asked you to surrender everything you love, Mr Drago?"

"It's Jonathon. Most people call me Jon." He stubbed out the fag and poured himself more coffee. "And no, she hasn't."

"I gave up everything to be with Marcelo. There was a world for me then. Now it is as though I am a child and he is my father. He is a strong man, you understand? I must do as he expects. That is all my world now."

Drago paused to drink his coffee. She was studying him. He let her do it, sat back gently and pointed at her forearm.

"That scratch," he began, "wasn't so bad, was it?"

Her nostrils flared.

"Alright, that was uncalled for," said Drago. "I'm being an idiot. I'm not used to talking to someone so lovely. I'm rather out of practice. Perhaps I can make amends. What would you say to dinner? I know the best restaurant in Otranto."

"No. I cannot. And you should not ask me."

Ariana stood up abruptly and took an urgent pace from the table. Drago made a tentative grab for her wrist, ended up clasping three fingers and was surprised when she didn't brush him aside. She half-turned, flicked her head again and shifted her weight onto one leg, lips pursed.

"I might understand more than you think," Drago said. "I know I want to see you again. What about tomorrow? Here at the spa."

The pause could have been a lifetime, but was probably no more than a second. Slowly, gently, she removed her hand from his.

"Give me one of your cigarettes," she said. He opened the pack. She took one and lit it, sucking the flavours deep into her chest. "Marlboros. They have a strong taste. Is that what you like, Jonathon Drago, strong tastes?"

"Not always," he murmured, "just sometimes."

"Tonight. The Castello. Marcelo has a charity, the Children of Otranto Foundation. There is a fundraising event. If you can get a ticket, come."

"And you'll be there?"

"Of course, I will." The elegant legs spun away from him and her hand gave a single backward wave as she headed for the steps. "I owe you a cigarette."

Eight

The Rules of the Game

The Castello Aragonese occupied the east of the old fortified town, its sloping six metre thick walls springing from the bedrock of the dramatic dry moat. The three great turrets surrounded a square courtyard. The fourth corner led to a peninsula bastion, speared to the sea like the prow of a beached sailing ship. The whole structure was the high point of once formidable fortifications which encompassed medieval Otranto and its maze of cobbled alleys, a city where the houses were piled on top of one another and streets and stairways ducked back and forth to reach the smallest of dwellings in the lofts and basements of slim buildings. By day it was dusty, hot and dry, the only respite the occasional breath of sea breeze. People went about business in the mornings before the sun beat too harshly, then again in the evening, when tourists and locals alike drifted into a pedestrianised heart, ate in the piazzas and paraded down Corso Garibaldi or Via d'Aragona exchanging greetings with one another in the traditional passeggiata.

It was one of those long lazy evenings. The sky was a mysterious blue and the August moon was competing with the last curve of an orange sunset to decide which god was greater. Tonight, the moon was winning.

It was well past nine o'clock as Drago walked from the villa to the old town and crossed the wooden footbridge over the empty moat. He paused in the Piazza Castello. People didn't usually stand in line in Italy and what passed for a queue had formed by the castle entrance. The melee resembled a large well-dressed rugby maul, moving gradually forward, always retaining its tortoise shape. He'd obtained a ticket directly from the castle box office. It had cost a small fortune, more than a seat at Covent Garden. For the cost he would be entertained with a dance, a charity auction and a buffet. None of it appealed, not ordinarily, but Ariana intrigued him. So too did Marcelo Sabatini. So too did the packages of money. So too did the scuba divers who, under cover of darkness, slipped each night into the waters off Otranto to retrieve and deposit them.

Drago had been back to Atlantis twice to observe the night time routine. The divers swam for about an hour. Once back on rocky land, they stripped off their gear and dumped several wet canvas packages into the rear of the Ford Fiesta. The second time Drago had attempted to follow, but lost them thanks to a traffic accident. Once clear of the two mangled cars, Drago couldn't trace his quarry. All he knew was the car headed south.

Drago took a tissue and wiped the dust from his shoes. He joined the rear of the gentle scrum as it slowly passed through the large oak doors. He waved the silver embossed ticket at the appropriate time, got the barcode scanned and was ushered into a narrow corridor which led to a large gloomy lobby, whose tallow brick work was the very expectation of a gothic mansion. He mingled with the crowd, listening for an out of place accent, someone he'd be able to talk to in English. Other than Italian, he mostly heard French or Russian. Unable to speak to anyone, although at a push his French would pass, Drago studied the décor, the low vaulted ceiling, the single faded tapestry and the coats of arms that dressed the walls. As he scanned the room, he searched for Ariana. He didn't find her. Instead, Drago picked out a uniformed waiter carrying a tray topped with prosecco rosé.

Nonchalantly, he took a glass and inspected his fellow guests anew. Well-connected people, he thought. A proliferation of tuxedos and evening gowns. He could tell by their manner as well as their clothes: the way people held themselves and cast slightly disparaging glances at the less well-attired. Drago was glad he'd progressed from Scott & Taylor to end of season Ralph Lauren. He couldn't stomach Lauren's real costs, those eye watering thousands printed in tiny numbers on tiny labels. To the people around him, those numbers meant nothing except prestige and position. It was printed all over their demeanour. Older female hands dripped with diamonds. Necklines glimmered. The elder male statesmen chuckled at the scenery, gloved hands resting on contented, cummerbund wrapped bellies. Young women in modern styles, shorter, daring, clung to the sides of parents. Flamboyant suitors competed with each other like strutting peacocks.

It was too congested and warm in the lobby. The hall seemed younger than the rest of the structure, not formidable enough to repel Venetians or Arabs. It might have been constructed after centuries of battle, the old walls torn down and to be replaced by something new, less warlike. Perhaps that was when the drawbridge was removed and the cannons rolled out only for show and ceremony, the moment Otranto ceased to be a mighty city and became instead a home to pleasure seekers. There had been a single siege, he recalled; maybe it was after that, when all the fight had been stolen from the townspeople, when hope was beaten back to the ocean and faith was the only certainty. He wondered how many of these people of distinction could trace their lineage back to that siege, back to the men who bore those armorial mantles and died for a cause their descendants could barely comprehend.

Drago left the past to its bejewelled audience. The outside courtyard was bathed in a muddy golden glow, illuminated with tiny yellow and green lanterns hanging in strings from the arches of the covered balcony. Beneath his feet the mosaic looked to have been steam cleaned. Potted palms had been imported. On the northwest ramparts a small, tidy orchestra played American smooth jazz relayed unobtrusively through speakers. A clutch of girls in short skirts, hot pants and strappy tops were swaying with each other to the music, hoping to impress the young nervous lotharios who watched them. A man kitted out with unsuitable sunglasses and a leather jacket loped around the arena, half-interested. A group of half-a-dozen serious looking men dressed predominantly in black congregated under one of the arches. They appeared as out of place as Drago felt among the assorted high classes. He edged closer.

"Good thing it isn't raining," he said to no-one in particular.

Someone did hear. A short, tousle-haired bespectacled man tugged at Drago's arm.

"English?"

"Yes."

"Ah. I took English and Philosophy at Keele, many years before I changed career. What brings you to Otranto?"

"The weather and the food."

"Ah, good reasons, good reasons." The man hesitated before asking: "Why are you here tonight?"

"Curiosity. I liked the idea of a charity auction. You never know what to do with your money these days, do you?"

"You have money?"

"I do now."

"That is good. You must bid in the auction then. It is a very good cause. The Children of Otranto Foundation. For the migrant orphans."

The man had a habit of speaking in short precise phrases. Drago liked the affliction. He sounded direct, to the point, unfussy.

"Do you have a lot of orphans?" he asked.

"Not so many, not now. You should come to the orphanage. You can see where your money goes."

"I might do that," replied Drago politely. "I take it you're something to do with the charity?"

"I am the pastor. Reverendo Lampedusa. Signor Sabatini has blessed us with his funding. God has blessed us with the Signor's kindness."

"I'm sorry, Padre. I didn't realise."

"It is no matter." The man waved his hand dismissively. It came to rest on his collar, conspicuously absent of decoration. "I am in disguise. Incognito. As you might say."

"Isn't that unusual for a Catholic churchman?"

"Then I am unusual. Is the prosecco good?"

"Very. You should try it."

"Alas not. I will save myself for the food. Signor Sabatini provides a wonderful banquet."

"He holds these parties often?"

"No. But it is the season for extravagant parties. A few weeks ago the exclusively rich spent the night at the Comte d'Orsi's residence. A melancholy place. It was a formal dinner and sometimes one must attend these functions. As must the rich. That was where I first met Signor Sabatini. Two years ago now. And also where I met his, his, umm, partner."

The man stumbled over the word. Not such an unusual Catholic then, considered Drago.

"She introduced us. She persuaded the Signor to contribute money to the Foundation. It all happened so quickly. They are now our joint patrons."

"She can be very persuasive," said Drago mildly. "She even made me come tonight."

"Oh!" The man's face brightened. "You know the Signorina?"

"We've met."

"Then you must know Signor Sabatini?"

"I'm afraid not. But I'd like to."

"Then I will introduce you."

Drago smiled thinly. Just like this afternoon, an opportunity to meet Ariana and Sabatini presented itself only this was not such a fortuitous event. Drago asked Paulo Vicino what sort of people attended the city's fashionable parties. Paulo assured him they were mostly stupid people whose money went further than the horizon.

"Most of them only want to be seen to do good by charity," said the Italian.

"What charity?"

"The Children of Otranto Foundation. A vanity project for those same rich faces. It's up on the hill behind the town, near your villa. If you want to speak with anyone sensible, talk to the pastor there, Reverendo Lampedusa. He'll be with the clergy, dressed in black no doubt."

Paulo reverentially crossed himself for the minor offence. And now here was Drago passing small talk to that same offended Pastor as if they'd known each other for ten years not ten minutes.

"I'd love to meet them," said Drago.

"It will be my pleasure. I don't think they will have arrived yet. Signor Sabatini enjoys an entrance."

Drago finished his drink and exchanged the empty glass for a full one. "Why does he want to help orphaned children? Is it to please his –" now it was Drago's turn to halt over the word "– partner?"

"I suspect that may be the only reason. Philanthropy takes all forms. Some wish to create a better society. Some wish to heal the sick. Some see it as a religious duty, a calling or an access to the keys of heaven. Others want to leave an earthly legacy or provide ergonomic necessities. And yes, still more are persuaded by love. Charitable work takes all forms, Signor – ah?"

"Jon Drago."

"Ah, Signor."

Reverendo Lampedusa held out a limp palm which Drago shook and almost crushed. If it hurt, the Pastor showed no hint. He was already distracted by something over the far side of the square. Drago turned. The guests who had earlier crowded the lobby were streaming into the open air, chattering animatedly.

"Ah. It is starting." Lampedusa pointed. "Look. Signor Sabatini and Signorina Ariana."

The audience parted for the big man. Sabatini was crammed into a tight fitting white jacketed tuxedo, the black trousers trimmed with teal. Even so, he moved with grace and purpose, cutting an elegant impression as he walked between extended hands, accepting compliments and exchanging pleasantries as if he was a returning Roman champion. Drago assessed him with a keen eye. Up close, despite being in his early sixties, the man was broad, strong, intimidating. Beside him, Ariana was slim, decorous, quiet.

Someone blocked their eyeline and Lampedusa stretched for a better view. With his diminutive stature and round spectacles, the Pastor suddenly resembled a child brought to the circus, fascinated by anticipation. Drago leaned in.

"I know you're incognito, Padre," he whispered, "but are you really supposed to enjoy all this?"

"The Lord will forgive," said Lampedusa with a tiny nod of his head, accompanied by an equally small shrug, like a marionette whose strings had been pulled. "Perhaps you will help restrain me from raising my hand during the auction?"

"You're not going to bid, surely?"

"No, no, but it would be a pleasure to win the prize."

"Why? What is it?"

"A dance with Signorina Ariana. She is a truly wonderful dancer. She will put any partner to shame."

"Another reason to not raise your hand, Padre."

"Alas so."

"Don't worry. I'm sure the bidding will spiral well out of the clergy's reach."

"Yes, yes. You are right. Here. Come here." Lampedusa grasped Drago's sleeve and yanked him towards Sabatini's entourage.

The big man's gaze swung their way. His whole body seemed to pivot on an unseen axle until he was facing Lampedusa directly. A smile as wide as his jaw erupted across Sabatini's face. It had all the pleasantry of angry polar bear. And then there was the eye. Drago's attention was unavoidably drawn to it. The orb seemed to glow. The aura flamed when light struck it and turned dark as the big head moved. One eye. A thousand eyes. All stared from the blackness. What was that cliché about windows into souls? It took Drago no more than a glance to open the gates. Sabatini's nature was fractured into tiny pieces but they all originated from a single unholy darkness.

"Signor Sabatini," Lampedusa switched to Italian, "Welcome, welcome."

"It is my party, Padre," replied Sabatini. "It is I who should welcome you."

The big man bent a little. Both paws reached out and encompassed Lampedusa's right hand. The two huge claws did not immediately release their hold. The men conversed. Despite them talking in Italian, Drago sensed the Pastor becoming uncomfortable. Once the hand was released, he seemed to breathe easier. Drago switched his attention from Sabatini's fake cheeriness to Ariana's almost ghostly indifference. He tried to catch her eye. She didn't avoid it, simply didn't respond, remaining silent and demure, her pose one of modesty, the hands clasping a small purse in front of her, the feet together, gaze slightly turned down so her fringe fell. It was only the stunning evening gown, sleek satin silver ,slashed almost to the waist on one side which spoke of a different natural animal. At her throat was a choker of stretched black satin augmented by a chunk of a diamond which seemed to blaze with intense white fire. Behind the two magical apparitions congregated what Drago could only consider where ghouls, dressed totally in grey, uncomfortable suits. Men from the yacht; he recognised the one who acted as manservant.

Lampedusa beckoned feebly and spoke in English.

"This is Jon Drago. A new donor for the orphanage."

"Really?" Sabatini switched languages with equal agility. His accent was heavy. The 'r' sound rolled for a long time across his tongue. "And how much have you donated, Mr Drago?"

"Nothing yet," he said. They did not shake hands. Drago noticed Ariana stepping forward. She tweaked the big man's sleeve. If he understood her intervention he made no show of it.

"I was hoping to win the auction," Drago continued.

"Oh? And what do you do for a living, Mr Drago?"

"Is that relevant?"

"The lot is expected to fetch a high price."

"I'm not sure I'd ever describe Ariana as a 'lot'."

Sabatini's neck twisted, his shoulders twisted, yet his hulking torso hardly moved. He looked for her. For the first time since they'd entered the courtyard, Ariana stood daringly forward. Drago recognised the pose. It was the same challenge she'd offered him at the spa: defiance.

"Hmm. Possibly not," muttered Sabatini.

"This is Jon Drago," she said urgently. "Remember, I told you about him. We met at the spa. He knows the woman who was in that horrible accident."

"Yes. I remember." Sabatini's shoulders turned back. "Are you hoping to spend your compensation before you get it?"

"No." Drago paused a moment. Sabatini was being deliberately rude. It would do well to let him bask in his glory before drowning him. Slowly, Drago pulled a fat leather bill fold from his pocket, one he'd bought specifically from a souvenir shop early that day. It was stuffed with fifty Euro notes. He flipped it so the big man could see. "I have my own source of income. It's amazing what you find on a beach these days."

Sabatini stared at the money long and hard. His eye, his one good eye, swivelled and peered at Drago from under a hooded brow. The false one seemed to glint with excitement. Sabatini reached into his jacket pocket and produced a big Cohiba. One of the ghouls was on hand with a lighter and held it flame-on while Sabatini puffed to ignite the cigar.

"Be careful what you wish for, Mr Drago," he said. "The waters are very deep around Otranto."

"I don't intend to do any more swimming."

"Good. I wish you luck at the auction." Sabatini watched as Drago replaced the wallet. A big cloud of smoke enveloped them as he breathed out. "Remember the rules of the game, Signor. Tonight all your funds must be to hand."

"Thank you for reminding me."

The big man stepped away. Drago swooped as close as he dared. "Wait, one moment, please."

Sabatini continued walking. His back was half-turned and he was striding towards a group of sparkling dignitaries, Ariana at his side, the entourage behind, the ghouls almost blocking Drago's advance.

"I'm not seeking compensation. I can assure you of that. I don't know Madeleine's intentions in that regard. Of course, her parents are very concerned and may press her to pursue a legal case."

Sabatini stopped.

"This is not the time or the place," he growled.

"She might have died."

The cigar had returned to the mouth where it became trapped between big teeth. Sabatini took it out and jabbed it dramatically towards Drago's face.

"Someone almost always dies, Mr Drago," he hissed. "It is an unwritten law in Puglia. You will do well to be mindful of the law."

Drago caught Ariana's solemn silence. Her face betrayed nothing, though her shoulders, her back, seemed to stiffen.

Lampedusa tugged at his arm. "You've upset him," he whispered. "This is a social occasion, Jon. Come. Come."

Drago allowed himself to be dragged gently from the fray. The ghouls were massing. They were an ugly razor-whipped bunch and he didn't fancy roughing it with them.

Nor would Lampedusa. Not ever. The Reverendo didn't like confrontation. He pleaded rather than demanded. He prayed rather than fought. The job with the orphans, its appeal to the soft heart fitted him like a glove. He'd learned solid English at Keele, but Drago saw the other afflictions he'd picked up, such as endless appeasement instead of action. Sometimes people in diplomatic positions never told it like it was; being easily frightened, afraid of criticism and reprisal. Was Lampedusa a frightened man? There might be another reason, considered Drago. It might be Ariana. He remembered the bruises he'd seen. The beautiful evening gown covered the blemishes. Drago remembered the anger in Sabatini's photograph; he no longer needed to wonder where it stemmed from. It was here, in front of him. Envy. Greed. Power.

Lampedusa led Drago far from the host. He had always been a good measure of a man's intent. He knew Sabatini had a burning ire. He saw it in the gritted face. It reminded him of the crude gangsters who sought absolution in the confessional box. Hatred, anger, lust and greed were what fuelled these men. For a second, as Sabatini and Drago spoke barbed sentences, he detected it also in the Englishman. Something latent, something hidden below the affable masque of respectability: it was something to do with death. Whatever argument the two men were starting it only had one outcome. The rules of this game were entirely different.

From his position on the stone canopied balcony, Bergamo also watched the incident. He wasn't dressed for the occasion. He was decked out in a turtle neck and a thigh length leather jacket. He knew he was conspicuous, but he didn't own a suit. After collecting one beer from the makeshift bar in the old armoury, he'd made his way carefully through the sparsely populated courtyard and back to the staircase which led to his current vantage point and an opportunity to hug the shadows. Bergamo had received his ticket in advance. As soon as the motor launch set off from the yacht, he had made his way to Piazza Castellano. He was mildly surprised to see the Englishman waiting in line, the man he now knew was called Jonathon Drago. His informant at the hotel had told him and explained the details of Drago's sojourn and the sad story of his girlfriend's accident. Bergamo didn't think the Englishman seemed upset. In fact, his pursuit of another woman might be considered somewhat indecent, but then you had to account for her undeniable beauty. Bergamo had weighed the conundrum in his head and found his scales had fallen, like the Englishman's, onto the woman's side.

The next hour or so proceeded almost without incident. The band continued to play, the dancing started, the buffet was announced and people swapped rooms and dance partners as regularly as they exchanged empty champagne flutes for full ones.

Throughout Bergamo moved carefully around the perimeter, watching the woman closely when she departed from Sabatini's side. When she was in situ, he took to observing the Englishman. Whatever this Drago did for a living, he wasn't daunted by the surroundings. He was equally at home conversing with priests as high society. Wealthy businessmen, elderly ladies, young women, hot headed men, artists, servants, everyone received the same appropriate deference, one which mixed uneasily with wit. Drago was a furbacchione, a smart-arse. He got away with it by being gentle in his manner. He talked, but more important to his audience, he also listened. That makes him different to Sabatini, concluded Bergamo, but did that make him more or less dangerous?

Drago talked with the Frattellis. They owned a wine emporium. Bergamo saw the Englishman had found a niche. He spent a long time discussing the merits of Brunello and Barolo. Later, Bergamo saw him chatting lazily with an aspiring foreign model and her hopeful cameraman who were taking personality shots among the crowd. The Englishman would glance across the courtyard to check on the whereabouts of Sabatini and Ariana. When they exited temporarily for the buffet, Drago followed discreetly. A few moments later, Bergamo too made his move, sneaking in via the service route. He took a hunk of bruschetta and bit down on it, shaded by an elaborate artwork, part of an exhibition of modern Italian sculptors. Drago didn't stay long and neither did Bergamo.

The band finished a jaunty number with a clash and disappeared for a well-earned break. In their place, came the auctioneer. He was a multi-lingual officious man with a pinched beard. A small stage had been provided for him on which stood a glass lectern and a microphone. He called for attention and then related a greeting and instructions, first in Italian, then English and lastly, badly, in Russian.

"Ladies and gentlemen, honoured guests, welcome to the highlight of the evening: a charity auction, the proceeds of which will be donated to the Children of Otranto Foundation."

He paused after speaking in each language and a ripple of applause reflected the impact the announcement had on its various. nationalities. The smallest response came for the English version.

Slowly, the auditorium began to fill.

"We have twenty-one lots to be auctioned this evening. Some are valuable, some are trivial, some are an obligation, all, in terms of the Foundation are priceless. So, let us proceed with lot number one."

Drago was bored quickly. Most of the auction didn't interest him: a vase here, a photographic album there, a valet service, that sort of thing. He yawned once, noticed someone looking, a tall man with a mop of curly hair and sideburns to his neck. Drago stared at him a few seconds too long. Their eyes snapped at each other. The man wasn't dressed for a fancy do. He wore a turtle neck, not a shirt and tie. And with that bulky leather jacket, he stuck out like the young men whose regard for propriety was so low they loosened ties as soon as they arrived. Drago had noted him before, just once, on arrival.

"That man's looking at you," said Lampedusa, who had materialised beside him.

"Yes. Do you know who he is?"

"No."

"Is he one of Sabatini's mob?"

"I have no idea. Why?"

"No reason. It's unsettling being stared at. Now I know how that model feels."

The comment was lost on the Reverendo.

"Do you still intend to bid for the dance?"

"Yes."

"You might lose."

"And it'll be fun doing so. I'd be interested to see Sabatini's reaction."

"Please don't antagonise him anymore." Lampedusa appeared genuinely worried. "It is not polite."

"Bother polite," said Drago swiftly. "He's a bully, isn't he? I saw how he reacted when my friend was hit by the speedboat. It was as if he didn't care. I've seen how he talks to Ariana. Not the words: the actions, the disdain. Look how he spoke to me. Come on, Padre, you don't make threats at social occasions."

"Nor do you discuss business, which you did."

"I don't accept that. There's more to Sabatini's business than meets the eye."

"What do you mean?"

"I mean he's not coming to Otranto simply to help migrant orphans." Drago dug into his pocket for his Marlboros, took one and lit it. "Shh. It's time."

The auctioneer rapped his gavel on the lectern.

"Ladies and gentlemen, the final lot, donated generously by our patron Signor Marcelo Sabatini: a single dance with his companion Signorina Ariana Morena. I am sure you are all well acquainted with the Signorina who has danced in all the ballrooms of Europe. A waltz with the Signorina is a dance of delectable delight."

Drago thought the spiel crude in translation, yet it had sounded charming in Italian. There was a round of applause. Sabatini held out his hand to exhibit his prize. Coy, Ariana performed a twirl, delicately spinning on high heels. Drago pushed his way closer to the front, the cigarette caught in his mouth.

The auctioneer rattled off the Russian translation then switched back to Italian for the bidding process. He opened at a relatively low one hundred Euros. There was plenty of enthusiasm. Prices rose quickly. Drago waited until the bidding grew tired. There were four or five interested parties. The price was tilting at five thousand. An astronomical sum for three minutes of fun, considered Drago; mind, it's only going to get worse.

"Five thousand three hundred?" said the auctioneer. "Thank you. Five-four? Yes, sir. Five thousand and five?"

"Six thousand," said Drago dramatically.

A little thrill ran through the crowd. The women especially reacted to the sudden increase in bid with excitement. One or two people turned to look at Drago, to check he had really said it and that he wasn't joking.

"Six thousand, sir, thank you. Do I hear six-one?"

"Six-five."

It was a Russian, Drago thought. The voice was blunt.

"Seven thousand."

"Seven-five."

"Seven-six." Someone else, one of the earlier suitors, a local businessman.

"Seven-eight," said Drago.

"Eight thousand," from the Russian.

Ariana peered into the audience. Drago didn't know if she could see him, but she must have heard his voice. Sabatini puffed on the last of his cigar. He tapped the ash and it fell in a tumble onto the clean mosaics. His one eye ranged across the audience, flicking from each gambler in turn. He twitched every time the price leapt up another notch. Drago wanted to make him twitch again.

"Nine."

"Nine thousand," confirmed the auctioneer. He swung the gavel extravagantly, seeking the Russian, hoping he would continue the fight. "Nine thousand Euros for a dance with the beautiful Signorina."

"Ten."

Another series of gasps. Drago had counted a stack of notes out of the canvas pouch, but now he'd forgotten how much he'd brought with him. His concerns were elsewhere. Sabatini's face was screwed into the same demented mask he remembered from that press photo. His free hand balled into a fist.

Lampedusa noticed it too. He crept forward towards the small stage. What was this? Anger. For what? What did Sabatini have against the Englishman? It was obvious he was not about to let Drago have his way.

"Ten and a half."

"Eleven."

There was a dramatic pause and the gavel swung again. The Russian suddenly said: "Fifteen thousand."

Sabatini's shoulders relented. He almost grinned.

Drago dragged on the cigarette. He raised his hand, the orange tip flashing briefly. The auctioneer understood the intent.

"Thank you. Sixteen thousand, sir."

The bids competed upwards, the Russian jumping by five thousand a time and Drago upping only an extra one to keep his nose ahead. When the figure reached forty thousand, the audience burst into spontaneous applause. Drago waited for the excitement to die before slowly raising his hand, just enough for the cigarette to be seen.

"Forty-one thousand Euros I am bid." This time the auctioneer was met with a long silence. He craned to find the Russian among the assembly. The man's interest or his wallet had peaked. "Forty-one thousand. Any advance?"

The auctioneer allowed two seconds of quiet, during which everyone expected the hammer to slam on the lectern. Instead a loud growl came from the stage as Sabatini said: "Fifty thousand."

The bid was met with astonishment. The host was buying his own lot! This is so romantic, the women tittered, buying a dance with his lover so no-one else could share her; a man truly in love. This is so selfish, the men replied, keeping her to himself. Why not just donate the money? He's showing off.

Drago creased his brow. Sabatini was baiting him. He couldn't have been any more blatant. How high would Sabatini bid to win the battle? Did he know Jon Drago's resources, the sudden income of €200,000 or was he guessing? If Drago bid, would Sabatini continue up and up until all that two-hundred grand had vanished? He was gauging Drago's ambition and inflating his ego in one swoop. Well, there was always one way to defeat a bully: humour.

"Fifty thousand Euros," gabbled the auctioneer, "to buy back your dance partner, Signor?"

"Fifty thousand," repeated Sabatini.

Casually, Drago raised his hand, the cigarette meeting its death as it smouldered between his fingers. Ariana looked uneasy.

"Fifty thousand," he began, "and one Euro."

Somebody laughed, a cautious giggling sound. The anger rippled across Sabatini's features. He understood where the mirth was directed and he didn't like it. The fist bunched once more. The big man was going to say something when Lampedusa pressed out of the crowd, a broad smile on his face, mounted the stage and clutched quickly at Sabatini's elbow, whispering. The big man's gaze settled on Ariana, silent and radiant, but Drago could have sworn the flickering false orb had swung his way. Sabatini's face broke into the most hideous of smiles. Something resembling laughter burst out of the shark-like mouth.

"Fifty thousand and one Euros," repeated the auctioneer. "Once. Twice." He banged the gavel. "A dance, Signor, for a generous Englishman."

The applause was suddenly very loud. Several people shook

Drago's hand, congratulated him on his spirit and his good deed, such a huge donation. The auctioneer was thanking everyone in three languages, explaining how much was raised, revelling in the fantastic sale. The band began to play again and people lost interest as fast as they'd gained it. Drago made his way to the stage where an official was assisting the auctioneer in collecting monies. The official asked politely how Drago wished to pay.

"Cash," he replied. "I don't carry that amount on me, but I do have it. Signor Sabatini can vouch for that."

The official glanced across at the host. Sabatini tossed the cigar aside. Ariana stood like a mannequin. She'd hardly moved through the whole scene.

"Mr Drago's credit is fine," Sabatini announced. "Which dance would you like the orchestra to play? Remember, Ariana is a very fine dancer."

Drago considered for a moment. It would have been easy to waltz. His mother and father had insisted he learned as a child. Later, for fun, Abbey Scott had persuaded him to try ballroom dancing, but his attempts at the foxtrot and quickstep were soon ditched in favour of the drunken vagaries of disco moves at night clubs, the shaky sambas and salsas people did without inhibitions or finesse, the preamble to a likely encounter and a dance of an altogether more erotic kind. The daftness of those mating rituals tempted him now. It just might piss off Sabatini even more. Now, what was the most sensual of those ballroom dances?

"What about a rhumba?"

Ariana's statuesque figure shook. She suddenly seemed to take in that it was Drago, standing before her, lighting another cigarette, that amused half-smile on his lips, the one she'd noticed at the spa in the sunshine beneath the awning. Meanwhile, oblivious to her, Sabatini chuckled. It was a sickly thing devoid of humour, as if even he accepted who was being made fun of.

"Alright, a rhumba then." Sabatini waved his hand airily, an act not of flippancy, but of disguise. "Tell the band to play it slow, very slow, so Mr Drago can enjoy every precious second. Ariana," he continued, "show our guest how excellently you dance."

"Will you watch, Marcelo?" she asked, but her eyes never

left Drago's face. The Englishman was crazy. He had to be. Yet he didn't look it. No. Instead, he stepped forward and held out his hand, an invitation to take the floor.

"No." Sabatini turned his back on her, pushed past Lampedusa and headed angrily towards his ghoulish grey entourage. "It would be difficult."

Nine

Spar and Spinnaker

The two chambers are called the Round Rooms. If a person stands in the exact centre of the first room and speaks, the acoustics bounce off the curved stone blocks and create an echo effect which changes as they step closer or move further away from the walls. The second room has a round bench in the middle. Two people can sit on opposite sides and talk quietly and it will sound as if they are whispering at each other's ears. Children have endless fun in the rooms. Most people though, never understand the attraction of either dormitory.

Sabatini knew of the room's properties. He sat on the stone seat and sucked on a cigar. The tobacco made a satisfying sizzle as it ignited. For a second he thought he could hear the echo. Somewhere, far above him, he could still hear the orchestra playing *Te Quiero*, a classic rhumba.

The man sitting with his back to Sabatini wore a leather coat. He had curly hair soiled with the gel he'd streaked in it. He smelt of bad food. Sabatini sniffed at the offensive odour.

"You are Bergamo?" he whispered.

The man shifted on his seat. Unaware of the properties of the room, Bergamo genuinely thought the Albanian was murmuring at his shoulder. He glanced over, saw Sabatini still staring at the wall and said loudly: "Yes."

"Turn and face the wall and whisper."

Sabatini let the instruction sink in before he continued.

"Bergamo, Atilla Ferrara engaged you to watch over my companion. That was a request I made of him because it is not possible for my own men to watch her without arousing suspicion. You have been an ideal replacement. I am told you are exceptionally thorough. Tell me, what do you know about Jon Drago?"

"Only what they tell me at the hotel," replied Bergamo.

"Whisper it."

"Please, excuse." Bergamo lowered his voice. "I have a man at the hotel; an informer. Drago is a journalist. He writes books. That's all I know."

"What is his interest in Ariana?"

"I do not know. Not for certain. They met today. They have never met before. They took coffee. I watched them on the cameras."

"Did he attempt to molest her?"

"No."

"A kiss?"

"No."

"Did he touch her?"

"No. Wait. They held hands for a moment."

"What else?"

"They talked. They exchanged cigarettes."

Bergamo inclined his head a little. Two guests, a man and a woman, entered the room, talking in loud half-drunk voices. They stared in sudden embarrassment at the two men who occupied the seat, apologised and tried to keep their chatter to a minimum. Occasionally the woman burst into a frantic giggle. Bergamo leaned back and twisted his neck. His next words were uttered straight into Sabatini's ear. There was something he remembered, an insignificant detail but the sort of detail the Albanian would want to know.

"She smiled a lot."

The rhumba had come to an end. Sabatini hoisted the fat Cohiba to his lips. Did it matter? he pondered. Of course it did. She was his and his alone. He'd made her that way. No one else should have her. Not now, not ever. He came to the conclusion and the resolution quickly as he did all ruthless decisions.

Bergamo detected a dull hiss. It was the cigar.

"Kill him for me," ordered Sabatini.

***

Te Quiero. Te quiero. I want you.

She glided smoothly towards him as if she was on ice, hardly a ripple on her shoulders, only a sway to her hips, the supple figure-of-eight. He held out his hand. She took it by the fingertips, allowing them to come together. As she stepped into his embrace, he detected again the amorous scent of oranges and cedar wood: deep, hidden, seductive. It seemed to encompass her, envelope her, become part of who she was and what she promised. His arm lightly took her waist and for one moment they were entwined, moving hip to hip, in unison. She spun away, one arm outstretched as if reaching for him and from him at the same time, the classic pose, the indecision of romance: to stay or to flee, what was her choice and where did it lead, what was his choice and why was he doing this? Was she thinking of those questions or was she so compelled by the slow-quick-quick rhythm that all else ceased to exist? Was Jon Drago a man attempting to seduce her, by music or design, or was he a mere cypher, a stranger, a totem of all men who had won her, lost her and abandoned her.

The music prowled the air. They crossed the mosaic floor, shoes and heels making light tapping sounds, adding to the melody. Drago wanted the dance to be slow. He'd rarely attempted the rhumba. It was the hardest ballroom for a man, for he was almost only a prop for the woman to parade around. The rhumba was her dance. He wanted Ariana to have the spotlight. The watching faces approved. People clapped. The women sighed. Occasionally, as she executed graceful open breaks or spun an underarm turn, he heard approving wallowing comments, breathed so as not to disturb the sensual, exotic scene unfolding before midnight eyes. He moved quietly, guiding her through a routine he felt she had learned by heart many years before when romance and love really existed. Before all this. Before Sabatini.

It was over almost as soon as it started. Three and a half minutes can fly past, Drago thought, when you are caught in a moment. And what a moment.

Ariana finished dramatically. She clasped his neck. He reversed on the balls of his feet, her body slanted on his, face buried on his neck, feet stretched impossibly behind her in a rhumba slide. At the end of the movement, her hands ran down his torso to his hips and she descended to the floor, to her knees, head cradled beneath her arm, afraid maybe or bashful, uncertain, a little girl once more on the threshold of life's great excitements. She must have skinned her legs on the tiles, but she didn't complain. His hand rested on her hair, the fingers caressing the folds, the tips pressing on her scalp, to let her know he was there. The applause broke. She knew it would. Now she turned her face up. The lips parted. She panted tearless sobs, the kind he thought women only cried when they made love. Drago stared at her long and hard, letting the moment become absorbed into his memory, the flashing silver evening gown, the black mane, the darkness of her skin, the agony in her eyes. His other hand took an arm and lifted Ariana to her feet. They were inches apart. Her limbs surrounded his neck. She pulled them together. Their mouths almost brushed. Her lips were breathing on his.

"Are you staying all evening?"

"No."

"Then take me out of here."

"Now?"

"Marcelo isn't looking. He isn't here. I can't see him."

"What about his men?"

"They won't do anything unless Marcelo orders it."

"What about you?"

She smiled, pulled away and led him from the dance floor. The band was playing again. Other couples were filling the space.

"I will say you kidnapped me."

"Thanks."

He sounded disingenuous. She detected it and became coquettish. "Do you want to be with me, Jonathon Drago, Jon Drago, or not? I won't ask you twice."

"Maddie was right," he said and took her by the elbow, leading her quickly to the main lobby. "Do you have a coat?"

"In this heat?" She gestured with a hand as if waving a fan.

"No. I guess not. Come on. People are watching."

One man in particular watched with interest. Bergamo had reappeared from the depths of the castle in time to see the couple exit the courtyard. He saw the confused faces of Sabatini's bodyguards. They had no orders to follow the dancer. One of them pulled out a mobile and started to make a call. Bergamo knew what the guard would be told: the chase was the preserve of a man who knew the town. The audience had closed again, moving onto the dance floor to enjoy a cha-cha-cha. Bergamo skirted the perimeter. He made it to the lobby in time to see the silver dress exit the hall. He was about to follow when a hand grabbed his arm. It was one of the priests. Damn! He dare not be rude to the clergy. Bergamo smiled, listened to the priest's entreaty while attempting to escape his attentions.

"I'm not a practising Catholic," he said, which was half a truth.

"You must return to the fold, my son. God will forgive."

But Sabatini won't, thought Bergamo. It took almost three minutes to extricate himself from the priest's attentions. Momentarily, Bergamo wondered why the Pastor was being so earnest and insistent.

When he finally allowed Bergamo freedom from his grasp, Reverendo Lampedusa gave a contented sigh. Sabatini had his good points – the money mostly – but the Signorina, ah, now that was another matter altogether.

Bergamo couldn't see them. It was dark. Everything was bathed in an eerie street lantern glow, shades of lime and tangerine and sudden bursts of snowy white mixed with the breathing blackness. He jumped onto the bottom rung of the drawbridge handrail. He scanned the tourists, a host of interchangeable faces. Something caught his attention. Was that a streak of silver? Working by instinct, Bergamo headed for the Porta a Mare.

Drago and Ariana walked swiftly up the sloping access way to the top of the gatehouse tower. Once the tower had been a customs house. Traders who docked in the harbour had to stop here to declare their goods. Now it was merely a belvedere. Everything was awash in sultry burnt caramel colours: the looming castle, the marina with its pretty illuminated yachts, the twin hills which hugged the town crowned by the new basilica and the ancient chiesetta. The band could still be heard strumming the last of the cha-cha-cha. A rapid drum beat interrupted it. A modern sound. Laughter, squeals of excitement. The gatehouse was linked via a slender wooden causeway to the Torre Matta. Atop that sea-facing watch tower was an open air cocktail lounge and nightclub. The bar featured a neon sign announcing: *Spar & Spinnaker*.

Drago had already been there once with Maddie. He'd spied the little footbridge and thought then it would make a useful getaway.

Little details like that stuck in his mind these days. He actively sought them in the same way his glances into driving mirrors no longer looked solely for traffic and his appraisal of men took in the cut of their cloth in case they hid something lethal. He'd never expected to use this route so suddenly. There was a gate. Drago vaulted it and helped Ariana swing herself delicately over the stile. The bridge was shaky, but stable. They crossed in a few seconds and hurdled the barrier at the far end.

Spar & Spinnaker's crowd shared an energy lacking in the stoic leaden feet of the invitation-only audience at the castle. Drago grabbed Ariana's hand and danced her across the tower esplanade to a booming techno rhythm. The sound system assaulted their ears. They liked it loud at Spar & Spinnaker. They shimmied through the throng to the balustrade. The night sky was sprinkled with stars, sparkling like the pretty diamond at her beautiful throat. The wind suddenly whipped across the wall and caught her hair. It swirled, got wrapped on her face. Drago tugged gently at it and she moved closer. She was grinning, cheekily happy. At last she resembled the woman he'd imagined, when he'd first spied her on *Diamantin*, beautiful and unselfconscious.

"This is crazy," he said above the music.

"Yes."

"Have you ever run away before?"

"I am always running. Maybe it is time to stop."

"What are you running from?"

Ariana produced a small silver grip from her purse and rearranged her hair. She didn't answer. Instead she declared: "That was fun. It's been a long time since I had fun."

"I'd call it impetuous. Won't Sabatini be mad?"

"Yes. But I know how to calm him."

Drago didn't venture further.

"Have you been here before?" she asked. "I know the man who runs it. Marcelo held a party here a month or so ago. We can get free drinks."

"I had free drinks at the castle. It must have cost Sabatini a small fortune."

"No. He charged it to the Foundation."

"That's hardly a representative act of charity."

"Was that a joke?"

"I'm not sure. Was it funny?"

Ariana started to giggle. Her hand went to her mouth to hide it, as if embarrassed, then went to her neck and fiddled nervously with the choker. There was an unoccupied three cushioned sofa nearby and he led her to it. There it would be easier to talk, barricaded from the noise by dancing bodies. Still, they sat conspiratorially close. A waiter came to collect empties from the small square table. Drago ordered champagne.

"The best. We're celebrating."

"What are we celebrating?" she asked.

"Our continued friendship," Drago replied. He perched slightly sideways on the sofa, one foot on the floor, the other lodged under a knee. "That's assuming we are friends."

"I don't have many friends. I wish to have you as one. You interest me."

"That's good because you interest me."

She dismissed the comment.

"Men often say such things. It happens to a girl." She looked at her fingernails. "A girl like me."

"What sort of girl are you?"

"I don't know what they would call me these days: a secretary or a companion? An escort, perhaps, or a whore. I am Marcelo's woman. That is enough to frighten most men."

"He doesn't pay you much attention."

"I am the window dressing. And I am other things, you understand."

"Yes."

"You are not shocked?"

"No. I think there are worse ways to live a life. Of course, I am extremely jealous. Of Sabatini, I mean."

She offered the flicker of a smile. The waiter returned with Kristal champagne, a brand Drago wouldn't have chosen if he'd known. He didn't want to fuss by returning it. When the glasses were full, Drago lifted his in a toast.

"Friends?"

"Friends," she repeated. "Now, tell me, Mr Drago, what is your interest in me? It isn't just about your injured friend, is it?"

"That's very forward."

"I cannot waste time. We may not have long to talk."

"If I'm to tell you my secrets, Ariana, then you must call me Jon."

"Jonathon," she answered emphatically. "I prefer Jonathon. It sounds reliable. Important."

"If you want," said Drago, "but every so often I wish women would simply call me Jon. It started with my mother. When I was born she insisted my name had to be long so it could be shortened. The irony is she now religiously calls me Jonathon. And so, for some inexplicable reason, do most women. I was hoping you might be an exception."

"Then I must disappoint you, Jonathon." She drank a little champagne and smiled. "That was an interesting story, but I must learn something more recent about you. Your career perhaps. Marcelo will ask. I cannot say we never talked."

"Ask away then."

"I am not interested in asking questions. Just tell me the littlest thing and I will make up the rest."

"I write books," he said, "and my parents taught me to dance."

"I wondered about that. You show promise."

"You're brilliant. The Emcee said something about you dancing in ballrooms."

"I did once. Marcelo likes to exaggerate. I toured North and South America with a revue. That's how I learnt English. When I returned I danced with Leo, at the Illyria Ballroom. It's in the Sheraton, Tirana. We lived off tips. Marcelo was in the audience and he saw me. He was rich, good looking. The rest is the same story the world over. It is as simple as that."

"That's when your relationship started?"

"It was seven years ago. My parents had died. I had no one. He was, what would you say, reliable?"

"I suppose. He's rich. I expect that helped."

She shrugged.

"Who was Leo?" asked Drago. He shook out a cigarette,

offered one and held out his Ronson for her. He lit his own. Ariana sipped the champagne and mixed it with a lug of tobacco. The entrails of Marlboros drifted between them. When she spoke, she seemed to be talking of another place and time.

"Leo? He was a wonderful dancer. Graceful. Strong. A brilliant interpreter. He had, what do they call it in English, musicality? Leo was tremendously upset. Maybe I broke his heart. He might have been a little in love with me. It happens when you work so closely together. When I stopped dancing, he tried to find another partner, but it wasn't possible. He teaches now, in a small school in Kukës. I have not seen Leo since I agreed to go with Marcelo. Nor do we talk. I am told he is well. It is a good town, in the mountains. One day, I would like to visit him there." She shifted back onto her haunches, resting against the heavy cushions. "I love those places. It reminds me of home; the mountains, Albania, the people. The soil is a deep rich brown, the grasses tinged with gold and the rivers as clear as the sky. Everything is pure, intense: we live life the way others can only describe. It is hard. It is poor. Yet it is as rich as heaven. We are a proud people who do not forget our past. We look after one another. Every village, every town is like a huge extended family. When I return to Albania, I think I will return to Kukës and all the families will help me."

"You make it sound romantic and very beautiful."

"It is. You must come and visit me. I will go there when Marcelo tires of me."

"Is Sabatini part of those families too?"

"I know what you are thinking." She gave a half smile. "Marcelo is a gangster, of a kind. He is ruthless in business, yes. He is part of the union, yes. He has a violent past. Look at his eye. He lost it in a fight. The black pearl, it flames in the dark, you see? Now he is rich, he wants to alter the way of life in Albania, change things, bring the light. So he has projects happening all across the country. Schools, museums, youth centres. I help him sometimes, to choose the locations, the names. That was how we came to the orphanage here. One day I saw the children and well, as I said, I know how to sway his mind."

"He sounds phenomenally busy." Drago said it obtusely. "Do

you think he'll ever grow tired?"

"Of me?"

Ariana exhaled a long smooth streak of smoke. He thought she was smiling as she did so, the corners of her mouth tipped up a tiny fraction and he saw the dimples in her cheeks glow.

"Yes. One day. I believe he cannot live without a woman. I expect I will cease to be of interest if another model intrigues him."

"Or this one is stolen."

Drago touched her cheek.

"Perhaps," she answered diffidently. "Now, you really must stop asking questions. This wasn't how I wanted it to be."

"I'm sorry. I'm getting carried away. Being here with you, the dance, this crazy scene, it's making me turn corners."

"What a strange expression," she said, "as if you are searching for something you can't find. What are you searching for, Jonathon Drago?"

He was about to reply when a shadow fell across them and Ariana, distracted, inclined her chin sharply. Drago expected it to be one of Sabatini's ghouls, but it was a slim youngish looking man, his hands held out in greeting. Ariana took the hands, accepted the proffered kiss and began talking in rapid Italian. The man's cheerful face switched to concern very quickly. He gave Drago a quick interested glance when Ariana introduced them.

"This is Roberto. He owns the bar. It is lucky we came here, Jonathon. Someone is looking for us."

"Are you certain?"

"Roberto wouldn't lie."

"Come," said the man, gesturing with all fingers. He vanished into the dancing throng. Ariana didn't wait for Drago's approval. Quickly, he doused his fag and followed.

"Who is it?" he asked when he got close enough.

"A man in a leather coat."

"Thigh length? Curly hair?"

"Yes. How did you know?"

"Instinct."

The uncomfortable looking man from the castle, his long leather jacket completely out of kilter with everyone else's attire. He must have been boiling in such a heavy coat. Now Drago knew it was for another reason. The man wasn't used to hanging out at posh functions. He was more used to stealing from the rich – or worse.

They were taken behind the bar, Roberto leading. As they dodged ice buckets and spinning cocktail shakers, Drago noticed a reflection in the mirror behind the optics. Curly hair. Swarthy. Bulky beneath a leather coat. Shit. They went through to the rear store room. Drago could hear some sort of commotion breaking out in the bar. Roberto showed them to a trap door in the middle of the storeroom floor, covered by crates of Smirnoff Black and Grey Goose. Drago helped ease them aside. The hatch creaked open on an upward hinge. Hidden below was a slim passage heading into the bowels of the tower. It was accessed by a stone stairway.

Urgently, Roberto motioned for them to go down, kissed Ariana's cheek and headed back to the bar where someone was still shouting.

Drago shut the trap door after him. He had a torch app on his mobile and switched it on. They took the stairs gingerly, one at a time, Ariana leading, the dust of ages rising as they stepped on each flagstone. The debris sprinkled blue in the shallow light. At the bottom they found another door, this one metal and fixed on the inside with top and bottom bolts and a standard Yale latch. Drago slid the bolts and opened the door. They were standing in a thin snaking street. The public entrance to the nightclub was to the right, towards the sea wall. A man with tight curly hair and a big leather coat was emerging from it onto the bastion. He was agitated and angry. He'd been forcibly evicted from the club. Ariana saw him too and dived down the alley. She seemed to know exactly where to go, turning into an even thinner crevasse, heading for the darkness of Otranto's winding medieval streets. The high walls of the apartments, peppered with barred box windows, guided them left and right, up and down. At one corner, Drago looked back at the misty yellow blur, thought he saw a man in pursuit. Ariana lifted her dress to her knees and led him down the sliver street, dodging a row of potted plants, a splash of colour on a ghostly scene. They emerged onto a small pizzeria, its tables occupied and the whiff of fresh tomatoes, mozzarella and basil emanating from plates and kitchens. They crossed at pace, up another steep alley, more shadows, a slight breeze, the scent of the sea, finally a sunken garden among the overhanging buildings, a few steps down into the foliage where they huddled together and waited, listening.

The hefty footsteps came, paused, carried on. Drago peeked over the parapet. A leather coat retreated down the opposite path, back to the sea wall and the bastion.

"He's going," Drago said.

Ariana pulled him close and kissed him, once, hard.

"What was that for?"

"I wanted to."

"I guess that definitely makes us friends."

"Yes. Let's go back to the bar."

"No. I know somewhere else. You'll like it."

Vicino's was still busy. Paulo greeted Drago with a clasp of hands. He cast an approving eye over Ariana and immediately welcomed her as if she'd been coming to his restaurant every day. There wasn't a spare table so he offered them seats at the bar and produced prosecco in big bowl glasses.

"Later," he said, "I will give you my mother's grappa."

"Is the grappa special?" she asked when Paulo had returned to his customers.

"He thinks it's an aphrodisiac."

Ariana cocked her head to one side.

"He thinks I need it?"

"He has a vivid imagination. Ask him to tell you about his childhood. He'll keep you entertained for hours."

They lit cigarettes. Ariana offered him one of her Camels. They talked, but if you'd later asked them what they spoke of, they would not remember. It was simple fare: music, movies, places, faces, food, love talk, the long preamble, the kind of conversation two people have where the words do not matter, all that concerns them is being close to one another and deciding if this one might be a little more special than the last. A second glass of prosecco arrived unprompted. They kept coming and so did the smiles and the laughter. Later too, when the conversation was finished and the decision made, Paulo joined them and Ariana asked about his childhood.

Drago had heard all the stories already. He needed the washroom and excused himself once the second tale started. He stumbled on entering. There was a step down and he missed it. His shoes cracked on the worn tiles. After using the urinal, he turned to the basin. He was flushed from the booze. He splashed water on his face and let it dribble onto his collar. It'd soon dry in this heat. His head came up, the intention to wipe his eyes. Instead the pupils, blown wide by the semi-darkness of the restaurant, focussed on something else. Reflected in the mirror was the dark skinned, side-burned, curly headed heavy they'd avoided at Spar & Spinnaker. Somehow the man had slipped unnoticed into Vicino's. He was leaning against the closed door, his right hand dabbing threateningly into his coat pocket.

The night became sober. Drago's eyes shifted left and right and back again. Near the still running tap, the ceramic soap dispenser was dripping lotion. He lowered his hands.

Bergamo said nothing. He took two strides forward, the hand slicing out of the jacket. The thin stiletto blade hissed its warning. Drago was already dropping a shoulder. His right hand grabbed the ceramic, his whole body turned, all movements at once. The blade cut the air an inch from his cheek, snagged on the lapel on his suit. Drago lunged forward. The little white pot smashed into Bergamo's face. Soap and ceramics splattered the two men. Defence became attack. Drago's other fist swept up, plunged into a soft stomach. The silver viper's tongue lashed again. The tip nicked his sleeve. No matter.

Bergamo was too wild. He was angry for being made to look a fool. The stiletto is best used for short, stabbing attacks. He was trying to scythe Drago into submission. The arm swept again. Drago saw it coming and snatched at the wrist. The two bodies came together with a crunch, breast bones snapping. Drago's fingers did not slacken. They held like cement. The two men tussled, teeth gritted, spun and crashed through the cubicle door. Beads of sweat and soap slapped out of Bergamo's shaggy hair. Drago forced him back against the toilet bowl, felt the legs buckle off-balance. He took the man's legs away with a sideswipe. Bergamo collapsed, his buttocks half in the bowl. Drago twisted the wrist. The knife tinkled on the tiles. He slammed a fist into Bergamo's nose and yanked on the old fashioned chain, activating the flush. As the water rinsed his arse, Bergamo scrabbled for the glinting steel finger. Drago got it first. He took a step back. The stiletto was very light yet it felt supremely powerful. His fingers wrapped instinctively around the hilt, the thumb over the top, ready to thrust the blade at its target.

Squealing obscenities, Bergamo jerked out of the toilet bowl. A suicidal ploy. Drago tried to avoid the mad rush, but the arena was too constricted. They collided with a sickening thud. Bergamo yelped. The knife stuck out between his ribs, blood spurting. Drago struck out with a single haishu blow to the neck. Bergamo catapulted across the washroom and landed in a heap by the door, dazed, wheezing and crabbing vaguely for the knife. Drago kicked out and watched the curly head snap back and become still and silent except for slow rasping snuffles.

"Shit."

Drago sucked in a long breath. The air tasted of lavender oil. Shaking, he turned back to the washbasin and dowsed himself again and again until the stink and the shock had passed. There were blood stains on his shirt. The body was blocking the exit. The chest, still drooling blood, was vibrating. Thank God; the man wasn't dead. Drago pulled the body away from the door and placed it in the recovery position. Buttoning his jacket, he went out.

Ariana was still at the bar. Paulo was regaling her with another story. Drago paused, making a rapid visual recce of the place. Nothing suspicious. The clientele was the same as when he'd left. Her eyes lit when she saw Drago then immediately darkened as she took in the state of his jacket and shirt. Paulo saw her mood change and half-turned to follow her gaze. His eyebrows raised in astonishment.

"What is this?"

"Unsociable business," said Drago. "There's a man in your bathroom with a knife in his chest. He just tried to kill me."

Paulo uttered a violent curse and made for the washrooms.

Ariana put out a hand and clasped Drago's fingers. She appeared almost unconcerned by the incident, as if she either expected it or its happening was no surprise, as everyday an occurrence as washing your face or taking a piss.

"Who was it?" she asked. "Was it that man?"

"Yes."

"Shit," she said.

"I thought so too."
"It must be Marcelo."
"You think?"
"I don't know. I thought I recognised him."
"He's not from the yacht?"
"No. Somewhere else." She paused for a moment, frowning. "The Comte's party. Yes. The party. He was at Tarantella."

Paulo reappeared, shaking his head. His reaction to the affray was like a drowning man, the effort was all too much. He reached for the telephone behind the bar and dialled. Drago didn't need to be told he was phoning the police and prepared to leave. Paulo's flat palm made him stay.

"It won't look good," he explained after making the call.
"Marcelo won't like me being here," said Ariana.
"You just told me it's his doing."
"I can't be here."

She said it firmly, but Drago detected apprehension, more in her body language than the manner of her speech.

"You don't need to be." He turned to Paulo. "Let's get Ariana out of here before the police arrive. Get me a taxi number."

The restaurateur's face sunk another fathom. Drago saw it, ignored it and said: "Please, Paulo."

With a sigh, Paulo took a business card from a stack beside the till and handed it over. "Do it quick," he muttered, "before I see."

Drago got Ariana to make the call on her mobile, in case anyone should try and trace his. He walked her to the front of the restaurant. Her face seemed to cloud over until only the diamond was lit by street lamps. A sparkling reminder of a spontaneous evening.

"Will you be alright?"
"There will be a launch and one of the crew waiting by the jetty. I will be fine."
"Are you sure?"
"Yes."

The taxi didn't take long. The faint hum of a police siren was edging up the harbourside towards them, Drago kissed her cheek.

"Will I see you again?"
"You know where I am each afternoon."

Ariana got in, the cab pulled away and in seconds she was sucked into the darkness. Everything, the fight, the clear up, the decisions, the phone calls and goodbye had taken minutes. The whirling police lights were in sight now and he retreated to the restaurant where the last remaining diners were choosing to ignore whatever fracas had occurred. Two of them, a middle aged couple, had already settled their bill, hoping to avoid whatever enquiries might come their way. Probably a wise decision, considered Drago, and he wondered how long his night was going to be once the real questions started.

Ten

Tarantella

Inspector Gigli would have looked at Jon Drago down his nose, but they were both standing up and their noses were on a level playing field. Instead, he half-closed his eyes and scratched an imaginary irritation behind his ear.

"You never saw this man before?"

"Never," said Drago. "Frankly, I'm appalled."

"Appalled?"

"People can't just walk around attacking you with knives. It's bad enough they get hit by errant speedboats. What's happening to the police service in Otranto?"

The Inspector half-smiled at the indignation. What was it the Wiki-page had said about this journalist come writer? 'Often considered arrogant – A wasted youth – Violent stories based on a semblance of his real life experiences'. Something like that.

"Whatever you may feel about the police service," said the Inspector, "the evidence does suggest you stabbed a man in a fight."

"It was an accident. I picked up the knife to throw it away, but he ran at me and the blade got stuck in his gut."

"So you say."

"Is he denying it?"

"He is on his way to hospital. He's not saying anything."

"Of course he isn't."

"If he did, I couldn't tell you." The Inspector gestured to one of the empty tables. They were all empty now. Drago didn't move. "I would like your co-operation, Signor Drago. I could easily do this at the station." He checked his watch. "If you like, you can come tomorrow morning. You know where it is."

"You're not arresting me?"

The Inspector took a seat anyway. He placed on the table a sealed bag containing the blood-stained knife and arranged it neatly, square-on to the edge. After several seconds the Englishman's ire seemed to calm down. It was all for show, he thought, thunder and bluster. He wasn't genuinely angry. He really wanted information.

"The man won't press charges," explained the Inspector. "Of course, I could arrest you, but then I'd have to go through all the paperwork and keep you locked in a cell and deal with lawyers and people from the embassy and the newspapers: 'famous writer on assault charge'. It'd be chaos and I don't think I have the time or the energy." He checked his mobile, which had peeped at him. "Neither does my wife."

Drago sat down and took out his cigarettes. He offered one to the Inspector, was turned down and decided not to light up. He saw Paulo standing stone still and nervous at the counter. The restaurant was closed, the concertina doors shut, the external lights off. Only the cool amber glow of the ceiling bulbs and the shadows of human statues revealed what life still existed in Vicino's. The Inspector too noticed the patron was hovering.

"Are you alright, Paulo?" he asked.

"I am. You won't shut the restaurant?"

"No, Paulo. This isn't your doing." The Inspector toyed with the corner of the evidence bag. He lifted his tired gaze back to the Englishman. "You, Signor Drago, are a different matter. I could ask you to leave Otranto, but I don't think you would."

"No, I wouldn't."

"You tell me you don't know anything about this man. You don't know why he attacked you."

"That's correct. I've been here all night. I like the food. I like Paulo. This thug jumped me. He must have thought I had money."

"You know I can find out if you are lying to me."

"I was at that charity shindig, at the castle, but I was bored, so I left."

The Inspector raised his eyebrows and took out his notebook. "You never said this before. Was your assailant there?"

"I doubt it. Did you see his clothes? Hardly the sort of kit for a posh do."

The Inspector ignored whatever it was the Englishman had said because he said it too fast. He scribbled 'No' in his pad and put a question mark after it. He sighed, closed the book and composed himself.

"I am going to tell you something, Signor," he began. "It might make a difference to you or it might not, but I suggest you listen and listen very carefully. There are people in this town, in this region, who you English call the Mafia. They aren't anything like the people in the movies. They are rough, tough low-lives. They steal and they exploit, they rape and they fight. They don't respect anyone. They don't care about anyone. They look after no one, only themselves. The man who assaulted you tonight is one of these men. I do not recommend you stay in Otranto. Someone will be looking for you, Signor. Life could get very dangerous for you here."

Drago said nothing.

"Dangerous," repeated the Inspector, "and short."

***

Drago drove the short journey to Santa Cesarea Therme the next day. As he swung around the cliff head, he could see the spa town spreading inland from the semi-circular bay, its beaches and promenades crammed full of holiday makers. It was impossible not to see Tarantella, perched on a dramatic hilltop overlooking the arena like some God-King's palace from centuries yore. It certainly looked as if it came from another era.

There had been a trend for the Moresque style of architecture in the late-nineteenth century. The coastal towns were littered with examples. This was a villa on an altogether more opulent scale. A huge tower dominated the structure. The peacock blue cylinder was laced with columns and topped by a roseate dome which peered over the tops of tall carubo trees. There was no pointer. The tower was signpost enough. Drago merely drove uphill to find it. One or two turns later and he came across the barred iron gates and the long seven- foot-high wall, both looking as if better days had passed them by.

"Tarantella," Paulo had said. "Here it is quite famous. A villa built over a hundred years ago by some crazy, rich old family. It looks as if a Moroccan palace was uplifted and planted on the Italian coast. Ugly thing."

"Who owns it?"

"Some other crazy man. A count. Very rich. Very lonely. What would you call him? You know, like that American Howard Hughes."

"A recluse."

"Si. Recluse. They hold parties there. Nobody sets eyes on him unless they get an invite."

"Very mysterious."

"Don't go there, Jon. It isn't worth it. Take the Inspector's advice and leave."

"And never see you again?" Drago stood up and downed the final grappa of a long night. He ruffled Paulo's hair. "How could I do that?"

"You are thinking of the woman again. I can tell it."

"Maybe."

Drago didn't make it back to the Villa Caprese until almost five in the morning. He slept awkwardly. Half his mind wondered what tale Ariana weaved to placate Sabatini. The other half wondered why Bergamo was following them. When he woke, he knew the answer to the second question must reside at Tarantella. His instinctive, journalistic juices were suddenly awakened. An old house. An old man. A Mafia hoodlum. It all read like the ingredients of a Hollywood movie, just like the ones the Inspector told him were a sham. He made the decision quickly, impetuously, ate breakfast and was away without telling anyone where he was going.

Drago parked the Fiat Panda a little way past the large, gated entrance. He inspected the gate and tugged at the bolt, despite it being sealed with a padlock and a chain looped through the bars. There was no bell or gatehouse. He glanced up and down the road. There was no car in sight and there weren't any houses nearby, just the long wall stretching along one side of the road. On the other, the tree filled escarpment plunged down to the town and the sea glittered beyond. Drago went back to the Fiat and re-parked it, much closer to the wall this time. He climbed onto the bonnet, onto the roof and was able to see over the parapet. The estate wasn't in good health. He could make out a grim driveway, a winding track of dry mud. Everything else was overgrown. Among the trunks of trees sprouted nettles, weeds and thistles. Some of the untended plants were enormous. He'd never seen thistles so tall. The wicked pointy thorns looked lethal. Sleeping Beauty would have loved it. The place needed more than a gardener. It needed an agricultural overhaul.

Drago reached forward and grasped the top of the stone fence. He hauled himself up and over the wall then dropped in an ungainly pile atop of a spreading mass of bougainvillea. The scent made him cough. Brushing off the petals, Drago made his way delicately through the forest of thorns. One or two scratched. The further he walked, the more he was aware of a curious farmyard odour. Eventually, he arrived at the drive and progressed up the path, sticking to the verge. The branches hung low. Threads of dead spider webs mingled with the leaves. The afternoon sun blinked through gaps in the foliage, turning the murky green barricade into bright verdant hedgerows. The track led all the way around the dramatic spur which elevated the villa to its godlike position. Close to the summit, the ground flattened off and became wet underfoot. He'd have expected it to be dry, but the ground was smothered by some sort of manure. It was the mulch which carried the unpleasant smell, now less like a farm, more like blocked drains or backed up toilets. Once or twice it caught Drago's throat. The sound of his cough was answered from inside the thicket. He tensed. What was that? A grunt. A rustle. Something moving. The undergrowth shook. Intrigued, Drago ventured forward, hugging a tree trunk for support, slipping on the gunge carpet of ground. He eased back a stilt like thistle, then another, and a third, stepped into the gap and froze.

The mammoth creatures stopped chewing and snorted.

Wild boar. Three of them.

Someone had dumped mountains of waste in this part of the wood. The pile was at least four feet high, gouged out on one side like a collapsed volcano. He could see the dregs of it spreading among the trees, moved by cloven feet, festering vegetable and animal remains, maybe even human excrement. He could see plastic, tin and cloth dotting the stinking pile. Vermin scuttled. The giant pigs, their grey-black hair matted with the shit they snuffled, stared at him. The big, baleful eyes didn't move. The snouts creased. One of them returned to the dung heap, head down, tusks digging at the smouldering slag, mouth slobbering.

Jesus, what the hell was this? Drago slowly folded back the thistles and made his way to the path. There was hardly any wind, but now he'd smelt the spoil its grossness clung to the air, pursuing him. Even a change to the prevailing breeze didn't help. Drago stepped onto the broken drive. He'd hardly moved a few metres when a fourth beast sauntered out of the bush. It twisted a wrinkled neck and growled. The track curved ahead. The last turn before the villa revealed itself. The boar was perched on the corner, waiting expectantly.

Slowly Drago crossed the drive, edging along the opposite side to the squat, four-legged guard. The boar's head and its strong brutish neck followed him. There was no sound other than the low bellow of its breathing. Condensation rippled on its flat nose. A steam of hot breath circled the jug lips and the empty expressionless brow. Drago stepped on a root. His foot slid. He stumbled, putting a hand down to break his fall. Instantly the animal leapt across the divide, jaws snapping. Drago's hand was on a fallen branch. It was thin, but long and still in leaf. He grabbed it, heard the scuttle of charging feet, the crunch of tooth on tooth. Desperate, he yelled, swung the branch and swiped at the gristled snout. Alarmed, the boar skidded short. Drago swung again and again, felt the branch collide with the animal's side. It gave an ugly scream then the incisors clamped down on his weapon. The branch was torn from his grasp, skinning his palm. Christ, the brute was like a goliath. The boar thrashed madly left and right. Drago was off and running. The boar turned and galloped after him, half the stump stuck in its jaw, the short barrel-legs carrying it at tremendous speed across the ground, groaning, gasping, gnashing. Now there was more commotion. Two more of the bastards were plunging out of the wood, thistles stuck in their hides, spittle dragging from craggy mouths, big trotters making loud crumping noises on the soil.

Drago rounded the corner and kept running. There was a small garden, its pool dry, its rhododendrons failing, juniper weeping. The villa was ahead, a huge two-storeyed mansion, bigger than he expected even with the tower. A staircase led to a wide canopied promenade terrace. There didn't seem to be anyone in the villa. The doors remained closed. Where the hell was everyone? Who tended these bloody beasts? The whole set up reeked of insanity. Drago headed for the stairs, the hogs in pursuit. He took the steps two at a time. The boars tried to make it after him, but their hooves clattered and skidded on the Lecce stone. They halted and their obscene grunting sobs echoed around the mansion.

Men suddenly appeared from several different directions. They advanced quickly from both sides of the house. Two of them carried shotguns. One of the gunmen passed Drago on the steps without so much as a glance, his only interest the angry livestock. He didn't raise the shot gun when he fired, simply hoisted it in the general direction of the boar and let rip from his hip. The sound was enough to deter the bastards and they retreated far enough to allow other men to come between them and the house in a classic pincer movement, whereupon they pulled out long handled tasers and used them to usher the angry beasts back to their rank rotting homestead.

Gasping, Drago watched the scene with interest and much relief. As the men fanned out, searching for other miscreants, he went down the steps and held out his hand to the nearest of his saviours.

"Thank you. Grazie."

The man, who was as unwelcoming and brutish as the boar, brushed past him and barked an instruction to one of the shotgun carriers. This man, while no more friendly, at least said hello. He then proceeded to talk in rapid peasant Italian, took Drago's arm and started to manhandle him towards the drive.

"I was hoping to see the Count," protested Drago.

The man ignored him. Drago repeated his request, louder each time. He shook himself free and when the man went to grab again, knocked the hand aside. This time the shot gun was hoisted. As Drago raised both hands, he had a moment of recognition. Looking directly at the gunman, it was impossible not to notice the obscene carbuncle on the side of his cheek. The abscess was unmissable. He'd seen the man before, in half-light, pulling on a scuba mask.

"I want to see the Count!"

"Arrestare!"

It was a different voice to the guttural tones of the estate men.

A new figure appeared on the top step of the staircase. He was older than Drago, but compact, firm, and dressed in a smart black suit with a necktie bound in a schoolboy knot. Something about his features didn't match the uniform. Despite this, Drago was relieved the man appeared calm.

"The Comte does not receive visitors," he said plainly, loudly and in English.

"It's about Bergamo," replied Drago, playing his ace.

"What of him?"

"He tried to kill me yesterday."

The man pondered the revelation for a second then made a single quick movement with his hand before returning to the shade of the terrace.

"Antonio," was his only instruction, but the shotgunner understood, pressed the barrel of his gun against Drago's side and motioned he was to return to the mansion. The man retained the gun in its rock-steady position as they walked. Drago finally had an opportunity to take in the detail of the building. Everything, except the blue tower, was faded oyster pink. The contrast was visually shocking. The two floors were surrounded by a colonnade, the arches formed of twisting decorated columns. The windows were massive. The terrace was smothered by climbing plants – a hibiscus, he thought – the tendrils and blooms enveloping two whole sides like a floral curtain.

Drago was led through the terrace, which was as big as a ballroom, and into a high ceilinged hall, its floor a geometrical maze of mosaic tiles, the kind of decoration normally reserved for Islamic mosques. The three men faced each other in a triangle at the centre of the big open space. It was dark. The windows barely admitted any light, being of stained glass and of a similar pattern to the floor design. Their footfalls made tapping sounds on the tiles. The place was battered. Wood panels were held on by the thinnest of nails. The paintwork was peeling. The grand seascape painted on the ceiling was no longer a deep azure blue, more a tobacco stained anodyne grey. Oil lamps, unlit, lined the walls. The place smelt musty and damp, was decayed and cold, even on a blistering afternoon such as this. Drago almost shivered. The gun hadn't lowered an inch.

"My name's Jon Drago," he said. "I'm a journalist."

"Atilla Ferrara. I am the valet for the Comte d'Orsi. What is this news of Bergamo?"

"I think I ought to tell that to the Count."

"I communicate everything to the Comte. What you tell me, he hears."

"And everything I don't tell too." Drago wasn't certain the valet understood his accusation. He didn't wait to find out. "Where is the Count?"

"Tell me what you know."

"I want to tell the Count."

"No."

The valet stepped forward one pace. Drago watched the muscles tense under the ill-fitting uniform. He'd developed a sixth sense for danger. This man oozed trouble. The whole place was a bad portent. The grimness of the house, the jungle full of evil beasts and their solemn keepers was bad enough, but he could have coped with that. Now, inside the dank world of whoever owned this godforsaken place, he was faced by something entirely more frightening. Atilla Ferrara was a wrong 'un, as bad as a cracked bell. He could tell by the coiled, reptilian movements. Ferrara was waiting to strike, always waiting, for one single deadly opportunity.

"What do you wish to tell me?"

This time the words came from behind Drago. Immediately they were uttered, the valet's expression changed. His body language altered.

"This man startled the boar."

It was said in Italian. Drago didn't understand, except he knew it was a lie. He turned and faced the new stranger. He was a tall man, slightly hunched. He was dressed in a grisaille morning suit, immaculate to his polished shoes, pocket square and single pink button rose. The colour of the cloth suited him. The man was almost entirely grey. The slate hair, tinged with silvery white, and the almost transparent skin, a weak dermis stretched over old bones, spoke of death. It hadn't taken him yet, but he was living it.

The man stood beside the ornate unlit fireplace, his hand on the mantle. He spoke with authority to the valet. The exchange was swift.

The old man turned and retreated into the next room. His hand never left the wall.

Atilla Ferrara indicated Drago should follow.

They walked through several interconnected salons. Doors led off to other rooms and passages. There was no change to the décor. They all shared the Eastern flavour: mashrabiya windows, lattice work shutters, columns, geometric patterns on walls, no carpets only scuffed floorboards, no rugs either. There were some fine fake tapestries. Large urns overflowed with neglected plant life. Cobwebs occupied corners. Dust. In one room a mangy cat was wrestling with a dead rat, one the pigs hadn't got to first. Drago noticed all the windows were closed which kept the odious air outside, but couldn't prevent the onset of a clammy internal atmosphere. Hadn't Ariana attended a party here? Halloween must have come early. She had to be joking. The room they stopped in was better than the others. The walls were furnished with family portraits and a series of display cabinets packed full of jewellery. The room still retained the villa's gloomy half-light due to the red and green panes of stained glass. The centre of the room was occupied by a long oak dining table and two solid straight backed chairs, one at the head, the other side-on at an angle to it.

The old man reached the table and ran his hand along its length as he walked. At the far end, he carefully turned and sat in the chair, crossing one leg over the knee of the other. He dismissed the valet with a wave of his hand and sat staring straight ahead.

Drago considered whether to say something, decided instead to walk towards the old man. His shoes tapped. The man's head shifted enough to observe him. The eyes did not move. The top half of him, grey or not, immaculately cast and clothed, could have been the stone bust of a Roman Emperor so still did it sit. It appeared to understand everything, yet it saw nothing. That was its power, for the Comte d'Orsi was completely blind.

"Who are you?"

The Comte spoke in English with a thick, heavy accent, almost impenetrable. It was only a keen ear which picked it, but Drago was alive to everything at that moment. He could have heard a pin drop. The place was like a morgue. Silent. Waiting for the breath of life to pass into it, acknowledge the tragedy and move on as if nothing more could be said or done, yesterday's news, today's chip paper.

"Jon Drago," he said. "I'm a writer."

"I don't read."

Drago wanted to say 'why not' but stopped himself. He shuffled uneasily on the seat. "You are the Comte d'Orsi?"

"I am. What of it?"

"I understand you have a man who works here. His name is Bergamo."

"What of him?"

"I want to know why he tried to kill me."

The gnarled head shook. "An unlikely occurrence," he hissed violently. "Who are you? Why are you here?"

"I told you. My name's Jon Drago."

He couldn't say anything more because the old man spoke over him. "The police have already called here today. Nobody calls here unless I request it. Now, you are here. Why?"

"Bergamo tried to kill me."

"The police say it was an accident."

"Who told you that?"

"Bergamo has worked with me for many years. He is a good man. Trustworthy. I have not spoken with him for several weeks. He is working in the city."

"Did your valet tell you that too?"

"Ferrara has worked for me many years. He is a good man. Trustworthy."

"He is?" Drago hoped he didn't sound doubtful. The old man didn't have a clue what he was saying. He was repeating words by rote. "Who else works here? Are they all trustworthy?"

The Comte's lips sucked over his teeth.

"You are an Englishman?"

"Yes."

"Tourist?"

"Yes."

"No! You come to steal from me!"

"You don't have anything I want to steal."

"I am a wealthy man. I have much worth stealing."

"Not for me." Drago stood up and walked around the room. The Comte followed his movements with a blank face.

"Your estate's in a mess. I've never seen a place so dilapidated."

"Tarantella," stated the Comte, "is the greatest villa on the Salentine coast."

"Maybe once." Drago reached the doorway and glanced through it in case the valet was listening. There was nobody in the adjoining room. He closed the door. Surprised to see a key in lock, he twisted it shut. Drago turned to face the Comte. "Of course, you haven't seen it lately, have you?"

He knew it was offensive and he meant to strike a chord. The whole grisly place, the people in it and the flora and fauna which surrounded it, the vile stench inside as well as out had made him nervous. He wanted away from here and soon.

"I know every detail of Tarantella, Signor," said the Comte. "I can tell you where everything is. Everything that is of value. Everything that is nothing. That is why you came here, isn't it? That is why Bergamo tried to stop you. You want to steal from me."

"What can I steal with only my hands? These paintings?"

"There are smaller things than paintings."

"The jewels?"

Drago peered into one of the cabinets. Even in the dullness, he could see the wealth the Comte spoke of. It glittered and glimmered.

"Stop there!" The Comte pointed directly at Drago, his hearing tuned by experience to the dimensions of the room. "Touch nothing! I know what you want. I know why you came here."

The situation was ridiculous, thought Drago. How could a blind man have come to such a conclusion so swiftly? Like the phrases he repeated, someone must have planted the idea. Someone he trusted.

"Who told you?" Drago asked. "When I first met you, what did your valet say?"

"They are good men. I trust them."

There it was again: words like an incantation, as if the more the old man said it the more likely it was to come true. Drago was walking along one side of the room. There was a portrait in front of him. It was the Comte as a young man, in a scene from history he could never have played or understood. Green fields swept away from him to a castle in the distance. His expression was as blank then as it was now. A lustrous red diamond was clamped to bis breast.

"Why are you interested in my portrait?"

"Is it here?" asked Drago.

"All my treasures are here."

"What made you say that?"

"So you do know about my treasures."

"No, the scene looks familiar."

"I know what you are looking at!" shouted the Comte. "The ruby! Il Papavero! You have come for it! You are a thief! I will not give it! I am not finished yet!"

Drago didn't know which version of the Comte to stare at most, the one in the portrait with the red ruby stone glowering on his chest or the one across the room, unseeing, frothing at the mouth like his pigs, leaning forward, hands gripped to the knobs of the chair rest. Drago stared at the portrait again. He'd not even mentioned the ruby. He'd only asked if the artist had painted the portrait on the estate grounds. Drago started to walk quickly around the room, scanning the display cases again, searching for the jewel.

"Don't touch a thing!" scoffed the Comte. "Ha! Don't think you'll find it there! You foreign bastard. Come to steal from me? Ha!"

Drago stepped up to the chair and jerked it sideways so he faced the Comte and the old man faced the windows. He leant in close. He tasted the garlic swelling on the man's breath, saw the remains of lunch tucked in his teeth. The wiry hands released the chair and started to form trembling grey fists.

"You need to listen to me, Comte," Drago said. "I am not going to steal from you. You can't see what's happening here. You live with a gang of hoodlums and one of them tried to kill me last night."

"Bergamo was in a car accident."

"No. I was there. I ended up sticking his own knife in his belly."

The Comte did not immediately reply. He thumped the arm rest twice with his left fist and declared: "Your accusations do not concern me. Your presence here is not welcome. I have informed Ferrara to contact the police. They will arrive shortly. Do not try to escape. We will wait for the authorities to arrest you."

Drago was very close to the old man. He could almost see the mind working behind the empty eyes, thinking, assessing, but which part of the warped imagination was the Comte using: the fantasy or the reality, the world he lived in or the lie he was being fed? Drago could see the muscles in the leathery fist clench again. He could see the button it thumped. An emergency call point inlaid on the fine oak chair, the kind of thing disabled people use to summon assistance. The lie was working.

"I'm not staying," he said.

The Comte's hand shot out and grabbed Drago's wrist. He tried to pull away. The tired looking fingers wrapped like a vice. The sudden strength bore no relation to the old man's faded appearance.

"You trespasser!" hissed the Comte. "I will protect my property by foul means or fair. You forget who I am, Signor."

"You're the Comte d'Orsi," Drago said angrily. "Let go of my arm."

"I am Il Padrino!"

"Let go!"

Drago wrenched free. Almost immediately the Comte made another grab for him, this time catching his jacket. Drago twisted out of it, clutching at one sleeve. The rest of the garment stretched between them, a rope of twisted polyester. The Comte yelled expletives. Shouts came from behind the door. The handle rattled. This wasn't what Drago wanted, not one bit of it. He ripped the jacket from the Comte's hand, pulling the crazed old man from his seat. The Comte's hands slapped on the table for support. In one movement, Drago lifted the second chair and carried it to the nearest window, jacket hanging from an arm. He jammed the chair forward. The pane shattered into several large chunks. Drago thrust again and rammed the chair sideways, back and forth, ripping at the lattice work. Most of the glass landed outside. Small shards hung loose. The door crashed open, the lock shattered by a booted foot. Three men charged across the room. Drago discarded the chair in their direction, wrapped the jacket over his head and shoulders and launched himself at the broken window. Something tore as he passed through. His hands touched stone as he executed an ungainly forward roll, coming up on both feet. There was a sharp stab to his hand. Drago was on the terrace, but to the rear of the villa. He vaulted the parapet and sprinted for the trees which flowed down the valley like a rippling green sea. Another goon, double barrelled shotgun to hand, tried to intercept him. Drago burst into the thicket and ducked just as the first shots cannoned into the dense quivering masts. Shitting hell! Right now, Drago fancied his chances with the boars.

He plunged on through the spiky foliage, losing all sense of direction, running blind. The irony made him grimace, as did the shouts of the hunt. Did he hear the growl of wild animals? Drago headed sidewards and always downhill. He ducked below the tall waving prickles. His hand hurt. A sliver of glass was embedded in the pleat of his palm. He stopped to yank it free, wincing with pain. Blood seeped down his fingers. Dammit. There they were. He caught sight of their heads. The same two men who carried the shotguns. One had the carbuncle: Antonio. The other, Drago had only glimpsed. They walked along the obvious trail: all those tall weeds bent, stems snapped.

There was a copse to his left. The small shallow clearing was occupied by three fallen, hollowed out tree trunks covered in fungi and lichen. Drago scrambled to them, glad to be free of the swinging thorns. The ground was bogged by the same manure he'd smelt and slipped on before. Feet first, he crawled into one of the logs, disturbing hundreds of huge wood lice as he did so. He squirmed and wriggled with them on his arms, his face and clothes in the dirt. Something prevented him going deeper. He had a kick at it. The obstacle came apart. It felt like building bricks. He rolled onto his side, squinting into the dark. Bags. Packages wrapped in black canvas. What the hell was this?

Drago heard voices outside. The squelch of footfalls edged into the close. He sucked in a breath. These were not booted feet. Drago saw the hairy trotters, the belly sagging low to the ground, the head casting this way and that, spit dribbling. A wild boar. Panic gripped. Where the hell had it come from? Was the tree trunk its warren? The hog's head swayed to and fro, snout furrowing. Did boar detect human scent? The ground was lacquered with that putrid soil. No, it couldn't; not through all that. Drago was covered in it. The thing paused, dug at the ground and snaggled something with a tusk. While it ate, the pig eyes seemed to fix on the tree trunk. Grimy sweat poured into Drago's eyes. He blinked the muck clear, fought to control his breathing, shallow, slow, no movement. The boar started to pass on. As the animal shifted from his eye line, others entered. There was a tribe of the bloody things, big and small, youngsters eager to forage, adults hardly caring. Trotters trailed over the ground, kicking up muggy clumps of crap. Where the hell were the gunmen?

Suddenly some sort of hell broke loose. The pigs bellowed and began to stampede, making a terrific noise as they leapt through the forest. There was an urgent, human call. A gun shot, three, four. Two horrified screams, not human, dreadful disconnected high pitched wails. He saw real feet encased in boots stomping over the ground chased by the brutes. Drago waited until the sounds of flight echoed away then he waited longer still. Convinced, he snuck out of the hole. The men had disturbed the pigs. A trail of richly thick blood laced the forest floor. One of the animals must have been hit. Drago spun himself around and reached head-first into the fallen trunk, activating his mobile torch. The interior had been deliberately hollowed out and was stuffed full of canvas bricks. Drago's feet had collapsed the neat pile. He took the nearest. It was just like the package he'd pulled from the sea bed a few evenings ago. He tore at the tape, freed a corner and just had time to take in the dense brown contents before new sounds of pursuit disturbed him. Drago tossed the package back inside the log. Heroin. It wouldn't do to be caught with that sort of contraband. He went for the trees again, sprinting straight downhill, ignoring the scratches and barbs. Speed was all that mattered.

A few minutes later, the forest of pines gave way to a series of meadows, golden in the sunlight, acre after acre. He couldn't tell whose land this was. A network of barbed wire stretched over his path. It seemed to mark the edge of the Comte's estate. Gingerly, he lifted the top rung, climbed through and made his way swiftly along the perimeter of the first field. He took a dirt track leading away from the forest. Halfway down it, he looked back. The dome of Tarantella was still visible above the tallest tips of trees. Standing on the edge of the woodland was a group of men, the same men who had saved him from the boar. They stared angrily at him. Shotguns heaved, but stayed silent. Whatever order they'd been given, it did not involve chasing across someone else's land.

Drago walked for almost two hours. He stopped at a stream to do some rudimentary cleaning. It didn't work. He smelt rank. By the time he returned to Santa Cesarea Therme he was a scummy, sweaty mess.

Inspector Gigli was waiting by the Fiat Panda, tapping out a message on his mobile phone. Drago saw him at a distance.

The policeman's eyes hardly took in Drago's soiled suit and mucky shoes. The Englishman's adventures had ceased to interest him. He wanted the journalist out of his town. Perhaps then his wife would stop nagging him, he could work regular hours and easy shifts again. Things could return to normal, the world of pick pockets and domestics.

"You are not good at taking advice."

It was a statement without sentiment. It was also another warning. Nothing fights fire like fire, considered Drago, and went on the attack.

"Who the hell is this Comte d'Orsi?" he said, pointing at the brick wall. "What the hell does he think he's doing?"

"We don't argue with the Comte," replied the Inspector. "He is very important. The people like him. They respect him."

"Well, I don't like him."

"He's an old man. He scares easily."

"He's a lunatic."

The Inspector looked offended.

"Don't let the people hear you say that."

"Why? Why's he so bloody special?"

"He is Il Padrino," replied the Inspector blandly. "Godfather."

Eleven

It is Best in Business to Understand Your Friends

Nrupal Patel was a little man who kept himself very much to himself. It was easier that way, he considered, always had been and always will. The world never changed for Nrupal. He had a wife. Two children had grown to adulthood and fled the coup, occasionally to return out of duty, for favours, money or good wishes, sometimes all four. It would always be so.

His sons were staunchly Italian. They'd been born in Bari. To them Italy was home. One of them didn't even speak Hindi. "Can't be bothered," he'd said in that thick Italian accent which always sounded out of place coming from his dark Indian skin. They'd spent so many years being bullied at school or fighting to prevent it, that assimilation was obvious to them. Nrupal and his wife felt differently. For them, there was always a link to the past, some point of origin.

For Nrupal it was 1950s Madhya Pradresh where he'd been brought up by an abusive father and mother, both of a lowly caste. He was thrown into the slums of Panna to clean streets for a few measly coins and had the luck of the devil to blag a job running errands for Big Lip Biran, the gregarious pawnbroker and goldsmith – so named because his lower lip jutted furiously away from his upper. By the age of sixteen, Nrupal was separating genuine diamonds from fake ones in Biran's main store a few paces from the Baldau Temple. Aged twenty-two, he'd graduated to the nice wood-panelled office at the back of the store and had a plaque on his desk which read: *Nrupal Patel: Chief Saudagar*. He'd married acceptably. He had a two-room apartment with running water. Life should have been good. India though was not for Nrupal. The effects of separation were intense in the north. There was still fighting and prejudice on all sides. For instance, Biran didn't accept Muslim trade, even when the jewels were of great value. It wasn't that Nrupal disagreed with the policy; he simply thought it immensely stupid to turn down an opportunity to make money.

In fact, very early on in his career as a jeweller, Nrupal realised his boss had left a window of opportunity open to his employers: they did not duplicate receipts. This allowed Nrupal, as the chief broker, to offer clients a lower price than he declared on the office ledger. Nrupal pocketed the difference on a daily basis. Should a client return to collect any goods, an event which rarely happened, they found their pay-out mysteriously higher than agreed. No one complained. It was a such rare occurrence anyway, Nrupal never worried. He became comparatively rich very quickly.

It didn't last. One day, Big Lip Biran visited the store to make an inspection of his premises and almost by accident, Nrupal's ruse was discovered. An old man was sat outside the store having surrendered the last of his gold teeth. He bemoaned the skin-flint compensation he'd earned. Biran was a kindly and cheerful owner who joked about his own nickname and was always quick to buy tea and pastries, so he stopped by the old man to discuss the nature of his grievance. It shocked him to be berated for such pinch-tight services. Biran set in motion an investigation which would inadvertently reveal the extent of Nrupal's deceit. The Chief Saudagar was lucky. It was lunchtime and one of his assistants found him at the tea house and told him Big Lip was on the warpath. Nrupal never returned to the shop. Instead he went home to his pregnant wife, withdrew all his savings from the bank, packed all their clothes into a battered trunk and took the train to Mumbai. He bought a berth on the worst steamer heading out of India. He could probably have escaped as easily by travelling to the next state, but Nrupal didn't see the point. The social system was holding him back. He'd never progress higher than the position he'd already attained. It was his for life, or as long as he wanted it, but he wanted more than that: he wanted just a little of the power Big Lip Biran wielded.

Three weeks later, Nrupal and his wife arrived at Bari and they never left. At first Nrupal found he was once again at the bottom of the social ladder. He had no language skills, no way to explain his talents and no contacts. He was back in the slums. Barivacchia. One room. No drinkable water. He managed to get a menial job cleaning cars, was grateful because it meant he could learn Italian quickly. He hid his money. He didn't want to spend it openly. The run down quarter, which looked as if it had not been rebuilt after the war, was rough and ready. Criminals roamed everywhere. Yet Barivacchia also had the redeeming feature of a community which co-operated and aided each other. When his wife's term arrived, they found the local women, always excited by babies, eager to help with the home birth. No one went to hospitals. They didn't see the point: no one had before, so why now? His first son was born and made Nrupal determined to utilise his talents fully, to give his growing family a life beyond the slums.

Luck once again played a part. In India he'd gradually weaved himself into the fabric of Biran's business, talking to the old jewellers that sat there drinking strong tea and mulling the day. He learnt and tested the skills of identification and evaluation during his evenings and lunchtimes. The old men used to tease him, but their eyes were weak and Nrupal found he was often called upon to re-identify pieces when they lost focus. He proved himself by stepping unannounced into position when one of the old men suddenly died. His Italian opportunity came in far more spectacular style.

Nrupal had taken to walking through the ancient markets. It got him away from the one room and the screaming baby. He liked to stare at the diamonds in the jeweller's windows. He'd often be shooed along by the irate shopkeeper. One day, he witnessed a violent street murder. It happened in broad daylight. An old, but intelligent looking man was knifed by a teenager as he sat in a street café. The body was left jerking madly on the pavement. The assailant sprinted up the alley. No one called the police. There was no point. It had occurred before and it would occur again and again. Nrupal's luck was that he knew the assailant. They had worked together for a few days at the car wash. Nrupal didn't go to the police either. He knew that would lead nowhere. Instead, he read the newspapers, discovered who the deceased was and attended the funeral. The dead man was Victor Ferrara, an important member of the Unione Sacre Croce.

During the solemn wake, conducted in the piazza adjacent to the church, Nrupal tied up his courage and approached the first man who appeared to be of standing. He was an extensive, lumpy man wearing a three-piece suit and smoking a long cheroot. He sported a drooping, Zapata moustache which made him look the worst of devils. The man listened without any courtesy as Nrupal explained he knew the murderer. At the finish, the large body trembled as it turned to face the little Indian.

"What do you want in return for this information?" he snarled.

"I only wish to be able to impart it personally to Il Padrino."

The moustache might have moved independently of the man's facial expression, Nrupal couldn't tell, but 'Zapata' laughed very loudly.

"You have i coglioni, little Indian," he declared. "Come, come with me."

Nrupal was taken to a trattoria and introduced to a rotund man, alive past his years, flanked by the oddest couple of accomplices, a young plain woman and a straight backed, middle-aged man who was permanently attached to his sunglasses. Neither of them spoke throughout the interview. Il Padrino listened closely before asking again, just like 'Zapata' did: "What do you want in return for this information?"

Nrupal gulped. He'd not intended to. He did it instinctively. The old godfather noticed and grinned. He stood up and stepped towards the little Indian. He was far bigger in stature standing than sitting, broad, big and bristling. The grey hair looked like iron wool, the face leather, the hands plates, fingers sharp as axes.

"Are you scared of me, little Indian man?"

"I am scared of what you can do."

Il Padrino gave a single snort, turned to his entourage and bellowed with laughter. "I like this man," he said. "Dominic was right. He has balls. Alright, little man, what do you want? Tell me and tell me quick."

"I have some money. Not much. I wish to buy a business. I was a pawn broker in India. I wish to be so again."

"What do you need me for?"

"No one will loan to a poor Indian immigrant."

"And you think this information will help sway Il Padrino to bestow some favour on you?"

"A word from Il Padrino will open many opportunities."

"Yes." The great head nodded sagely. "I can also sweep them away. Remember it, little man. I will help you, but in turn, occasionally, we may need you to help us. Don't forget that. Now; tell me what you know of this killer."

Nrupal heard nothing about how his information was used, but two months later, and without warning, he was visited by Dominic, the man with the Zapata moustache and the never ending cheroot, and presented with the keys to a small shop on Via Fragigena. It wasn't the best location, but Nrupal knew he could make it work. He handed over almost all his savings, rolled up his sleeves and started all over again.

Today, Nrupal crinkled his long, tapered nose and screwed the eye glass into his left socket. Those memories all seemed such a long time past and yet here he was, with a new reputable establishment at the north end of Via Roberto in the shopping district of Murat, a nice apartment in the suburbs and a nest egg of money on which, if he wanted to, he could retire. Yet he was still doing the work of gangsters.

This was another exceptional piece. A white diamond. Flawless. Cut. Namibian. Rare. A little freckle of blue at its centre. He wanted to cry. Such rarities.

"Where do you get these stones, Laszlo?" he asked as he turned the diamond over to inspect the rear faces.

"If I told you, you wouldn't believe it."

"This is the twenty-sixth gem I've taken from you," continued Nrupal. "Some of my customers are very intrigued. They would like to buy more, if you can get them."

"I am only the middle man," Laszlo replied. "I can't divulge my sources and contacts. I only bring you the diamonds."

Nrupal looked at the strange couple who stood the other side of the glass partition. They'd visited almost a dozen times over the last nine months, sometimes with one stone, usually two. They looked as if life treated them very badly. The man was unshaven, his eyes permanently bloodshot and his bulky coat sagged. In cold or hot weather he, or the coat, stank of cannabis and tobacco. In hot weather the smell spoke of everything else as well. The woman was rake thin and wore clothes more suited to teenagers. She may have still been one. It was hard to tell. Her teeth, rimmed with grey, were the teeth of the geriatric. There was always something dirty about her appearance. One day her hair looked unwashed and knotty, on another she wore a pretty patterned skirt, but it was frayed and torn and her knees and shins were scabby. On the third visit she was sick in a waste basket.

The next time they appeared, Nrupal employed his assistant, a young whippersnapper of a boy, to follow them. It always paid to understand who you were dealing with. The assistant didn't contact him for several hours. When he returned, he explained he had needed to hire a taxi to follow the couple as they had driven off in a car. The assistant had taken a series of photos using his mobile's camera. Nrupal studied them and listened to his excited employee's report. Once Nrupal saw where and how Laszlo and Maria lived, he understood exactly what business they were involved with. The diamonds, he concluded, were stolen, although he did not know who stole them.

Nrupal stared unblinking at Laszlo. "I understand, your concerns," he said. "But do remember, there is a good market for these diamonds. I can help you, if you want to sell more."

"We'll remember that," injected the woman. She rarely spoke. She seemed very nervous today. Much more than normal. "How much for the diamond?"

Nrupal shrugged. He knew a good client, a businessman in the techno-trade, who might want to set it in a ring for one of his mistresses. He'd purchased two of these illicit jewels already. Everyone was making good on the deal. Laszlo got his money. Nrupal made a profit. The client got his gift. The woman got her keepsake. The only one to lose was whoever had been robbed and clearly they didn't notice. The insurers had probably paid handsome compensation. Nrupal expected the diamonds were stolen one by one and from different houses, prised from rings and necklaces. A large theft would arouse the police. The other possibility as that the diamonds had already been stolen, perhaps from a cache lifted many years ago. Occasionally Nrupal was presented with objects looted during the war, handed down from generation to generation, hidden by families waiting for a big pay day. Perhaps, he mused, these jewels too were the spoils of conflict. Still thinking on the gemstone's origin, Nrupal wrote his price carefully on a receipt.

"I'll need two days to get the money."

"Alright," she said. "We'll be back in two days. Give us the diamond."

She almost snatched it from his palm.

Nrupal watched them scuffle through the door. He tapped lightly on the desk with his forefinger. He considered again whether he ought to contact the Unione, and then dismissed the notion.

Three minutes later, the front bell rang. Nrupal activated the lock and a swarthy looking man pushed the door open. He held it for his companion. Both men entered the pawnbrokers confidently. They did not look at the showcases and made directly for the counter. Both men wore tight fitting suits, had very dark hair and rustic complexions, bunched hands used to strong work and no fine detail. Their faces did not smile. For the first time in many years, Nrupal felt a twinge of apprehension. This wasn't the Unione. They looked like it, but his accustomed eye recognised the flaws, just as it would in a diamond. The men wore straight cut t-shirts under their jackets.

He'd seen them around. This kind ran with the ruthless foreign cliques, the new gangs and pimps, the drug dealers and pushers, the Albanians. The first man approached the counter and spoke in rough Italian.

"Are you the owner?"

"Si."

"Good. Lock the door. My name is Grigori. We need to talk about diamonds."

***

Atilla Ferrara watched Marcelo Sabatini as the Albanian lifted the cigar to his lips and took an excessively long pull. The pall of smoke slipped from his nostrils and mouth as he spoke and made him resemble the mythical minotaur, all piercing eyes, bull neck and chest, his knuckle forehead an alternative to horns.

"You see Atilla, my friend, it is always best in business to understand your friends as well as your enemies."

They were sitting in Peccato di Vino, a three-tiered basement establishment on Via Rondachi in Otranto's old town. Ferrara had waited impatiently in the lower section by the bar while Sabatini and his woman consumed the last of their meal. He watched them eat by staring at the mirror behind the bar. He envied every beautiful morsel of food which crossed their lips. Eventually, the woman was dismissed with a brief goodbye. She left accompanied by one of the heavies. Ferrara was finally asked to join Sabatini. The seat was warm where the woman had sat. The table was big enough for four, but Sabatini commanded it, the proprietor and the restaurant. The place was empty. They'd eaten exceptionally late and the trattoria had closed to everyone but the Albanian once he arrived. Ferrara had not even set off from Tarantella until midnight. Now it was almost two and he was tired. Instinctively he knew this was Sabatini's game, the Albanian's time and place. Respecting that, Ferrara did not reply to the statement.

"You volunteered to distribute my heroin throughout the Salentine. I was sceptical of your abilities, Atilla. However, I was pleased by your suggestion of an undersea rendezvous. It is far safer than boats. I like that I am able to shift distribution and drop off points along the eastern and western coastlines without interference from the police. I am also grateful for the man you send to monitor Ariana. It reassures me. In addition, Atilla, you have been swift to pay me the monies I demanded." Sabatini paused and took another long pull on his cigar. "Too swift."

Ferrara shifted uncomfortably. His mind was working fast, searching for an answer. More importantly, he was trying to compose the question.

"It appears, Atilla, that you have not been entirely honest with me," Sabatini declared. He flicked the ash from the cigar into an empty wine glass and called for two espresso coffees and two Galliano shots. He waited without sound or movement until the proprietor returned with the drinks. Sabatini dismissed the restaurateur, asking him to return when he called, and the man made his way back to the kitchen, dousing all but the lights on the mezzanine floor where they sat. Satisfied they were alone, Sabatini continued.

"I know where you get your money from. I know it because my

men followed you and the conspirators you employ. It appears for many months you have been selling Namibian diamonds to set up cannabis factories in and around the Salentine. The man you use to market these stones is Nrupal Patal. He works on Via Roberto in Bari. Three of your factories are based in Galatina, Melpignano and Zollino. We know this because we have visited them and made enquiries. Your people are easily interrogated, Atilla. You really must try to get better trusted employees. There appears to be a flourishing market for cannabis in Puglia and Basilicata, but it doesn't amount to enough money to pay me the thirteen and a half million I requested for the first shipment of heroin. Nor would the diamonds, as expensive as they are, afford more than the few small factories you have procured."

Sabatini paused and relit the cigar.

"So, where is this money coming from, I ask? Let me tell you. My men watched your movements, they watched your men. I have Albanians all over the peninsula, remember, men loyal to me. You have not moved anywhere without someone spying you. I discovered you have a house in Matera which you use as a base for your other operations. From there you have been observed making several visits to I Campo di Mielle, the seat of the Sada Family and the Unione Sacre Croce, an organisation you claim to despise. It is obvious, however, from the dates supplied to me of your movements and the dates of the down payments, it is the Unione who is supplying you with my money."

Ferrara finally decided it was time to broach his story. He took the espresso cup and drank its contents in one gulp. When he replaced the cup, he pushed the saucer aside and placed his hands carefully on the table, fingers steady and locked. It wouldn't do to display any nerves.

"I don't need to explain where the money came from, Signor," he said, "only to ensure you receive it. Our arrangement never stipulated anything else. That is a mistake on your part. On my part, I have created an operation which has deceived the police for over a year. I am distributing your heroin swiftly and effectively. I and the Unione are both making money. You are making money. Your concerns are irrelevant."

Sabatini's one good eye shut. The other blankly stayed open.

For a moment the candlelight struck it and bubbles of blue, amber and tangerine momentarily fizzed. He rolled his bullneck. The muscles across the back tensed. He sipped the Galliano and said nothing. The Albanian stayed quiet for so long, Ferrara assumed the interview was over. He stood up to leave. The other eye opened.

"Where are you going, Atilla?"

"I have nothing more to say."

"But I do. You don't think I'd bring you all this way at this late hour without having something to say to which you must give serious thought?"

Ferrara found his exit blocked by a guard, a hulking man with half a day's growth of stubble. The man's hand hovered close to his pocket.

"A fight is not advisable," said Sabatini. "Sit down and listen."

Ferrara returned to his seat, took the glass of Galliano and, like the coffee, downed it one mouthful.

"You stole the diamonds from the Sada family," declared Sabatini. "They in turn had stolen them from a beached shipping vessel in 1944, an opportunistic old fashioned scavenger hunt which delivered sudden riches to a once poor Mafioso. This of course is supposition. No one admits it happened, but the shipping records note a cache of one-hundred and sixty-seven pure white uncut diamonds from Lüderitz, Namibia. The insurers paid out millions. Slowly, over a number of decades and in a number of outlets, some of these diamonds, now cut, have surfaced. The paper trail leads nowhere. Unfortunately, the Comte d'Orsi is old and blind and susceptible to flattery. When my companion asked him of the diamonds in his collection of wonderful jewels, he told her, innocently as if it was joke, where those diamonds originated from. The mystery of 1944 is no longer supposition."

Ferrara knew the story was true. The blind old man had said so himself during one of his maddening rants. And now Sabatini knew. There was no sense in hiding it anymore.

"The Comte knows the diamonds are not there. He is the only one with the safe combination. I have to ask for access. We sell the gems for repairs to the estate."

"What repairs?" Sabatini laughed out loud. "You are lucky

your employer is blind and half-mad. You've done no work on that house for years. Well, nothing worthwhile." Sabatini waited for a reply. When he didn't get one, he continued regardless. "So, what do we do, Atilla? I could tell your employer, the Comte, or I could tell your money lender, the Capo, or I could do nothing. What I prefer to do is enter into another arrangement, one which you may find of interest."

Sabatini clicked his fingers and the second bodyguard opened a briefcase and took out a laptop which he spent a few minutes activating. He spun it so the screen faced both men. The screen revealed an artist's impression of a blood red diamond, multi-faced, intricately carved.

"We call it Il Papavero, the Blood Stone Poppy," said Sabatini. "It's an ancient jewel once owned by Skanderbeg, Albania's national hero, but it was lost in the fifteenth century. Do you recognise it?"

Ferrara nodded.

"It is the same diamond carried by the Comte on his portrait at Tarantella, are we agreed?" confirmed Sabatini. "I have no idea how it surfaced in his hands. Perhaps it was on that beached ship, although the manifest has no mention of it. Perhaps it has been possessed by the d'Orsi family – not the Sada's – for centuries and he inherited it by default when his father bought him that title. However, it is definitely in his portrait of that I have no doubt."

At a signal from Sabatini the guard switched pictures on the laptop to one of Ferdinand's portrait. Sabatini pointed with his cigar to the large red stone which sat clasped to the Comte's shoulder.

"There. The exact same stone. I even asked the Comte, politely, if he possessed it. He may be going crazy, Atilla, but he isn't as stupid we believe. The old man refused to answer. He chuckled and chuckled and made small talk with my mistress. Did he tell you that story, Atilla? No. Of course he didn't. He really is no fool, this blind Count."

Ferrara offered a vague shrug.

"I admit, I don't extract all his secrets," he began. "The Comte has been very compliant over the years. I administer medication to keep him that way. I am lucky the Capo shows no interest in the Comte and is easily deceived. The men on the estate share in our spoils. They cooperate because the influx of heroin and cannabis benefits them financially. Their wives like it, their children too and their whores. It is a good business, smuggling and running drugs. Uncomplicated. Unsophisticated. No trouble. Just the occasional strong arm tactics to extract a debt or an envelope full of cash to the local police. But the Comte, if he knew, even in his old age, there would be no forgiveness and that might bring the wrath of the Unione. You see, I must tread carefully sometimes."

"Of course. I don't doubt your integrity in that aspect. In fact I am grateful, for it aids my business too." Sabatini blinked once. The eyes glimmered equally dark for a second. "I only ask a small favour. I'd like you to think it over. You can think on it for a few minutes while I explain."

Ferrara bristled at the instruction. Manoeuvring himself into the role of intermediary between the Banda Family and the Unione Sacre Croce was suddenly more complicated than he imagined. This, though, was the reality: being ordered by a superior. Atilla Ferrara was nobody's underling. He proved that by his ability to create a durable business in direct opposition to his own Unione. He remembered when his father fought alongside the Sada family, brokered agreements with their Sicilian brothers, controlled the police, how he was a man of power and position. To have the position snatched away by murder, to have lost it all by the decision of a youth. And the humiliation for Ferrara, to be abandoned for twenty years as he suffered in jail for taking revenge. The Unione said they could do nothing because he had killed in public and there were witnesses. He knew it was a lie and the knowledge festered as he passed those years isolated in prison. They never let him rot, but they never lifted a finger to free him. Ferrara was trapped, a wounded beast in a snare, and a trapped animal enrages quickly. Ferrara had such a beast within him. Frequently, it rose from slumber. Now, his animal rage confronted an angry minotaur. It wasn't about the instructions: it was about the past, about what he'd lost and what he wanted to gain. He wanted what Sada had. He wanted what Marcelo Sabatini had. He wanted influence and power and control. He remembered this as he sat and listened.

"I have a man on my staff, a thief of exceptional capabilities," continued the Albanian. "He recognised the chimney vault installed at the Comte's estate. It is, he says, a crude design, usually employed by once wealthy families who lack insurance and wish to protect jewels and family heirlooms, wills and important documents. If I asked him, he could break into the safe and I am certain he would recover Il Papavero. Am I correct?"

Ferrara had seen the gemstone twice. It was in a little locked drawer below the main body of the safe. He'd seen the Comte remove it and run his hands across its surfaces, as if it was a beautiful woman he was touching for the first time, his blind man's hands mapping the contours, every curve, line and corner, as if they were cheekbones, noses and lips. The stone sat in a brass clasp, moulded to grip precisely at the six points. It didn't seem worthwhile arguing its existence, so he nodded.

"The stone is very important to Albania. It is also important to me. I collect many great jewels. I have Faberge eggs, for instance. I have the sapphires from the Peacock Throne. The Burmese Ruby. I plan to display them in a museum when I retire from public life. The building is already under construction in Durres. And I want Il Papavero. And you, Atilla, are going to allow me to steal it. In return, I will keep supplying you with heroin and allow you to continue your deception of both your masters, the Comte and the Capo. All I ask is one diamond and your loyalty."

Sabatini remained perfectly composed. He twitched some ash from the cigar. His one eagle eye studied Ferrara's face. The beasts were combined: hawk, serpent and bull, all twisted into that wretched façade. It reminded Sabatini of his own festering spirit. He half expected the man to spit venom.

Ferrara slowly nodded. It was only one diamond. It made no difference to Ferrara. It was only the blind Comte who would miss it and then only with his fingertips. Vaguely, he wondered if there might be a more prosperous deal on the horizon. He didn't mention it, but already a plan was forming. He needed time to form it. He needed to stall the Albanian for a few weeks or even months.

"I will tell you when I can arrange it," said Ferrara.

"Good. A Galliano to celebrate?"

Sabatini called the proprietor from the kitchen. Two more glasses were poured. Ferrara drank his immediately and got to his feet. Sabatini watched him, the cigar descending slowly from his lips. There was something he hadn't noticed before, something in Ferrara's expression which he didn't like. He saw it occasionally on the face of Ariana. He could wipe it from her with his hand. Not here. The countenance remained. Contempt. Disdain. Hatred.

After the Italian had gone, Sabatini turned to his bodyguard and said: "What do you make of him, Grigori? What's he going to do?"

"I am surprised you ask, Krye. He's done it already. Betrayal. The Comte. The Capo. Next time it will be you."

"Is he that dangerous?"

"A man can't have more than one master. He's got three. Four if you include money."

"Indeed." Sabatini sucked on the cigar and took the last of the Galliano. "We need to remove him. When the time is right we will speak to the Capo. This arrangement has gone on far too long already."

Twelve

Ariana

Drago watched *Diamantin* that evening and the following day. He knew, deep down, that he ought to take Inspector Gigli's advice. There wasn't any sense in antagonising these bastards any more than he already had. But he still had questions to which he wanted answers because they would become his story, not one he could take to the police: one he could write. The ambition was burning.

He had discovered what was in the canvas packages the divers collected from the seabed. Either they contained money, like the one he'd appropriated, or they contained drugs, like the one discarded at Tarantella. Between the water skiers and the scuba divers an exchange was taking place. He regretted not holding onto the heroin and passing it to the authorities, but if the police started sniffing around the yacht, Sabatini would no doubt hightail it off and any remaining evidence would be destroyed. None of it explained why Bergamo attempted to kill him. The Comte d'Orsi admitted the hoodlum worked for him. Drago casually assumed the spiteful valet controlled Bergamo. The extra question was: who controlled Atilla Ferrara? Not the Comte, except on a superficial level. Blind from birth, living isolated in that dreadful mansion for decades, the old man had begun a descent into mental illness. After Ferrara's prompting, the Comte convinced himself Drago's intentions were dishonourable. Was there something Drago had misheard? He turned over the strange conversation in the big, dark dining room again and again. The singular. The Comte kept using the word 'it'. One thing. Only one thing mattered to him amongst all that finery. What on Earth was 'it'?

Finally, while *Diamantin* was clearly the base for the smuggling operation and Tarantella the base for distribution, what was the relationship between Sabatini and drugs? He was a powerful man in Albania, the head of the biggest union, someone people looked up to, possibly a man with political ambitions. Schemes like the Otranto Foundation and the National Museum were flamboyant vanity projects. They didn't demonstrate political knowledge, only a man whose ego had to be constantly on display, like the black opal in his eye. It was born of arrogance. Sabatini was a rich man with a beautiful mistress, a fabulous yacht and opulent surroundings. He didn't need to continue to run drugs. He did it because he could and it excited him. If he could, he would tell everyone about it. Sabatini wanted people to know he was powerful and influential. The extravagant parties and philanthropic donations covered how the man acquired his wealth: through foul, illicit means. What was it he'd said about life? Somebody always dies. Drago suspected the rules of Sabatini's game were intense and entirely deadly.

Inspector Gigli hadn't waited for an explanation. He ordered Drago to attend another interview at Otranto's police station the next morning where he would be issued with a warning and a fine.

On his way back from Tarantella, he paid a visit to Lore at the Spirito Spa. She wrinkled her nose and hands at his state of dress, but spoke to him ever so sweetly.

"Signorina Ariana hasn't visited the spa today."

"That's odd, Lore. You said she came every day."

"Si. Every day."

"But not today."

"No, Signor."

Drago studied the yacht during the evening, eating cold meats and cheese with a glass or two of Fatalone Primitivo and some sparkling water. The Villa Caprese kept an excellent cellar. The yacht's stateroom lights flickered on. There was movement. He could make out Sabatini's bulk. Of Ariana there was no sign. He waited and watched until all the interior lights had been extinguished and only the security lamps at the prow and stern glowed. Afterwards, he slept badly.

When Drago woke, he hoped Ariana might emerge for her dawn swim. She didn't. He showered and dressed. She didn't appear for breakfast either. Drago telephoned Vicino. Paulo was sleepy. His voice suggested he'd been offended his English friend had not visited the restaurant last night.

"What?"

"Can you come to the villa?" asked Drago. "I want you to do

something for me."

"You woke me up."

"I know. I can tell."

Paulo objected, but Drago was insistent and persuasive: the bottle of Fatalone was still open. Eventually, the unusually grumpy patron arrived looking as if he really had just woken up, unshaven and still in a loose pair of joggers and an oversize t-shirt. Drago offered him the shower as well as the wine.

"I want you to watch the yacht while I'm gone. I'll be no more than an hour. I have to pay a visit to Inspector Gigli. If I don't, I'll be in trouble. Thing is, I haven't seen Ariana since the fight at your place. I'm worried. If she does come ashore, I don't want to miss the opportunity to speak to her."

"Don't you have her mobile?"

"No."

Paulo shook his head. "English! Alright, what do I do if she comes ashore?"

"Call me. Then follow her from the marina. You'll have plenty of time to get there."

"I'm not a detective."

"Not a problem. She'll recognise you anyway. You could probably hold hands."

Outside the front door was parked a green Maserati Spyder III. The top was down. Drago peered at the interior, the pine dash, the bold black leather seats and the almost spartan instrument panel. A sleek two-seater built on a wheel base shy of eight feet and with a two-litre bit-turbo engine, it would purr along the beautiful coastal roads and probably accelerate with a gorgeous pull of speed, even at twenty-five years of age.

"Do you like her?" said Paulo.

"Very beautiful. The bonnet's higher than the original, isn't it?"

"Yes. And the wheels are an inch wider. Seven spokes. She cuddles the road."

"I bet you've even got a name for her."

"No. But she is my only lover now. Everyone else has gone," Paulo said wistfully. "Maybe I'll let you drive her one day. She's the best car in the Salentine."

"I believe it." Drago made his way to the robust Fiat. "I'll hold you to that drive. Don't forget about the yacht."

"No, no."

As Paulo retreated indoors, Drago started the car then took the shortest route into town. He needed some provisions from the shops. He got those first and then made his way to the police station. Drago expected more sage wisdom. He didn't get it. The Inspector's phone pipped and he turned to leave without a word. Just as well, thought Drago; I doubt I'll be taking his advice.

Drago dutifully paid the fine with his Amex. He could have used the stolen Euros, but was cautious about arousing suspicion. A tourist carrying that much cash was unusual these days. Almost two hours had elapsed before he returned. The Maserati was still in place. Vicino was steaming.

"Come on, come on, it's almost twelve. I have to be at the restaurant soon."

Drago chuckled and let him go. He watched the emerald beauty slip down the lane blowing smoke from its exhaust. He ate a pastry and made coffee, lifted the binoculars and resigned himself to a long afternoon. He was glad Paulo had been in a hurry and neglected to ask what Drago's urgent appointment was about. It saved a long explanation.

Neither Ariana nor Sabatini appeared for lunch. Then, just as Drago was contemplating his own snack, there was movement on board. Sabatini, his bulk filling a light grey suit to bursting, appeared on deck. He issued instructions. Half a dozen men, dressed exactly as they had been at the charity event, ranged about him. Three of them organised one of the motorboats, unhitching it from the rear pontoon. Sabatini descended the ladder with ease for such a big man. He took a seat in the rear. All his accomplices had to stand. The Captain, identified by the pips on his shoulders, took the helm and manoeuvred the boat sedately to port. Drago followed them through the lenses of the Cavalry 10 x 50. A big Lancia was waiting for the group, black, with tinted windows.

For a few moments, Drago considered following it. He withdrew the thought, sat back and waited for Ariana.

It was almost the usual time for her daily escape. She came out dressed in a pair of below the knee pleated shorts and a blue and white striped round-necked shirt. It was the sort of thing he saw in Tommy Hilfiger, but was probably much more expensive, some fashion house like Biagiotti or Lora Piano, no doubt. Her eyes were covered with wrap around shades. Drago pressed the binoculars to his eyes. She was arguing with the steward. For a moment it appeared she wasn't going anywhere, but after a heated discussion, the steward tired of her antics. Normally Ariana came ashore alone. Today, because they had already used one boat, the steward came with her. As the launch departed *Diamantin*, Drago was already slamming the front door on his way out.

She disembarked at the harbour, the two speeders docked side by side. The steward issued some instructions which she ignored. Drago watched the play with some amusement from the cab of his Fiat. She strode off, head thrown back in a dramatic huff. The steward was out of his depth dealing with a feisty woman. He released the lines and steered the motorboat away from the harbourside. Drago caught up to her at Piazza Madonna del Passo.

"Hello."

Ariana wasn't shocked to see him, nor did she greet him warmly. Instead, she kept walking.

"Are you worried you're still being followed?" he asked, falling into step.

"You are being too persistent, Jonathon."

"Let's call it curiosity. I was wondering where you've been."

"I stayed on board."

"And in your cabin."

"Yes."

"Because you wanted to or you had to?"

Ariana halted and flicked her gaze up to his. She was wearing pumps, so stood shorter in flats, but no less impressive.

"This is very difficult for me, Jonathon. You must understand."

"You told me you were always running away. I don't understand why you've chosen to stay."

She shook her head.

"It is not easy, leaving."

"What's he going to do: kill you?"

"Do not joke." Ariana breathed deeply. "I'm not going to the spa today. I'm going to the orphanage. It's the only reason Blaku let me come ashore. Come with me. Perhaps then you'll understand."

They walked through the town to its outskirts where farmland took over from tarmac and the riverbed split the valley. Set in an acre of open land was a renovated white stucco chapel with long elegant arches ruined by time. Attached to it were two new constructions which resembled barrack buildings. Shuttered windows ran along the sides. The building was surrounded by a fence three wires high. What might have once been grass had been turned mostly to dust by playing feet. Children played on it now, running and skipping. Some of the boys were kicking a knackered tennis ball, pretending to be Lionel Messi. Seated on a neat wooden bench was an olive skinned lady of indeterminate age, older than forty, younger than sixty, lips like eighty, unkissed, frugal, simply the age all good nurses always seemed to be. Ariana waved and the nurse rose to her feet and made her way through the children. Kisses on cheeks were exchanged.

Ariana introduced Drago as an Englishman who had given a big donation to the charity. The nurse wasn't remotely interested. The two women embarked on a discussion in Italian during which Drago spent his time watching the children, kicked the ball back when it came too close and marvelled at how innocent childhood was. The kids were a mixture of ages, sexes and races, yet they played together as if ethnicity and religion never existed. They had more colour in their young lives than all the shades of black and white and grey adults lived with. Ariana went with the nurse to the sandpit and spoke to the kids messing in it. She ruffled a boy's head, picked at a loose thread on a girl's blouse and offered to get it mended. She looked alive and spirited. She didn't mind her fashionista knees getting a little dusty and dented, not if the kids were happy.

After a few minutes more, she came back to Drago and they went inside. The vestibule was cool, high and whitewashed. The two new blocks led off it, as did a refectory, a canteen and some offices. The original chapel had been shrunk in size to accommodate the changes. One of the office doors was open and the nurse led them to it.

Reverendo Lampedusa sat at a spartan wooden desk, his

fingers poised over the keyboard of an ancient home office system. He stopped typing immediately and stood up, face beaming, to exchange more greetings. He switched to English at Drago's arrival.

"Come in, come in," he said and then in Italian told the nurse to bring coffee. "You have arrived at an opportune moment. I was writing thank you notes for the donations from the charity ball. I do not appear to have your address, Signor Drago."

"You don't have my money either. If I'd known I was coming here, I'd have brought it with me."

Drago gave the details of the Italian villa and the London flat. Lampedusa looked puzzled. He wanted an email. Drago dictated it. He sat down next to Ariana, who was trying not to giggle. The settee was bumpy and looked like it would mark his clothes, but as Ariana didn't mind, he overlooked it. The coffee arrived quickly. It must have been brewing already.

"Of course, it was a wonderful occasion," continued Lampedusa once the nurse had left them alone. "A feast for the eyes and, eh, the account of the orphanage. I can't say such things with Signora Trevelli present. She does not approve of such demonstrations."

"She takes the money," said Drago.

"Unwillingly," said Ariana.

"Everyone was excited by your dancing. They say you made a beautiful partnership, if I may? I was disappointed you disappeared so soon, Ariana. Signor Sabatini was worried. He sent a man after you."

Drago looked at her.

"Did he?" she said.

"Yes. An uncouth gentleman. Curly hair. Leather." He made a vague swish of his hand and nonchalantly started to pour coffee. "I spoke with him."

"Oh. Bergamo." Drago said the name to gauge any reaction from Ariana. There was none. "We got the message."

"I'm glad you are both alright. I'm sure Signor Sabatini was relieved at your return, Ariana."

"He was."

That was said without any warmth. Lampedusa handed her a

cup and saucer. She accepted it gingerly. Lampedusa let out a delicate sigh.

"Remember, Ariana. We can always talk."

"Thank you, Padre. Not today."

Drago caught a slight inclination of Ariana's head. It bent his way. He took the coffee cup offered to him and said: "Ariana is an excellent dancer. I was pleased I won the auction."

"I had no idea you had that much money," she said.

"I didn't until a few days ago."

"Yes?"

"Yes. A happy accident."

Lampedusa chuckled. An attempt to ease the tension. He sipped his own coffee. "Now, did you see the children, Ariana?"

The conversation diverted to the running of the orphanage. Ariana took a keen interest in the welfare of the youngsters, asking several specific questions and mentioning individual names. She was impressed by their achievements, worried by their health and sad if they left, even if an adopted child had been placed in a good home. Prospective foster parents were vetted extremely carefully by the Foundation's team. Drago wanted to contribute to the conversation, but the Foundation was Ariana's scene and his interest was only in its benefactor. During a lull he said: "This seems an excellent enterprise, Padre. Exactly how many children live here?"

"At the moment sixty-three."

"There's only half that in the playground."

"Some have local school places. We aim to provide as much as we can. Education, other than the barest of language, is not our calling."

"Did Sabatini build this place?"

"Marcelo paid for the extension," said Ariana. "Without it the children were crammed into the vestry. It was horrible."

"Yes," agreed the pastor. "Awful conditions."

"This used to be a church?"

"Yes. There was an altar piece here once. I had it removed. We have all religions here. I will not press children to convert. Of course, if they are interested, that is another matter."

"How are the plans progressing for the girls' washrooms?"

said Ariana.

"Ah. Yes. I have had some luck. Wait. Let me show you." Lampedusa closed down his Word document and fiddled with the mouse to bring up a letter and a facsimile copy of an architect's plan. He printed a copy and handed it to Ariana for inspection.

"It seems very expensive," commented Ariana.

Drago wasn't a builder, but he had to agree. The price of the small extension was as high as some flats in London. He viewed the plan at some length, started searching on his Samsung for online details.

"Who's the architect?" he said.

"Vëllezërit Caldo," replied the pastor. "Very reputable."

"According to whom?"

"Marcelo Sabatini is paying for the installation. It was he who engaged the firm."

Drago already had the website on his mobile. "An Albanian company. Will he be engaging the builders also?"

"I expect the architects…"

"I think they might be taking Sabatini's generosity a little for granted." Drago handed back the plans. "Did anyone do due diligence on this firm? They're associated with the N.M.T.; that's Sabatini's union isn't it?"

He said it with half an eye on Ariana, but she didn't reply.

"Listen, Padre," Drago continued, "there's a man whose villa I'm staying at; he's an architect. Email me the blue prints and I'll see if he can't make some more cost effective suggestions."

The discussion seemed to make Lampedusa uncomfortable.

"It is not always right to object."

"Nonsense. I bet he'll get your material costs down. All this stone's coming from Albania."

"No. You don't understand." Lampedusa opened his hands reluctantly. "Sometimes there are certain people you must trust. Certain people you must pay."

Drago again glanced sideways at Ariana.

"You're throwing money away," he said. "All those Euros raised at the charity ball and half of it is going to these cowboy developers. The kids won't see a cent."

"No." Ariana's voice was sudden, sharp, like an axe chopping. "You really don't understand, Jonathon." She stood up to avoid his gaze. "Now, perhaps we should leave the Reverendo to his letters."

"Alright." Drago extended his hand to Lampedusa, who looked shocked at the sudden exit. "I'm sorry if I've offended you."

"No. Not at all. Please come again." The Reverendo inclined a smile. "With your donation, this time?"

Drago nodded. "I won't forget."

Ariana kissed the Reverendo and led Drago outside. One of the children rushed up to her, the same one whose dress she'd toyed with. She was holding a posy of tiny bright yellow blowballs, picked from the verge, tied with some of the loose thread from her fraying blouse. Ariana squatted, hugged the girl, spoke to her, kissed her forehead and held the pretty weeds as if they were the most delicate flowers in the world. Momentarily, her face brightened then turned dark as the little girl scuttled shyly back to her playmates, who teased her for the silly demonstration. Something caught in Ariana's throat. She rose and turned aside, heading for the main gate.

"Why are you doing this, Ariana?" Drago fell into step beside her. "I mean honestly. You don't have to. Sabatini isn't interested in these children. It's only good for lining the pockets of his union friends. It's all for show: media philanthropy."

"You don't understand."

"I do." Drago was angry. Not at her, but at what she was refusing to deal with. "He's stroking his ego, Ariana. It's a smokescreen for whatever else is going on. Things like this auction and the Foundation. You know he's not everything he says. And I know it too."

"How do you know?"

"It's obvious." Drago clutched at a reason. "Come on. Look at that thing with his eye. Conspicuous extravagance. Something for people to talk about so they ignore the real issue."

"Which is what?"

She kept walking, her pace faster by the stride.

"He's using you."

She strode on, noted he'd drawn to a halt and stopped herself. She turned to face him, hand on a hip, the pose familiar from the spa only this time she did not remove her glasses. "So, now you insult me, not only the Padre."

Drago blustered.

"Fuck's sake. Alright. Alright." He came slowly to her. "You're right. I probably don't understand. I'm on the outside, looking in." He reached out and stroked her arm with his fingertips. "That's not where I want to be."

The sobs she'd held back since the playground came freely now. She pulled a tissue from her handbag, turned her back and dabbed her tears, folding the tissue carefully to catch the drops as they fell from under the glasses. Flustered, running out of hands, she dropped the posy of flowers and left them in the dirt. Drago wanted to embrace her, but he sensed it would be inappropriate. Eventually calmness and composure took over. She stared at the flowers a long time and took one deep breath.

"I am sorry," she said. "I wasn't expecting to see you today. This is, what would you call it? Overwhelmed."

"That's pretty close. Would you like me to go?"

"No. Do you have a car?"

"It's at the marina."

"Walk me back. You can drive me somewhere. Marcelo will not return until much later tonight. He has an important meeting. Business."

They detoured back to the marina to avoid being spotted from the yacht. They strolled quietly, side by side. Occasionally they caught each other smiling. Drago thought she'd looked very happy with the children, very beautiful, even more so than when he'd seen her naked, as if the form of Venus suddenly inhabited more than sex appeal. He found it intoxicating and wanted to discover more of her secrets.

When they settled into the Fiat, Ariana noticed the plaster across the ridge of his palm. "What happened to your hand?"

"That's a long story. I went to visit the Comte d'Orsi yesterday."

"Oh. How is Ferdinand?"

"He's insane."

"No. He's a lonely old fool."

"He bloody isn't. I'll tell you on the way." Drago started the engine. "Where am I driving us?"

"Go north. There are grottos up there. Most of them are sign posted for tourists but I know a secret cave where we can swim."

"I don't have a costume."

"Neither have I."

He raised a speculative eyebrow and pulled away from the kerb. As promised he related the chaotic scenes from Tarantella. She laughed at his initial run in with the boar.

"Yes. They stink the place badly," she commented. Later, when he mentioned the bags of heroin, she became silent, pensive.

"So, who's this man Ferrara?" asked Drago casually.

"He's a valet. Ferdinand relies on him for everything. I don't like him."

"Bergamo works at Tarantella as well. Did you ever see him?"

"I might have recognised him. I don't know all Ferdinand's employees. It was dark, remember?"

"I thought the whole set up there was very odd. Afterwards, I was sort of arrested by Inspector Gigli. He told me Bergamo was part of the Mafia, that the Comte d'Orsi was the Padrino, the Godfather, I wonder –"

"Mafia?" interrupted Ariana.

"Yes. Do you know anything about that?"

"No."

"Does Sabatini?"

"Why do you ask?"

"Just curious."

"You should have asked the Comte about it before you jumped through his window."

"Probably."

Drago wanted to mention the scuba divers and the packages of money, but her mood had lightened and he didn't want to spoil it. The afternoon had become lusty. They skirted the coast, the sky vanishing into opaque seas. Drago followed a train of cars easing through the twists and turns, back and forth, like the sun-speckled waves rolling endlessly to the horizon and home again. Inland, the greens and reds and golds reflected the sunlight in strange earthbound rainbows. Flocks of honey buzzards took off in extravagant arcs as the line of cars dazzled past.

Ariana's mobile rang. She studied the call log before choosing to answer it. She spoke in a language Drago assumed was Albanian. She was immediately agitated. The conversation ended on a defiant note. The mobile rang again a moment later. She declined to answer and then switched it off.

"Who was that?" he asked.

"Blaku, the steward. He wants to know when I will return. The yacht only has two speedboats. Apparently, they are both required tonight and I must be on board before the second boat leaves."

"What time is that?"

"I didn't ask. I was too angry."

"How many men are there on the yacht?"

"Other than Marcelo and Captain Belzac, there are seven."

"And no women."

"The cook. She's the only one."

"Does that bother you?"

She stared blankly at him. Drago couldn't see behind the dark tint of her sunglasses, but assumed she was squinting with puzzlement.

"I mean, you don't worry about being on board with all those men?"

"I told you before. I am Marcelo's woman."

"Yes. You did."

Drago let the matter rest. The call disturbed the light-hearted mood. Ariana was pensive for a while. She turned on the radio, some Italian pop station. They mouthed the words to the songs they knew, Drago to Adele, Ariana to Marco Carta.

After a while, they approached the lazy fishing village of San Foca, which once landed boats by the hundred. Now the harbour plied a small seasonal trade and the rest of the town was given over to the inevitable tourists. An obstinate watchtower stared at nothing. Its walls spoke of stories to be told, sometime, somewhere, witnesses to danger, destruction, to love and the debris of dreams.

Ariana directed him through the town, past all the popular grottos until, with a flourish, she gestured to a small track half obscured by overgrown laurel bushes.

When Drago brought the Fiat to a halt they were at the tip of a cove in a tiny secluded gravel car park. She got out and pointed at the coastline. He could make out a low niche cut off by centuries of waves and beyond the opening, darkness.

"The Siren's Grotto," she explained. "There are lots of caves along the coast. Most of the tourists go to the Grotto dell' Amore. It's a big round lagoon. Too dull and too busy. Then there is the Cave of Poets. They say two lovers took refuge there one day to shelter from the cold spring wind, but the tide came in and they died in each other's arms. They say you can still hear them sigh."

"That's a nice story. What about this one?"

"It's haunted: a Siren's call."

"I'd like to hear that. A bit of temptation never hurt anyone. How do we get there?"

"There's a small boatyard by the beach. The owner knows me. Come on. Get your things."

"What things?"

"Your wallet."

She was already on her way. Drago followed, jogging to catch up. The short track led to a series of steep steps cut into the cliff side. At the bottom was a small wooden jetty with two battered old Riva speedboats, double-seater in-boarders with faded mahogany treads, hitched to rusty iron mooring rings. Ariana negotiated. Drago paid. They stepped into the boat and, with the owner's direction, Ariana managed to reverse from the tiny harbour and set out across the sedate oscillating sea.

"You steer very well," said Drago.

"Marcelo taught me. You never know when you might need to be a pilot, he told me; so I learnt. Of course, I rarely go out alone."

"You're not alone."

She stared back at him from behind the big black glasses. He stroked her hair which had come loose in the breeze, but she pulled away from the intimacy and returned to the task of playing Captain. She pointed to a battered locker under the passenger seat.

"Have a look. There's usually water in there."

Among the bottles, Drago also found a creased navy blue pilot's cap. He tossed it to her. Ariana placed it at a jaunty angle on her head.

"What do you think?"

"I'd follow your orders anywhere."

"Do you mean that?"

"Of course."

"You are joking. Don't joke about love, Jonathon."

"I'm not."

"Love is a serious thing."

"You believe that?"

"Isn't it for you?"

"I'm not sure. Love is extraordinary and painful."

"What curious words you use." Ariana paused for a moment to realign the speedboat. Another boat was heading out of the cave. They passed within metres of each other, exchanging greetings as the bow waves crashed.

"What was her name?"

"Who?"

"The girl who broke your heart."

"Someone. Anyone. It's not important."

She snorted in disappointment.

"What about you?"

"Marcelo broke my heart."

They'd almost reached the cave. Ariana shut the throttle and let the boat idle at the entrance. The low arch stretched seven or eight metres across. What Drago assumed to be darkness was now revealed as a deep aquamarine. The waves sucked the little boat and its two passengers into the bowels of the cave. Above them, hundreds of sugar white stalactites hung like lances. The walls glowed with sea colours: zaffre, cobalt and autumn sand, the phosphorous deposits casting a cool sheen across the cavern and prism-like ripples in the sediment mirrored the ocean tides, washing in and out, back and forth. Silently they drifted into the centre of the pool, transfixed by the rainbows of the sea.

Ariana depressed the throttle and the motorboat moved ever so gently into the throat of the cave, a long channel bearing right. There was a small shale beach, the stones glinting silver-grey in the cave light. With a jolt, the prow of the boat beached on the spit of stones and she cut the engine. Ariana grasped the wheel hard with both hands.

"I wanted a son," she said. "When I became pregnant, Marcelo made me lose it. I hate him for that."

Drago said nothing because there was nothing to say. He remembered how he'd seen her with the little ones at the orphanage. Her sorrow was everything and her life was nothing. It was hollow, filled at intervals by good works, emptied by entrapment to a man she had learned to loath.

"These things can change," said Drago. "You can still have children."

He thought she'd like that. Instead. she turned aside and began to dismount from the cockpit.

"It's time to swim."

They left two bundles of clothes on the beach. Drago discreetly turned his back as they stripped. When he looked across to where she'd stood, the sunglasses rested on the pilot's cap on top of her clothes. She was already up to her thighs in the sea. He stepped forward. The water was cool to his toes, perhaps too cool, but he soon warmed up by slicing into the blue and using long, lazy breast strokes to catch her. Drago tapped an ankle and she turned. He blinked. Had the translucent air tricked him? Ariana's face, her left eye, was swollen badly, a small cut on the eyelid. He retreated from her, uncertain if she meant him to see it. He remembered the bruise he'd spied on her shoulder, how the evening gown had so casually covered it.

Ariana continued to swim. She called out from the centre of the pool: "Don't worry. Carlo promised me he'd not rent another boat today."

"Why was that?"

"You paid him four times the rate."

"That was naughty."

"I know. I want us to be alone. Just us and the wind and the waves."

Drago swam after her. It was a beautiful, blissful few minutes. They played like children, tag and splash, laughed and dived, caught feet and hands and occasionally, by accident or design, they brushed against something intimate. The fairy tale atmosphere of the Siren's

Grotto wrapped them in its spell, each touch magical and unforgettable and chaste, their nudity no more than fish scales, flashing in the cyanosis.

Eventually they retreated to the little beach. Drago sat on his buttocks, dripping. Ariana lay on her front, head on hands, the damaged eye hidden by an arm. On her back, there were fresh bruises, festering under the skin.

"He's a bastard," Drago said.

"It was never like this, Jonathon, not when we first met. And then one time it happened. I called him what you said. Bastardo. Bastardo. I was angry with him. He wanted what all men wanted and he took it. I was scared. It was very bad. I hated him for being like that. Afterwards everything was fine, as if it never occurred. But it was not fine. He hit me too hard, too many times, and I lost the baby." There was sudden tension to her voice, as if she'd never told the story before and the telling was stretching her vocal chords until they burst. "He isn't always like that. He is an impatient man. He wants things immediately and without question. And sometimes, well, I can't, you know."

Her face turned to his. She propped herself on an elbow, to study him better. Drago understood. She didn't need to explain. Sabatini, with his hawk eyes, his brute presence, was an animal, hunting, feeding, digesting and spitting out the waste. When the shark has had his fill, he discards the carcass and leaves it to the scavengers. Sabatini was abandoning his woman. She was becoming part of the leftovers.

Ariana's beautiful wide mouth parted. The teeth gleamed. The tongue almost poked out then retreated. He bent over and kissed the mouth, quickly, lightly, and then harder until their lips hurt. His hand softly touched one beautiful breast and she pulled him towards her. When the kiss broke, one single hot gasp escaped her chest. Slowly, deliberately, Drago pulled away.

"I don't want it to be now," he said.

"Why?"

"I'm not sure. This isn't the right moment."

"Because of Marcelo?"

"No," he said. He couldn't tell her why because he didn't

understand either. His throat closed up. "Just because."

"Because?"

"I'm worried I might be falling for you."

"I'm worried too."

"I want it to be different, Ariana."

"You mean with flowers and wine?"

"Perhaps. You see, I don't want to steal you from Sabatini and I don't want to share you. I want you to leave."

"I suppose I have," she murmured, "at least in my mind."

"Perhaps we should both walk away now."

"It's gone too far for that."

"What do you want to do?"

"I don't know."

"You must tell him."

As soon as he said it, Drago knew it was wrong. Sitting beside him in this unreal world was someone soft, but also hard and very real, torn, tattered and yet still magical; a woman who he imagined could spirit away all the troubles of his world and wrap them in a frivolous Pandora's Box, bury them deep, never to be seen again. You didn't let someone as charmed as that disappear. And yet, he knew, soon she would do exactly that and he would once more be alone to face the cursed world.

"It won't be easy," she continued. "He's working towards something, something very big and important. I feel he needs me."

"But I need you!" Drago said it in a whisper, but it was hard and almost cruel. Envy burned. He couldn't help the anger. "For Christ's sake, Ariana, you want me, I want you and Sabatini's got nothing to do with it!"

"I know, Jonathon." Her fingers pressed his lips to silence. "That's why it is so hard."

She kissed him once more, gently without anticipation. He placed his arms about her and they lapsed into silence. Ariana's breath tickled his skin: the sweetest, bewitching of breaths. They lay like that for a long time, listening for the siren's call.

Thirteen

The Heist

The insects of the night were in song. Blaku dropped from the stone wall and immediately started to make progress through the overgrown gardens. His skintight clothing was dull enough to camouflage him among the darkness of the forest. Stretched over his head was a balaclava. His eyes were covered by a thick set of night-finder goggles. His hands were encased in fine mesh, wire and wool gloves, thin enough for close work, thick enough to prevent imprints. Slung crossways over his torso was an empty canvas holdall and attached to the webbing belt at his waist was a tool bag. It had been several years since he'd last been required to use his equipment. Too long, he thought, since I performed a proper duty for the Krye. The excitement spurred him.

  He moved toward the house. He knew there was an alarm, but he also knew where the power source was. Tarantella was old. Its rudimentary, inefficient heating system was still fuelled during the winter months by an oil fired boiler located in an outhouse on the near side. He was glad of that. The opposite side was where the forest became a jungle and where the boar roamed wild. He could smell them and their trash everywhere. The stench clung to the forest as if it was delivering a scented warning. Blaku was careful to heed the advice. He did not relish an encounter with these vicious beasts. Quickly, he crossed the pathway.

  The outhouse door was fastened with a standard bolt lock. Blaku took out his screwdrivers, undid the heads and lifted back the lever. He could see the bolt inside and, using pliers, slid it across. The door swung open. Blaku located the fuse board. Once there, he carefully traced the lines. They were not marked, but prior knowledge told him the alarm required an isolated fuse. He found it, removed the plug and placed it on a shelf.

  Blaku left the outhouse with the door wedged shut. He moved towards the villa, rejected the stairs and instead scaled the parapet to the terrace, rolling flat on the floor between two columns. There was a broken window, patched up badly with panel boarding. Blaku scratched his stubble thoughtfully, rejected the idea as too noisy and continued along the terrace to the first set of French doors. His shoes made no sound. They were adapted from the style worn by free-form mountain climbers, good for grip, padded, noiseless. Blaku squeezed a surgical-sharp knife in the crack between the doors, felt the lock click and silently pulled. It creaked. He measured the sound against the noise of the night. It was just another low hoot, another meaningless solitary grumble among dozens. Blaku positioned a strip of sticky board over the latch to stop it closing on him. With an exit secure, he entered.

Blaku had visited the villa before with the Krye and knew internal layout. He made his way swiftly to the study, the room with the broken window. It more resembled a dining salon than a study. A big table was in the centre. There were no bookcases, nothing to learn from. Instead, ghostly portraits hung on the walls and display cases packed with family trinkets stood beneath them. Blaku ignored them all and moved to the far end of the room, which was occupied by the chimney breast and the small iron fireplace, its grate caked in soot. On the mantel sat a large bracket clock. He inspected it. His fingers scrabbled around the edge seeking the catch. Nothing. Carefully, he prised open the casing to reveal the clock face. It was decorated with an elaborate Romanesque scene. One of the Roman faces looked badly aligned. It was cut out from the rest of the scene: a neat rounded button. Blaku pressed it. God knows how the blind Comte ever located it. Practice and more practice. He probably found it first time, every time. There was a crisp snap as the locks disengaged. Blaku held the clock face open for a moment, listening. Nothing. Not a sound. He replaced the casing, then eased open the door. The whole mantel, clock included, swung back on an axis to reveal the cavity behind it. No one used the fireplace anymore. The chimney was blocked up to contain a steel-lined safe, four feet high, cemented into the brickwork. It was impossible to remove it, unless he drilled through the wall from outside. If the mansion had been unoccupied that would have been Blaku's first choice. However, this was not a smash and grab heist. It was one for an expert.

In addition to waiting on tables in Tirana's finest restaurants, Blaku received his best tuition from the greatest of experts. Long before he was employed by Sabatini, Blaku had run with a gang of cat burglars. The extra income was always useful. It meant occasionally he'd been able to eat at the same kind of establishments he worked in. It also helped him gain women, temporarily. Best of all was the thrill. You could never take that away. Blaku felt the shiver of excitement once more.

The safe looked snobbishly confident in its housing. This might take longer than he expected. It was a digital lock. A Rotter Sydney 65, sealed by a four digit combination. There were millions of possible solutions. Still, nothing was ever a problem. Blaku didn't touch the key pad. Instead he produced a tiny infrared micro-light torch from his bag. It was attached via a thread thin cable to a hand held monitor. Blaku switched the equipment on and slowly ran the light beam over each of the ten number buttons. He could tell from the surface blemishes four of them had been pressed more often than the others. What the beam didn't reveal was the correct sequence of numbers. Blaku carried a list of important dates culled from the Comte's family and personal history. He checked and rechecked to see if he could discern an outcome. All he needed were number combinations of 0, 1, 5 and 9. There were twenty one alternatives. The most obvious was the year of the Comte's birth: 1950. Blaku would normally reject this date as too obvious. Yet no other combination seemed likely from his list. Carefully, he tapped it in 1-9-5-0-enter.

Nothing.

"Mut!"

Blaku reversed the numbers but still came up empty. A droplet of sweat clung to his eyebrow. He took a deep breath and retreated to the only chair in the room, one which stared along the length of the dining table. He leaned his backside on a velvety arm for respite. A second chair was broken into three pieces and had been tossed carelessly into a corner underneath the portrait of a military man. Blaku considered the remnants and then the portrait. It was a youthful representation of the current Comte, Ferdinand d'Orsi. Not a bad likeness, but a painting made to resemble all the others in the room. Blaku had seen it before, when he toured the place during one of the

Krye's visits, a dull party with bad food and a terrible orchestra playing all the wrong notes to old fashioned dances. He pulled out a pencil torch, raised his goggles and walked to the portrait. He flashed the torch over the surface, catching the blind Comte's young face, the detail on his uniform, the meadows in the background which once might have been how the estate looked before it went to ruin and there on the man's breast, set in a gold brooch: Il Papavero. Even the elaborate hawk's claw setting that Blaku recalled so clearly from other paintings was the same.

***

"There's no denying the likeness," he said. "The resemblance is uncanny. The artist must have seen the original paintings."

Ferrara shrugged. He stood holding a half-full glass of prosecco. Blaku had finished his. Neither man should have been drinking; they were both on duty. Blaku listened to the orchestra. If they stopped playing, he ought to reappear swiftly. Sabatini's expectation was that he should always be in attendance. He'd escaped for a brief respite from the party. Not even the food had interested him.

"Or he must have seen the real thing," said Ferrara.

"That's what I was thinking." Blaku scratched his beard. "It's exactly like the ruby in the painting of Skanderbeg on *Diamantin*. You know the story, Ferrara?"

"It is a fable."

"Well, in Albania, over the centuries, every-so-often people would claim to know of its existence. Yet every search has proved fruitless. It would be astonishing to find it sitting in that old fashioned safe."

"It doesn't matter how the stone got here. Here it is."

"And you've seen it?"

"I've seen a big fat ruby."

Blaku's heart quickened. Could the Comte d'Orsi really possess Il Papavero, the fabled red diamond of Skanderbeg?

"Of course, I can't promise it is the real Papavero," said Ferrara, "but I can promise you lots of other diamonds. The Comte sells them occasionally for money."

"The Krye only wants me to steal Il Papavero."

"And do you do everything the Krye wants?"

"What do you mean?"

"You used to be the best thief in Tirana. I heard they employed you across the continent. The theft from the Rijksmuseum, to order I understand. The Munch's from Oslo. That princess's bracelet lifted from Van Cleef and Arpels on the Place Vendome. And it was only in for repair. Now, look at you, Blaku. What has happened?"

"The police got too close to me. It was safer to take a reliable, inconspicuous position, to keep my head below the parapet."

"You've stayed below it too long." Ferrara took the steward's elbow and gently squeezed, lowering his voice, moving closer, exactly how his father used to at moments of high importance. "In that safe, Blaku, are dozens more diamonds. White Namibian stones. I know they are there because the old man occasionally uses one to pay for repairs. Or so he thinks." Ferrara chuckled. "I do a little work. The rest I have used for my own enterprises. Of course, I could steal them myself, but it wouldn't be possible without my killing the old man. The Comte may be blind, but he's no fool. When he enters the safe, he can operate the mechanism all on his own. He keeps everything well covered from me, never shows me or tells me the combinations. I am the only other person allowed in the room and once the chimney breast is open, he listens until he knows I'm standing with my back to the door. That's one of the things about this villa: excellent acoustics. It's the curved ceilings.

"Now, your task is to steal Il Papavero for Sabatini. While you are there, Blaku, you can steal the other diamonds for me. The Comte will believe everything has been stolen. But he won't report it to the police. The diamonds are not on an inventory nor are they insured because they themselves were stolen, picked off a damaged freighter during the war. They'll simply be lost. Oh, he'll be angry, but Sabatini, the press, the police, they will never know. And during your next furlough ashore, you can give the diamonds to me. I will invest them into my narcotic operation, which is expanding slowly, but steadily.

This will be the influx of extra funds I need to really make inroads into the Unione's territory. The money will start rolling in my hands. I'll cut you in a percentage, Blaku. Soon, you and me, we'll both have enough to retire and live in luxury."

Ferrara turned to the iron chimney breast. "Let Sabatini have his red diamond. We can take the rest."

"How many diamonds are there?"

"More than enough."

"What makes you think I want to do that?"

"I can see it written across your face, Blaku. It's the same expression I have." Ferrara finally sipped the prosecco. "You want to get your freedom."

***

Il Papavero? thought Blaku. Again, the torch beam picked out the famous delicate oval shape, the sides cut to accommodate the fangs of the famous talon clasp atop the mace. The artist had even replicated a semblance of refracted light, the blood-like crimson thinning to a youthful burnt pink. It showed good technique. Who was the artist? wondered Blaku. He played the torch beam across the frame. Rodolfo. A pleasant enough painter. Nobody exciting, judging by his work here. Blaku blinked. The inscription read: *Composta dal 5 al 9 Ottobre 1969.*

5. 9.10.

Blaku shut off the torch and pulled his goggles down. It couldn't be a coincidence. It simply couldn't. Excited, he returned to the safe, automatically flexing his fingers. He breathed out once and tapped in the combination: 5-9-1-0-enter. The lock slid back with a click and the door popped open. A tremble of fear ran down Blaku's spine. He almost expected an internal alarm to activate, the sort of trap these old safes used to contain. When silence prevailed, the fear turned to euphoria.

The safe was split into small compartments. A number of documents tied with ribbons in the manner of old parchment papers sat on one shelf. On a second was a slim leather wallet full of ancient Roman coins. Another carried boxes full of pearls and brooches. An ancient pocket watch. Sleeves full of preserved currency from the Kingdom of the Two Sicily's, almost two hundred years old. Below all this was a stocky-looking drawer. Blaku pulled it open. Several cloth bags rested inside. He took one and parted the draw string. The bag contained about a dozen small paper envelopes, each one embossed with braille writing. The insignia meant nothing to Blaku. He saw some carried the same figures. Perhaps it revealed the weight and description of the contents. Blaku carefully opened one envelope. A single white diamond was inside, in a tiny sealed plastic pouch. Fascinated, Baku opened the pouch, rolled the immaculate stone between his fingers, imagining the furious wealth as it glinted under the last of the threaded moonlight. Reluctantly, he replaced the white stone and put it back in the bag. He counted the envelopes. Yes, an exact dozen. And there were four bags. He nearly whistled. Blaku inspected each bag in turn, opening a couple of the envelopes, just to check. The Comte had quite a collection. Different sizes and cuts, some like lentil grains, others peas, a few larger still. He transferred all the bags into his own holdall.

Now; there had been no sign of the stone he needed – where was the red diamond? The drawer was now empty and, peering closer, Blaku realised it had a false back. There was a small hinge to one side, with a tiny keyhole cut into the metal. It was a simple lock and Blaku opened it with two pins. Inside was a single gourd, much heavier that the others and better padded. Blaku removed it, pulled the strings and the contents fell into his hand. The huge red diamond, resting in its golden clasp, sat in his palm.

Blaku contained an audible obscenity. He was the first Albanian for centuries to hold Il Papavero. A trembling thrill ran up his spine. Even in the virtual darkness of the villa, the ruby had an unexpected shine. Blaku grinned, replaced it in the bag and slipped Il Papavero with the other stones into his holdall. Quickly, he restored the other antiquities to the safe, closed it, reset the lock and swung back the hidden door. It clicked shut and Blaku headed noiselessly for the hall.

Half-way, he stopped. He heard something. He listened. No

sound. An owl hooted. His imagination was playing tricks. The noise had been outside. No one else was here. The estate workers didn't live at Tarantella; they travelled in from nearby villages. Only Ferrara and one other stayed in the villa overnight. And they wouldn't want to stop him; after all, it was Ferrara's special 'doctor' who gave the Comte a sedative with his sherry every night . All Blaku wanted was a big, fat red diamond, a present for his employer, a chance to show his loyalty, like he used to with the old thieves in Tirana, and a chance to escape the drudgery of service.

The sound was nothing. His ears were playing tricks. Blaku crossed to the French doors and removed the sticky pad from the lock. A loud clatter echoed from the back of the lobby. The lights came on. Dear God! Astonished, he spun. At the top for the stairs stood the Comte d'Orsi, in his night clothes, his face staring blankly but directly at Blaku. His hand was raised and in it he held a small automatic pistol. The hammer was drawn back. The eye of the barrel pointed directly at Blaku.

"Chi è che?"

The thief didn't wait. He swept the door open and stepped outside, closing it with a crash. Simultaneously the pistol barked three times. Glass shattered. Blaku felt something tear below his left shoulder. Goddamnit! He could hear the Comte shouting as he sprinted over the terrace and down the steps. What the hell was happening? What happened to the drugs Ferrara was supposed to give the old man? The bastard must have the constitution of an ox. Or was this a double cross, a way for Ferrara to maintain his links with the Unione Sacre Croce. Either way, Blaku was injured and he wanted out of Tarantella. He winced at the throbbing pain in this shoulder. He ploughed through the forest, weeds whipping at him as he ran through the dragnet. Tarantella was coming alive. Lights were switching on. Among the trees, he heard the snorts of waking wild boar.

Blaku reached the wall, leapt at it, his shoes giving him excellent all-round grip. His hands found the top bricks. His chest slammed into the tablature. His left shoulder screamed. His chest began to ache with a dull continuous thump. He bit his lip to stop his own screams. The bullet must have wedged against a bone; he could feel it. Blaku tumbled over the apex and landed in a pile at the base of the wall, winded and grimacing. He got unsteadily to his feet, ripped off the balaclava and the goggles and shoved them in the kit bag. He set off at a stumbling run, eyesight fractured by pain, thankful for the darkness.

He struggled for almost fifteen minutes before he reached the motor launch. It should have been a pleasant walk, like the one he took in Oxford in 2000 after the Ashmolean heist. That job had been a joy. This was torture. Twice he almost passed out. What the hell was that pistol loaded with – barbed wire? If felt as if his whole shoulder was being torn apart. God forbid the old man loaded his guns with expanders, the kind of bullet you could only buy on the black market. The Comte was so old he probably had them from the war.

Blaku's breathing became short. He winced continually. As he approached the stone pier, he almost tumbled down the steps.

Simeon saw him staggering wildly and came to help. He almost recoiled from the bloody man, whose chest was soaked in gore.

"Christ! What happened?"

"The old man woke up. He shot me."

"But he's blind!"

"I tell you –"

Blaku coughed and the first bubble of blood burst out of his mouth.

"You need a doctor," said Simeon.

"No; *Diamantin* first," wheezed Blaku. He'd worked with Sabatini for over a decade. He couldn't cover up this mess. Better to confess his mistakes quick. It was bad enough that foolish woman hadn't returned from the orphanage. Now, he'd been shot. And he'd stolen all the diamonds. That was three mistakes in one night.

"I have the jewel," he croaked. "The Krye must have it."

Scared, because Blaku was sweating horribly and bleeding profusely, his breath coming in short gasps, Simeon sat his companion on the rear seat, strapped him in and proceeded to unhook the lines. He was heading back up the coast within minutes, easing the speedboat up to twenty knots, the white bows skimming the black waves, the single lemony spotlight his only illumination. The shore was a good navigator and he kept it well within sight, using the landmarks to identify his whereabouts. Occasionally, Simeon turned to check on Blaku, but other than the fact the steward sat upright, he couldn't tell if he was alive, alert, unconscious or dead. Otranto came up suddenly, the twin lighthouses marking the wide entrance to the bay. The promenade lights were still on, the parties just dying. *Diamantin* was waiting. Simeon cut back on the throttle.

Occasionally the electric white beacon from Otranto's lighthouse passed over the yacht. Simeon didn't need it to guide him. *Diamantin* was outlined by the incandescent shadows cast from the windows of the staterooms. Someone was already on board.

***

Like those lovers of ancient times, they'd drifted asleep. Luckily, there was no tide to wash them to their doom. Drago woke with a snap. The beach was cold. It was almost pitch black. He scrambled to find his phone and switched on the torch app. A thin mist condensed above the water. The entrance to the cave was a black hole leading to a silver speckled sky. As the torch beam arced across the walls, the eerie blue phosphorus light flickered. He shook Ariana awake. Instantly, she became panic ridden.

"I must get back. I must."

"I thought you wanted to leave him."

"Not now. When the time is right."

They both seemed to want that, so Drago didn't argue. Quickly, they dressed and Drago eased the motor launch away from the shale while Ariana started the engine. Drago hopped in and they trundled back to the jetty as he dried his feet and pulled on his shoes and socks. The single headlamp picked out the wooden pier and the other boat. Ariana guided them to the quayside. A note from the owner was pinned with an old nail on one of the posts.

"What does it say?" asked Drago.

"He says we owe him money for keeping the boat overnight."

"We may as well take it all the way to Otranto."

"That is an idea."

Drago thought she was joking and said so. Ariana's face was set. She twirled the keys around her finger.

"If we take your car, I can't get back on board," she said. "They'll have taken the second boat, remember?"

"You could wait at the harbour."

"I could be there all night. I don't know where they are or how long they'll be."

"You're being silly." Drago spread his arms in mock exacerbation. "What exactly are we going to do with the boat?"

"Marcelo will return it," she said, as if it solved everything, "or you could."

"Great. Thanks. And no."

"Well, I'm going. Are you coming with me?"

Ariana was already climbing back into the little speedboat. He frowned, thought about the car on the cliff, thought about how dangerous it was to travel so far in such a small boat at night, thought about Sabatini's reaction, thought about how stupid it really was, like when you're lost but you keep moving and make a rescue that much harder, he thought a whole multitude of unconnected issues, most of all he thought how ungallant he might appear abandoning a woman to the sea. He jumped in after her and started to loosen the lines.

"Alright," he said sharply. "We'll take turns. I've steered these things before."

"You never told me."

"Up until now you were doing a good job."

Ariana swiped the navy cap off her head and plonked it on his.

"Aye, aye, Captain."

"Don't take the piss. If you're intent on doing something dumb, I ought to make sure you don't."

"You take the wheel then."

Ariana fired the motor and stepped aside so Drago could occupy the helm. He slung the throttle into reverse and guided the craft carefully away from the jetty, before spinning the wheel and accelerating forward, picking up speed outside the cove.

She watched him as he concentrated on the manoeuvre and ran a hand idly through her hair which was blowing in the cross wind. She wondered about Jonathon's past, how she knew so little of it, only what Madeleine had told her at the spa. He never spoke of himself, he only asked questions. Jonathon said he was a journalist and a writer, but she couldn't even remember the books he'd written, if he'd even mentioned them. Maybe he wasn't being honest. There were scars on his body, awful ones, which looked as if the injuries had been life threatening. She could even see the tell-tale sign of plastic surgery on his left shoulder where the surgeons patched him. He was stronger than he looked. She remembered the calmness Jonathon displayed dealing with the thug at Vicino's. He barely took a breath. There was much more hidden under those scars, she thought.

He caught her looking. Ariana liked his eyes. Green was an underrated colour, she considered. It suited his considerate, slightly impish manner. They could also be angry, she supposed, but mostly they stayed calm, faintly prying. Jonathon didn't so much look at her, considered Ariana, as look inside her. It made her quiver, something that hadn't happened since the first time she met Marcelo. Of one thing she was certain, despite the holes to his story, Jonathon Drago was nothing like Marcelo Sabatini.

"I like you when you're being protective," she said. "Do you often rescue damsels?"

"It's become something of a habit."

"Does that explain the scars?"

"Maybe."

Drago turned back to the sea. Far off the portside the outline of a cargo ship was making slow steady progress, probably to Bari or all the way to Trieste. To starboard lay the coast, a blackness interrupted by flashes of pearly white. Occasionally, when towns and villages tip-toed to the shore, a trail of amber harbour lights floated in mid-air and dozens of small fishing vessels, their nets hung up to dry against the masts, buffeted the stone wharves.

After a while he let Ariana take the wheel and said: "I don't like to talk about it, Ariana. I've done some terrible things. I'm not very proud of any of them."

"You mean you're a gangster like Marcelo?"

"No. Nothing like that."

"Then what?"

"Just terrible things."

He took off the cap and ran a thumb nervously around the brim. "Would it affect how you feel about me if you knew?"

"I don't know how I feel about you."

"Good."

"Why do you say that?"

"When I embark on a love affair, it usually ends badly."

"Is this an affair?"

"I don't know."

"Then nor do I." Ariana smiled. Her reaction was a relief and it made him chuckle. "You are making me laugh," she said, "and I told you not to joke about love."

He was silent for a moment as Ariana negotiated a rising wave. The boat crashed onto the surf with a bump. Drago tightened his knees against the roll. His hand gripped a little tighter on the rail. She seemed to enjoy his fear.

"You don't have sailor's feet. You look scared."

"It isn't the sea that frightens me."

Ariana understood. She knew his green eyes would have that inquisitive look to them again, the one which made her quiver.

"When you want to tell me, Jonathon, I know you will."

"Yes," he said, "I will."

The journey became increasingly jumpy. The speedboat rode the breakers and cut across the waves. Drago clung to the rail and rode the dipping, rising turbulence. He would have sat down, but was fearful Ariana might miss some obstacle in the sinking twilight and thought four eyes better primed than two. The warm night air cut across his face and the sudden bursts of sea spray became a welcome relief. Ariana shifted portside to circle a tall rocky spit, early moonlight glinting off the wet rocks. Beyond the spit Drago could make out the shadowy silhouette of *Diamantin* identified by the tiny red and blue port and starboard lights. There was no other sign of life. The yacht was a curtain of darkness, the white zeppelin hull a curious slate grey, the whole edifice oppressive on the sea. They sidled up to the rear of the yacht, cutting the engine early to allow the prow to drift into the holding pen. Drago jumped onto the runner and started to hitch the lines. Ariana was suddenly a jangle of nerves.

"Quickly," she said. "I don't know how long they'll be."

"Don't you know where everyone is?" Drago asked.

"I didn't ask. It is safer that way."

"Until you forget to return home."

Ariana picked up her shoulder bag and gave him a withering look. "Do you always make silly remarks at silly times?"

"Yes."

"Why?"

"It helps relieve the tension."

"Jonathon, you are a clever man, but sometimes you talk like an idiot."

"I get that a lot. Go on. I'll follow you."

"There. You say it again: something stupid."

There was a hinged set of steps locked in place beside the pontoon. They led up to the rear deck. Behind them was a pair of water tight doors set in the stern, just clear of the waterline, probably storage for the boats when the yacht was cruising. Ariana stood clutching the ladder and watching him tie the lines. When Drago finished, he straightened and smiled.

"I'd like to have a peek around the boat, if that's alright?"

"Marcelo won't like it."

"Do you have cameras?"

"No. I mean, not after I deactivate the alarm."

"He won't know then. Anyway, I'm your guest."

"You are impossible."

"Go on, Ariana. Turn off the alarm."

With an astonished shake of the head, Ariana ascended the ladder. Drago waited below and heard the sound of a door swishing open followed by a series of pips, which halted after a few seconds. A moment later, Ariana reappeared at the rail and gestured for him to join her. Once on deck, Drago was able to take in the yacht at close quarters. The two runner decks stretched away on both sides, surrounding the main superstructure which appeared to be constructed from glass and steel. Everything was slimmer than he imagined. The yacht was perhaps only ten metres wide. The hull veered sharply into the water. She was built for speed. Beneath his feet the boards shone even at night, the wood pine polished to within a whisper of being nude. Chrome fittings glimmered. He could even see his reflection, darkness or not. The tarpaulin was rolled out to cover the table and chairs he'd observed being used for breakfast and lunch. The furniture was not upholstered in leather as he'd assumed, but white PVC. The table was fixed to the deck for safety. Drago ran his hand over the surface. It was cool, like marble; porphyry, the imperial stone, the rarest of minerals found in only a tiny corner of eastern Egypt. They buried emperors in porphyry, he reflected.

Ariana was inside the lounge, the glass concertina doors folded back, and she activated the lights. In a series of flickers, arcs of white started to sweep across the gimcrack decking. She was already moving through the huge room. It was conspicuously plush. A long row of real leather bound sofas ran down each side and at intervals matching armchairs nudged teak tables. The carpet was springing; inches thick. Drago's feet got sucked into the deep pile. He noted too the pillars flashed with white marble. The décor was the same off-white as the chairs, with chrome finishing added to the teak. It all shared a sleek, minimalist touch. Every joint and screw head was hidden, cupboards lacked handles, doors were pitted glass, corners and edges were flat, sharp, common. It lacked glamour which made the rich items stand out. *Diamantin*, like its owner with his opal eye, was beautiful in a functional, brutal way.

Drago's gaze flitted around the room. All the neatness betrayed no security system. Maybe it was behind the mirrors. He confined the thought to the back of his mind. If the ship had CCTV, it was too late for him not to be seen anyway. Drago walked to the far end, where there was a ubiquitous cocktail bar, the counter long and thin, but without seats. The optics and shelves and a row of glass-door refrigerators contained expensive wines, champagnes and spirits. Behind the bottles, where one might have expected to see a mirror, was an ugly painting of a crown prince in full military regalia. It seemed out of place in the magnificently stark room. The ceiling lights were all spots. The place blazed, but did nothing to illuminate the dull picture. After the dimness of the sea-ride, the bright atmosphere hurt his eyes. Drago squinted.

Ariana whipped off her shoes and pranced towards him. She paused to fiddle with the air conditioning controls.

"So, you've seen it," she declared. "Don't stay, Jonathon.

Please."

"You seem genuinely concerned for me," he replied. "I like that."

He hoped his smile might have twinkled, but from her reaction he doubted it. Drago walked behind the bar and poured himself a neat scotch. He heard her take a sharp breath, rattled in a couple of ice cubes and took a sip. He replaced the bottle on the rack and stared again at the painting. Something was familiar about the offending work of art.

"Who's this?" he asked, waving the tumbler at the sitter.

"Skanderbeg."

"Who?"

"He's an Albanian hero. Not really a king, more a dictator. He lived in the fifteenth century and threw out the Turks. Or tried to."

"What's he wearing?"

"The helmet?" said Ariana. "It's very famous. They send school children to the National Museum to see a replica. In some schools, it's compulsory."

"Where's the original?"

"Vienna. After he died, Skanderbeg's treasure was taken to Italy by his widow, Donika, and it was sold off to various princes and kings."

The helmet as depicted looked to be made of white metal inlaid with gold, attached to the cap was a golden ram's head which looked both benign and menacing. It wasn't the helmet Drago was interested in. Attached to Skanderbeg's ermine cloak was a large ruby coloured jewel set in an elaborate hawk's claw clasp. He pointed to it.

"What's that?"

Ariana rolled her eyes.

"You also?"

"What?"

"Marcelo goes on and on about that jewel."

"Does he? Why?"

"They call it the Blood Stone Poppy: Il Papavero. It used to sit on the handle of the royal mace. They say it came from Ethiopia and that Skanderbeg stole it from an Ottoman general. Unlike the Italian treasures, there is no record of purchase. The ruby disappeared.

Treasure hunters have been searching for it for centuries. They say some sultan had it, but no one has ever proved anything."

"Is it valuable?"

"I don't know." She shrugged. "Millions."

Ariana could have said hundreds for all the emphasis she put on the word. Drago downed the whisky. He stared at the many sided, blood-red stone and poured himself another measure.

"I've seen it before," he said.

"No. Marcelo paid millions for the painting. Although this is a replica too. The real one is in his museum."

"No. Not the painting. The jewel. It's the exact same ruby featured on the Comte's portrait at Tarantella."

"Is it?"

"You didn't notice?"

"To be honest, I've never really looked at Ferdinand's paintings. They are scary pictures."

"I'd agree with you there." Drago drained the glass a second time and placed it on the counter. "I've seen the painting online too when I was researching Sabatini and this fabulous yacht. *Diamantin*: the diamond. A bit cryptic, isn't it?"

She shrugged. For a moment, they both stared silently at the painting and its depiction of the ruby gemstone. Drago said abruptly: "What's the rest of the boat look like?"

Ariana shook a frustrated head. Drago went to the door beside the bar. It led to the ship's interior. He was in a small atrium with a wide square-spiral staircase in the centre and a small elevator inside the coil. A short corridor was lined with doors leading to washrooms, small lounges and offices. It ended in another set of doors. Beyond these Drago could make out the swimming deck, bathed in cool blue light. He came back to the atrium, where Ariana waited impatiently, smiled and went up the staircase. Gingerly, she followed. The next deck featured two spacious opulent dining rooms, one inside, one out. The interior room was all polished oak, chandeliers and a central marble fireplace, porphyry of course, its fake coals cold. Forward of the atrium was what Drago could only call an observation deck. An intimate lounge, its appointments were arranged facing the prow of the ship and the floor-to-ceiling windows were all retractable to allow fresh air to flow. Above the lounge was the bridge deck, scrupulously clean, jammed with an array of sophisticated ultra-modern navigation and engineering equipment which meant nothing to Drago. Too many digital screens. He couldn't even see a compass. A final tier of steps led to an isolated sundeck perched above the bridge. The only company for a sun worshipper was the radar column and satellite dishes.

Drago called for the lift.

"What are you doing now?" asked Ariana.

"I told you. I'm having a look at where you live."

"You are looking," she snorted, "but not for that."

"Let's just say I'm interested in Sabatini's undersea activities."

Ariana didn't say anything. They stepped into the elevator and in the filtered light Drago saw her face up close, past the bruising and the twitching smile and glimpsed a flicker of fear. She bit her lip. They stood in silence as the elevator descended below deck and came to a restful stop. The doors pinged open on another corridor with plenty of doors.

There were twelve guest rooms, each one comfortable and appointed in the same sanitary manner. The master suite occupied space in the bow. Ariana put a restraining hand on Drago's arm. It was too late to stop him. He opened the door and paused on the threshold. The unmistakeable tang of cigar snoke still hung in the air. He saw the enormous bed, immaculately made, the doors to the his-and-hers dressing rooms, the marble columns and lying on the smoked-glass-topped table the leather restraints, the choker, the ball gag, the sort of thing kinky people used in their love games. Beside the cuffs was the flogger, tasselled with long thick threads. Only at the end of the strips were stitched small steel bolas which would sting and score and bruise. Drago's eyes fixed hard on the weapon and thought about the bruises he'd seen on Ariana's body. He felt her hand pull at him again. Slowly, Drago shut the door, his anger rising, just as it had in the grotto.

Fourteen

Thieves

Simeon guided the speedster up to the pontoon. There was a battered little motorboat sitting in the next pen. His brow furrowed. Who was this, a thief? He started to worry. It hadn't been right to leave the yacht. Blaku hadn't been thinking straight. Too keen to show off his skills. And then he got himself shot. Silently, Simeon cursed.

    He looked behind him at the slumped unconscious figure. How the hell was he going to get him on deck? It didn't matter. Blaku wasn't going anywhere yet, not until whatever was happening above was resolved. Simeon's hand shook as he tied the lines and ascended the ladder. He wasn't used to this end of the business. He left it to the professionals. He was a look out, a carrier, an informer, a messenger, the cabin boy.

    Upstairs, all the lights were on and the saloon was as bright as day. The lounge doors were open. Swiftly, Simeon followed the route of the intruders: an open door to the lower levels. The elevator indicator displayed -2. The crew's quarters. Slower now, Simeon trod down the spiral staircase. He couldn't hear a sound. No, wait. There it was. A door opening or closing. Somewhere below. He descended to the next level, where the crew ate, slept, laundered and lived. The noise had come from where the galley was located. Simeon approached, wary of surprise. The kitchen lights hadn't been turned on, only the blue tinge of the security lamps breathed any life. Cupboard doors swung open where they'd not been properly sealed. That was odd. The chef knew better than that. At the far end the galley storeroom was ajar. Did he hear voices? Simeon breathed in slowly. Tension swept up his spine. His palms become suddenly greasy. Thieves always come at night, Blaku told him. So, it was true.

***

Ariana tried to stop him, but Jonathon behaved like a lunatic. He opened every door, looked into every crevasse and cupboard. She thanked God he'd not spent any time in the bedroom. Not because she had anything to hide, but because it wasn't where he ought to be. Jonathon was better than that, wasn't he? Looking at him now, she wondered. There was a controlled frenzy to what he did. Ever since he'd seen the painting and asked her about Il Papavero, he'd become determined, arrogant, careless. He'd rifled through the crew quarters, left some of the cabins in a mess, which she tried to tidy, and then started on the kitchen. When he found the storeroom, Ariana grabbed at his shoulder, almost pulling the jacket from his back.

"What's the matter?" he said.

"Don't"

"Why not?"

She couldn't answer.

"Let's have a little look, shall we?"

Ariana took her hand away and trembled as Jonathon opened the pantry door. His hand searched for the light switch. When he found it, she bit her lip. Jonathon entered, his eyes scanning the racks of expensive, exclusive provisions. He selected a caviar jar, read the label and put it back; peered at the water butt with the live Brittany lobsters; stroked the vacuum sealed Wagu ribeye steaks. He picked his way carefully through the shelves until he reached the pile of sacks at the very end of the store.

"How long do you stay at sea?" he asked.

"I don't know," she answered, nerves cracking at her throat. "A month, maybe two."

"You eat much rice?"

"Sometimes."

Her voice wavered. She couldn't help it.

"Ariana, you told me Sabatini's a gangster. You're very good at saying what you want me to hear. How about telling me something you want to keep a secret?"

"I don't know what you mean."

"Yes, you do."

She bit her lip again and he saw it.

"You have a gambler's tell, Ariana. You've got to stop biting your lip."

Jonathon patted one of the sacks of rice. She knew what he was going to do and knew she ought to stop him, or at least try, but the determination etched on his face hadn't altered. He was as controlled now as Sabatini would be. It both repelled and fascinated her. Not how it had with Marcelo, when money and riches had swayed her and blinded her to his wrath, but in an altogether more potent combination: righteous anger and a sombre, settled retribution. He was doing this because of Madeleine and the accident. He was doing this for some crazy sense of Biblical justice. An eye for an eye. She ought to stop him. It would end in people getting hurt. Probably Jonathon. It was too late. He was already lifting the first 25kg sack, feeling its weight, the way the rice rippled and bunched at one end. He dropped it on the floor and picked up the next one.

"No chef needs a hundred sacks of rice," declared Jonathon. "Not for a month."

Six sacks down, he stopped. The contents were no longer moving. They were jammed solid. Whatever was inside had compressed by the weight of the sacks above it, but the ten packages were still clearly defined. Jonathon dug his fingers through the thick paper sacking, split it and yanked out a parcel. He held out the canvas brick for her inspection.

"Care to tell me what's in it, Ariana?"

She shook her head.

"It's heroin, isn't it?"

She still couldn't answer. Her tongue had ceased to function properly.

"Are you going to tell me Sabatini never mentioned this?"

She half-nodded, half-shook her head and backed away towards the door, shaking. It was a shock and a relief at once.

"Of course I know it," she stammered. "It wasn't hard to discover. All his men talked of it. They tried to hide it from me at first, but I heard them, more than once. Even the crew discussed it. When I challenged him, Marcelo bragged about it. He said now I knew, it would be even harder for me to leave him. I realised some of the people he entertains at his mansion or here on the yacht were suppliers and distributors. I've met them all, Jonathon. If I leave, it won't be just Marcelo looking for me."

"Alright," said Jonathon, although he didn't concede any ground. "That explains why you're so reluctant to leave him. Now, tell me, what is this stuff?"

"Afghan heroin," she explained. "They bring it by donkey train from the Nimruz mountains and smuggle it across the border at Gushgy in Turkmenistan. We visited once; that's how I know. The mayor explained it all to me. I danced with him. Marcelo uses me for things like that. I soften his hard edges, you understand. They tell me things they shouldn't and I tell Marcelo. The mayor was good to me. He gave me a mink coat. But he's a corrupt man who wants to make as much money as he can make before he dies or gets thrown out of office. Marcelo offered him a half-percentage point for every kilo allowed safe passage through the border zone. The mayor did better than that: he allowed Marcelo access to the domestic freight terminal. For shipping rice, of course."

Ariana was in full flow now. It felt good to tell someone what she knew. The weight was lifting. The recipient of her confession was listening closely, his expression softening.

"The planes can't make the journey all the way to Albania, so Marcelo has them stop off at this place called Mary. An ancient town. They don't ask questions there. They only want the money. Marcelo's lieutenants feather the pockets of the officials. He's got his own men at the airport. They log every flight as a mercy mission delivering Afghan rice to the Albanian poor. Of course, fifty percent of the shipment is genuine rice, from the Turkmens, in case anyone asks."

Jonathon patted the sacks with a shake of his head.

"Once in Albania, the big sacks are sifted, the drug packages unpacked and resealed. They're stored in huge warehouse in Durres, waiting for distribution. The police don't ever inspect it. Marcelo has them paid up."

"A tight operation," commented Jonathon. "Do all the drugs come over the Adriatic?"

"No. I mean, I don't think so. There is too much for Marcelo's yacht."

"Then what's he trying to do?"

"I don't know exactly. He's trying to create a new market. It is hard, he says. Marcelo told his suppliers the Italian Mafia have the business sown up. That's true, I think. He's still trying to breakthrough. He's been laying the groundwork for two years."

"And has an accomplice in the Comte."

"I'm not sure the Comte knows."

"Well, someone at Tarantella does," said Jonathon tersely. "It doesn't really matter who. However you dress it, you're still sleeping with a man whose primary business is shoving heroin into the arms and minds of addicts."

Ariana opened her mouth to say something, yet not entirely sure what: some apology, a defence, a justification. It all seemed so weak now. A sound came, but not from her mouth, from outside. It wasn't a word. It was a metallic clang, like a saucepan falling from its hook.

Jonathon's eyes swept over her shoulder. Ariana stepped back into the galley, pulling the door to. At first she didn't recognise the figure pressed against the worktop. The shadows hid his face. The figure spoke, in Albanian.

"Miss Ariana!"

"Simeon! What are you doing?"

"I thought you were a thief."

"Where is everyone? The yacht is empty."

Ariana thought the young man looked relieved. He must be scared. He'd not been with the crew long. He was hardly even a proper sailor. Marcelo employed him and another young man as well as the female cook to ensure the crew didn't look too intimidating, too rough, too much like modern-day pirates. They brought a sheath of respectability to proceedings, both on board and on shore, without it there would be more than the usual insignificant questions.

Simeon didn't answer her. Instead, he grabbed her hand.

"Quick, Miss! Upstairs! In a boat. Blaku is hurt. Come quickly!"

"What?"

"Blaku!"

She didn't fully understand, but the young man's urgency made her leave the awkward interrogation with Jonathon and follow Simeon back up the spiral staircase, through the lounge and to the stern rail. Below her lay the soulless sea, two motorboats and, in the seat of one, Blaku's motionless body.

"How do we get him up?" asked Simeon.

"He needs a doctor," she protested.

"He won't go."

"Why not?"

"He has something for the Krye."

"He can give it to me. He must see a doctor."

She descended the ladder. Simeon was even more worried than before. The mistress wasn't part of the Banda Family. She was only the Krye's woman. She shouldn't be giving orders. Agitated, Simeon glanced at Blaku's motionless form and surrendered his will. It wasn't worth arguing: he was glad she was making the decisions.

There was blood all over the boat. Even in the dim shadow of the stern, Blaku looked as if death had already seized him. It was only the slight movement of his chest which told Ariana he was alive. Blaku's hands were clutching a bulging leather holdall to his stomach. Ariana tried to prise it loose, but his fingers coiled even tighter. Blaku stared directly at her and mouthed a word, which she thought was "No."

Men. Stubborn idiots. As if it wasn't bad enough having Jonathon on board, now this. Ariana shook her head, tried to break Blaku's grip and failed.

"Sheets," she said suddenly. "We'll lift him. Can you open the bay doors?"

"Probably."

"Come on."

Ariana climbed the ladder, Simeon followed and sprinted back inside and downstairs. She tore into one of the guest suites and ripped the clean, pressed linen from the mattress. Half of her mind wondered what Jonathon was doing. She couldn't worry about that. Ariana hurried to the rear of the passage. A second set of stairs led over the engine room to the back of the ship and the entrance to the pontoon. Simeon was there, spinning the watertight lock.

"We'll wrap him in this," she panted. "I'll help you."

The doors sprung slowly open. Ariana stepped onto the jetty and tossed Simeon the sheet. "Get it under his shoulders," she ordered.

Blaku was a heavy man and they struggled to manoeuvre the sheet beneath his draining body. Once done, they tied the corners together and used them as handles. Blaku's fingers clung to the leather pouch. Ariana took the feet end and between them they dragged Blaku up out of the boat and along the jetty.

"Through the engine room," she instructed. "Take him to the crew canteen."

They negotiated the path through the second sealed door and past the two big Deutz turbines. The engine room door wasn't locked and led directly to the crew quarters. They had a small shared canteen and galley between their cabins. Ariana hadn't often been in here. It stank of cigarettes and men. She never asked the cook how she coped with the smell. They half-carried, half-dragged Blaku to the comfy settee and laid him on it. The white sheet was soiled in a vivid sticky crimson. The steward's head flopped. The eyes glazed over, dull and lifeless. A tiny groan seeped between his lips accompanied by a bubble of air. His fingers slipped from the holdall.

Ariana knelt beside him and took it, surprised at its weight. Blaku's head nodded once. Blood spurted from his mouth in a sudden belch. The body wrestled with life for a few more seconds and then the head settled back and everything was still.

With a cry, Simeon retreated to the table and leant against it, his hands going to his face to hide the sobs. Ariana placed an arm about his shoulders. Whatever was happening here was a result of Marcelo's orders. Simeon knew that, even if the result appalled him. She'd seen this before, once or twice, when terrible things had occurred, when the guards had stepped in to protect the Krye, when the opposition tried to fight back. The sight of death shocked her less and less; it was the dying which upset. Yet once it was done, death no longer held a sting. It was simply one of fate's many faces. As she held the young man, Ariana became aware someone was watching.

Drago took in the scene quickly. A frightened young man, crying. Ariana consoling him, hands covered in gunk. The dead body. The blood. The kit bag lying abandoned on the floor. He walked straight to it and opened the buckles. He peered inside and saw an array of tools, such as knives, jemmies, gloves, goggles, a stethoscope and a fob rammed with keys. There were also several cloth pouches.

Drago reached in, took one and shook it. There was a delightful tickling sound. He opened it and pulled out a few of the small white envelopes. He noted the braille insignia, opened one and saw it contained a small cut diamond. So did a second and a third. He let out a low whistle. Drago returned to the kit bag and extracted what had caught his eye first: a tied leather gourd. He opened the drawstrings and pulled out a huge diamond, red like the blood which suddenly seemed to be everywhere and flashing fantastically real in the stained artificial light, as if just by its appearance the ruby could promise life and death and riches. It sat in a golden hawk's claw brooch.

Ariana stared at him. So did Simeon.

"Il Papavero," whispered Ariana.

"Yes," said Drago.

"Who, who are you?" said the young man in Albanian.

"This is Jonathon."

"Who?"

Ariana soothed his arm. The young man wiped the tears angrily from his eyes. Drago could sense the questions forming in the man's mind. He could see tension and worry etched across his face. This wasn't one of the tough nuts who attended the charity dance. He was younger, less capable, out of his depth, which was presumably why he was usually left on board. But not tonight. And now he'd seen death, diamonds and strangers his mind was working too fast for its own good. Drago sensed trouble coming, if not now, later. Try being nonchalant, Jon.

"Is this Blaku?" Drago asked.

"He's dead," said Ariana.

"Poor bastard. The bullet must have disintegrated on impact. A dum-dum round. It probably busted his shoulder and punctured a lung. I'm surprised he lasted as long as he did, assuming he was shot at the mansion."

"What mansion?"

"Tarantella. Where he stole this."

Drago held up the diamond again. He was watching the young man who appeared more and more tense. Slowly Drago replaced the jewel back in the leather bag.

Simeon didn't understand who this man was. He recognised

some words of English. There had been some talk among the crew of an Englishman. He'd caused trouble on shore. Trouble for Miss Ariana. What was he doing here? How did he know about the diamond? The Krye would want to know. Whoever this man was, he had to be stopped. Blaku was dead. It was his turn to take charge, to rectify a terrible night. Simeon wasn't sure if he moved in fear or in anger, but he moved fast and desperately, pushing Miss Ariana aside and lunging across the room towards the stranger.

Immediately Drago dropped his shoulder. Simeon clutched at air. Drago's right hand was already out of the leather holdall, the thief's jemmy firm in his grasp. As Simeon passed, Drago stuck out a foot. Simeon sprawled towards the floor and Drago brought the steel bar crashing down on his neck. Ariana squealed. The body twitched and moaned. Drago hit him again on the skull. Stillness. Silence.

"You killed him!" Ariana gasped.

Quickly Drago checked the young man's pulse.

"Thankfully, no, but he'll need stiches and some aspirin." He busied himself putting Simeon into the recovery position. "Who is he?"

"Just a crew member. He's new. Why did he attack you?"

"Why not? I shouldn't be here, remember?"

"Oh God!"

"Looks like we're both in trouble now."

The realisation seemed to hit her. She shivered, suddenly in shock. Drago thought she might faint, took her to a seat and got her a glass of water. He rifled through the kit bag again. In addition to the big red diamond, there were four more cloth bags. He placed them on the table. The big red diamond he twirled it on his palm.

"I don't think this is going to help matters, do you?"

Ariana shook her head.

"I didn't know he had plans to steal it, Jonathon. He doesn't tell me everything, you know. Blaku, the steward, he's a thief, a proper one, a professional, at least he was before Marcelo employed him. He could steal it."

"Someone must have caught him in the act."

"Who?"

"The Comte?"

"He's blind, Jonathon."

"It hardly matters. What are we going to do with this?"

"God knows. It's bad you being here like this, seeing all this. If it was only Blaku, I'd maybe get away with it, but Simeon too. Do you know what Marcelo will do? He was bad after the dance. This will be –"

She was panicking. Drago detected it in her urgent, rambling sentences. He knelt in front of her, put a hand lightly over hers.

"Come with me," he said. "Now."

Ariana stared at him.

"Bastard," she said, but she said it at a whisper and without malice. It was a fact and she presented it plainly. "You are both bastards."

"That's not fair, Ariana." Drago would not be wavered. He squeezed her hand. "It's not about coming with me. It's about not living with Sabatini. You said you wanted to run away. Now's your chance. Whatever's happened, it's completely fucked up. Me being here just adds more fuel to a bad fire. We're both better off escaping."

"He won't let me go."

"He'll have to."

"Why would he? He never has before."

"Because he's plotting something big, like you said." Drago considered the statement for a moment. "A big plan, big riches, wealth, position, power, all of it built on narcotics. You aren't part of that plan. You're just his window dressing. People look at you and they forget the kind of man he is. Sabatini won't change. He'll always be fighting, grasping, winning, everything for his benefit."

"What about the Foundation? The children?"

"He's forming allies, Ariana. It's a front. A distraction. Politicians do it all the time. He's just taking their lead."

"I don't understand."

"He's lying to you, Ariana. He always has been. You know it. I think you've always known it."

Briefly, Drago thought she smiled, the sallow one permanently tinged with sadness. She lifted the diamond out of Drago's palm. It flashed a quick ochre shadow across her face. "Where does this fit in?"

"Vanity." Drago paused a few seconds. "Fuck it. I don't know. I don't really care. Let's take it. We can return it. It doesn't matter. We've got to get out of here."

"Do you think we can do it?"

"I do."

"It won't be pleasant."

"If there was any other way, I'd take it. Come on."

"No."

It was said with unexpected calm assurance as if a decision had been made and resignation was all that lingered. Her voice sounded frozen. The passion seemed to have drained from her since those hours at the Siren's Grotto. The face of a joyful woman had vanished. It's replacement was only the ghost of beauty. This was a huge decision for her, one she ought never to make in a moment of crisis. He had pushed too hard. Even if their friendship remained nothing more than that, she surely had to escape the life she was leading, one which failed to make her happy and kept her embroiled in a gangster's empire of deceit, death and decay.

"Why?" he asked quietly.

"I have a better idea. You can get away. You are a journalist. You have contacts, don't you, people you can talk to about Marcelo? You have the evidence. You can expose them."

"What about you, Ariana?" he said, desperation rising in his throat.

"Jonathon."

She held his hands in hers. Her eyes blinked. She bit her lip. He understood. He knew the decision she had taken: to save him.

The silence was broken by the buzz of the ship-to-shore radio, an extension of which was located in a niche near the canteen's doorway. A scratchy voice demanded an answer.

"Marcelo's coming!" Ariana hissed.

"Shit!"

She ran into one of the crew cabins, stared out the porthole. "He'll be here in a few minutes. I can see the forward light on the speedboat."

"I can't take the boat. He'll see me."

"I'll explain it." She was back with him, suddenly all orders and hustle. "Come! Quickly! You have to tie me up."

She led him back to the master suite.

"Use these."

Drago squirmed at the array of bedroom paraphernalia. He hesitated.

"Put the gag in my mouth, use the cuffs."

"What about your feet?"

"Tear my blouse. Hurry."

He did as he was told. Before Drago placed the ball gag over her head she said: "Go out past the swimming pool. Use the bow anchor line. You can reach it if you hang over the rail."

"Ariana, are you sure about this? There's still time for both of us to make it."

"Wait. My dressing room, on the left. There's a waterproof bag. I hang it on the rail. It's got a pink zip; you see it?"

Drago went to it. It was big enough for wallets and phones and blood red diamonds. He dropped his valuables into it, including the beautiful gemstone. As an afterthought, he scattered the contents of Blaku's bag onto the floor, knocked over a chair, pulled the sheets from the bed and smashed a glass ornament. Satisfied, he returned to Ariana.

"What will you do?" he asked as he slipped the gag over her head.

"Act." He looked incredulous and she almost laughed. "Don't worry, they teach you that in dance school too."

Drago kissed her quickly, dispassionately, and shoved the ball between her lips, drawing the gag tight. Finally, abruptly, he pushed her over. She fell in an ungainly heap. There was a muffled squeal. He refused to smile, swallowed hard and sprinted for the door.

The rumble of the motor launch was audible as he tore up the stairs. They must be getting close. Drago went down the corridor and outside onto the forward sun deck. He kept low. At the front rail he could make out the anchor chain. Through a gap in the rail, he saw the pilot boat heading for the stern. They would have difficulty docking. Both pens were occupied. That would be in his favour. He watched and listened. As soon as the headlights vanished behind *Diamantin* and the engine changed tone, skidding to neutral, Drago stood up and swung his legs over the rail. The wind was unexpectedly strong. Heavy clouds were rolling across the moon. It might be rain. Below him, the sea was even more choppy than earlier. The surf slapped against the hull, the waves more menacing by the second.

The anchor chain was a metre or so lower than the deck and he had to stretch precariously to get a hand on it. Once done, he allowed his legs to drop and his body was suddenly hanging in mid-air. His fingers became slicked with the salty grime crusted on the links. Several times they slipped on the fat iron rings. He descended hand over hand until his body was almost wholly in the sea. Then he let go.

Immediately a wave crashed over him. He took on water. The salt tore at his throat. Hell. This was madness. Slowly, Drago struck out from the yacht, trusting that whatever was happening, was happening aft. His intent was to get as much distance as he could from *Diamantin* before cutting towards land.

Another wave swamped him. The swim became even harder than he anticipated. The wind was strong, the waves regular and heavy. He'd hardly gone more than thirty metres before he realised his clothes were dragging him down. Drago shrugged everything off except his boxers and the watertight bag. Suddenly its weight, its value, its significance, its theft seemed so much heavier than clothes.

Fifteen

Into the Salentine

There was plenty of light to guide him. Otranto seemed never to sleep. The promenade, the restaurants, the castle fortifications, the winking lighthouses, the harbour, all alive, a misty skyline glow diffused by the salt water that racked his eyes. Like a moth, Drago headed toward the brightest light: the Atlantis Club. The party was in full swing on the pontoons. The sounds of trashy Euro-pop filtered across the expanse of dark sea, the drum and bass percussion beating in time to the waves lapping at his ears.

Drago swam with a straggling, unsteady speed. A chopping breeze forced the currents south. Breakers crashed across his path. Soon his arms ached with the effort. His legs grew tired. His belly groaned. Several times a huge wave bounced over him and he tasted the sea, spat out the brine in a fury, his throat complaining as the spiteful water gripped. Halfway, he paused, trod water and looked back. *Diamantin* was a luminous white whale basking under the moonlight. Drago's stomach curled anew thinking of Ariana and how she might explain what had happened on board and what punishment might be dealt. He put the thought aside. There was nothing he could do except swim. She'd given him the opportunity to escape and he mustn't waste it.

When Drago's feet touched the shore, he thanked God for those hours of toil at the gym. He shook off the wet and stepped warily to avoid the sharpest rocks. Clumsily he mounted the weather boards which marked the extremes of Atlantis. Further on stood the big shack, its cocktail bar and dancefloor humming with activity. Crowds young and old lined the stretch, milling aimlessly, drinking and dancing. The music wafted with the sea salt scent of the surf. Drago felt exposed in his underclothes, but no one paid him any attention. Still dripping, he perched on a chair at the extremes of the pontoon and dug in the bag for his mobile. It was bone dry and only took a moment to detect a signal. He dialled Vicino's.

"Paulo?"

"Oh, God, what now?"

It was said in Italian. Drago got the general gist.

"Can you come and pick me up? I'm in a spot of bother."

He didn't explain much. Paulo reluctantly agreed to drive out and fetch him. Drago made his way gingerly towards the entrance, hugging the edge of the crowd. A clutch of scantily-clad made-up girls giggled at his state of undress and called out. He forced a smile, stole a beer from a busy table and toasted their good looks. There was an abandoned shirt lying over the back of a chair. The young couple necking on the next seat didn't notice Drago pick it up. It was a girl's floral blouse. He slipped it on, ducked under the barriers and headed for the exit and the car park. He waited ten minutes, drying in the warm breeze and slugging the beer as he watched the sparkling yacht and felt guilt seize him over and over. Drago exhaled a grunt of acceptance, necked the lager and tossed the bottle into the hedge where it nestled with all the other discarded trash. Forget her, Jon. You've work to do.

The green Maserati Spyder, top up, swung down the road and came to halt. Paulo greeted him with an amused grin.

"What happened to you?"

"I went swimming."

"You like swimming after midnight?"

"Less crowds," said Drago and opened the passenger door.

"You're still wet."

Drago ignored the comment and got in.

"Alright," sighed Paulo, "where to?"

"Villa Caprese."

"Where's your car?"

"I left it at the Siren's Grotto."

"San Foca? That's a long swim."

"And an expensive one. I lost all my clothes."

"You joke, yes?"

"Yes. I came from the *Diamantin*."

"The yacht?" asked Paulo. "What about the girl?"

"I had to leave quickly. Sabatini was coming back."

"I see. What's in the bag?"

Drago didn't want to show him, so he said nothing. After a second's pause, Paulo slipped the car into gear and drove away from the beach, back over the gully and circled the town. He turned into the drive of the Villa Caprese and stopped by the front door, engine humming. Drago accompanied it with a resigned sigh.

"I need something else," he said. "Your car."

"What?"

The poor man looked incredulous. Paulo's fingers curled automatically, possessively around the steering wheel. "Why?"

"There was an incident. A robbery. Someone was killed."

"Holy Mother!"

"His corpse is on the yacht."

They sat in silence for a minute, then Paulo said: "She's not worth it, Jon. No woman is worth that much trouble. Leave her alone."

"I can't do that. Anyway, it's more than her, at least it is now. You see, I seem to have become an accessory to burglary."

"That will only cause you more trouble."

"Probably," Drago said thoughtfully. "I need to take that chance. You see, I have a way out, for both of us, her and me: a bargaining tool."

"Blackmail?"

"If you like."

"But why isn't she with you now?"

"She's given me time to escape. A flimsy alibi. Anyway, they'd find us immediately if she came with me. Ariana's too well known."

Paulo nodded.

"Where will you go, Jon?"

"North," he said, "somewhere north."

"Good. There is more space in the north."

Paulo didn't sound convincing.

"So," started Drago, "the car?"

Paulo muttered something low in Italian. It could have been a curse, Drago couldn't tell. It didn't sound complimentary and was exemplified by much head shaking. The fingers twitched on the wheel.

"I can't."

Drago must have looked disappointed because his friend added, as if to justify his reply: "You know she's the best car in the Salentine. I can't lose her."

"I know that, Paulo, but my car's in San Foca. And if I had it, they'd probably track down a rented Fiat Panda easily enough."

"You'll be spotted in this too."

"But I won't be recognised," Drago argued. "People will think it's you. Look, I just want to drive north. Bari, maybe. I'm not going anywhere else."

"You promise to take care of her?"

"Like I do all my favourite girls."

"You make a joke out of something serious. How does this benefit me?"

"Because I have something Sabatini wants and there will be a hefty reward for its return."

Drago cautiously opened the zip on the bag and showed Paulo the contents. Even under the porch lamp the Italian could see the magnificence of the gemstone. His face lit up for a second. It darkened just as fast.

"This is not good. What is it?"

"They call it Il Papavero. In Albania it's known as the Blood Stone Poppy, one of the world's rarest diamonds. It used to sit in the sceptre of the Imperial Family, you know King Zog and all that."

"I am not a history man," Paulo shrugged, "nor am I an artist, but I know great beauty when I see it."

His fingers traced the outline of the stone exactly how they'd stroked the steering wheel, gently, soothing, a loving caress. When the fingers withdrew, Drago saw the hand was trembling. The precious stone had the same effect on everyone. He closed the bag.

"You're right," he said. "It's supposed to have been lost for centuries, but it appears to have turned up in sunny Italy."

"Where?"

"Tarantella. It's the Comte's."

"No!"

"That blind man isn't half as much of a fool as everyone takes him for. He's kept this hidden for decades. Until Sabatini stole it. I'm fairly certain the Comte will want it back." Drago placed a hand on Paulo's shoulder. The man's brown eyes flickered a little. "Or if he doesn't, the rightful owners in the rightful country at least. It'll fetch enough to buy twenty Maseratis."

"Is this your plan?"

"Something like it," answered Drago. "I need to lie low for a few days. Let everything calm down."

Paulo switched off the bubbling engine and with a movement suggesting reluctance, he held out the key. Drago grasped the nervous outstretched palm and swiped the little slice of metal.

"Thanks, Paulo."

Drago made to go, but Paulo stopped him with a soft restraining hand.

"Be careful with her, won't you, Jon."

"I promise."

They got out and stood looking at what bound them. They shook hands; a feeble gesture. Drago wanted to embrace him, but his state of undress made him self-conscious. He was glad when Paulo moved to run a hand across the warm bonnet.

"You promise?" he said. "Take care of her, yes?"

"Yes. I owe you, Paulo."

"That you do."

Paulo circled the car, his expression tipping towards sadness, before he retreated on foot down the hill without as much as a glance. Maybe, thought Drago, his mind was full of red diamonds and new Maseratis.

He went inside, took a shower and put on clean togs. Drago trained his binoculars on the yacht. It was lit like a beacon. He could see people moving inside the lounge and along the deck. There was no sign of Ariana or Sabatini. No sign of a hospital boat. All three speedboats were strapped to the rear jetty. Drago grimaced at the sterile edifice, the fey cleanliness, that steely, marbly sheen, all for exhibition and show, to hide what was really happening in the murky depths, not in the sea or in the yacht, but in the soul of its owner.

He shut the bad thoughts away and started to pack. He was finished within ten minutes, leaving the dirty items behind to make it look as if he planned a quick return. As an afterthought he left plenty of Sabatini's Euro's in the wardrobe, still wrapped in the canvas bag. He shoved more than enough for a few days in his jacket pockets. He wouldn't be using charge cards on this trip. Then it was lock up and back to the convertible.

Drago immediately put the top down. He tested the pedals and the gear shift and made certain he was happy with the seat position and the mirror alignment. Sitting in the driver's chair felt intoxicating. Despite the events of the evening, the long hard slog through the sea, the fear which hung over him, this was new, exciting, invigorating. He felt in control again. He released the handbrake and slipped the car into first. The Maserati eased up the rambling street. The engine, tuned to perfection, purred rather than growled. Drago headed for the coastal road. The chafe air whipped over the windshield as he hit sixty.

The Spyder drove beautifully. It clung to the tarmac, taking corners with speed and comfort, the 24-valve engine responding to every gear change with nothing more than a mechanical sigh. He travelled swiftly, despite not taking the obvious route. There was hardly another car. There was a hardly a light. Hillside villages clutched to their lonely domestic shelter, staring blankly at the close blackness of the Adriatic, their mustard colour existence only visible in the Maserati's front beam. After forty miles of dark, dramatic coves and silent lives, Drago swung inland and circled Brindisi.

He continued north, competing for speed with night trains and heavy goods' lorries. Occasionally, he glimpsed a new set of headlights behind him, but the snaking suspicion of fear didn't haunt his rear-view mirror. The twin eyes came and then they went, replaced a few miles further on only to vanish once more. Towns came and went too: Ostuni, Fasano, Conversano. Eventually at something like four in the morning, the highways emerged from the night and street lamps became their watchmen. There were more cars now, solid forms among ghostly atmospheres. As he turned towards Bari, the earliest tips of an orange dawn were piercing the clouds in front of him.

Drago pulled up outside the Moderno. He was lucky. They had a room. He paid in cash for five nights. The proprietor had seen him arrive and he enthused about the Spyder, said it must be the most beautiful car in the Terra Di Bari. He couldn't have been happier to have the owner of such a car stay at his hotel. Cheerfully keeping up the pretence, Drago asked for coins to pay the parking meter and went to collect his luggage.

Once alone, he threw the case on a chair beside the bed and took another shower. It was a small, spartan room. This wasn't low budget: it was no budget. Drago didn't care. He was tired and hungry. He pulled on a few clothes and returned to the lobby, asking after some food. The proprietor apologised. There was nowhere open at this hour. However, could Signor wait? The portly man poured Drago a black coffee from the filter jug and promptly disappeared for several minutes. When he returned, he carried a tray on which he'd placed two plates each covered by a tatty white napkin. A small decanter of red wine and a glass sat beside them.

"Prego, Signor."

"Ah, prego, si, grazie."

"It is nothing for you, Signor."

It was the Maserati's doing. There was wood-baked friselli on one plate and on the other, smothered in virgin oil, cuts of air dried ham, three cheeses, sliced preserved pepper and olives. Drago ate in his room, slowly, the oil dribbling down his chin. His mind was still whirling. Why was this diamond so important? He took out his mobile, grateful he had a local Wi-Fi connection, and searched for 'Blood Stone Poppy' and 'Il Papavero.' The usual mixture of nonsense results accompanied the first page, the second mostly wanted to talk about real poppies. Drago tapped in 'red diamonds' and found his way to De Beer's *How to Recognise Diamonds* information pages.

Red diamonds were pure carbon, just like white gemstones. An extremely rare deformity in the atomic structure had the side effect of colourising the stone with a deep red pigment. The stronger the hue, the greater the value. Apparently, they showed up best by candlelight. Curious, Drago took out the diamond, lifted it and flicked on his Ronson lighter. He studied the result for a few seconds, detected not the slightest change in the gorgeous crimson tones and tossed the bauble on the bed. The values were certainly eye-catching. Rough estimates suggested over $100,000 for a mere fifth of a carat. Christ, and one carat weighs the equivalent of a five pound note. The diamond he was carrying was heavier than a golf ball, a phenomenal weight. Examples of recent sales, like the Moussaieff Diamond, scored in excess of eight million dollars. At the bottom of the page was a little section about lost or mythologised gems and there he saw it: the Blood Stone Diamond, not a poppy as he'd constantly been told, yet definitely Skanderbeg's great jewel from Ethiopia. The article itself listed it as a myth because there was little tangible evidence of it ever existing. Suddenly reverential, Drago picked the diamond off the bed sheets and placed it back in its bag. This thing was immeasurable.

"Not a bloody legend now, are you?"

Aware of the true financial value of the gem, or at the very least a wild estimate – fifteen, he thought, maybe twenty million – Drago's concern stretched. Sabatini couldn't report it missing to the police. Nor, Drago suspected, could the Comte. Both parties would need to take other measures. And it wouldn't take them long. He thought about Ariana. She could have come with him, but had ordered him to go and he'd obeyed. That had become a dutiful recent habit between him and women and not a good habit. Ariana's lies wouldn't last. Simeon was the problem. His story wouldn't match hers. The cracks had probably opened already. Was this jewel of millions really worth a woman's tears?

Drago suddenly resented the trouble the jewel was causing. He'd do well to be rid of it, twenty million dollars or not. Angry now, he scooped the last of the oil onto the bread and took a final mouthful of wine.

Let's get rid of it, he thought, an idea forming. Whatever he did, there was little time, only the minimum of hours it took to drive from Otranto to Bari. Drago set his mobile's alarm for three hours' hence and collapsed fully dressed on the creaking bed.

When he woke it was almost nine. The alarm hadn't pinged. He'd woken before it buzzed. The room was already stifling. Drago slipped on his shoes and went out. Earlier, he'd spied a small supermarket-type shop down the street. Inside, he found and bought wrapping paper, parcel tape and for good measure a copy of *Coriella della Sera*. Back in his room, Drago opened the waterproof bag and gazed at the deep crimson stone. Carefully, he took it out, wrapped it, refolded it into the bag and wrapped that, tying it stiff with the tape. The package looked amateurish, so he undid it all, took out the box for his Canon A2300 camera and emptied the contents. He stripped off the zip bag, which was too bulky, and used more newspaper on the stone. When he placed it in the box it looked as snug as it did in his palm. Drago stuffed the loose space with spare socks before tightly wrapping the box with tape. He tore a sheet of paper from his notebook, the one crammed full of recipe tips he reckoned he'd never use and wrote out one of the few addresses he knew by heart. Finally, he attached the makeshift label.

Drago didn't ask the receptionist where the post office was. Instead, he headed into the morning sun, walked three blocks and asked a stranger. The directions were appalling. He eventually arrived in an uncomfortable sweat and had to wait in a disorderly, hot queue. Fifteen minutes later, he was paying for a registered mail delivery up to the value of a digital camera.

When he returned to the hotel, Drago showered again, spread his toiletries around the bathroom and changed his clothes, leaving the ones from yesterday on the bed. He picked up only the car keys, his passport, mobile, wallet and spare money. He departed without checking out. Drago took the Maserati across country before doubling back down the SS7, past those old Bourbon towns and through the sunny plains of Murgia, where everyone made wine and ceramics and dozed in the heat. He pressed hard on the accelerator, ignored the speed limits, overtook rashly, killing the engine, and turned the stereo up to maximum, anything to keep his mind occupied, anything to stop thinking of Ariana. Drago had never intended to stay in the north. Sabatini's brute menace conjured sickening thoughts. The bastard would extract confessions and information from Ariana and then, one way or another, the enemy would be onto him. He could only hope Sabatini didn't damage her more than he already had. It was enough to have Madeleine on his conscience without adding to the rising bile. Yet Ariana had told him to go. She had wanted him out of her way, out of her own conscience and in doing so she had walked into a trap, one from which there could be no easy escape.

Drago stopped at a lonely petrol station, using cash to prepay for fuel, and went into the little shop adjacent to buy two litres of water for his parched throat. There was a copy of *Mezzogiorno* on the newspaper rack. Drago scanned through the pages, looking for any mention of Tarantella or a 'furto' – a burglary. Nothing. He paid and returned to the sports car. A third of the bottle had been drunk before he got there. It was baking. Nonetheless he kept the top down, undid his shirt almost to the navel and set off once more, sunglasses down, eyes on the road and the mirrors, driving almost on autopilot, his mind occupied with Ariana, with Sabatini, with jewels, heroin, money and death.

***

For hours Ariana had sobbed, trying to regain composure, trying to focus on anything other than the immediate future. She'd made a hideous mistake staying onboard *Diamantin*. For perhaps the first time, she realised whatever she wanted was never meant to be: happiness, a child, a better life, one without guilt and blame.

She'd never known there was CCTV. She knew about the security alarm and cameras the crew switched on when the yacht was empty. But she'd never seen inside the locked cabinets at the back of Sabatini's study. When he was alone in the office, the door was always locked and her presence unrequired. It was his domain and she rarely visited it.

After they untied her, the men brought her straight to it. There was no 'Miss Ariana' now. They called her 'bitch' and 'whore.' As she entered, Simeon was leaving. He looked frightened, but relieved. Her heart beat faster. Grigori pushed her inside the room, his big hands on her wrists, bending them into the small of her back.

Sabatini was puffing contentedly on a cigar. On the desk top were scattered a multitude of diamonds. He playfully tossed one in his hand.

"Blaku was always a thief," he said genially. "He just couldn't resist it."

"Leopards don't change spots," said Grigori.

"Indeed not."

Sabatini held up the diamond for a moment, stared through it and past it and directly at Ariana.

"Shut the door."

Captain Belzac obeyed and returned to his position to one side of the room, sharp to attention, as he always was. Sabatini flicked away some ash, dropped the diamond with the others and sat down in the big leather swivel chair. The cupboard doors were open and the bank of monitors visible, each one showing a view of *Diamantin*'s interior or exterior, the rooms and corridors. Sabatini said nothing. He picked up the remote and replayed the whole of the evening, switching from camera to camera when necessary, fast forwarding, pausing and rewinding. Occasionally, he would zoom in on something that interested him. He didn't look at her once. Grigori didn't alter his grip. Only footage of the brief fight with Simeon made him tense. She winced as his fingers twisted tighter.

When the recording finished and the cigar had burnt to almost nothing, Sabatini stubbed out the Cohiba and spun the chair so it returned to face the big desk. He folded his hands neatly in front of him, fingers interlocked, avoiding the stones, and stared at his woman.

Her bruised eye was mocking him, as if whatever respect he had punched into her had been repulsed by contempt. Ariana occupied a haughty, chiselled air. He recognised the look. A defence mechanism. She'd used it when they first met, he remembered, after she danced the beautiful rhumba at the Illyria Ballroom. It fascinated him then. He'd wanted to tear down the wall which hid her true likeness. That look, one he only saw when she danced, seductive, superior, obscure and haunting; that look, the one he'd become foolishly besotted with for seven years. He thought he'd struck it out of her. Leopards never change spots, they say. Nor do women, he concluded.

Sabatini felt revulsion. It had first happened in the early months of their partnership. She had said something to displease him. He couldn't remember the incident, something to do with her dance partner, a trifling matter that should not have concerned him. Yet the suggestion another man took precedence over him and the Banda Family came like an insult. The Banda Family had become the most important thing in his life, the most powerful entity and she must understand that. He remembered how he taught her the lesson. It was strange, he thought, how insignificant things prompted people to commit callous acts. Jealousy, he wondered, or mere rage? Euphoria too, for in his moments of triumph he would use her as a slave – it had always been so from that very first moment.

"Do you have anything to say?" Sabatini asked.

Ariana didn't reply. His one good eye inspected her. The other seemed to burrow inside, force out the answer she didn't speak.

Sabatini was torn. He wasn't a young man, but he could still attract women, seduce them with ease and deceit. If that failed, he could buy them. But he didn't want any woman. He wanted this one. She'd become what he needed. Despite what he always told himself, he did depend on her. No one else could act how this one did. They hadn't been trained to do so. Every so often, such as now, he had to confront the fighter which still clawed in her, control the untamed beast, reteach the leopard what she refused to learn. It appeared the final lesson was about to be taught.

Casually, he picked up a diamond and inspected it. A half-smile crossed his lips. With no emotion, he addressed the Captain. "Lock her in one of the guest suites. I have business to attend to."

"Tie her?"

"Yes," he said, "and take away her clothes. She won't need them."

Belzac offered an unintelligible grunt. He reached into his back pocket and produced a sailor's knife, the kind he might have used when he served on the fishing fleets or fought in the alleys of ports around the Mediterranean. He stretched out a single rough hand, seized the front of the torn blouse and inserted the knife. Within seconds her clothes lay in ribbons on the floor at her feet. She stood in her panties taking huge breaths, trying to calm herself. Involuntarily, her knees gave. It was only Grigori's unwithering grip that stopped her falling. Ariana was dragged out of the study and down the corridor. They threw her into one of the smaller suites and tied her wrists to the bed posts. After they left, the lock clicked shut.

Ariana cried, on and off, all night. Occasionally, she'd managed disturbed restless sleep, before the tears had taken over. Now, daylight started to creep beneath the curtains. The lock slid back and the door opened.

"Good morning, my dear."

It was Sabatini, bristling, yet strangely calm. He was still wearing the dinner suit from the night before. His gaze took in her helpless state and he gave a single nod of approval. He shut the door quietly, removed his jacket, loosened his bow tie and carelessly tossed them over a chair. He moved a second chair next to the bed, sat and loosened the top buttons on his shirt. Slowly his hand stretched out. His fingers dabbed at her calf, felt their way up her thigh, past the elastic of her knickers and on to her breasts. The touch repulsed her. Ariana wanted to struggle, to kick out, but she was paralysed, not from fear but indecision. Did she fight, fly or die? At that moment, only her tears moved.

"You appear to want to leave me," he said.

"Because you are a monster." Ariana couldn't help herself. The vitriol came out of her mouth like a hurricane, all obscene languages at once. "Bastard!"

"I agree." Sabatini remained serene beneath the barrage. "But even a beast must have his beauty." He stroked her cheek with one fat finger, poked the tip into the dimple. "That is the fairy tale, is it not?"

"It is a nightmare!" she shouted. "What have you done for me?"

"Everything."

"Nothing! I am nothing with you. I have no life. I have no laughter." The next words hurt. "I have no son!"

Swiftly, Sabatini's huge fist grabbed her face and squeezed. The thumb and forefingers dug at her cheeks. Ariana had to stop talking or she'd bite her tongue. The assault was familiar from many years ago, when she'd first learnt how ruthless a man her suitor could be. Then, she'd bitten often and her tongue had bled many times.

"Silence!" he said. "You forget your position here, Ariana. You are an important accessory to me. People adore you. You give me respectability. They like your history: that you gave up everything to be with the man you love, an old fashioned tale with old fashioned values, the sort of story which appeals to cheap journalists and bad writers. Remember you let it be so. You surrendered your life to be with me."

Sabatini released her with a sudden thrust.

"I was a fool," she said.

"Yes. You were." He took a cigar from his top pocket, lit it with two long puffs and placed the smouldering torpedo in a glass ashtray on the bedside table. "You thought you could change me, didn't you? But it is I who changed you: materialism, worldly pleasure, riches, travel, who needs a life when you have all this?"

"What do you mean?"

"This is all you have, Ariana. This world. My world. There is no way out for you. Not with Jon Drago. Not with an orphanage. Not with dancing. Not with a child."

"You never wanted a child. You took it from us."

"I did and I enjoyed it."

Sabatini took intense joy in what he was saying. His eyes creased into tiny slits, like the mountain eagles that flew over the Sharr Mountains, the hawk-eyed hunter, the emperor of all he surveys. Sabatini's face was set like stone, like the great marble busts of gods or Caesars. How alive they appeared on the outside and yet how dead they truly were. He had transformed himself. He was the god-king, both alive and dead, in the world but not of it, a man caught in limbo, a man waiting for the boat to cross the river into Satan's realm. Sabatini looked, she thought, as if death had taken him already.

"No one can take precedence over me," he growled. "I saw how you wanted a child. I saw in those few months of waiting how you altered. It was not what I wanted. You gave me no choice. You see, I want you, Ariana, and no one else shall have you. I have decided it will be so. You will have nothing except me. No life, no beauty, no lover and no son."

The words hit her like a punch. The breath was sucked from her chest. She could merely gape. Sudden sharp convulsions erupted in her throat. She wanted to shout. Nothing came. She was numb, as if some deadly poison was eating her. The crag face revolted. Its words assaulted. Its intent angered. There was nothing to keep her with this man. Everything was lost. The poison crept up her gullet. She spat. The stream of gunk hit its target square on the chin. Sabatini lashed out with the back of his hand, caught her flush over the jaw.

Petrified, Ariana could only watch as slowly, deliberately, Sabatini reached out a hand and removed her underwear, snapping the elastics. He inspected what he saw. The hand reached out again and touched her. She closed her knees to protect what was intimate. His response was swift and cruel. He pushed her legs apart, tried to invade her with his hand. She battered at him with her knees and feet. His hands fought her off. His lust was overpowering. Suddenly he was loosening his belt. He was on top of her, one hand clawing at her chest, the other controlling a flailing leg. Ariana struggled. He smothered her. A brutal thick arm attacked her throat. Curses echoed in her mind. His elbows and knees acted like missiles, damaging her. His big ugly mouth descended on hers. She tasted his breath, that hot smoky unctuous odour. Gurgling, her lips were crushed. Desperate, she returned all her bleedings and bit the vile tongue.

It stopped. Blood dribbled into her mouth. His heart beat hard on her breast, a drum thudding. First his mouth, then his hands came away from her body and he sat upright on the mattress, the good eye angry and intense, like ox-blood, the opal as black as death.

Sabatini stood, rearranged himself and took up the cigar. A trickle of blood ran out of the corner of his mouth and he swatted it away, all the while studying the figure which lay in front of him. He took up the cigar and blew down it, reigniting the tip.

"I remember when we first met," said Sabatini, smoke wrapping his face. "You were stubborn. You had to be broken like a wild horse and I enjoyed the breaking. Now, it seems, you must be broken again."

Ariana flinched. Slowly the cloud disappeared. Sabatini, his eye as hot and fiery as the cigar, fixed on her taut bosom. The burning point came down hard and jabbed home.

Sixteen

Temptation Bites

Drago travelled non-stop all the way down the west coast, his melancholy a drifting like a summer sun across an empty sky. He drove fast and furious until he reached the furthest south a man could drive.

The town of Santa Marta di Leuca sat on the very tip of Italy. In Puglia they called it the End of the Earth. Drago got out and stared at the horizon. He was dangerously close to Otranto and Sabatini, and Tarantella also. There was something reassuringly perverse in hiding in plain sight. Drago still had his phone. It had stayed silent. He'd almost expected Sabatini to call. It wouldn't have taken much to trace his number. Perhaps that type of intimidation was too obvious. Turning back from the glassy sea, Drago walked around the marina, admired the motor yachts and sailboats. If there was anyone tailing him, he'd not seen it on the roads. Nor here either. Drago planned to keep hidden for as long as the Italian overseas postal service operated. Four days, maybe five, he'd been told. He'd paid top whack, but that didn't get you much these days. It was time to do as he intended: hide in plain sight. He'd go back into the Salentine, visit those ancient villages, find a cheap hostel and mix with the locals in somewhere like Soleto or Galatina.

The Maserati enjoyed the challenge of the coastal roads. Drago slowed a little, considered again the evidence he'd uncovered on *Diamantin* and the mess he'd abandoned. Blaku must have stolen Il Papavero to order. Perhaps the other diamonds as well. He'd been shot in the moment. Drago hazarded a guess it had been one of Tarantella's armed thugs, which added Ferrara into the mix. It was Ferrara's goons who retrieved the drugs underwater and replaced them with money packages. The Comte was Mafia, Il Padrino, and the Godfather must surely know about the drug trade; he probably instructed Ferrara, had probably struck a deal with Sabatini during one of those evening dinner parties Ariana had mentioned.

So, why was Blaku stealing diamonds? Was it really a case of Sabatini's ego? It was a reckless endeavour and like many such expeditions, it met with a summary execution.

The death wasn't his fault, but Drago felt the impact keenly. Blaku's cold corpse embraced by blood, a life vanished, a grim extinction. These moments had come too often for Drago of late. He'd seen people killed. He'd participated in the killing. When it happened, it always happened unexpectedly, a moment detached from the world and his place in it, a moment when death, when killing, became the only pure thing. Yes, that was it, purity. It wasn't like that when he was younger and he'd fought like an idiot with and against other idiots on the terraces and in the streets of Brighton. That was a hot-blooded rush. You pumped yourself up for it. The football match was either the prelude or the sequel, the main event as sharp and unforgiving as a red-hot poker. Things got rough. Out of hand. But no one ever set out to kill anyone. Drago had fought, won and lost and escaped. He believed he had left all that violence and agony behind. His belief had changed a few years ago on the wooded slopes of the Hrad in Brno, when the frost had bitten his hands and his hands had killed for the first time.

Now, he always thought of death as cold and pure and unstoppable. Odd, he thought, to compare death and its accompaniments to something as virtuous as purity, as incessant as love. What had Ariana said? Don't joke about love. A serious subject. He wondered if that was why he pulled away when they kissed in the Siren's Grotto, because it wasn't pure, because she was someone else's, even if that someone was Sabatini. The right moment, he'd said, that was what he wanted. Was there ever such a thing? You can never choose the time to die, that was how the Fate's told it. Perhaps you can never choose the time to fall in love. He'd known it during that awkward conversation with Madeleine on the terrace of the San Pietro. He'd known it when he took coffee and swapped cigarettes with Ariana. He'd known it when they danced the rhumba. Maybe he'd always known it.

Last night she'd hardly turned a hair, not at the fight, the diamonds or to Blaku's death, not even a shake of fear, no tears. Ariana was not naïve in the nature of crooks; but now, having left her with the chief of villains, all she had to rely on was her own sense of justice and stealth. None of it reassured him. A sense of sickening guilt bloated in his gut. Briefly, he remembered the kiss, not the first one in Otranto's dark streets, or the hushed desperate clinches in the Siren's Grotto, but the last one before he'd tied her in the bedroom. It felt like a kiss goodbye, formal and polite, a fleeting press of the lips. She didn't look at him as he shut the door. Her mind was elsewhere, beginning the act she would need to play, the same one she had enacted for seven years. Drago knew it and understood it.

There was a turn to the left which headed inland. He took it on a whim. The road twisted uphill, crisscrossing the steep incline of a dry river gorge interwoven with farmsteads. Lone houses backed onto fields peppered with olive vines and fruit trees. Goats chewed at brown grass. Dry stone walls separated the acres and terraces. Wild flowers pushed between the cracks, their petals waving in the noonday heat. The road crossed the river by an abandoned dam, built to hold back the winter rains. The sun was baking again and Drago felt as dry as the riverbed. Across the bridge rose Gagliano del Capo, its patchwork of houses tumbling down the escarpment until the dusty pastel pink and white squares were absorbed into the green orchards.

On the other side, an unpromising dirt track was marked by a finger post indicating a restaurant and hotel. Drago impulsively relished the idea of eating. He'd skipped breakfast. A late afternoon lunch would be perfect and might release some of his tensions, remove those ill thoughts. He followed the badly pitted road, driving at a crawl. The track opened onto a make-do carpark outside a rambling old farmhouse guarded by half-closed lattice-work shutters. The dirty white washed walls had seen better days. The sign read *Il Candela*. 1950s Italian jazz blared from a radio inside.

Drago slid to a stop, turned off the engine and got out. The doors were propped open with Victorian irons allowing for what passed as a breeze to penetrate the half-gloom. The ceiling fan was on strike. It was almost as warm inside as out. The restaurant looked in decline. The tables were scrupulously laid, but the glassware and cutlery was chunky, old and so rustic-looking he expected to see wooden plates and bowls. White tablecloths were spread corner to corner to protect what was left of the varnish. The floor was a hopscotch mess of big broad tiles and cement infill. The walls were unadorned save for tobacco stains and one huge gilt framed mirror.

The music came from the galley kitchen. A plump, middle-aged woman was immersed in preparing pasta even if no one was eating. Drago smelt fresh herbs and tomatoes. Steaming water bubbled. He stepped silently between the tables, reached the rear exit and stepped back into the daylight.

There was an outside eating area, peppered with a dozen tables, not a parasol between them, nor a customer in sight. The terraces sloped along the hillside; first a kitchen garden full of vegetables, then an olive grove; lastly an orchard with neat rows of almond and cherry trees bursting with fruit. Beyond the garden he could spy three stone trulli waiting patiently for occupancy. Heavy leafed cacti and dwarf palms littered the flower beds, some so big they made a nuisance of themselves buffeting against tables and chairs. Drago raised his sunglasses. Half-hidden behind an enormous palm leaf or two, he could make out a head of luscious black hair resting on the pillow of a sun bed. He coughed. No reaction. Cautiously, he moved forward, his shoes making crunching slaps on the shale path. He circled the bush, not wanting to startle whoever rested.

She was sunbathing. Her walnut skin seemed to suck up the sunlight. Even at distance he could make out tiny beads of perspiration resting on her shoulders, in her cleavage and her belly button. She was wearing a small fuchsia pink bikini, the material so thin it was almost see-through, and a pair of big plastic sunglasses, the sort you bought in supermarkets. Drago couldn't tell if she was really asleep or not, so he coughed again. The head turned towards him, but no other part of her body moved. He couldn't see if her eyes were open, so he said: "Excuse me."

Lazily, the girl propped herself up on an elbow and lifted her glasses. She gazed at him as if uncertain what to say.

"Buongiorno," said Drago. "Voglio mangiare."

The girl studied him, squinting in the light. She couldn't have been much past her school days. She still had the slight puffy look of young girls. The lips were full, unpainted, the expression puzzled. Her cheeks and brow should have been immaculate, but were instead cursed with acne scars. She frowned. Her lips stared to form shapes. He realised she was searching for forgotten words.

"You are Inglese?" she ventured.

"Si."

"Ah ha. We closed. Everyone knows it."

"I don't. I'm a tourist."

"Ah ha," she chimed and carefully rearranged her bosom with one hand. "You must come back later."

"That's disappointing," said Drago. "It all looks so appetising."

The girl took a deep breath through her nose. It came out like a snort. Drago found the sound oddly appealing, as though the girl was unspoilt, lacking the manners she ought to have been taught. She swung her long legs off the bed and stood up, appraising him, slipping her feet easily into a pair of plastic sandals. She raised a long tapered finger.

"Wait."

The girl made her way back to the building. The material of the swimsuit strained over her muscles. She stretched on tiptoe to shout through a window, her buttocks taut, strong stilt-like calves tight. The rapid exchange ended with her settling back on her soles and returning to him, the sandals making slapping noises on the path. She indicated the terrace with a vague gesture and offered a pleasant, informal smile.

"Please. Sit. Any table, yes?"

"Yes. Thank you. That's very kind."

Drago took a seat at her end of the garden, but closer to the restaurant, positioning himself so he could see the sweep of the terraces as well as the building. He lit a cigarette. The girl went inside and returned a minute or two later. She had wrapped a small patterned shawl around her hips, barely covering what Drago had already seen. Four-inch heels replaced the flats and made her legs appear even longer. She carried a menu in one hand and a wicker basket stuffed with bread and jug of olive oil in the other. She placed them on the table and stood with all her weight on her right hip.

"Would you like drink?" she asked slowly. "Beer?"

"No, vino." Drago opened the menu, a fat, worn leather book, and turned to the wine list. He randomly picked a name. "The

Salento."

"Ah ha."

She disappeared again.

The menu was in Italian. Drago inspected it curtly and put it aside. He ate some of the bread, dipping it in a pool of warm oil that he poured onto the plate. The girl came back with a pitcher of water and two big wine goblets.

"To refresh, yes?"

"Yes."

She filled one glass. He thought she concentrated more on him than the work. Her head dipped a fraction too far, her shoulders sloped, the contours of her breasts an invitation Drago struggled to resist reading. When she straightened, the girl deliberately ran a hand along the fringe of her hair, framing her face in a shade for a second, accentuating her figure, before striding away, allowing him to witness the sway of her young hips. She's a cocky little thing, he thought.

The girl came back with the wine, cork already pulled, and poured half-way. She waited while Drago tasted, but didn't wait for his judgement.

"Is good, yes?"

"Si, grazie."

"Ah ha, grazie." She filled the glass. "You choose?"

"I couldn't read it." Drago handed her the thick volume. "A green salad and some orecchiette."

The girl took the menu. One finger flicked at her lower lip and she made that snorting sound again.

"Together?"

"No. One at a time, if you can."

"Ah ha."

She gave a little twirl for his benefit and went to deliver the order.

Drago was left on his own for a while. He smoked, drank some wine. When the girl returned, she carried a large white bowl in which some greenery had been sprinkled with cherry tomatoes, artichoke hearts and mozzarella, dappled in sweet virgin oil. She bent closer to position his knife and fork and her thigh brushed his elbow. Drago enjoyed the touch. His skin tingled and his fingers automatically twitched.

"Do you live here?" he asked, trying to make the inquiry sound both casual and polite. He couldn't tell what she thought he intended.

"No. I live in other place. Mama owns this."

"But you work here?"

"No. I use garden. For sun."

"It's very quiet. Does no one come to eat?"

She shrugged.

"They work all day. In the fields. The beach. We are not big city." She shifted her weight and her hips jutted out. "I don't like work. Today, I do Mama favour." She winked. "You also."

"Thank Mama for me."

"It is pleasure."

She dragged the word out, rolling it over her tongue.

I'll bet, considered Drago. The salad was excellent. When he finished, the girl immediately reappeared as if he'd rung a magic bell, her smile filtering across her lips, her eyes watching his to see where he was looking. This time he studied her navel. He thought it exceptionally pretty.

The pasta came in a light mascarpone sauce, with chopped garlic, rapini and crumbled ricotta cheese melting into the jus. It was divine, the little ear parcels soft and succulent. It really needed white wine, but it was too late now. Having delivered the dish, the girl retreated to the sun bed, spent a few moments rearranging it, stripped off the scarf and lay on her side facing him. She picked up an emery board and began to manicure her nails, idly glancing over the rim of her cheap sunglasses. Drago watched the little play. She'd arranged the furniture to allow him the best possible view of her body, temptation no more than ten metres away. After a few minutes, the girl put down the file, turned her back and idly slipped the catch on her brassiere. She lay on her front. The sun-bronzed back revealed no tan lines. The squashed flesh of her bosom poked invitingly clear. Drago thought she sighed.

He didn't hurry his meal. When he finished, he continued to eat the bread and drink the wine and water, his attention distracted by the near-naked girl. After some time, the older woman came out of the kitchen, muttering to herself. She collected Drago's debris and spoke to her daughter in a raised voice.

"Shh, Mama!" came the reply as the girl sat up and repositioned her bikini, offering Drago a brief glimpse of a beautifully formed bosom. She swung her legs and sat facing him.

"You want sweets?"

"No." Drago chuckled and lit a cigarette. He indicated the bottle. "Do you drink?"

The girl frowned.

"Cigarette?"

She nodded and skipped off the recliner. It was his last one. He lit it for her. She took it and their fingers tingled. The smile flashed once more. She stood in her heels, that beautiful belly inches from his elbow. He made an effort to look only at her sunglass hidden eyes.

"What happens here? It's a very quiet town."

"Nothing. Why you come?"

"I told you. I'm a tourist. I'm just driving around."

"Why here?"

"Your place looked nice."

The little snort was acknowledgement enough to tell him she knew he was lying.

"I'm on my way to Melpignano," he said.

"Big concert in Melpignano tonight. Busy. Busy."

"Is that right?"

"Ah ha."

Drago poured the last of the wine.

"You speak very good English. Where did you learn?"

"From movies. School. I am talented girl."

"I can tell. Like your mother."

She frowned quizzically.

"You like my mama?"

"She has great talent too. She cooks wonderful pasta."

"Ah ha." The smile returned. "I will tell her."

"Grazie. What do I owe?"

"Thirty Euros, maybe." She shrugged and sucked on the cigarette. "More for my tip."

Drago dug out his wallet and slipped three notes under the wine bottle. He took out another three and pushed them across the table towards her.

"Thank you for the view."

"Prego."

She smiled. A hand snaked out, took the money, folded the notes and deposited it quickly and with no qualms into the front of her bikini bottoms, casually flipping the gusset with a thumb to flatten the line.

"And now?"

"What now?" asked Drago.

The girl finished the cigarette and equally casually deposited the stub in his half-full wine glass.

"You have car?"

"Yes."

"I did not hear it."

"You were asleep."

"I see it?"

He nodded. Drago led her through the restaurant and outside. Mama watched them pass the kitchen, her eyes suspicious. The girl didn't bother to dress, once more tying the scarf around her hips. When she saw the deep emerald sports car, she gave a long squeak and grabbed his arm. Her nails scratched.

"It is yours?"

"No. I borrowed it."

The girl ran her hand along the hot bodywork, cooing with excitement. She leant over the driver door, backside jutting, gazing at the interior. One soft hand manipulated the gear stick.

"Do you drive?" he asked.

"Not yet."

The girl turned around, leaning against the bodywork, one long leg crooked, breasts and belly flush. Her bottom lip juddered loose. Urgently, she said: "Take me in it."

"Where?"

"Anywhere."

"Melpignano?"

"Yes."

"I don't think Mama would approve."

"I am not baby."

"I can see that." Drago reached out and gently eased her away from the car. "But Mama doesn't think so."

The girl gnashed her teeth and raised her sunglasses. A disappointed sneer enveloped her beautiful lips. He expected her to spit.

Drago settled into the driver's seat and started the engine. Mama was watching from the safety of the restaurant. The girl gazed at him. He considered saying 'Get in' and wondered where it would lead if he did. There was always something exotic about youthful beauty, an indescribable frisson which pulled at the lusty heart and the wicked soul. The girl was temptation. The apple for Adam to bite. He wasn't about to take the bait. Drago pulled his own sunglasses onto his nose to hide the truth. Without a second look, he struck first and headed down the lane. He imagined the cheeky bitch was scowling, but not half as much as her mother.

Seventeen

Melpignano

It was one of those lazy Otranto nights which had metamorphosed from a lazy evening and an even lazier afternoon. The lanterns were flickering beneath the trees and pillars, the young and old still walked arm in arm and bought their last romantic ice creams and the sea was still gently pushing the sprite air over the walkers on Lungomare. Beneath the awning outside Vicino's the air was heavy with conversation and thick palls of tobacco.

Drago and Maddie had visited the restaurant twice in quick succession. This was the third visit and already Paulo treated them as part of his family.

"It is hard to find a table in Otranto," said Paulo, "but for you, Jon, if you wish a table, I will find it. You know, I read one of your books. The one about Iraq. Very good."

"I didn't know it had been translated into Italian."

"I bought it online," explained Paulo, "and copied it with Babel translator. I am not sure the Tower of Babel understands modern English. Some of it read funny."

"I'm not sure how to take that."

Paulo laughed and went to collect another order. Maddie tutted. "Just be glad he's bought one of your books. It's more than I ever have."

He expressed surprise.

"You've never read them?"

"You mean you haven't noticed?" Now it was her turn to look shocked. "Most men that visit my flat snoop a little. You know, bookshelves, trinkets and that."

"Most men? How many were there before me and –"

Drago stopped before she interrupted. Maddie wrinkled her nose so her spectacles jiggled.

"You promised we wouldn't talk about him," she said plainly, "and yet there you go again. Guilt sits badly with you, doesn't it?"

"Not usually."

"Does that mean this is more than a carefree holiday in the sun?"

"It's complicated."

"You're making it complicated," she said with resounding finality. "Eat your food and drink your wine. You're less conceited when you're pissed."

Drago did as he was told. He didn't mind being verbally spanked. They drank a superb Menhir Primitivo and gorged on risotto di mare, packed full of squid, octopus, clams and prawns, soaked in rich Arborio rice.

Now, as midnight fast became 1am, they sat outside in the low heat, smoked and drank grappa di laurel with Paulo and his mother, the old matriarch who ruled the kitchen with a sharp tongue and a cackling laugh. They had friends with him. Alberto and Luisa were cheery people. The Italians were swapping stories. Drago and Maddie listened to the rolling Roman vowels and wished they could speak the language of love, at least for one evening.

Luisa turned to Drago and in a sharp, yet melodic voice, she said: "Paulo tells me you write."

"That's correct. Yes. Books. Libres."

"Si. Libres. You write of Otranto?"

"No. There's already been one great novel set here."

"Not yours?"

"No. *The Castle of Otranto*," said Drago. "*Castel del Otranto*, by Horace Walpole, the first gothic novel."

She shook her head. Maddie intervened on his behalf.

"He's talking about really old books. Jonathon writes adventure stories, thrillers with spies."

"Not quite like that." Drago made a dismissive roll of the eyes. "My hero's more a fish-out-of-water."

Luisa didn't understand.

"Anyway, he's stuck for ideas," said Maddie. "I don't suppose there are any good stories about Otranto?"

Luisa paused for a moment, inclined her head and said: "You know La Taranta?"

"No. What's that?"

This one word seemed to get Alberto's attention. The grey tousle-haired man pushed back his chair an inch or two so as to have a better view of the pretty young English girl with the freckles and glasses. He ruffled his moustache.

"Tarantism," he declared, "is the spider's song, an old folk tale. It is village music. They play music concerts all month in the Salentine to celebrate the tradition."

"What's the Salentine?"

"There are several towns north of here, like Calimera, Castrignano, Soleto, Sternatia, nine pretty towns, a little cluster of life in the heart of Terra d'Otranto. The Greeks came here centuries ago when the Byzantines still ruled half the world. They brought many traditions. Some of those traditions still survive. No one knows why. Maybe no one cares. It is history now. Myth. Folklore. Like La Taranta."

"You excite too easily, Alberto," jostled Paulo. "Do not listen to him."

"What is it," Maddie asked again, "some sort of pagan festival?"

They didn't quite comprehend paganism. Drago lit another cigarette. "Yes. What did you call it: spider music?"

"Ah, the music," soothed Luisa, "that beautiful sound. Whenever, wherever it is played, people want to stand up and dance. They are captivated by the rhythm. It is like, ah, a reazione, a reazione chimica, a physical reaction. The rhythm spreads through the body like vibrations on a spider's web."

"All the nine towns have concerts," Alberto continued. "That's the real spider's web. Melpignano is at the centre and on the last Saturday every August they have the biggest concert."

"Alberto, Alberto." Paulo tried to restrict his friend's melodramatic impulses. His words vanished into garbled Italian. The two men argued, gently. Mama slapped at her son's arm. He ignored her. Mama said something to Luisa and the two women cackled together. Luisa turned to Maddie.

"She says men don't understand the dancing or the music. The emotional feelings. The love. The madness. The madness of love. The songs are not like modern songs, you understand. They are a link to a tradition long past."

"No," said Alberto suddenly. "It is a link to La Taranta. Tarantism is the real thing."

The statement was greeted with general mockery.

"You don't believe me," he argued. "Listen, I believe my mother. She was still a girl when she was sent to work in the fields picking tobacco leaves. She remembers another young woman, maybe only a teenager herself, who was bitten by the tarantula and was driven into madness, frenzy, hysteria. It was only when the musicians came and made her dance that the tarantula's spell was broken. She danced and danced and danced until she could no longer dance and then she writhed on the floor to the rhythm until the evil left her."

"Sounds like some sort of primal scream therapy," said Maddie. "People don't still believe this, do they?"

"Some do in the Salentine," answered Paulo. "Of course, it was different before. Women were inferior, subordinate, and dancing the pizzica to free their bodies from madness was a moment of liberation."

"Pizzica?"

"Pizzica," repeated Mama, waving her weathered cook's hand for attention. She started to explain something in rapid Italian, which Paulo and Luisa made quick not over-successful attempts to translate.

"Each dance has specific rules and movements. Each dance empowers the woman. In the past, if a woman wanted to dance, she had no place to dance alone, so the spider's bite was an excuse, a subterfuge to dance. Then it perhaps became a sort of music therapy, so each sickness required a different dance to cure it. So a woman who was melancholic, would dance to a different tune to the one who was crazy. But always the songs kept the same strong rhythm and that is what defeated the cholic. It was a medical cure and an emotional outlet."

"Some of the songs are so old," continued Luisa, "they can only be sung in Griko."

"What's Griko?" asked Maddie.

"The local language. It's almost extinct. They still speak a little Griko in Melpignano and the nine towns."

They fell silent for a moment. Paulo stood up, went to the

sound system behind the bar and twiddled with the knobs. First a swaying fiddle and then a rolling drum punctured the air leading to a vibrant stampede of sound that echoed under the awning. When the song reached its refrain, Luisa began to sing, a deep pitched, calling tone, splintered and yet magical. Drago had no idea what she sang, but he listened intently. Four youngsters strolling past stopped to dwell in the moment, hummed and clapped as the chorus reached a climax and passed on when the song was sung. Mama grinned and gabbled her appreciation. Alberto gazed at his wife, wonder set on his face, pride in his eyes and love in his heart.

Paulo poured more grappa.

"Even when one believes that everything must be forgotten, that there is no more memory and no more witnesses, these traces of ancient life stay all around us," he said and gestured towards the departing youngsters. "People like them, today's youth, people like you, like me, we all have demons to exorcise too, personal tragedies, struggles, financial problems, no work, no religion, no love. Yet music has this magic. It takes you to another world, does it not? It heals."

"Yes," agreed Drago, "it does."

***

It took Drago two hours to reach Melpignano, the journey getting slower and the roads more congested. Close to the town there were several warning signs. Coaches had pulled up and parked in fields opened to the public for a small charge paid to the local farmer. Eventually, Drago could make it no further and he turned the Maserati into an orchard and found the last space, hooded beneath branches overburdened with ripe peaches.

Cheekily, he nicked a couple of peaches, saved one and split the other. The flesh was soft and the juice dibbled on his tongue. He set off casually, shoving a €5 note in the collection box. The route to the town centre was hardly any distance. The road led to a line of bus shelters and a triangle of open land, potted with palms. Further on, the road became a broad dusty corridor of commerce, all souvenir shops, crappy cafés and hot tiny places ridiculously named 'supermarket,' fans and air conditioners buzzing endlessly. The sun was inching towards sunset. The blistering afternoon started to dissipate. The sweltering buildings began to relax. Shade eked over the roads and trattorias.

He turned off Castrignano and found a bustling piazza surrounded on three sides by a colonnaded arcade, behind which hid more trattorias. Metal columns of night lights had been lifted and would make a pretty scene when the day turned dark. A small open-air stage had been erected to one side, but no one was playing there now. The square was dominated by the church and its bell tower. Over the west porch a relief depicted San Giorgio slaying the dragon. The door was ajar. Folk music spun from inside. Drago passed under St George and escaped the blinding heat by entering the cool nave. Straight ahead was a fine marble encrusted altar which protected an east window and another view of the saint at war. Paintings hung at intervals and had similar interpretations to tell. Seated in a small semi-circle in front of the altar was a sextet of musicians strumming mandolins, clapping tambourines and finger-rapping drums. The music rose and fell dramatically with a vigorous, vivace quality, reminding Drago of the haphazard material film composers wrote for cheap historical romps, only this had fewer orchestral strings overburdening the overture. He took a seat to the rear of the audience and closed his eyes to the church and his mind to the world. He could have been back in Otranto with Alberto gesticulating wildly as Paulo translated his mother's words and Luisa elaborated and expounded the virtues of La Taranta.

"It could be called delirium, how the women compete with the musicians, how they fight with the drums to constantly upstage one another, to see who will tire first. That is the Panno Rosso, the dance of the red cloth. And opposite is the Panno Verde, the green cloth, slower, melancholic, for an altogether different kind of tarantism. Then there is the spallata and the morisca, each a different time, a different beat. It was believed the victim of a tarantula's bite was held in thrall to the spider's song, and until that spell was broken, they would replicate aspects of the creature's physiognomy. They might suffer headaches or nausea, hot or cold fevers, listlessness, paranoia.

Each symptom had to be purged separately and musicians would fashion cadences to match a spider's venom and perform a musical exorcism, nature's medicine."

After a time, the music altered. The new tunes were less dramatic, less thunderous. A flute replaced a drum, and the pounding became more of a stroke, the fingers caressing the pigskin so the infectious rhythms gave way to a wistful melody, where the strings harmonised, singing rather than fighting to be heard. This was the Panno Verde, the dance of the green fields. This victim, this spider, must be suffering from a distinct case of melancholy. Drago smiled. It was all hokum. Tarantulas don't carry enough venom to kill a human and most victims sweat the poison out in a few days. Nonetheless, it was a lovely baroque story.

The concert relaxed into a series of beautiful, slow melodies. There were some speeches. The words sounded different to Italian, the emphasis unusually strong on certain syllables. It had to be the Griko dialect Luisa had spoken of.

Outside, the air was clammy. The last strokes of daylight tapered to vicious orange, tipping the wings of incoming rolling clouds. The Piazza San Giorgio was going to be noisy tonight. A DJ's booth was being loaded onto the small stage, a bank of speakers on each side and an arm of revolving lights above. There were more people on the streets now, moving through the square and heading vaguely for the convent. Most were young and dressed down for an evening of dancing. Drago found a corner bar. People sat outside and in, sipping beer and water, eating snacks. Ceiling fans rotated and pushed the hot air reluctantly around the interior. The taranta was playing on the sound system. There was a stool at the bar and Drago hitched himself onto it, ordered a Moretti and watched the bubbles rise as the condensation fell. The beer was deliciously cool. It slipped down fast. He took the second peach from his pocket and bit into it.

A female voice called out. A couple of nearby tables were occupied by a big group of youngsters, students possibly, dressed for the sun and fun. A flirtatious girl was trying to attract his attention. Drago, as was his habit, explained he was English.

"She wants to know where you got the peach," replied one of the men. "She likes fruit."

"The orchard."

The man translated. The girl looked forlornly at the fruit and said something in Italian. The man said: "She wants to know if you have any more."

"No. Scusi."

"Okay," she said.

"What's going on here?" asked Drago.

"Music festival," said the man. "Night of the Taranta. It's famous. You like the music?"

"I don't know it."

"You'll love it. Where are you from?"

"London."

"Holiday?"

"Yes. Of sorts. I write books."

The man translated again.

"Wow," said another girl.

"What do you write about?"

"Thrillers. Crime."

"You looking for stories in Melpignano?"

"Maybe."

"You won't find anything tonight. Maybe pick pockets. It's all music and dance. You going to stay?"

"I expect so."

"Most people head to the big stage. By the fields and the old convent."

Drago followed the man's vague throw of an arm which didn't tell him any specific direction. He swallowed the last of the fruit, drank the beer.

"What time does it all kick off?"

"An hour or so. When the sun has gone. You should come."

"I might do that."

Drago ordered another Moretti and a packet of Marlboros. He turned back to watching the road. Someone was propping up the doorframe. He looked like a scarecrow. Thin ugly wisps of straggly, curly hair peeked from under a battered cap. The eyes were sunken into his skull as if someone had dug out the originals and decided on inferior replacements. Clothes hung on his frame, including a long overcoat completely unsuitable for a summer's day. He had no need to stand where he did. The whole frontage was open to the street. The doorway, positioned at the corner, caught the last of the sunlight. The scarecrow squinted at the occupants before slowly making his way to the bar, shaking as he walked. He took up a position next to Drago. An earthy smell permeated the immediate vicinity, so strong it made the beer taste funny. The scarecrow ordered from the barman, got it and slumped against the wall, legs stiff and straight, exactly as he'd propped up the doorframe. His mobile chimed. The scarecrow muttered an obscenity, pulled it loose from his coat and squinted at the screen for some time before replacing the gadget and shuffling his back further up the wall so he finally stood upright.

"La taranta," he said loudly. "Noi amiamo la taranta."

Scarecrow swigged at the bottle then tapped Drago's shoulder with it.

"Se amate la taranta?"

"Scusi," said Drago, "mi Inglese."

"Oh. Inglese. Capisco."

The bottle tapped again.

"You like taranta?"

Scarecrow slurred his words badly and they ran into each other.

"What?"

"The music. You come for the music?"

"No. Well, sort of. Yes. Si. La musica."

"No mi piace."

"What?"

"Oh. Scusi. I don't like it."

"Then why are you here?"

"Business. Drink. Girls."

Scarecrow didn't seem capable of conducting any kind of business or of attracting girls. Drink had enveloped him already. He was the sort you tried to avoid. He'd likely kick up a fuss. The barman kept a watchful eye on proceedings.

"It is hot, yes?"

"Yes."

"It will rain."

"You think so?"

Scarecrow tapped the bottle against his temple.

"I know it."

"I could do with a sixth sense."

Drago's attempt at humour fell flat. Scarecrow lurched from his position and leant on the counter, head down folded onto his arms, bottle still in hand. He came to rest inches from Drago, one bleary eye staring. Two fingers pinched the material of Drago's jacket.

"Nice. American?"

"British."

"I show you something."

"You don't have to."

"Yes, my friend, yes. See here."

Scarecrow fumbled into a deep inside pocket of his coat and pulled out a small plastic bag of dope, which he shielded from the barman's sight. His voice lowered to a whisper, but it was suddenly sharp enough to be heard plainly, even under the music.

"One hundred euros to you, my friend."

"No, thanks."

"It is good. Real good shit. You get many girls for fucking if you show them this shit. One long cigarillo," he mimicked a demonstration, waving two fingers and puffing through them into thin air, "and you will fuck all night."

He made what sounded like a laugh but it had a more lecherous intent. He slapped the bag against Drago's thigh.

"Take it."

"No."

Scarecrow pushed back his hat and the straggly hair moved with it. He stared hard at Drago, who decided enough was enough and gestured to settle his bill. He asked for a bottle of water to go. The barman spent most of the transaction watching the drunken interloper, who either didn't notice or ignored the subtle threat. Drago paid with a twenty and took his change. As he went to leave, the bottle touched his elbow.

"You have money. Give me it."

"I said no."

Drago didn't wait to be asked again and left Scarecrow slumped half-on half-off the counter, the barman wiping around him and making not-so-subtle aggressive comments. He'd decided not to lose any more customers.

Drago lit a cigarette and drank the water. A solemn dusk was descending. He'd forgotten how quickly day turned to night. The group of youngsters poured out of the bar. The man he'd spoken to earlier poked at his arm.

"Hey, Inglese, you come?"

"Why not?"

"You had trouble with that guy?"

"He was drunk."

"He's a shithead. Come. Come with us."

"Si, si," called the flirtatious girl and made a grab for Drago's arm.

"Stick close. She doesn't only like peaches."

Drago laughed.

"Come. Come on." The man hugged Drago's shoulders and the group nudged their way towards the centre of the road. "There's not much time."

Drago was propelled along the little lanes until they turned into Via Roma. The street was filling up, funnelling the numbers into a tight space. He dropped the fag in the crush. The stoic walls of the Pallazzo Marchesale watched them pass, perhaps wondering when it could be returned to more peaceful virtues. Beside it, by contrast, the ruined castle bastion seemed to welcome the invasion of bodies. He could hear musicians tuning in preparation for the concert. The girl and the guy kept talking to him in a mixture of fast Italian and pigeon English. The air was hot, even as the sky turned the deepest ice blue. Billows of grey cloud secured the horizon. That bloody scarecrow had been right. It was going to rain. Drago could feel it now; the humidity, the strong wind.

Via Roma opened onto an expansive plaza, unencumbered with walls or buildings, its only monument a barren monastery, the Convento degli Agostiniania, its decapitated façade looming golden over the mass of people clustered beneath it. The main stage was pushed slightly to one side. An elegant canvas roof stretched over its loudspeakers and platforms. A long banner announced *La Notte della*

Taranta. A large orchestra packed full of mandolins, violins, drums, accordions and flutes was busy tuning and mic testing. The audience, not a chair in sight, was standing and sitting on a plateau which ran three football pitches wide across empty land. At the far edge, before trees took over, Drago made out a series of temporary wooden stalls, probably selling food and beer to the masses.

Everyone was very friendly, if a little smashed, but Drago didn't mind that now. He felt safe and secure and unseen. The musicians took their places, the singers bowed to an opening cheer and slowly, amongst rolling applause, the hypnotic heartbeat of La Taranta started to soar.

Eighteen

Night of the Taranta

The music delivered an energetic life force to the crowd. Hands were raised, heads shook, shoulders jived, bodies twirled, sometimes in time, sometimes not, always rapid, weaving movements, as if the hands and feet were forming a web to trap a friend, a lover, an enemy.

The fast songs resembled a fandango. The sound slithered through the air, rolling and intertwining, percussion instruments blending with strings, competing with the vocals and overarching accordions. There were women dancers on stage with the singers, their long silk dresses split to the thigh, high necked, bare armed, bracelets and jewellery glistening, hair ruffled, pulled back, lips made-up to a fantasy pout, an earthen gypsy look, women of the world as well as in it. They were barefoot and their feet moved in two-beat time, the ankles snapping and stamping as the hips swivelled and swayed, four steps forward, four steps back, spiral, turn and tuck. They danced together, hugging each other as if scared to be parted. Fascination swept over them, the movements an intricate entanglement, hands forming confused, ritual patterns, heads thrown back, eyes still and straight.

With a male partner, they embraced each other at a respectful distance, until the music demanded their obedience, demanded they came together and fought for their love, an erotic courtship, a rapid Paso Doble, no matadors here, just tarantulas and maidens waiting to be stung by the madness of love. They danced and lived those songs, danced until their souls overflowed. Drago wasn't sure he could dance as hard as that, but the performers and most of the audience seemed able too.

Eventually, he left the colourful youngsters and moved through the rousing crowd. He preferred the slower songs. Maybe it was an age thing. Nights like this didn't happen often for Drago. He couldn't remember the last time he'd gone to a night club or even a party. When he went out, it was usually to the restaurants or pubs he liked. A bottle of wine, a pint or two, a kiss with his date, a stroll back to Fulham and a warm bed overlooking the Thames. Dancing never came into it, not of the vertical kind anyway. A young restless body brushed against him. Drago grinned. Not the vertical kind; what was he thinking? He gave the girl a quick up-and-down and eased his way further from the melee. He'd had enough of music and dancing. It was making him think of Ariana.

Drago made it to Via Roma as the first rain drops started to fall, big cannonballs of wet, smacking onto scalps and shoulders. The crowd initially didn't react. Then there was a stretching of arms to welcome the offering from the sky. They needed cooling after the forty degree heat. Drago shuffled sideways towards the first available trattoria and hunched under the eaves watching the monsoon descend, bouncing off bodies and rattling tables and chairs. Even the cobblestones seemed to vibrate.

He was about to go inside and order something, when a long-coated scarecrow lurched into the space beside him. Drago almost groaned. If it was possible, the man had become more intoxicated. His straggly hair was matted by the rain, long threads plastered on his face. When he spoke, he was less convivial.

"Hey. Friend. I still have that weed."

"I told you I don't want it."

A hand crawled out and took Drago's elbow. The fingers bit into the joint. Drago tried to pull away, but the limbs of the spider resisted.

"I have to show you this, friend."

"I don't want to see anything."

Drago placed his hand on the scaly fingers, attempting to prise the claw free.

"Yes. You do."

The words came short and sharp. Scarecrow was suddenly not so drunk. The unshaven face pitched closer, pungent breath rasping between sour teeth. Drago flinched. The stench didn't help matters. Neither did the knife placed blade side up against his belly.

"Don't move, Drago. This is sharp. If I turn it, you will be cut. Horribly."

Drago stared directly over Scarecrow's shoulder. No one noticed his plight. Scarecrow had covered his antics well. The weapon was covered by his body and coat, unobtrusive, professional, as if this was two old friends meeting. The pouring rain did the rest. Another man, unseen until now, took hold of Drago's shoulders.

"Move."

All three moved at once. Together the two men hustled Drago along the street and into a dark alley. The new hands shook constantly. The rain jumbled with them. The music drummed over everything. Drago could see tattoos on the man's hands and arms. Spider's webs. There was a busted old Cinquecento parked on the corner and a third man, equally shabby, thrust open the door.

Drago was thrown into the rear footwell. Wet, Nike clad feet stamped on his chest and neck. The soles smelt of shit and the car smelt of hash. Lots of it. they set off without a word. The noisy engine buried the sound of music. Soon he could hear only the shamble of spinning wheels, pellets of rain and rumbling exhausts. The feet vibrated on his thigh, all out of tune. The journey was undulating, bumpy, erratic.

Quickly, Drago became disorientated. The cramped posture didn't help. As the car turned, he rolled against the seats, the feet battering his arms and body to keep him still. He ignored the discomforts and tried to rationalise the situation. It wasn't looking pleasant. Scarecrow had called him by name. This wasn't an innocent hold-up. It could be a kidnap, but he doubted it. This was Sabatini's work. Damn. He'd stayed too close to the enemy. The wild Salentine had not protected him. Scarecrow had earmarked him in the bar, got close to confirm who he was and then contacted his friends for assistance. The foolishness of Drago's decision seemed obvious now. Obvious and dangerous. Instinctively, Drago's body tensed. The vibrating feet reacted to his anxiety. A heel pressed down, digging at his throat. Drago gurgled, tried to twist away and received a kick from the shaking leg. Wincing, he resigned himself to a cattle class ticket.

Between his shoulder, a tattooed leg and the door frame, Drago could make out a patch of uninterrupted dark clouds. They'd cleared Melpignano, then; no more buildings or telegraph poles crossed his view. After a few more minutes, the car turned sharply and came to a halt. The doors opened and Drago was dragged out, the knife tight to his stomach again. The driver, who was a younger man, stayed with the car, lit a herbal cigarette and fixed his earpiece. Sounds of the taranta echoed at full blast from his iPhone, even over the storm.

They'd stopped outside a dilapidated farmhouse, shutters down, creases of wan light eking at the frames. Joined to it was a collection of buildings in an even worse state of repair, all broken brick and corrugated roof panels. In the next three or four fields, protected by a wire fence stood an army of solar panels, silent, uniform, dark grey and threatening, pointing back the way they'd come, where the lights from the soundstage lit up the roofs of the town, hazed by the chatter of rain. Drago reckoned it was two or three miles back to the music, his car and freedom.

They waited by the ruddy coloured door. Nobody knocked. It kept raining. Eventually the bolts were pulled and the door swung inwards with a creak. A sickly looking girl stood in the half-light beneath a weak unshaded bulb which hung on a wire from the ceiling. Her unwashed denim shorts and cropped vest hung on her bones.

"Laszlo," she said.

Scarecrow grunted.

The men took Drago inside, their shoes scraping echoes on a stone floor. It might have been an agreeable home once; it was so dark, he found it hard to tell. The best light was in a corner near the television which was tuned to a sports channel. A football match was in progress somewhere. To the left where the main bulk of the farmhouse should have been, there was only another bolted door. Odd that it's bolted from this side, thought Drago. Old mattresses with dirty sheets were strung randomly about the floor. The place should have been cool, yet it was chugged by the all-encompassing green whiff of strong tobacco and stronger cannabis. Paint was peeling from the walls and littered the place with dust on top of dust. Adding to the illegal smell was the mouldy hum of human piss. Beneath the T.V. screen, Drago could make out several of the same brick-sized packages he'd seen in the hold on *Diamantin*.

Scarecrow did not release the knife from Drago's midriff. His friend, who was shaking all over, not just his hands and feet, made several attempts to light a fat rolled up cigarette. It wasn't only his arms and legs he'd decorated with tattoos, but his face and neck as well. The spider's web probably covered his whole body, infected him like some ancient legend. Maybe he blamed the blood of the tarantula for the incessant shakes and the sweat that pierced his brow.

The stray girl, whose age was indiscernible but young, shut the door and wandered over. She lit the man's cigarette, tiptoed past him and sat on a mattress, coiled up and cross-legged. Behind her was the kitchen. Drago could see scales and spoons: utensils for cooking of a different kind. A familiar looking parcel was sitting, unwrapped, on the prep table. At last Scarecrow, who Drago assumed was called Laszlo, eased the blade away a tad.

"It's our good fortune to find you, Drago."

"How do you know my name?"

The girl pulled a mobile phone from the pocket of her shorts and scanned through the apps. She held up the device. On the screen was a picture of the Maserati Spyder.

"You have a nice car," she said. Next, she showed Drago his own picture, one of him sitting in the café where Scarecrow / Laszlo had first approached him. "We checked it against your Facebook page. We wanted to make sure it was you."

"We have to keep you here," added Laszlo. "It won't be for long."

"I suppose a drink's out of the question?"

Laszlo dug the knife in. Sharp, but safe.

"Give Maria your phone."

Drago removed it from his pocket and tossed it to the girl. It landed on the mattress at her feet. She slipped it into her back pocket. Returning to her own mobile, she began to tap out a text.

"Who do you work for?" asked Drago. "Sabatini? No. You seem too shabby. Let me guess. Ferrara." Nobody said anything. "A nice line of business."

"Not your business."

"I've seen those packages at Tarantella. But you don't seem the type to deal with the Comte."

"What?"

"The Comte d'Orsi. What are you up to, stealing his diamonds or his heroin?"

Startled, the girl looked up from her phone, staring wide-eyed at Laszlo. The two of them stared to converse in rapid Italian. Maria stood. An angry disagreement entailed. As the confused scene unfolded, Drago became certain who the brains of the outfit was. The girl stepped right up to him.

"How do you know about the Comte?" she said urgently. "Who told you? Nrupal?"

"Who?"

"How do you know about Nrupal?"

"I've no idea what you're talking about."

Everything was held in suspended animation for a second: Maria, close and afraid, her diseased teeth snapping the questions; Laszlo's knife edging again, too close to the belly; the tattooed man rocking forwards, agitated, cursing in Italian, his gaze fixed on Drago, all of it laced with loathing. Rain rattled the ceiling and added its own constant discord to the chaos below. The football commentary shouted over everything.

Maria's mobile buzzed. The ring tone was set to maximum volume and the sound jerked everyone. The movement almost got Drago ribbed by the knife.

"Steady, Laszlo. Your boss will want me in one piece."

"Shut up."

Maria muted the television, answered the call and spoke fast and in a low voice. Afterwards, she gave orders to Laszlo, controlled and deliberate.

"We wait," she said to Drago. She gestured to the tattooed man. His eyes were still fizzing. The confrontation had stirred his blood. Whatever he'd rolled in the reefer had no effect. The shaking, sweaty hands took hold again and Drago was guided towards the bolted door. The iron shafts were slung back with a thump and the door flung open. A hot rush of air invaded the already warm interior. Drago saw white lights and row upon row of wooden trestle tables festooned with greenish plants. Someone shoved him forward. Laszlo kicked out at an ankle. Drago plunged to his hands and knees. He spun in time to see the door smack shut and hear the prison bolts slam.

It was bright and hot and the brightness stung his eyes. Everything was silvery white: the walls, the ceiling, the plastic sheets on the floor. Only the tables were a different colour: off-white, mixed with earth and dust and plant feed. Across the iron roof were strung a series of electric cables and bare light bulbs hung at intervals, blazing down on the habitation. Makeshift reflectors had been created by pinning sheets of aluminium foil to the walls. They added an all over intensity to the vivid glare. He couldn't hear the television. The drum of rain on metal reverberated too loudly. Under it, he could pick out the ever-present bore of an electric generator, probably somewhere just outside the hothouse. The place stank worse than next door.

    Drago got off his knees and coughed, trying to clear his throat of pungent, hot air. He considered the situation anew. Something rankled. Something the girl had said. Walking carefully, Drago inspected the tables. The cannabis plants looked about to flower. The top leaves were long single veined leaflets and below them the foliage ballooned and the leaflets split into seven, eight, ten, eleven veins. He twigged at a tendon, it was rough, arid. This was a good solid crop. Something moved among the fibres. He peered in, saw nothing, only waxy green. Probably a draught. There must be holes all over the place; from the outside the building looked half-collapsed. Unsurprisingly, occasionally, he felt more breaths of air as he began to hunt around the factory. If he was staying, it would do well to check the facilities.

    There were none, except a standing tap in the middle of the floor and an electrical junction box mounted half-way up the far wall to which all the light bulb wires converged. There was a time switch attached to the box. Cannabis plants can prosper in complete artificial light, but an enforced period of dark aids a healthy survival rate. Laszlo, or whoever erected the factory, was obviously aware of this. Also against the wall stood a row of neatly spaced kerosene drums, old ones with the plugs removed. The fuel was still widely used to heat greenhouses. Looking up, Drago saw they stood in line with the overhead lights. Cautiously, he climbed on one and found he could touch the big wooden beams to which the lamps were nailed. Laszlo obviously used the drums as makeshift ladders. There was that draught again. He hadn't imagined it. Returning to ground level, he ran his hand over the wall, feeling the silvery sheet crinkle under his touch. He tapped it. the wall wasn't constructed of brick. It had a hollow, wooden echo. The crumpled foil threw off a vague greenish tint from the plants. Once again a leaf or two shivered. Drago saw it in the tin mirror. The breeze, perhaps. He moved closer to the nearest plant. Something grey scuttled very fast across the tabletop, half-hid by the foliage. Most likely a field mouse. He should have expected as much out here in the countryside.

Drago completed a full circuit of the factory. Unexpectedly, there came a loud click and the lights dimmed to nothing. From squinting in the bright light, Drago was suddenly absorbed by blackness. The afterglow passed in front of his eyes, red and white spots, furiously buzzing, then they too vanished and everything was total darkness. He stood perfectly still, listening. The generator buzzed outside. The hard rain abated. The television was still on. The only new sound was his shallow breath.

Drago wondered if the timer had an override switch. He shuffled towards where he thought the junction box was, hands held out for guidance, dodging tables. Something ran over his foot. Idly he kicked out at whatever it was. His hand caught an outstretched branch. He flicked it. A spider's web straggled between the leaves. He shook it off and kept going. After bumping into more tables, he made it to the junction box and wrestled with the handle to open it. He dug in his pocket for his cigarette lighter, wondered why he'd not thought to use it before, and flicked it on briefly to inspect the inside. Drago wasn't entirely sure what he was looking at. He wasn't helped by haphazard workmanship. The box was packed full, a jumble of wires and fuses. Hopeless. He felt that breeze again, this time by his ankles. That was odd. Why would air come from ground level? Air bricks, he surmised. In the dark, he felt along the wall, tapping again. It wasn't wood, but plasterboard. There was some kind of cavity behind it. Flicking on his lighter once more, he identified the line of staples stamped into the foil. He grabbed at the edge, tearing the thick sheet several ways until he'd exposed the boards beneath. Using the lighter, he could see the badly sawn join. Fat nails had been used to hammer the boards into whatever was behind them. At ground level there was a slim gap, ankle high, and it was through this the breeze blew. Drago lay on the floor, flashed his lighter at the entrance. Nothing but debris. Then something moved, maybe a mouse, scurrying out of the halo of light, across the ground, up a partition. Drago angled the light, trying to get a better view of the scaffold. He thrust his other hand through the gap and tried to grab whatever it was. It was metal.

Kneeling now, Drago pulled aside more foil. The board was a metre wide and a good two or three high, cut badly to size. The shape was less of a concern than the condition. He wasn't sure how much noise he'd make pulling the nails loose. He ran his hands down the edge until he found a point where he could get his fingers underneath. It was tight, but the board had some give in it. The fixings were tired and rusty. He managed to force his fingers in further, scratching and scoring them. He tugged outwards. There was a sharp pop and the wood bowed outwards.

Drago stopped and listened. A light tapping. The last of the rain. The hum of the generator. Behind the door the football. The sound level rose. Drago shoved his hand further into the gap between the board and the wall mount, waiting. Suddenly there was a loud cheering sound. The commentator's voice soared. A goal! Drago yanked hard. Something snapped. The simultaneous sounds covered his assault. The board was riven. Rotten as shit. Probably from the humidity. He moved one section clear. A slender shaft of bluish light penetrated the darkness. Drago could now see the board was attached not to a wall but to the remains of an abandoned milking parlour. Jagged sections of cement and tile stalls lined the length of the near side. At some point it had been knocked through to create a huge space adjoining the farmhouse. He squinted inside, searching the cramped interior. Pale night light was coming from several long slit windows set high on the farthest wall. That was it. Escape. In the eerie glimpses of light, he could see the floor was moving.

"Shit."

Drago snucked back. What the hell was that?

It was deathly still in the factory. The television still churned its high pitched noises. Drago shuffled back, considering his situation. Yes, escape was paramount, but there was a lot of illegal money tied up in the hothouse. An idea started to take shape. Laszlo might be a dab hand with a knife, Maria might have taken his mobile, but they were both as out of focus as their tattooed friend. The idiots had shut him in a room packed full of combustible materials and left him his cigarettes, lighter and a load of old oil drums. Quickly, Drago moved to a table down the aisle. He emptied out his fags and opened the papers letting the tobacco rest in one of the plant pots. The leaves hung so thick they enveloped the side of the trays. He pushed the plants closer. He had tissues in his pocket and added them to the mixture. Next, he picked up one of the drums. It wasn't completely empty. Something liquid sloshed in the bottom. It was awkward to handle, but Drago upended the barrel and the remains of the kerosene tipped out all over the table and the plants. He repeated the trick with a second barrel.

Satisfied, Drago took out his Ronson, rolled open the aperture and turned the lighter on its target, aiming the nozzle at the pile of tobacco.

The long flame shot out and licked at the dried leaves. The tobacco flared quickly and died within a few long seconds. Damn. He'd blown it.

Then, slowly, the darkness began to shine with a tiny sliver of orange. The oil had taken. Instantly, the flame leapt and rushed along the length of the spillage. The vivid orange fingers slapped at the parched leaves. They crumbled, sparked, took the heat. The little bushes smouldered, smoke crackling in wispy spirals. The longer the oil burned, the more damage the flames were doing. Dozens of angry candles were flickering off the spidery plants. Already the whole of one side of the table was alight with tiny fires. Suddenly, as if a trigger had been depressed on a flame thrower, the bushes exploded with a leap of incendiary fire. The whole table was swept up by the pyre and burned bright and harsh. The flames spread out big and wide, tickling the next table and the next. Leaves crinkled, smoked and burnt. Two, three, no four tables were instantly aflame. Drago backed off. Pungent acrid smoke was pouring into the turgid atmosphere. Fire lit the arena. It was time to leave.

Drago dived for the busted hoarding. He shoved it aside with a shoulder and ploughed into the old parlour. Immediately, he ran through strings of spider's webs, fat ones that clung to his face and arms. Smoke was wafting through the gap, swirling in the breeze from the broken window. Ignoring the webs, Drago went for the window, treading on something soft. He spun, slipped. Now something on his arm. He jerked, flapped, but the bastard was still there, clinging to the lining of his clothes. Another was on his leg. They were on the floor too, everywhere, backing away from the increasing inferno. They knew the danger. Their eight legs scrambled. Their bulbous bodies writhed with movement. The poison claws jabbed. The mass of ghostly grey fur moved fast and terrified in the fluttering, licking light. The place was rammed full of tarantulas.

Drago cried out in alarm. It was a natural fear, born from childhood memories of huge black creatures that crawled out of plugholes, that you dreamed would crawl into your mouth, into your food. Even now, when he saw a house spider, he extinguished it quickly, irrationally; scared of such an insignificant animal. Now, he was surrounded with big menacing bastards. They were the size of his hands. Bigger. They moved at speed. They didn't creep, so much as scuttle. They looked evil. Possessed. Eyes as black as death. Hair on stalks, alarmed. They moved with a primitive, almost reptilian gait, head switching left and right, just as Drago had dreamed. The image petrified him. The spiders were climbing, pawing. He closed his mouth, his eyes. The felt feet padded over his skin. The sack-like stomachs bounced. They bit you, remember. They poisoned you. They turned you mad, didn't they? Was that why the tattooed druggie outside was permanently wasted? Had he been driven insane by the venom of these wicked creatures? Drago knew it was a lie. Didn't he? He shuddered. Something crawled along his collar. Up his cheek. The little nippers seemed as big as boots. The eight legs scrambled over his nose, his eyes, he saw through panicked slit lids the tiny hook-like pincers, dripping with animal perspiration, primal fear. If it was terrified, would it attack? There were more of them, clambering clumsily, rapidly everywhere, finding all the nooks and crannies. Everywhere he looked the place was alive with a seething mesh of crawling, creeping grey and black.

The shout of alarm from the factory jerked Drago into action. Ignore the bastards. They're small. Insignificant. Get out of here or bigger bastards will find you.

He flung his arms out, brushed at the thing half on his face and tossed it aside. He turned to the window. The glass was cracked. He reached for it, scrabbled with the spiders up the wall, the mortar turning to powder as he did so. His fingers clung to the lip. One hand thrust at the rusty lock and the whole window fell with its frame, tearing away cement, enlarging the hole. Already the tarantulas were swarming over the ridge. He leapt upwards, forced himself through the aperture, breathing the sweet scent of freedom. Halfway through, there was a sudden yell and a thunderous crack. Wood splintered. The tattooed man was leaping after him, the shattered plaster board flung aside in a tattered heap. The fire was raging bigger than ever. The man's clothes were sparkling with ash and ingots. The heat came at Drago in a rush, the flames attracted by fresh oxygen.

The man yelled and flung himself at the dangling legs. Drago lashed out with a foot. A shoe smacked into bone. Blood spurted down the crazed face, but still he climbed. Drago kicked out again and saw the tattooed body tumble backwards. Drago rolled over the sill. He landed with a thump in an ungainly pile, half in a stinking overflow drain, streams of tarantulas vanishing into the beckoning fields.

Drago skirted the building, feet sliding. The fence to the next field was only a few metres away. The solar panels loomed orange in the firelight. The Cinquecento stood unattended. The driver must have gone to help save the harvest. Drago ran for it. The car was unlocked, but the keys were not inside. Drago grimaced. As he straightened, Laszlo appeared in the doorway, his unkempt hair unmistakeable. The two men stared at each other for a second. Without a thought, Drago sprinted for the wire fence and dived over. He half-ran, half-stumbled, sneaking an over-the-shoulder glance. The factory, so badly maintained, was fully ablaze. Soon the farmhouse would be too. Maria appeared from the raging hell, desperately throwing heroin parcels onto the driveway. Meanwhile, seemingly from nowhere, Laszlo had pulled a large revolver. Drago wondered why he'd never seen it before. Perhaps he'd always carried it. Curious thought, at a time like this.

Laszlo took aim and fired.

Nineteen

Pursuit

Drago dropped like a stone the second Laszlo's hand raised. The shot echoed. The bullet ricochet with a zing. He rolled over in the wet grass, rose to a crouch and sprinted for the nearest structure, a white steel storage container festooned with danger triangles. The second and third shots pranged off the metalwork. Drago huddled behind the building long enough to get his bearings. There was no sense in waiting. He ran towards the first row of sloping panels. They were angled at forty degrees and faced due south to catch the all-day sun. Big stanchions supported the panels and thick heavy cables linked each section to the nearest substation, snaking dangerously over the ground. Occasionally, the silver tiles flashed pale in what passed for moon-glow in the brooding overcast night.

Drago squeezed between the first two panels. Some distance on he could make out a wide central aisle, which he assumed must run the length of the field. To his left was the road. Drago thought he saw Laszlo, silhouetted by flames, moving urgently towards him, one oversized hand stretching out. Drago dived early. He rolled under the wings of a solar panel. Gunshots echoed. The bullets died somewhere between the silver beasts. Drago edged backwards, counting bullets, uncertain what kind of shooter Laszlo possessed, what the range was. Another shot. This one pinged close to his face, snapping a cable, which hissed up like an angry serpent. Drago wormed his way backwards through the dirt, on his elbows and knees, passing one panel and the next until he made it to the central aisle. He turned a corner, praying he was out of range, and ran for it. If Laszlo saw him, he didn't answer the challenge. Drago sprinted down the aisle, upright, his feet sucking into the sodden grass, half an eye on the fire. The blaze illuminated the whole vicinity with a crackling orange glow. Clouds of soot enveloped the highway. Two cars had slowed almost to a stop.

That was why Laszlo hadn't fired: witnesses. Drago seized the opportunity, pushing harder, passing block after block of metal sails until, breathing heavily he reached another wire fence and a field of rustling corn. He climbed the barrier, pausing a moment to take in the chaos at the farm. The drivers had left their vehicles. The scrawny girl tried to shoo them away, protecting the illegal stash from unwelcome eyes. Only two cars? Where was Laszlo's Cinquecento? Drago found a grassy path heading away from the road. He hoped to find a farm track which might take him closer to Melpignano. His luck continued. There was one, splattered with fast drying puddles. Even at night, the heat absorbed everything. Except his sweat. Drago felt it welling up in big drops, running down his face, neck, back and thighs. It stuck to the dirt and crap on his skin and clothes and oozed garlic and wine. All that booze and good food. Not the best preparation for a midnight pursuit.

Ignoring the stench, secretly wishing it might rain again, Drago made a stumbling way along the undulating potholed track, sometimes running, sometimes walking. He passed a big farmhouse with a gated entrance, then a collection of rundown homes, barely alive; lastly a makeshift metal graveyard full of rusting motor cars and tractors. An athlete's stitch started lancing across his belly. He sucked in big breaths to cure it. The road gradually bent towards the shimmered outskirts of Melpignano, the low yellow houses clustered around tight woven streets. The hum of the taranta echoed louder and louder. Presently, Drago broke out of the fields and onto a tarmac road which led to one of the main streets – Castrignano, he thought – a wide expanse lined with souvenir shops and trattorias.

Exhilaration swept over him, burying fatigue for a few moments. He'd thought he was fit. Swimming was one thing; running something else entirely. He ached badly, his legs like lead. Ignore it, Jon; almost there; all you have to do is locate the Maserati.

The makeshift carpark was on the opposite side of the bus station. He saw a little patch of green ahead. A tree lined square he recognised. Yes. There was the Central Bar where he'd first met Laszlo. And there was the bus stop, two winsome girls chatting on a seat, fingers flicking at mobile phones. People were dancing under the branches. A different sound hummed overhead, more drum n bass than violas and guitars. He crossed the street and through the bodies caught sight of a knackered old Cinquecento parked at angles across the road. Beside it was a dark blue Lancia Thema, all cool gangster-chic. Laszlo was talking animatedly to a second man, who incongruously wore a suit. No one wore a suit in Melpignano tonight. The man stared intently at Laszlo, his expression and demeanour never changing whatever tale was being weaved. Even at distance, Drago recognised the sharp features, torn by the goblin-like mouth: Attila Ferrara.

Drago spun. He'd never get past Ferrara's men. He moved at a canter trying to make haste without attracting attention, forcing tired limbs to move while addled thoughts tried to reassess the situation. Half of his mind was occupied with trying to reach the Maserati. The other half was piecing together the jigsaw puzzle he witnessed. Ferrara and Laszlo. The two men were connected, perhaps through the Comte or perhaps through Sabatini. The drugs, the diamonds, the money, all of it illegal yet still none of it made any proper sense. The only thing he knew was that Laszlo had been searching for him and now so was Ferrara. Laszlo's druggie girl had alerted them. That phone call she'd taken. It was the only way they could have got here so fast.

He joined the crowds heading for Piazza San Giorgio, risking a glance up the street. He shouldn't have. Ferrara didn't see him. Nor Laszlo. It was the driver, the boy with the iPhone. He gestured instantly. Ferrara's head craned, the neck twisting without the torso moving, eerie and silent, staring straight ahead.

Drago thrust himself into the crush, a swarming party, all hip-hop vibes and half-naked dancers, people waving sparklers and light sticks, the revolving spectrum dipping and flashing above the heads of gyrating bodies. The square was alive with people milling like ants over one another, the big illuminations throwing ghostly shadows across the mess of activity and turning the arcades into dark sullen caves of secret, where lovers and strangers kissed and fondled. Drago hugged one of the lamp posts, checked across the piazza, seeking signs of the hunter. Nothing. Maybe the crowd had smothered his flight. He didn't believe it. Ferrara probably knew the town. Laszlo certainly.

He saw them. Two camouflaged outfits, the same uniform the

thugs wore on the estate. The jackets that blended so well in the woodland stuck out sorely here, announcing that danger was coming. People veered away from the pair. Drago ducked his head, searching for sanctuary in the bustle of life. He scooted past a man selling chestnuts. Tourists, dancers and carnivalistas mingled, all bodies making for Via Roma.

Drago pushed on through. The crowd wheeled past a corner trattoria, its eaves festooned with flower baskets, the petals sprinkling customers. Drago ducked inside. The fresh hum of walnuts and gorgonzola caught his throat. The zim of espresso mixed with grappa, red wine and cassis sucked at his senses. The place was full to bursting, hardly a spare seat and shoulder to shoulder. Drago forced his way to the counter, taking a corner position where he could watch the doorway. He thought he'd wriggled free, but a few minutes of furtive glimpses revealed a tall, thin angular man, the green and brown jacket a giveaway. He had a nasty carbuncle on the side of his neck. The gamekeeper, Antonio. Drago shuffled further into the shadows. Antonio was making his way methodically through the bar, one table at a time. Drago could see his accomplice too, a fat man, one of the rough bastards who'd tasered the wild boar. The pit of Drago's stomach screwed tight as he watched and waited for the inevitable. They'd find him soon. All he had was safety in numbers. He didn't want to fight them, not in public.

He caught his reflection in a mirror. Even in the dark hubbub of the bar, he looked pale, drawn. His muscles were tensing. He recognised the situation. He remembered the sensations. They were still with him. He never forgot, even after all those years. He'd been holed up with Kent Galloway, his best mate, a drinker, a fighter, a property developer during the week, a football hooligan on Saturdays. They were cornered at the Race Hill Tavern, a vicious little wing-ding off the Levels, Brighton. The bastards had come down from Millwall, lost the game and were out for blood. It was bad bloody luck they still wore their Seagull's scarves. Brighton was a shit team. The crew had ceased going for the football; fighting was all that mattered. Nonetheless, this sort of confrontation wasn't on the agenda. Too close to home. Too many of them. Too little room to manoeuvre. Banter started it, verging from comedy to the insults. Kenny took it amiably until his personal space was invaded. Jostled at the bar, spilling his pint, Kenny snapped. Later, he said it had been a comment about his mother. Zidane had used the same excuse about a similar head butt. Hell, appropriately, broke loose. Sixty seconds and almost a severed thumb later, they were sprinting down Lewes Road, Drago praying for an ambulance, blood gushing from the waggling finger which looked as if it might drop off at any moment. He fainted eventually, more from the beating, he reckoned, but they'd taken out three of the fuckers before scrambling out the door into the rush of a Christmas night. Boxing Day never had a truer meaning.

Drago blinked the memory down. Antonio was only a few tables away. The fat man was working his way up the near side, closing on Drago's position. Unbelievably, they hadn't seen him. It wouldn't be long. Safety in numbers? Drago didn't reckon it. There was a new sound. New music. A sudden skipping thump. His heart. His blood. Beating between his ears. There were three doors behind him, two marked with pictograms for 'male' and 'female.' Another fight in a toilet? Not on his list right now. The third was a swing door sporting the words 'Privato - Personale.' A large, happy waitress came out, chattering furiously over her shoulder to someone inside the kitchen. She carried three dishes swaddled along her arm and began orchestrating a path through the melee, squeezing against Drago with a wicked loud laugh and "Grazie, Signor. Prego! Ha!"

The movement attracted Antonio's attention. He started forward. There was no indication of surprise on his face, only a pinching urgency. Keen, he sought his quarry like a dog. Drago went for the kitchen door. The waitress couldn't restrain him without spilling dishes, but she was in Antonio's way and refused to let him pass. He made to grab her, but she was large enough to intimidate even this thug. His ire didn't help. The locals didn't like it and the hunters got caught in the hubbub.

Drago poured through the kitchen with sudden speed. One chef grabbed at his sleeve. Drago shrugged him off.

"The back? The back door?" he shouted. "Uscita?"

The chef waved to the rear, his face lined with confusion and anger. He shouted something obscene. Drago tore on, that baked walnut zest pinging at his nostrils. The door was open, leading onto a side street. A rat munched on slops in the gutter. Further on, a man and a woman stood and squatted beside each other, urinating in tandem. Drago offered them a sheepish smile as he hurried past.

He turned into the main street, running into the crowds, running on instinct, safety in bloody numbers. The festivities converged on the Convento, past the Palazzo, past the castle. Drago tried not to look back, only forward. The bastards wouldn't be far behind. There must be more of them. Had to be. He jostled everyone, pushing down the long sweeping spine of Via Roma, at its tail the bell tower of the convent. Small alleys and lanes opened on both sides, a honeycomb of medieval streets, interlocked at strange angles, grit on the cobbles, effigies of saints staring out of terracotta grottos. And cutting through the sound of his pounding heart came the crash of the taranta. He was sucked into the huge open forum, the façade of the convent now bejewelled by flashing stroboscopic lights. The images and patterns formed a mad kaleidoscopic haze, switching as the music altered pace and rhythm, red for fast, blue for slow, white for hot. The flat turret loomed omnipotent over the town. Below, the peasants played for their king. The musicians and dancers on the stage struck a hypnotic dramatic accent, the sound rising, falling over the heads of thousands crammed into the theatre, a swelling, half-drunk, dancing animal, its body a crazed heaving mass milling through the backlit spectral hue.

There was no sign of Antonio or the fat man. Drago's tired eyes picked out the souvenir stalls at the forum's far side. He made for them, pushing through uncooperative partygoers, steam still rising from wet clothes. He arrived at the pine cabins, their hatches down, lamps flickering, laden with t-shirts and trinkets, pizza and beer, a summer cousin of a Christmas market. Time to look the part, Jon.

Drago swiped a hat from a stall selling tarantula toys as souvenirs. The hat was shaped like a spider, furry and uncomfortable. Drago sank deeper into the market, moving through the crowds, heading for the corner of the expanse and another rabbit warren of twisted alleys where he could circle back to the car park and the Maserati. He zigzagged between barrows and people, all occupied with their own lives, frivolous, unbeknown. He forced a route through, brushed an arm, knocked a beaker of coffee, swapped insults, stopped dead.

Ahead, Attila Ferrara, flanked by Laszlo, was striding purposefully through the stalls. Christ! How in God's name? Drago barely finished the thought. The bastard's mouth curled with violent satisfaction. Drago plunged between two cabins and back into the thicket of thriving bodies, the mad musical muster beating overhead, trapping the heat. Every chord seemed to suck him further from safety. Disorientated, Drago fought to put distance between hunter and prey. All he could think of was the car park. Where was the bloody orchard – to the west, the south, where? Shoving against the sway, he started craning left and right, forward and back, seeking Antonio's dark camouflage or Laszlo's straggling hair. There! Was that the thug? Laszlo? A pincer movement. With no time to think, Drago switched direction, pushing, apologising, ignoring. He crammed past a big whirling group of young women, oblivious to their joys, only the surrounding crowd, the gaps which opened up. A girl grabbed his hat, lifted it from his head, laughing. Panicked, Drago stopped.

Suddenly, Laszlo hurtled through the throng, grasping, lips drawn back, teeth exposed, a tiger to pounce. A small space opened between them, an arena of minute significance. Drago automatically tensed. Reflexes built up over years of danger, years of practice on the karate mats, years of violent memories. Weariness mattered not. This was instinct. Survival. Running down Lewes Road.

They came together with a thump. The gun was in Laszlo's hand. It lodged across Drago's stomach, pointing away from him. He ignored the weapon and went for the diaphragm. He jabbed hard with rigid pointed fingers. Instantly, Laszlo choked and curled, the pain almost causing paralysis. Drago tripped him, his bladed hand striking at Laszlo's neck. The body jerked once and went limp in mid-step, landing spread-eagled in trampled mud. Drago brutally trod on his spine, heel down. He exited, left boot snapping at the exposed face. There was an obdurate groan. People closed in, more feet kicked the fallen scarecrow, accidentally this time. Someone cried in alarm, tried to attract attention.

Drago vanished into the mess and confusion, shoulders slumped. He spied another camouflage jacket or thought he did.

Sweat was pouring into his eyes. His body ached. He'd been running hard, muscles strained and stretched with tension and action. He'd avoided one fight, triumphed in another, but was losing options and places to hide. His body sagged. He felt it. The stitch first. Now his hard blowing breath. His thighs complained. The ankles swelled. Mouth dry, throat parched. He was out of condition, his body unable to respond. That last brutal episode had sucked at his reserves. No! He had to respond. Had to. He must go to ground, rethink his tactics, but where in this madness, this furious fandango of noise and colour, could he go? He was exhausted with the effort, exhausted with it all, the Albanians, the Italians, Mafia, men or women, diamonds and drugs, the whole bloody lot of them, this whole whirling seething Hieronymus Bosch interpretation of hell. Everything good felt so far away, London, his apartment, everything secure and stable, not this wicked game of life and death. It was happening all over again. Brno, Abu Dhabi, Crete, everywhere he went the fucking devil followed him.

Through the macabre pantomime he glimpsed Antonio easing his way around the rim of the arena. And there was another green jacket closing in. The fat man. No respite. Shaking, Drago hunched over, taking refuge in the shadows. Maybe he could create a scene, get the police involved, an arrest, something the hunters couldn't interfere with. No. He remembered Inspector Gigli. The reluctance of the policeman to be involved in the Mafia's business. Get out of Otranto, he'd advised. About time you listened, Jon.

The scent of singed sausages from the cabin's stove wafted over him. People hustled past. He was a muddy statue, something to be ignored, to be trapped. He wiped his sleeve across his face, clearing the dirty perspiration, clenching and unclenching bruised fists. It would only be moments before they caught him. And when that moment came, he had to strike first, challenge and combat and then run like a fox flees hounds, run again. Drago's muscles tightened, coiled, ready to spring and bite. The contractions pulled at him. The numbers were against him. The next impending tussle would be a brief affair, he felt, hand-to-hand, a knife, a gun, and a dead body hurled and abandoned like a drunken sot. Then at last it would be finished.

Gunshots barked. Startled, Drago looked around, then up. A midnight firework display! Worried the flashes of colour would betray him, he turned into the shadows, away from the ecstatic bodies which sweated and trembled and cooed as the big explosions ripped overhead. Out of the hugging, grinning, shouting figures swirled a slim girl, clad in a barely-there white mini dress, a long white silk scarf wrapped loose at her neck. She stopped directly in Drago's eyeline.

"Buon sera!"

He stared hard at her, not immediately recognising the youthful walnut looks and the long jet black hair. A warm sensation came over him. It was the flirtatious, pouting girl from the restaurant. She looked different without the bikini.

"Hello!" He forced a grin. "You made it."

"Si."

She studied him, flicked her lips with a finger.

"You look shit."

"I'm in trouble."

She cocked her head to one side. Perhaps she hadn't understood.

"I'm in trouble," he repeated. "I need to get to my car."

The girl considered his request. After a few seconds, she held out a hand and he took it, her long fingers curling around his.

"Come," she said. "Is it police?"

"Yes," he lied.

"Police are bastards. Come."

She led him into the forest of bodies, around the outskirts of the forum, towards the convent and the stage and the scaffold erected around it to hold the spotlights. Drago bent to her shoulder. In heels, she was almost as tall as him. She pulled him closer. Over the sweat and grime, Drago smelt an extravagant perfume. Givenchy, maybe; no, Lolita Lempicka. The bergamot betrayed it, that hot sweet scent. Drago breathed it in and cradled her waist, so close he was almost blind to everything except the beautiful odour and the thrilling, fervent smile, all teeth and plump welcoming lips. She felt it, grinned and guided him further through the chaos.

"Your car. It is at bus station?"

"Yes. The carpark on the edge of town."

"Si. I saw it. You are lost. You go wrong way."

"How did you get here?"

"Bus. I go to my friends. I am late. Mama she need help in Il Candela."

Drago nodded: Mama's luck and mine.

They neared the corner of the stage. The music howled. Dancers were on the scaffolds, gyrating madly, a midnight devilish impersonation of the medieval taranta, when women and men would writhe on the ground, grapple and curse and sweat the poison from their bodies. Drago shivered. It was only a myth. But the fear was real. He remembered the soft legs that had crept across his face, tickling his eyes and ears, the claws wondering if Drago was a beast worth biting. His eyes caught something green and brown, close to the entrance and exit point. The fat man.

"There's one of them," he said urgently.

The girl didn't question him. She placed the scarf so it trailed around their heads, necks and shoulders, caught in the midnight breeze, faces inches apart. Instinctively, she wrapped her lips onto his. They tasted as wonderful as they looked: ripe, choice fruit. They kissed long and hard, her tongue running along his teeth, exploring. The girl seized his face in her hands, held onto him until they were through the gap and behind the convent. Free of the confusion, the girl released Drago's mouth and giggled. He couldn't help but grin with her. If he believed in these things, he'd have thought her eyes twinkled. She grabbed his hand and started to skip up the avenue. Even Drago, who thought he was burned out, discovered an extra spring to his step. They circled the town, found the orchard and the Maserati within it. They settled into the welcoming bucket seats. The rain, dirt and shit on the upholstery was going to annoy the hell out of poor Paulo.

Drago turned the ignition and breathed a satisfied sigh as the engine gorgeously rumbled. His tiredness vanished. Behind the wheel, he felt a surge of adrenalin. Here was something he could control, something he could master, make his own, a little piece of the world where nobody could touch him, where he wouldn't be afraid.

Suddenly excited, he ran through the gears and was heading out of Melpignano in seconds. He was grinning. The bastards had not expected love to come to the rescue. Or lust, he corrected.

"Where am I going?" he asked.

"You must wash," she said by way of an answer.

"I don't have a hotel."

"Okay. My house. Drive fast. Very fast."

"Prego."

Drago saw no reason not to oblige. As they cleared town, she pulled out her mobile and tapped out a text.

"For my friends," she explained. "They miss me."

There was a brief to-and-fro of messages, some of which made her laugh, then, finished and happy, she pushed back the seat and wrestled off the belt.

"How fast you drive?" she shouted.

He touched one hundred. Laughing, the girl placed her hands on the dash and knelt upright, the hot wind rushing over her, blowing what passed for a dress tight against her taut breasts and smooth swallow belly. She almost lost the scarf, caught it and a metre and a half of expensive silk trailed behind them, snatching the shallow moonlight and the obdurate headlights of other cars as the Maserati swept past them. He couldn't help but look. She was as tempting now as when he'd first met her half-naked and stretched across Il Candela's patio. She was young. She was beautiful. She was intoxicating. She was giddy with restlessness. His foot pressed hard on the accelerator. He didn't reduce speed until he reached Galliano and she finally sat down with a deep moan, a hand clutching her bare throat.

The girl's apartment was a few streets from Il Candela. She led him up the battered stone stairway and through a creaking door. One single lime green lamp illuminated the room. The place was small, compact and untidy. A week's worth of laundry was littered across the floor. Without a word the girl shut the door and pulled him close to her. Their lips met. It wasn't like before, not hot and cunning. This was a tingling kiss. The sort you pray for, the sort which reminds you how love should always be. But this wasn't love. It was play-acting of the most virulent kind.

When Drago emerged naked and dripping from the shower, she was lying on the bed, shoes kicked off, propped up on an elbow, toying with her long hair. Gaze lingering, she knelt and reached out, panting as they embraced. Drago thumbed the hem of her dress, lifted it over her head and tore down her panties. She didn't stop him. This time the kiss was more of a bite, urgent, violent and primitive. Drago's hand moved to her knees and thrust them apart. She lay back. All he could smell was the wicked bergamot. All he could see was the amorous white of her tempestuous teeth.

Twenty

Touched by Death

It was like being touched by death: an impersonal sensation: the cool point, about half an inch in diameter, pressed against his cheek just below the eye socket. Slowly, Drago's eye lid cracked open.

It was still dark. He was looking at the gun barrel of a Tanfoglio pistol. The combat switch was off. The hammer was back. They called this 'condition one.' Ready to kill. Nasty. Not the sort of thing you made any sudden moves against. Beyond it, framed in the moonlight shimmering through the open window, was Attila Ferrara.

"Shh," was all he said before stepping back, gently removing the gun from Drago's face. "Get dressed. Slow and quiet, please."

Drago slowly peeled back sheet and planted his feet on the cold floor. As cold as the muzzle of the gun, but not as scary. He was unclothed. He took one look at the still sleeping girl. She was out. Too much booze and weed between fucks. He didn't regret it, but this wasn't how he'd wanted it to end. Had it all been too much of a coincidence? They'd found him easily in Melpignano. The girl knew he was going there. And then she'd appeared at the festival. She'd seen his car. She'd been texting her friends. Her little heavenly hovel was dozens of secluded miles from the noisy crowds and fireworks. No more public confrontations, no more fights or chases, just a quick night of love, a quiet kidnap and one hundred Euros stuffed down her knickers.

"The girl?" he asked in a low voice.

"Yes, but we'd have found you anyway."

Drago pulled on his trousers and fixed his socks and shoes. "You think so?"

"You drive the only decent car in the Salentine."

"I've been told that already."

Drago put on his shirt and bent to grab his jacket. Her face was turned his way and he could still see lipstick spoilt on her mouth.

"Regrets?"

"No," said Drago. "I don't even know her name."

They went outside into what wasn't quite dark but couldn't be called day. The dull time. It weighed heavy on Drago's shoulders. The blue Lancia was stationed in the road outside, next to the Maserati, which even in the dull time seemed to sparkle like a polished gem.

They left the jewel behind. The fat man drove at a steady careful pace along the winding roads of the Salentine. Ferrara sat in the front and Drago was squeezed on the back seat between Antonio and another ugly mug, name unmentioned and unnecessary, silent as the night heather. Only the gentle sway of the car as it took a bend disturbed their posture and made them breathe in or out. They could have been Greek statues, remnants of the region's once powerful landlords. As dawn banished twilight, vivid colours took form and the Hellenic influence dissipated. The famous whitewashed terracotta villages gradually dissipated, house by house, into dusty reds and pinks, speckled with earthen brown, as if the people wanted to demonstrate by the decor of their abode who they lived for, to leave the bland Orthodox for the ruddy Catholic. Choices made in heaven, thought Drago, history falling away from him as they pressed higher into the heel, past Lecce and into Brindisi, where the ships never came and Spartacus was double-crossed, where the Apian Way was only paved with crucifixes not gold. Drago offered a wry smile as he gazed at the crackling wheat fields. Who betrayed Spartacus? A slave woman, perhaps. The thought struck as almost ironic. He must do more research on irony.

They turned vaguely west, cutting across the instep towards the coast where the industrial wastelands bruised the pastel paints of the early dawn canvas, the cranes and rigs and storage yards sprouting like waking giants from the sleeping land. They continued sedately up the SS7 into Basilicata, possibly the poorest of the poor south, famed for its rugged cut-off cliff-hugging townships, its cacti and constantly chirping crickets. Occasionally, a naked village or a ruined castle rose on the crest of a low horizon, disturbing the flat tranquil sea of green and yellow, wheat for the nation and bread for the world. Here, the once isolated land seemed to well up out of the soil and inhabit the surroundings, its antecedents, its myths and legends pursuing the car as it rambled through the fertile unhindered landscape, talking to it, beckoning, begging, until Drago swore the sound of long buried voices inhabited the wind. Quickly, he closed his eyes to the thought. Just as quickly, he was jostled awake.

They'd been travelling for almost three hours. It was hard to gain speed on the perpetual bendy roads. The town had barely woken. The faintest stirrings of life: an old woman brushing stone steps, a flower seller on his way to his pitch, a photographer catching the sunrise. Somewhere a radio played the latest hits as the day's first coffee was filtered. Above and on both sides, the city fanned out along and up the steep ridges, capped by the impossibly tall bell tower of the cathedral. Tinged amber by the sleek morning sun, Matera was a bleary, silent effigy, its elegant facades hiding the caves behind, the extravagant creations on the scar of a dizzying ravine.

They entered from the north along the winding path of Via Madonna della Virtu, out to the edge of the canyon, where only a stone wall seemed to prevent the city from tumbling over the precipice. The fat man parked the car in an unmarked bay, its panorama the cliffs on the opposite ridge, where Drago could make out still more desolate caves.

Without a word, they disembarked and Drago was led up an unmarked path, steps cut into the sandy stone, the occasional block of paving cement the only sop to modernity. Doorways were bolted shut, sheets of steel screwed into the rock, keys thrown away. Sometimes a window had been crowbarred open and Drago glimpsed cold interiors splattered with the remnants of twenty-first century life, a waste tip, a dog's coffin, a hollow shell. They continued up the path, the unnamed man taking Drago's elbow in a pinching grip. There was an old café at one level, advertised by a scratched wooden sign. Two creased women sat outside watching the blood-bleached sunrise, cigarettes in hand, black shawls over heads. They stared at the group, but said nothing. The eyes betrayed what they already knew. The world never changes in Matera; life and death goes on beneath the blistering sun, accompanied by tourists and insects. The day was already hot. Drago could feel the sweat mounting on his shoulders.

They stopped by one of the steel doors. Ferrara produced a key and cranked open the lock. The metal squealed as it moved. He hit a chunky, old-fashioned switch and the gloom became light.

The place wasn't as awful as Drago anticipated. It was clean and airy. The walls had been given a fresh lick of lime mortar. There were two central light bulbs. The shelves cut in the walls might have once held books, but had cloths and provisions stacked on them. A small open fire was arranged beneath a chimney breast, in reality a hole cut into and up through the rock. Cold ashes scattered across the hearth from when it was last lit. There was a table and several chairs, leather covered. A small archway led to a second room, this one with a bed in it. Further back another, larger arch had been hewn out of the rock face leading to another space, barriered by a curtain. Beneath Drago's feet a huge cistern had been dug from the floor. The original rock channels from above had eroded and been replaced by plastic pipes depositing cool heaven-sent rainwater into the massive tank. A barred hatch prevented anyone dropping bodily into the pool.

While the fat man went to shut the door, Antonio swung out one of the chairs and placed it in the centre of the room. Ferrara took a second seat and arranged it a metre from the first. He sat, right ankle on the left knee, the gun resting on his thigh, and gestured to the empty chair.

"Prego, Mr Drago."

Antonio slapped a hand on Drago's shoulder and thrust him onto the seat.

"Let me explain what is about to happen," continued Ferrara. "You can tell me what I want to know, in which case we will be finished quickly, or you can refuse to tell me. That action may take considerably longer."

"I guess it depends on what you want to know."

"Mr Drago, first, let me say I admire a man with spirit and what you English call 'guts'. There is a time when it can be useful and madly exciting. Soldiers, naturally, but also more mundane pursuits: boxers who get themselves needlessly punched to pulp, highwire stuntmen or trapeze artists, the drivers at Le Mans, the Palio horsemen, running with the bulls, perhaps too those who give personal sacrifice and, maybe in sorrow, suicides. There is no need for you to show guts. No need to be punched to oblivion. We do not need to argue. We can settle this very easily."

"Who's arguing?"

Ferrara didn't reply, only inclined his eyes to Antonio, who gave Drago a hefty, openhanded thwack on the back on the skull. He almost toppled from the seat with surprise.

"Alright." Drago winced. "What exactly am I supposed to tell you?"

"Il Papavero," stated Ferrara. "Where is it?"

The question wasn't a surprise. Drago didn't say anything. He had to: amongst all the excitement, the good food and wine, the music and the sex, he hadn't prepared a decent lie to tell anyone who asked. Something of an oversight, Jon.

"We know it isn't in your car," continued Ferrara. "We checked."

"I hope you didn't damage the Spyder. My friend will be upset."

Another slap.

"Superficial grazes," Ferrara said sneering, "unlike what may happen to you. We also searched the Villa Caprese in Otranto and your hotel room in Bari. We even checked Il Candera in case our girl was trying to be clever."

"She's too smart a cookie."

Ferrara snorted just how she did, which made Drago wonder on the niceties of their relationship.

"No clever comments, please. Tell me, where did you hide it?"

"I have no idea where it is."

"Please tell me you didn't lose it?"

"No."

"Then?"

"Why's Sabatini getting you to do his dirty work, Ferrara?" No reply, so Drago carried on. "I understand Sabatini's obsession with the thing. Heroin is replaceable. Splendid gemstones are not. The thief took all the diamonds in that safe, or at least a good four bags full. How are you going to keep that from the Comte?"

"A minor complication. Plans must be fluid. Whatever arrangement I made with Sabatini will soon be changed."

"What arrangement have you made?"

"That does not concern you."

"You're selling his heroin. He's robbing your boss. I take

it you're getting a hefty cut all round." Drago paused. "And you've used that money to set up your cannabis factory. I'm afraid that's not going to bring you any income any longer."

"You are very astute." Ferrara shrugged. "It is no matter. I have other warehouses."

"Looking to overthrow the old empire?" Drago noticed the smirk which flashed across the man's creased features. "And you can do it with Sabatini's help. Is that why you're so keen to do his bidding?"

"My men know the Salentine better than his."

"Good thing too, because they'll be searching a long time."

"Oh?"

"Yes, because I have no idea where the jewel is."

Drago was expecting a slap. Ferrara merely sat. The forefinger of his right hand tapped on the barrel of the pistol. The tinny sound echoed in the enclosed space. The wait went on for several minutes during which nobody moved. Outside the cicadas began to breathe.

"Vito. Antonio."

The third hood came over and made a grab for Drago's right wrist. He moved to prevent it and found his other hand was being snared by Antonio. The two men snapped Drago's wrists into a pair of metal cuffs, held tight behind the back of the chair. The hoops cut into his skin.

Ferrara went to the shelves. He set down the gun and picked up a bottle whose content was obscured by the rough waxy coat applied to the outside to keep the spirit cool. He poured a slug into a small shot glass and made his way over to Drago, tumbler in hand, bottle in the other. He waved the glass under his prisoner's nose. It was grappa. Drago detected the sweet sickly scent, the residue of more than one bad wine, skins and juice and stems together, reduced, fermented, a pomace as bad as rotten eggs, not stored well, not refined at all. This was a strong dose. Homemade hooch of the very worst kind.

"Here," said Ferrara.

"It's a little early for drinking."

"You must accept hospitality, Mr Drago. This isn't a choice, you understand."

Ferrara downed the shot. It was a signal. Immediately, the two men grasped Drago's shoulders and pulled his head back, opening his jaw with thin smelly fingers. He struggled against the wiry grip. It was impossible to fight when his hands were tied. Ferrara leaned across him and tipped the bottle so the spirit trickled into Drago's mouth. It stung. He tried to spit it out, succeeded, but the trickle became a torrent and when his mouth was full and his throat couldn't stop the tide, he gulped and wretched and the powerful liquid slipped down his gullet, stinging all the way. His eyes watered. He gasped. They repeated the offense. Drago's head swam.

"We can go on like this all day," said Ferrara, indicating the row of similar bottles that sat on the shelf, "if you want."

"I don't know where the bloody thing is."

"You lie so badly. The girl has already told Sabatini you took it."

"You're lying."

Again his head was jerked back. Again the hands swept over his lips, opened his mouth. Again the spirit dashed into his throat. Again. Again.

Drago threw up. The brownish gunge splattered across yellow rock, speckled Ferrara's trousers, who paid it no attention and lifted the bottle once more. Drago whipped his head aside, trying to break the hands which held him. Some of the stuff went in his eyes, on his shirt. The neck of the bottle was shoved right between his teeth. Ferrara upended it and the shit gushed down his throat, drowning him. Everything swam, the faces leering at him, the sulphur-grey ceiling, the ammonia taste, the sound of the questions, the smashing of broken glass and then in a delirious moment, Drago passed out.

When he woke, the sickness bit. Drago hacked. Half of what was in came out. He couldn't focus on anything. The world was a blur. His belly was churning. He vomited again. Nothing stopped. There was a fresh uncorked bottle making its way to his mouth. They held back his head, opened him up, poured the grappa like it was a soda fountain. His throat burnt under the assault.

"What's he done to her?" he said vaguely.

Ferrara laughed. He said nothing. They tossed his head and the whole bloody process started over and over.

Drago spewed out the last of the third bottle. He couldn't stay upright anymore and he toppled sideways, dragging the chair with him. His head cracked on the rock and his groans ceased. When he came to, he gurgled like a baby and wet himself like a child. His head lolled on his chest. He could have opened his eyes and said something. The words 'bastards' and 'shits' came to immediate mind. He stopped the words forming, forced his eyes to stay shut and the world closed in again, this time for longer.

It was like an enormous cloud. Everything was white and sparkling. Rain drops. It was cool and it was clear and it was soft. For the few minutes, the few hours, he stayed in the cloud he saw icicles form, saw the mists of rain, the wet season's condensation tremble and fall, speckles on an endless sheen on white and out of the whiteness he saw streaks of glistening ice cold water, chandeliers of it, rippling light shone through it and around it, huge hundred, two hundred piece arrow headed patterns flickered across the whiteness, patterns of ruby and gold, coral pink, beryl, copper and cobalt, damson, a sweeping, swishing curtain of rainbow prisms. How he wanted to see the rainbow's end, like his mother told him as a tiny child, safe, over the rainbow, where the sunbeams lie, damson sunbeams. He breathed a long shallow breath, so long he wondered if his respiratory functions had ceased. Damsons. Blood diamonds. Il Papavero. Post boxes. Delivery times. Time. He had to fill the time. They mustn't find out where he'd sent it. They say you can fight torture. They say you should concentrate on a single thing, the one thing which is important to you, the one thing which keeps you wanting to live. Ariana. Her face drifted into his mind, pixilated and reformed, an apparition solely for his torment. What had she confessed to Sabatini? How easy had it been? Or how hard? Had he used the flagellator? Did she struggle? Jesus Christ. Pain. Fucking Christ. More pain. Madelaine. Ariana. Jon Drago. His addled mind didn't have the luxury of comprehension. His drunk, tired, confused brain ached and time, that single vicious commodity, seemed to swell and compress with the beat of the blood in his veins. Slowly he opened his eyes, vision wheeling.

They had abandoned him on the floor, lying in his own mess. He could feel a light breeze on his cheek. It was coming from somewhere behind him. Through half-open eyes, Drago watched the four men eating cold sausage, talking and drinking coffee laced with that same sickly grappa. Had he told them anything? He couldn't even feel his tongue. His head pounded. He took big heavy sucks of dusty air. Think of her: think of Ariana.

When they came back, a decision had been made. The cuffs were released and Drago felt his wrists expand with relief. He flexed his dead fingers. The moment of temper hardly lasted. They were on him quickly. Vito carried a short curve-bladed knife, something you'd see farmers using, and he sliced at Drago's clothes. They fell away in strips. His shoes and socks were yanked off. Dragged to his feet, Drago almost collapsed. The alcohol racked his body. His insides were battered. His head was empty of everything bar a thumping grinding ache. They dragged him to the rear of the cave, under the curtained arch and up the wooden staircase which led to an open vent and the outside. That explained the breeze then. Antonio shoved him onto the rocky outcrop.

Drago knelt on bare hot stone. It was a makeshift, whitewashed rooftop patio, surrounded on three sides by the jutting pitched walls and roofs of other caves dwellings. A cheap table and chair stood beneath a parasol. The umbrella was fixed into a hole cored in the rock. It was folded down. The heat bore onto the limestone, scolding his toes and knees. It was a sun trap. The rock shelf faced due south. Drago stared across the expanse of blazing tufa buildings. Below, the ravine cut into the world, its sides sharp and unforgiving. Above, somewhere further up the escarpment, behind the litter of the Sasso Barisano was the Piazza Vittorio Veneto, the gateway to what had become a personal hell.

The men moved the furniture and detached the shade from the parasol, leaving the slender steel pole. Drago vaguely took in the hook at its summit. He was made to stand against the pole, the cuffs were snapped back on his wrists and his arms were pulled above the frame, the chain snared through a hook. It was supremely uncomfortable. He could hardly move left or right. Ferrara scratched his chin, inspecting the half-tanned body, raw and pasty under the sun. He made an indistinct gesture. Antonio leant over, pulled at Drago's boxers and ripped them away. Already he was scalding. It was hotter than Hades out here. The sun seemed higher than ever, the sky so pale of blue it could have been white. Big dollops of perspiration started to form on his forehead and chest. Whatever wind there was couldn't dent the sweltering steam-bath atmosphere. One single cloud had the audacity to pass in front of the sun and offer temporary respite.

"You look as if you need a little colour," said Ferrara. "Too many nights in restaurants and discos, Mr Drago. They don't prepare you for the outside world. Not this world."

Ferrara gave silent instructions with his fingers. From the back of the terrace the two thugs dragged over a wooden sunscreen and began to unfold it. Drago hadn't noticed the unlikely item of equipment because he'd had his back turned. The men placed it so Drago was half surrounded. The screen wasn't made of wood on the inside. Long mirrors replaced the panels. Ferrara inspected the arrangement.

"The Chinese Communist Party are renowned for their elaborate torture methods, Mr Drago," he explained, "methods which can almost be deemed accidental acts of nature. The wardens at Deyang prison in Sichuan have devised a method known as 'warming up' or more romantically 'the sunflower torture.' The temperature in Deyang is known to regularly exceed 40° Celsius in the summer. The cement parade grounds frequently touch a ground heat of 70°. Prisoners on military drill are known to faint. Particularly belligerent prisoners are isolated in a small cell for weeks, months, even a year, with no access to sunlight. When the temperature is appropriate, they are taken out into the sunlight and forced to stand in the parade square beneath the sun. They are denied water. They suffer excruciating sun burn. I have refined the method. For my stage one, I use alcohol to increase dehydration. Today the temperature is already 39°. I've always wanted to test stage two."

Drago began to understand what was happening. As the slow-witted cloud dragged itself free of the sun's glare, the rays struck the pinnacle of a mirror to Drago's left and instantly he felt that spiky, warm sensation you get from direct hot sunlight. His left arm first, but gradually the sensation spread to the whole left side of his body, his shoulder, chest and leg, his groin. He tried to curl away from it, but the heat caught him as if he was prodded by an iron. During the fresh winter months, he might have escaped major punishment, but today was high summer and a roasting was going to be a roasting.

The sweat came fast from his pores. As fast as it seeped, the sun soaked it up. His dry skin puckered and pulled at muscles, uncertain how to react to the sudden violent attack. His mouth and throat was already parched from the grappa. He tried to refrain from licking his lips, but the effort was too great. He felt his eyes begin to dry. The world became still. The only sound was the occasional mocking call of a motor car somewhere below. That and the damn crickets. Drago twitched. Flies buzzed at his salty skin. Beads of sweat eked from his pores. A little river dribbled from his chin and neck. His chest hair turned the stream into a delta. He said nothing. He heard a click of fingers followed by footsteps and the scrape of wood on rock and the concertina unfolded. He closed his eyes to the thresholds of pain.

This must be what hell is like. He was bludgeoned by a great pulse of heat as if someone had opened a blast furnace. Instinctively, Drago tried to turn from it, but there was nowhere to turn to. He tried to fight the bonds. Too damn tight. He gritted his teeth, hissed an obscenity. He rolled his head aside, only to find the reflections encased him. The screen was wrapped and closed except for a slim partition through which Ferrara's face glowered, almost as ravenous as the sun.

There was hardly any air inside the box. Drago tried to control his breathing, thinking quickly. Everything was in the back of his mind, all the information, but he tried not to focus on it, tried to think of cool streams, of clouds of ice and crystal chandeliers. It was an impossible task such was the force of the heat pushing on his chest, his face, his genitals. Something must be burning. Was his hair singed, his blood boiling? He rasped for air. Everything contorted, tighter and tighter, his brain, his lungs, so tight he couldn't live. He knew what they wanted. He buried the information. Snapped it shut into a locked box in his mind. His heart snapped with it. His flesh surely was baking. The walls of the makeshift sweatbox seemed to bend and twist. The mirrors shimmered as if waterfalls had invaded this private hell house. His bones were turning to blubber. His mind was an uninhabitable desert, miles of painful, shifting sand. And as the torturous swords of sunlight cut his skin, the bright white pulsing disc seemed to mutate into bloody inexorable red and one thought stayed clear, one secret must stay closed: Il Papavero.

Twenty One

Sada

It was agony. Drago's eyes were seared shut. Gradually, the lids creased apart. The doors to the world were flickering, the slits of his lashes masking what was beyond: a half-lit interior. He closed them again. His whole body was sore. His nostrils were filled with a pungent tang. It reminded him of holidays on the Costa del Sol. Torremolinos, bad sandcastles and mothers rubbing lotion into fair skin. He curled. His skin tightened. He delicately ran his fingers across an arm. It was dry and leathery. Hairs jutted out of the pores. Drago brushed at the offending limb. Broken, reptilian scales crinkled loose at his touch. He raised his hand to his nose and sniffed. Calamine.

Torremolinos it was then. Except he couldn't hear the sea and there was no mother to scold him.

Drago tried again. This time the lids made it past half-way. He took in the white sheets that swaddled him, stained pink by the offensive medicinal application. The room was in half-shade. Heavy drapes were pulled across the twin windows until only a graft of orange gloom remained, swathed by the net curtains. They billowed gently. The windows, floor to ceiling constructions, must be open. He could hear nothing except the reverberation of his heartbeat. There were no car engines, no music, no voices, none of the aural sounds you'd expect in a big town, perhaps the whisper of a chattering bird. He must be in the countryside and a long way from civilisation. The walls were lined with walnut panels. He was reminded of Tarantella, that tomblike, cobwebbed shadow of a mansion, and the leering effigy of the Comte staring blankly from his armchair, the sparkling droplet diamonds that clung to the chandeliers, like water, like poison, cyanide to be breathed in. God, he wasn't there was he?

No. This place was clean. There was no dust, no wrinkled decaying carpets, no ornamentation. Even through the waft of calamine, he could tell the room was aired, fresh and invigorating. There was even a vase of flowers positioned on a chunky table near the window. Drago stretched his muscles a little, first his arms and then his legs, twirling his ankles, bending his knees. Everything creaked. He was stiff and sore. The memory didn't need to come back to him. The flashing sunlight. The heat and fire that penetrated every pore. Eyes closed to the vicious white intensity. Mind closed. Skin crawling, baking, crackling. He must have passed out. He might have told them something. If he had, they had not stopped. The whole exercise was an excuse to indulge in sadistic pleasure.

Drago's tongue poked out and lapped at stung lips. His throat was a desert. He absently rolled over, felt his skin groan and grimaced. There was a glass of water on the bedside table. The glass was chilled to touch. He dragged it towards his face and took a sip. The shock of the cold made him choke. He dribbled rather than drank. He exhaled long and hard, replaced the glass and collapsed on the pillows, head absorbed in cool cotton, staring at the ceiling, all dark panels and one single unfussy lampshade of green crinoline.

He may have slept again. He wasn't sure. He could smell the lotion. He could also smell coffee, Italian, dark, strong and comforting. He hauled his biting body onto its elbows. His beard was scratchy. He'd not shaved since, since when? How long had he lain here? Drago inspected the room in more detail. The leaf had been pulled from the table and a linen cloth spread. Sliced bread, yoghurt, preserves and fruit had been placed neatly in a circle. His stomach gave an appreciative rumble. He forced himself to sit up. The sheet dropped to his waist. He was still naked. He looked at the calloused skin, blotchy with the lotion, red with pain. Some areas revealed big plum-coloured scabs. He touched one near his left breast. It was like bark. It took a tremendous effort not to pick at it. The patches itched. He caressed one or two in an attempt to relieve the pain. It returned twice as bad, as if he was stung by hornets.

Slowly, Drago swung his legs over the side of the bed and stepped onto swollen feet. He yanked at the sheet, pulled it free of the mattress and wrapped his body in it, a corpse blanket set to torch. The irony wasn't lost on Drago. He sipped more water, noting the crystal tumbler was clean and untouched, no tell-tale calamine prints stained the engraved pattern. He sat at the table. Two places were laid on opposite sides of the extravagant floral display. Next to the coffee pot was a tiny brass bell. Drago pondered a second, lifted it and delivered a sharp one-two. The tinny echo was like thunder in the quiet chamber. He almost jumped at the sudden intrusion of sound. He started to eat. The knife rasped as it cut into the bread and drew a line on the China plate. The fresh coffee gurgled like a baby when he poured. The warm handle made him wince. He heard himself chew. His muscles relaxed, tensed, relaxed, the jaw working in time to the steady tap-tap of oncoming footsteps.

Drago's right hand tightened on the knife. He raised the cup to his lips. He sipped, sucked in air to soothe the parched lips, eyes swivelling. A figure appeared through the net curtains. She was dressed in a beekeeper's smock. The head covering had been removed and was tucked under the woman's arm. The thick dark hair was parted in the centre, exposing grey roots, and tucked into the smock at the rear.

"Hello, Mr Drago."

She spoke in good, schooled English. The words were accompanied by a wide smile which formed creases on the strong peasant face.

Who the hell was this? He took another bite but did not relax his grip on the knife.

"Hello."

"You've been sleeping all afternoon. I was beginning to be worried."

"Me too."

"I expect you are wondering who I am."

"It crossed my mind." Drago popped the last of the bread in his mouth. "But first, tell me: am I a guest or a prisoner?"

"A guest," she replied easily. "I don't take prisoners, Mr Drago. If I considered you any sort of threat, you would already be dead."

"That's reassuring. Where am I?"

"I Campo di Mielle, my estate. You would call it 'Honey Fields'. I cultivate Ligurian bees here, some of the time."

"And the rest of the time?"

"I own and manage the estate. We make bread here also. Do you like it?"

"Very much." Drago put down the knife. "Can I offer you some coffee?" He reached for the coffee pot and flinched again. The woman shook her head.

"Stop that. Let me. You're like a stubborn child."

She threw the hat and smock on the floor, crossed to the table and poured for him. She wore a practical dark blue sweater and slacks combination. He thought she smelt of myrtle, that delicate earthy blossom.

"You never stop talking," the woman continued as she sat down and pulled the cup towards her. "You should hear yourself. Do you know you talk in your sleep?"

"I expect I was delirious."

"Who's Madeleine?"

Drago raised an eyebrow.

"I said that?"

"Yes. Once or twice. You also mentioned Ariana, Monty and your mother."

"Monty was a cat."

"A cat?"

"I don't have pets any longer. I assume you know who Ariana is?"

"Is it obvious?"

"No. But you must be something to do with Atilla Ferrara or else I wouldn't be alive now, and if you're associated with him, you'll know I'm involved with Ariana and that she's Sabatini's woman. That's why I was being hunted down."

The woman made no reply. She sipped the coffee. Her eyes were like warm teak. They watched him without any judgement.

"My men reached you sometime after you passed out. Ferrara had abandoned you on his terrace. You've been asleep all afternoon. Your injuries are painful, but they won't leave any permanent marks."

"I suppose I ought to say thank you," he said.

"There's no need. Ferrara is no friend of mine. He is, what would you English call it, a loose cannon? I shouldn't trust him."

"But you do."

"He helps my business."

"Which is what exactly?"

"My name is Sada. I am Capo of the Unione Sacre Croce."

Drago watched the dark, chiselled face. She seemed cold, detached, as if a cloud had landed on her shoulders. The moment passed and the warmth came back as suddenly as it had departed.

"The Sacred Cross," Drago confirmed.

"Yes."

"You mean the Mafia?"

"We don't have any Mafioso in Puglia," replied Sada, "not the Hollywood version or whatever you might be thinking. But, like everywhere in Italy, we have organised crime. There are ruffian pickpockets on the streets of Bari, gangs of car thieves in Lecce, brothels throughout the Salentine, smugglers along the Adriatic coast, venal politicians in Brindisi or corrupt developers in Taranto and dishonest policemen everywhere. So, yes, there is crime, but we do not live by an unwritten code of honour. We are not dictatorial families, unlike our neighbours in the Two Sicily's.

"That does not mean we are not tenacious, often vicious institutions. We both subjugate and protect. I am both God and Mother to the union, God and Mother to the populace. The Sacred Cross has risen through the communities it employs. We reward individual and collective endeavour if it adds value to our corporate portfolio, albeit operating in the blackest of markets. Because we value everyone, we call ourselves 'Unione'."

"What exactly is your line of corporate business?"

"I sell drugs."

She paused. The expressive dark eyes squinted. Another fleeting moment, less than a second. If she'd been a gambler, Drago would have reckoned it was her tell. Once gone, she stayed immaculately composed, and picked up the China cup from the linen baize as if it was a winning ace of spades.

"It isn't pretty, Mr Drago. I make no apologies for it. I had no choice in the matter. My grandfather had a son, but he was born blind, a medical complication. Grandfather couldn't trust him with the family business if he couldn't see friends and enemies. He was bought an estate and an old extinct title. A life of retirement. Some people still think he is the godfather, but the responsibility has been mine from an early age. Grandfather refused my mother, his daughter, the rights to teach me the woman's world. It is only now I've become a gardener, cook and lacemaker. I was raised tied to the organisation. If I had not officiated over and subsequently reformed the Unione, my grandfather's legacy would be unbound and that was not an option. This is the way of the world here."

Drago pondered his host. She'd clearly been his saviour, yet something clawed at his throat and eventually the words burst out, carefully, methodically, as if he was directing a dissection, not wanting to miss a single incision.

"I'm not adverse to the odd drug being passed, but you're making a killing with it, Sada, both in monetary terms and in lives. I don't believe that's the way of the world anywhere."

"Then your version of the world doesn't tally with mine, Mr Drago."

If he expected anger or disappointment, there was none. Sada remained unfettered. She sipped her coffee as if the words hadn't been uttered and watched as Drago resumed his meal. He dug into an unmarked pot of fresh honey culled from the hives somewhere beyond the net curtains. He poured more coffee for them both, ignoring the sharp pain in his fingers. When they had finished, Sada stood up.

"You need to bathe," she said and turned to retrieve the discarded apiarist's uniform. "I have a nurse. She will help you wash and redress your wounds. Take a walk in the grounds and don't eat too much. I eat at nine and I wish you join me for dinner. You are a lucky man, Mr Drago. Do not forget it."

"That sounds like a threat."

Sada smiled.

"I have guards. It is very safe at Honey Fields. I can keep people out. I can keep people in. Please, accept my hospitality and do not attempt anything foolish."

***

The Ligurian bee crawled along the edge of the flower basket, its abdomen heavy with pollen, a black and yellow patch on the green and pink of the interwoven geraniums. It took flight for a second and jumped over the thicket of leaves, perched precariously on a feather-like petal and carefully extended its proboscis.

Marcelo Sabatini watched the performance from distance. The insect was so large that when it flew from flower to flower, a flat midday shadow was cast on the paving stones. He drank coffee. It was rich, chocolatey. He sat under the shady eaves of Sada's summer house, surrounded by an endless sea of geraniums and beyond them row upon row of wooden hives. Sabatini contemplated the benign nature of power. Here, everything was provided, as it once might have been for a Roman Consul: the meat, the bread, the wine, the fruit, the milk and honey, the harvest and the wealth, provided by beasts of burden, both animal and human. And how easy it must have been and must be to take one of those beasts and crush it, on a whim, and still retain the wealth and influence. How easy, he considered, must it be to take everything and leave nothing. Hadn't his father abandoned Puglia, Basilicata and Sicilia because of this recurring fate? Hadn't he deserted and fought for Shehu's partisans because there was nothing in the Salentine for him; nothing except childhood fairy stories? Or had it really been love? No, there was little of that.

He imagined his mother kneeling here, tending flowers by his knee, just as she would darn a sock or a trouser when she sat beside his bed in the cramped room they called home, her fingers delicate, her proud face a mask of concentration, her eyes burning, twin embers of coal, the passion always testing the restraints. And now he imagined his father, tall, huge, filling the chair with his torso, the bottle beside him on the bare boards. He remembered the day when one of the mice, having returned from the fields and nestled in the cupboard as usual, decided to be foolishly brave. As it scuttled across the floor, his father swooped down fast from his perch and stamped hard. He crushed the offending rodent with a single blow.

Now, too, he remembered as a growing child kicking the bushes along the trackside, making the bees swarm as they gathered nectar, running from them as they angrily dived and spun. He watched as his friends were attacked. Later they'd plucked out the stings with blunt scissors. His mother scolded him. She was as angry as the bees and swatted him as she spoke. He didn't understand. They were only insects. Insignificant drones. There to serve, not to think. He hit her back. They fought. When his father returned, he was whipped and made to eat beneath the table. It was the first and last time he struck his mother. It was also the last time she disciplined him. That became his father's responsibility and beatings became a regular occurrence until he was too strong for his father to damage him. It took years of pain. He never again kicked the bees. How simple it might be, thought Sabatini, to now reach out and crush that large furry black and yellow blob. If she were alive to see it, his mother would hate it, but she would not scold him. Yes. Power. There to serve.

"What are you thinking, Signor?"

"I was thinking of my mother. She loved wildlife, the trees, the flowers. She would have loved this beautiful garden."

Sabatini put down the coffee cup and shifted so he could look Sada directly in the eye. This woman held power. She wasn't on this earth to serve. No one had ever swatted her. If they had, their hand would have been crushed, like a defenceless insect. She occupied a position equal to his own. He should have negotiated with Sada from the start. He'd tried the back door and it wasn't working. It was time to enter business from the front.

"You didn't come here to tell me of your mother."

"No."

"You came here to discuss business."

"There is no harm in taking a moment to reflect on the world we live in."

"I think for you, Signor, that is unusual." Sada lifted her coffee cup and took one small sip. "How is the luxury boat business?"

"It could always be better. As you know, I am always seeking to expand into more lucrative enterprises. Projects with a faster return."

"I understood you had already discovered one."

"Yes. Unfortunately, my partners are proving unreliable."

"I could have told you that," said Sada. "Atilla Ferrara is a novice. He came to me two years ago, before he made business with you. Ferrara needed my financial resources to pay your initial deposits. Subsequently, the Unione Sacre Croce has taken a significant slice of his profit. Without my support, Signor, your heroin would never even have made it onto the shores of Italy."

Sabatini showed no surprise the Capo knew of his contract with Ferrara; to do so would have displayed ignorance and weakened his negotiating position.

"Indeed," he said casually. "Are you aware, however, that he charges you an obnoxious overinflated price for my goods? He asked the assistance of my accountants to cover the subterfuge. I acknowledge the arrangement has also benefited me financially. Ferrara has used these excess funds to create a new market, homegrown cannabis, which his own caporegimes grow in facilities spread across the Salentine. These facilities and the goods they supply run in direct opposition to your own Mexican output which you land every month at Taranto. Ferrara is making excessive profit out of us both. Speaking as the Krye of the Banda Family and speaking to Il Padrino of the Unione Sacre Croce, I am no longer satisfied with the results this brings me. Being an injured party, I assume you concur?"

Sabatini watched Sada closely. The dark eyes remained static. Not even a fluttering lash. If the revelation was news to her, Sada had no intention of showing it. She had stones for blood. Sabatini recalled how his father never displayed emotion unless it was for emphasis or righteous anger. The temperament was identical. When angry, Sada would be ruthless. He wondered how angry Ferrara's deception had made her. Outwardly, there was no indication. He reached for the coffee pot and poured for them both. Sada nodded her thanks and took a sip of the refilled brew.

"There is no need for barriers between us, Signor. However, I am not Il Padrino. I prefer Capo. It shows a more military taste. I believe in order."

"Like the bees?"

"Like the bees."

"And I take it our mutual friend is breaking that order?"

"Ferrara has taken us both for fools, Signor. I am not one. Nor are you. What do you propose?"

"We cut out our middleman. I sell my products directly to you.

It will be more convenient for me and will involve you paying less. I will charge you the same as that paid by Ferrara. I do not intend to increase my price merely because I have removed an obstacle."

Sada wrapped her hands around the coffee cup. Sabatini saw the movement. It was a natural gesture, but the woman was deep in thought.

"How do you propose to remove this obstacle?" she asked.

"The Comte d'Orsi, your uncle, Ferrara's employer, lives at Tarantella," began Sabatini. "My mistress and he share each other's company. He dotes on her. He considers her very beautiful. For a blind man, he is an exceptional judge of beauty. They talk of many things. Occasionally, the old Comte forgets himself and tells Ariana many personal or private secrets."

"Loose tongues are a menace."

"They should be spiked."

"Indeed."

"Would you smite your own flesh and blood, Capo?"

"Would you?"

Sada's eyes flashed. The darkness in them seemed tinted with fiery red. It died as soon as it lived. Sabatini forced a smile. The lid shut over his one good eye. Sada watched the other. The sun caught the opal and it blazed prism-like. They sat for a while, contemplating each other's unspoken answer. There was hardly a sound. The gentle hum of the big black bumble bee. The whisper of a breeze. Eventually, Sabatini opened his eye.

"Capo, you possess the Comte, as it were, while the Comte possesses something I desire. This may be upsetting for you, but please indulge me."

Sabatini waited for the tiny gesture from Sada. It took several seconds for the fingers to uncurl and beckon.

"I know the Comte has in his vault one of Albania's greatest lost treasures, the Blood Stone Diamond, Il Papavero, once part of our Imperial Crown Jewels. Tonight, while I eat venison tortellini at a municipal function in Lecce, one of my lieutenants will steal it. It has been arranged. Atilla Ferrara has offered to administer a minor sedative to the Comte which will enable him to sleep. The Comte often has difficulty sleeping at night. He told Ariana this. It is a small matter to Ferrara. My lieutenants could have stolen the gem without Ferrara's input, but this will make it more convenient. Ferrara naturally believes it will cement our partnership."

"But my family loses Il Papavero."

"You will gain much, much more. Allow me to explain. I am in possession of a vast stockpile of Afghan heroin. It is sitting in my warehouses waiting to be shipped across the Adriatic. My operations with Ferrara have only tested the market. My cut is much finer than your Mexican draught, Capo. Its quality is not in doubt. The price can be kept artificially low for a year and then can be steadily increased once all other avenues of distribution have been eradicated. I am prepared to offer you full distribution of these goods. We will split the proceeds fifty-fifty. My only request is that you allow me to retain Il Papavero. Of course, there is the small matter of how to dispose of Atilla Ferrara."

"That would not sit well with some of my caporegimes. I can't be seen to be involved in murder."

"Capo, I also have a reputation. I have planned this very carefully. Perhaps you were not aware that Ferrara has been procuring disused warehouses and creating cannabis factories. We will lure him from his cage on a false pretext. He has some unreliable subordinates in Melpignano. There will be an accident. A fire. A few bodies. It will be most unfortunate. A small matter. All I ask is you do not interfere."

"It seems the Unione is giving you two things, Signor: an obstacle to remove and a precious jewel to steal." Sada put her coffee cup back on the saucer and twirled her left hand extravagantly through her hair. "Neither of these is a direct threat to my organisation. Why should I accept your offer?"

Sabatini understood her gesture. The porcelain patience was cracking. Across the expanse of flowers, he could see Alessandro, the tall, tough looking lieutenant, heading back from his sentry position. There was only a minute or so for Sabatini to convince the Capo before being dismissed.

"We are not at war, Sada," Sabatini said, "but we could be. The implications of that are worth contemplating."

"This is my home, Signor," she snapped. "Do not abuse my

hospitality."

Sabatini held up two open palms.

"I apologise, but you must understand: I make no idle threats. I am a powerful man, as well you know. It would be no issue for me to take over the Unione Sacre Croce in the same manner I usurped the Banda Clan or the Lorenz family. But I don't need to do it. I would prefer to share a working relationship with your Unione. All I need is Il Papavero. Once I have it, I plan to return to Albania and place the Blood Stone Poppy in a museum, where it can be admired and revered as it should be. The adulation will bring me respectability, status and influence. It will be a launch pad for my position in politics. A position of real power. I plan to diversify my business, place my own lieutenants in charge of the narcotics operation. And you, Capo, can continue to blithely run your own respectable businesses, like your farm and this honey making emporium. We can both turn a blind eye to the heroin trafficking while the profits continue to prosper."

Sada raised the hand again. Sabatini saw Alessandro slope to a halt, marooned among the flowers, sweating gently.

"Halve the price," she said.

"Done."

Sada nodded. She brushed back a single strand of hair which had fallen over her left eye. When she spoke, there was surprise in her voice.

"You bargain badly, Signor."

"You won't say that when I am President."

She did not reply. The inference was clear. As Sabatini rose to greater power, so she would expect greater reward.

Sada beckoned to Alessandro and ordered some vintage Falcone. "To cement our business partnership," she said.

When the spirit arrived, they tossed back the thimblefuls, offering a toast to each other before they drank. Sada didn't like grappa. She found it too bitter. In fact, she disliked all the old trappings of business, but her people appreciated she maintained the traditions. She would not be their Capo if she did not. Sabatini was talking, rambling about his future life as a politician, but she wasn't listening, already her brain was calculating figures, yields and profits. The sums were astronomical. After a while, as Sabatini's monologue drifted into a few satisfied chuckles, she allowed her forehead to crease. The deal struck was phenomenally advantageous to the Unione. It appeared also to benefit Sabatini's long-term ambitions. So how had the operation with Ferrara turned sour so quickly? The heroin was making excessive profits already, distribution was efficient and everyone, even the addicts, were happy. There must be another secret, something she'd not been told.

After more formalities, Sabatini stood to leave. He held out his hand, but Sada refused to shake it. Instead, she inclined her head.

"Tell me, Signor, out of curiosity, why does Atilla Ferrara have to die?"

Sabatini slowly withdrew his hand. Caught half in the sun, Sada resembled that two-faced Roman God Fortuna. She might have uttered the wise words of the Aurelian Caesars: 'accept the things to which fate binds you.' He shook the thought aside. Superstitious nonsense, the sort of rubbish Belzac talked about when he went into raptures about the sea and the sky.

"I like to use people," explained Sabatini. "There is always a motive. It burns and then it is extinguished. Atilla Ferrara's time has expired. I trust him no longer. His crude attempts at gainsmanship rankle. I can only take sorrow in his treachery. You see, any man who betrays his master is always worth investigating. A man who betrays two is a suspect. To attempt it three times makes him a liability."

The Ligurian bee was floundering across the path, close to his feet. Sabatini watched its progress.

"Ferrara has proved himself less of a man and more of an insect, feeding on other's debris. I don't like insects, vermin, lice, maggots, the leeches of the world. They are insignificant. Like my father before me, I crush them. So shall it be with Atilla Ferrara."

He headed up the path, stepping deliberately, dramatically on the defenceless drone as he went. Behind him there was one single intake of breath. It was the first emotion Sabatini had got out of the woman in an hour and it gave him a warm pleasurable feeling.

Twenty Two

Restless Sleep

He came to her again and again and he kept coming. The big Cohiba glowed. The sting was administered. Again and again. She wasn't given food, only a glass of water, once every few hours. She wasn't washed. The bed became stained and her body developed sores. She squirmed to avoid her own faeces, found it impossible. Eventually, sheer tiredness won and she'd slept in the soils. It was a difficult, restless sleep, just how it had often been over the last seven years, wondering what would happen when he woke.

There was no comfort, only misery. As if her own predicament wasn't enough, her thoughts were full of what she'd lost. The past, gone. Leo, the present, the Children of Otranto Foundation, a sham, all of it gone. How she'd never realised before didn't matter. She knew now. How much more of his life, or her life, was a lie? And she'd stayed with him seven years. And now not just those seven years were gone. Gone was the future. To see a child, her child, be born and grow, to love and protect a family. The future, gone. She saw it only in moments. The moments he came. The moments of pain. The moments of fearful rest. Her mind held one thought and one thought only: the moment of revenge that would come. She didn't know when or how. Part of her thought it might be Jonathon, appearing like some tainted saint with a sacred cavalry.

As each moment came and went, the thought retreated. He had been gone too many hours. Why would he come back? Because he had the jewel. It was the only thing which would keep him alive. Without Il Papavero, Sabatini wasn't going anywhere. The yacht had not sailed. And if Jonathon was alive, there was always the possibility of rescue, however faint. And rescue could mean revenge. Not for her, for her dead child. A blood debt to be paid. They still lived like that in the untamed mountains. They still lived like that in the Clans and Families. They still lived by the Bible's code.

Every time the slow hand and the wicked eye bent towards her, every time she convulsed, she thought of revenge. You take an eye. You take a life. Revenge. Death. It was in the heart, the soil and the blood.

Sabatini saw it in her. Every time he held her face, the fist bunching at her jaw, making her stare deep into his baleful edifice while he uttered what he demanded of her: obedience, penance, loyalty, fealty. Ariana never replied, her eyes intransigent. Two cool lagoons that flashed with solemn hatred.

"Revenge," they seemed to say. "When it comes, Marcelo, your death will be sweet."

***

Sada rarely ventured from I Campo di Mielle. Basilicata was home. Tarantella was not. The sight of that dreadful palace in the hills above Santa Cesarea Therme made her choke. It wasn't the welcome she wanted after the long stuffy journey south. She hadn't expected the telephone call from the Comte. Despite what Sabatini had told her, and his reassurances, something had gone wrong. Her uncle had been excited and frightened all at once. The thrill of the shooting had intoxicated the old man, but the shock of losing the gemstones struck him. Like any person subjected to a burglary, the sensation of being personally invaded and desecrated was palpable.

The Mercedes Benz pulled up to the gates. The driver rang the bell. It was one of the lesser men who came to the gate, opened it and escorted them through the overgrown forest. Sada watched him carefully through the tinted, bullet proof glass. He wore a camouflage jacket, like a mercenary, and military boots. He offered no formalities. He walked beside the car with a surly gait. The man didn't give a damn who the visitor was. Years ago, the man would have doffed his cap, like they had to her grandfather. It wasn't because she was a woman. It was because the man no longer recognised her as his Capo. This development was unexpected. Something Marcelo Sabatini had told her resonated: a man who betrays his master is a liability.

She instructed the driver to park close to the mansion and wait in the car, with the windows and doors locked. Her bodyguard, Alessandro, would accompany her. Sada sniffed at the air. Alessandro wrinkled his noise.

"Fucking hell," he muttered.

Sada gave him a reproachful look. It was only the obscenity she disliked. The sentiment was apt. Whatever they kept in the gardens shifted her stomach. What in God's name was happening here?

Once inside the mansion, the man finally attempted to integrate himself, but Sada silenced him with a whiplash order: "Is my uncle washed and dressed as I instructed?"

"Si, Capo."

It was said without any reverence.

"Where is he?"

The man jerked his head towards the ceiling.

"Go and tell him his niece is waiting for him." Sada snapped the order. It brought the man to attention. "Have coffee prepared and bring it to the salon. Where is Atilla Ferrara? I will want to speak with him."

"He's not here."

"Where is he?"

The man shrugged.

"Very well. Get on now. See to my uncle."

Sada watched him depart, loping up the stairs.

"What's the matter with these people?" asked Alessandro. "Don't they know who pays their wages?"

"They have another source of income now, Alessandro, a lucrative one. Let's do what we must and be away. I don't intend to stay any longer than necessary."

Sada walked through the gloomy mansion, her finger twitching across the dusty shelves. Alessandro followed at a discreet pace behind. His eyes scoured each room, searching for anything suspicious. His right hand never left his waist band, close to the gun tucked into a holster fixed on his belt. In the study, Sada stopped, her attention immediately taken by the hoarding placed over the broken window. Alessandro thumped it with a flat hand. The board shook.

"Rubbish," he declared.

"Was that how the thief got in?"

"No." Alessandro walked carefully around the room. "Your uncle said he shot him in the lobby. This is from some other incident."

"Perhaps he chose to leave through the front door?"

"Why would you do that when you've already made this hole?"

Sada had to admit the logic of the argument. The one-two step of a man's careful footsteps alerted her. Memories flooded back of teenage years spent in the old villa, fussing over her uncle, when she'd longed to be in the sea or sitting in cars with boys, eating gelato and drinking cheap beer. Her years had been lost to dutiful service and criminal education. For decades Sada had tried to depress the memories and disappointments.

When the Comte d'Orsi appeared in the doorway, it was Alessandro who took an arm and led him to the chair at the head of the table. He was dressed in a thick dressing gown, despite the warmth, and beneath it he was still in his pyjamas. Comfortable, loose-threaded house slippers were on his feet. Hardly dressed at all, Sada considered. She thought his skin greyer than usual, a tiredness creeping under his eyes. He was shaking.

She loosened her hair and let it fall about her shoulders, how the Comte remembered it and liked it, and knelt beside the chair, placing her hands over his.

"Uncle Ferdy," she said prettily and with all the sounds of concern she could muster. "Uncle Ferdy, goodness, what has happened?"

"Sophia? Is that Sophia? Come here, my darling. Let me see you."

She brought the frail hands to her face so the starchy fingers could stroke her features. His hands clawed at her hair.

"My dear, my dear," he said affectionately. "It has been too long."

"Yes, uncle. I'm sorry."

"Why do you never visit Tarantella?"

The accusation stung.

"You know I hate it here."

"Or your uncle Ferdinand?"

"Don't talk nonsense, uncle."

The Comte pulled a face. His hand continued to stroke Sada's hair.

"You lie so beautifully. It is no wonder my father wanted you as Godfather."

"I am the Capo, uncle. You will always be Il Padrino."

He chuckled.

"You have lost none of your guile."

"I was taught well. By you as much as old Andrea."

"It saddens my heart to see my niece no more than twice a year." His hands fell to her shoulder, her forearm and squashed the muscles. His mouth became set. "You have grown slender. Do you eat well?"

"I have nothing to worry of except you. You look sick."

The hand released her. He waved dismissively.

"I am strong enough to shoot," he said indignantly.

"When I heard, I was worried. I came straight away. I thought you had also been shot."

"Do not worry about your old uncle Ferdy. Come, you see I am perfectly well." He beat his chest and coughed.

"Stop it, uncle."

Sada took hold of his hand. The sleeve slipped well past the Comte's wrist. There was a bruise on the underside of his forearm. An older mark was higher up, where the vein wouldn't take anymore. Regular injections. It was just how Sabatini had told it. No wonder her uncle was becoming indiscreet. The poor dear was being slowly drained of his faculties. Uncle Ferdy was never good at talking business. He was distracted by his memories. And now he was distracted by drugs.

"Let's have coffee," she said and looked sharply at Alessandro. "Tell me exactly what happened."

The bodyguard too had seen the evidence. His hand tightened on his waistband. He nodded once and went to fetch the lacky, who'd not returned with the refreshments.

"We were robbed, Sophia. I was asleep. I sleep lightly now. That Ferrara, he wants me to sleep longer, you know. He feeds me medicine. The doctor prescribed it. A pharmacist comes from the town every evening. The medicine used to work. I used to sleep peacefully, so peacefully. Now I am restless and I have nightmares. I don't tell him. The last time I did, he increased the dosage. Now, you understand, I've grown immune. Ferrara can't tell when I'm asleep or awake any more. It's these blind eyes, you see, they look as if I'm asleep all the time."

"Or poisoned."

The Comte didn't seem to hear.

"The injections used to send me to sleep, but no more. I hear them sometimes at night, outside, in the grounds. I hear them working, moving. I don't know what they do, where they go, what cars arrive, who comes in them. The last two summers the activity has been prolonged."

"Why did you not tell me this?"

"Why do you not visit me?"

Alessandro returned with the coffee on a large, quilted tray. He gave an apologetic shrug and delivered the three cups, placing the Comte's close to the edge of the table. Sada had ceased talking while the ritual was performed. The silence allowed her to avoid the question.

"You shot one of them, uncle?"

"Yes. I would not have called you. Ferrara would have dealt with everything. But Ferrara has been gone since last night. I have no one else to trust."

"Do you still trust Ferrara?"

"He has been a loyal servant."

"He has been poisoning you."

"I am a nuisance in the evenings."

"Are you sure?"

"He would not betray me."

"If you insist." Sada looked at Alessandro. He frowned, shook his head slightly. Like her, he recognised the confusion of age. "Tell me, uncle, what has been stolen?"

"Everything."

Sada already knew it. For her uncle's benefit, she ought to check. While Alessandro stood guard, Sada activated the lock to release the fireplace and punched the combination into the safe. She wondered how the thief had got the numbers. He must have been an exceptional expert. Sada glanced at the portrait of her uncle which hung on the wall. Perhaps it was time to change the safe completely, this one gave up its secrets too easily. There were no cloth bags inside the safe drawer. Every gemstone was missing.

"Has anyone else been in the safe, uncle?"

"No."

"What about Ferrara? Does he know the combination?"

"Of course not." The Comte spoke as if he was admonishing a child. "Sometimes we need money to support the finances of the estate. Ferrara is in charge here. Sometimes he asks."

"Asks you what?"

"I never told him the combination."

"No. But he knew what was in it, didn't he? He knew about the diamonds and you gave him some."

There was a long pause. The Comte's hand reached out for the coffee. Alessandro placed the cup in his hand and the old man sipped, blowing first on the surface.

"Twelve," he sighed. "I gave him twelve."

"Oh, uncle." Sada felt her heart flutter. The poor old man; deluded, misled and she'd let him down by leaving him to the wolves. "Ferrara has taken much more than twelve."

"You think this is his doing?"

"I have learnt much about Ferrara these last few days."

"No. It was the thief."

Sada closed the safe and ensured it was locked, taking care this time to change the combination. Alessandro pushed the fireplace closed. Something was badly amiss. Sada's instinct told her Sabatini's thief would not have stolen more than what was ordered. There hadn't been any repairs carried out on the estate, not unless you included those awful pigs. Certainly not enough to occupy the sale of all those precious stones. What was Atilla Ferrara attempting to prove, stealing from everybody he knew? How many masters did he require? The Capo, the Comte, the Kryre, money-lust or sheer reckless vanity. The total was creeping up. Sabatini had been correct in his assessment. Ferrara was becoming an inconvenience. If the Albanian wanted him killed, so be it.

"How did you hear the intruder, uncle?"

"I heard him moving. I told you. I don't sleep." The Comte became animated, his expression taut and excited. The memory of the gunfight was fresh and unlike his visitors, he could still smell the scent of gunpowder on his clothes. "The study is below my bedroom remember. When the safe was opened, I heard the mechanism. It was like a coffin lid opening. I thought I was being buried. I listened. I could hear him breathing. He smokes you know."

Sada couldn't resist a smile. Uncle Ferdy was imagining things again. Or it might have been the effect of the drugs.

"I still keep the gun beside me. Loaded. I took it. I surprised him when he left the lobby. The men tell me there was blood on the door and the terrace. I must have shot the English bastard."

"English?" repeated Sada. "How do you know he was English?"

"It was the same man who came to visit me a two days ago. I am certain of it. He asked many questions about the diamond."

"Did he? Who was this man?"

"Jon Drago. A journalist. A thief. Ferrara dealt with him – after he broke that window. A good man, Ferrara."

"Ferrara never told me of it," said Sada. "Just as he never told me of the robbery. Why isn't he here, uncle?"

"I thought you knew. He said it was Unione business."

"Of course," she said it carefully. "I forgot. Thank you for reminding me, uncle. Come, let's take our coffee on the terrace. We haven't spoken about the old days for many years. I want you to tell me some of those stories again."

"You are lying again, Sophia, but I'd like that." The Comte chuckled. "You always laughed at my stories. Perhaps you'll do so today, heh?"

He was suddenly like anyone's elderly doting uncle, not irascible or stubborn, not blind, merely doddery in his movements, shrill of voice and his face swept with childish joy. Sada walked to Alessandro and she lowered her voice.

"I want to know what Ferrara's being doing with my diamonds. Speak to Cavanni. He's always informed before. He'll know if anyone has been selling them on the black market. If he doesn't remember, remind him."

"Yes, Capo. What about this man Drago?" said Alessandro. "We know nothing of him."

"I agree. Find him. Quickly."

***

"So that's how you found me," said Drago as he popped a black grape into his mouth, something to take the edge off the piquant cheese.

"It wasn't easy," replied Sada. "You moved around fast. The fire at Melpignano helped us. We thought it was Sabatini's men."

Drago nodded. They were seated in one of the mansion's dining rooms. It was well presented in plaster and pine, with stucco coving and an elaborate ceiling mural, beasts and nymphs at leisure interrupted only for the brass chandelier, an antique, Drago assumed. They had eaten a four course meal, antipasti, pasta, carne and cheese. The dishes were small, which suited his current appetite, and they drank water not wine. The pinching sensation from the burns was already on the wane. He needed to keep hydrated or the skin would tighten and roughen. Regular baths were recommended. The nurse had been helpful, if a little rough. Drago didn't object. It seemed unwise.

"I was disappointed Ferrara had abandoned you at Matera. It would have been a perfect opportunity to eliminate him. Killing Vito hardly sufficed."

"So you said," Drago murmured. Occasional ruthlessness cut through the Capo's calm exterior. Earlier she'd described Vito's execution. She'd told it quickly, dispassionately. He put aside his revulsion and concentrated on the cheeses.

"What I don't understand," he said, "is why?"

"I made an arrangement with Sabatini," began Sada. "I let him steal the diamond. It is very precious, yes. But it isn't irreplaceable. It is only a gemstone, however large. Jewels, Mr Drago, are the pebbles of the Earth, gold the clod which binds them. Like land, both have a price and my price was to maintain the monopoly on the heroin distribution in the Salentine. It was a very small price to pay."

"I suppose."

Drago didn't agree with the Capo's business operation. He'd said so twice over dinner. Once, he received stony silence. The second time, he was subjected to a veiled threat. Their differences were to be forgotten while he rehabilitated, however long it took. Once more, he detected a stern glance. He deflected it with a raised palm of contrition.

"And now you know Sabatini doesn't have it."

"Vito was quite clear about that," stated Sada. "He was also very clear that you knew where it was, that you stole it from the real thief. Men do not lie when faced with imminent death. Ferrara chose a foolish method to interrogate you. Of course, I would prefer not to interrogate you at all."

"That's a relief."

"For both of us. I thought perhaps we could strike a bargain."

"You have nothing I want," said Drago.

"Sabatini does."

"Ariana?"

"Yes."

The Capo's dark eyes watched him. Drago was used to asking questions, not the other way around. It was odd, he thought, how this woman extracted what she wanted without ever making a direct query. He found her tantalising. She offered only goblets of information, nothing permanent or even important, only what she needed to, yet in return, without realising, he'd offered her almost his whole story, from Madeleine's accident to the sunlit torture. The only episode he missed was one he couldn't tell: what had happened to Ariana. Drago ate another grape.

"She's still alive?"

"As far as I can ascertain," Sada replied. "I don't have direct contact with Sabatini. That would not be advisable for either of us. I know he needs her. His ambition is to become Albania's Prime Minister, or President, one or the other. He told me so. The woman serves a purpose for him. She smooths his rough public persona, a pretty, public face among his entourage. Her disappearance would cause some trouble for him, reputationally. He's been using her as a front for some charity projects. I understand she is the patron of several orphanages, both in Albania and Italy."

"Yes. I've been to one. The Children of Otranto Foundation."

"A complicated tax evasion. Sabatini hasn't paid more than the minimum in personal taxes in years. Charitable organisations allow him to store his income without penalisation. My auditors uncovered this as soon as he contacted me. It is always best to discover something about one's allies as well as one's enemies."

"Have you discovered which one he is yet?"

Sada delivered the same graceful smile which always crossed her face at moments of awkwardness. It was a delaying tactic, an opportunity to perfect a reply. Drago preferred to consume food or drink to the same effect. Sada's mind was made up quickly.

"On balance, he is an enemy."

"And what am I?"

"I told you. You are a guest." She paused. "If you wish me to help the woman, I believe I can, but you must help me in return. Tell me where you hid il Papavero."

Drago continued to eat the grapes and cheese until his plate was clean. Sada said nothing more. The room was still except for his movements, the cutting of the knife and the delicate grind of his teeth. Occasionally, when the breeze was right, the flutter of falling water from the fountains outside penetrated the silence. Drago had walked the gardens during the twilight before dinner. The nurse, a stout middle-aged woman who spoke very little English, walked with him as if she was a bodyguard. The flower beds were immaculate. Magnolia, oleander and myrtle nestled next to each other. Neatly coiffured laurel hedges ran alongside each pathway. Marble statues of ancient mythological gods lined the avenues, their names etched onto the plinths, reminding any visitor of who the forebears of the land were, of where power now resided. Three huge ornate pools each with an elaborate tiered fountain and exotic fish on patrol complimented the almost Roman grandeur. The walk had been longer than he expected, but it felt good to be moving and to know he was only superficially damaged. Back in his room, the nurse let him doze before dinner. He was provided with a smart, short sleeved shirt and soft cotton trousers, minus a belt, which would chaff the tender skin. They were both, amazingly, a perfect fit. The nurse had encouraged him to keep hydrated and she fussed even as he dressed. Sada had done everything to make him comfortable. Drago recognised his barriers collapsing. He didn't want to disappoint such a good-natured host, even one predisposed to killing people. Sada seemed the lesser of many evils he'd met in the Salentine. Her offer might be the best thing for Ariana.

"Do you have a pen?" he asked.

Sada made a tiny movement and the waiter appeared from outside, where he was standing out of earshot until summoned. On instruction, he produced a ball point pen from inside his jacket and handed it to Drago.

Quickly, carefully, Drago wrote an address on the white linen napkin which had sat on his lap since the first course had been served. He held up the napkin long enough to demonstrate he'd not faked anything, folded it in four and placed it in his trouser pocket.

"When Ariana is here. I'll give you the napkin."

"I might have memorised what you wrote."

"I'll take that chance. You're a woman of your word. You told me that. When you get the diamond, will you give it to Sabatini?"

"Yes," she replied, "and the others also. I have no need of them. I have a more pressing want."

"Which is what exactly?"

Sada stood up and walked to the open doors. The candlelight caught her face and for a brief moment it seemed to be cut in half, like the benign Fortuna who stood outside in the garden of gods.

"I expected Sabatini to assassinate Atilla Ferrara," she continued. "Usually I would expect an arrangement such as this to be honoured. However, Ferrara has stolen from me and my uncle. This evening I received word from a close associate in Bari, a man called Cavanni. He has discovered that a broker in the city, a man of lesser scruples called Nrupal Patel, has been providing fine cut Namibian diamonds, discreetly, of course. My associate was able to view one for verification. He informs me it is from the missing cache. The man who provided the diamonds to the broker was Laszlo, the same man whose warehouse you destroyed.

"Ferrara has established a string of warehouses across the Salentine to be used almost exclusively to manufacture cannabis.

Laszlo explained they sold the diamonds to raise funds to set up the factories. It was quite difficult for him to say so. You injured him badly. His jaw is broken. Coincidentally, Ferrara's action arrived at the same moment Sabatini's new, higher grade heroin arrived in the region. Competition began to get heated. There had been a number of incidents, some fights, even a murder; that is not the way of the Unione Sacre Croce. We knew of the heroin, but not the source. Ferrara knew and came to me with a proposition: to enter into an agreement with Sabatini to buy and distribute his heroin. He would act as a middleman. However, Ferrara is not a businessman. He is merely greedy. The cannabis isn't making him enough money, so he's been artificially raising prices for the heroin. Unfortunately, Sabatini is not a fool and nor am I. We don't need Ferrara to take a cut of our profit.

"And then there is another problem of which I have recently become aware. Ferrara has been poisoning my uncle, the Comte. He has a doctor, who I suspect is not a doctor at all, to inject him with heroin every night. It helps keep him docile. I have little regard for my uncle. I spent many summers with him at Tarantella. I detest the place. He lives in a world which no longer exists and people pander to his ideal. Ferrara exploits his weaknesses. He's exploiting the Unione. His actions, for whatever reasons, and none of them a justified, are not acceptable. I aim to permanently stop him.

"I was not made Capo to officiate over thieves and liars. I struggle day-by-day to maintain an order, but even as I struggle, every so often I must trample on the dispensable. I intend to change the parameters of my agreement with Sabatini. He can keep Il Papavero and all the other stones. For my part, you can have Ariana and I will kill Atilla Ferrara."

Drago took a meditative sip of water.

"So, this is about revenge?"

"It is about power."

"You sound like one of those Roman gods you keep in the garden."

"When you are in control of so many, they expect you to sound and act like a god. If you don't they will never follow you."

Sada turned and once again Drago thought her face strangely

split by the shadows. "And you will be abandoned to the fates."

***

Drago couldn't sleep. The night sounds from the gardens pricked at his consciousness. He may as well have had a ticking bomb in the bed with him. The sunburn didn't help. Despite the lotions and the baths, his skin stayed tortured. It ached to move. If he didn't move, he seized up. Sleep was not an option. His mind was active, springing with the information Sada had imparted. The Capo was taking decisive and dangerous action. However she intended to play it – bluff, double-bluff or blackmail – she was stirring up a hornet's nest making enemies faster than friends.

What buoyed Drago was the knowledge Ariana was still on the yacht and that, to spite Sabatini, Sada planned to bargain with him, using a horde of Namibian diamonds and the blood red Il Papavero as dubious currency. Drago wasn't convinced the cat's cradle of a scheme would succeed. It denied Sabatini's own ruthless ambition.

Moonlight shone through the crack in the shutters, forming a soft, bluish rectangle on the far wall. Drago pushed back the sheets and went to the shutters to close the outside window. The guest suites were in the far wing of the mansion. There was a view across the wide rear patio and the maze of flowerbeds which led to a summer house and the apiary, the wooden hives standing like soldiers awaiting orders. The clouds bunched up with one another, curtaining the moon. Everything became dark and still. Very still. Fear had drawn a veil across the sky. When the veil was pulled back, something or somebody moved, something beside the summer house. Drago blinked, watched. There it was again: low down, fanning out across the gardens: three, four, maybe five shadows crouched low against the vibrating silent flowers.

He crossed to the armchair where the nurse had thrown his clothes. Wincing, he shrugged out of the pyjamas and pulled on the shirt, trousers, socks and shoes. Drago gently depressed the door handle and went outside onto the patio, making his movements as light as possible so as not to disturb the nurse who was sleeping dutifully in the next room. Guided by streaks of moonlight, he walked, half-bent over, towards the other wing and Sada's accommodation.

Everything seemed quiet. Too quiet. Where were the insects? Where was the relentless buzz that had prevented him sleeping? He heard footsteps and low urgent voices and immediately pinned himself against the balustrade. He was caught in the open, as good as exposed. He watched from the shadows as the figures he'd seen crossing towards the mansion now retreated from it. In their haste, they didn't look his way. As they scurried into the gardens, Drago noticed the bay doors had been left ajar. A trailing lace curtain blew in the breeze. He should have sought assistance, but a sudden intense curiosity spurred him. Still using the low walls as cover, he went to the bay doors. The crickets had started to chime again. Whatever had occurred was over. Normality had resumed. Except Drago knew something abnormal was happening. He waited and watched for several seconds. There didn't seem to be any more movement, just a low scuffling sound behind him. Drago twisted and glanced back at his guest quarters. There was another silhouette, no two, moving against shadows. They were seeking him out.

Drago went swiftly to the open doors and eased the curtain back. The sensation hit his nostrils as if it'd been thrust beneath his nose. It was almost unmistakeable. They say it doesn't have a scent, but it does. Blood. Death. A raw, putrid tang, the reek of freshly butchered meat, a slaughterhouse. Eyes not yet adjusted, he stepped in and his foot collided with something. It was one of the butlers, a night porter he guessed, lying on the floor, blood and everything else oozing from a horrific wound in his throat. Drago gulped down the sickness.

There was an upright armchair further in the room and he could make out a figure sitting in it. The breeze was blowing long locks of greying hair about the figure's face.

"Sada?"

Drago pressed on, his shoes squelching on the wet mess that covered the floor. He was close enough to see her face. Moonlight shone for a few seconds, illuminating the whole body and the single vicious cut across her throat. Blood coated her night gown. It still pumped from her useless neck, from every angle. Drago baulked, put out a hand to steady himself and rocked the chair. The figure moved an inch and in diabolical slow motion the head dropped from the shoulders and rolled across the floor, coming to rest in the pool of crimson, eyes staring at nothing.

Drago almost fainted. He staggered backwards, supported himself on the edge of a leather-topped desk and started to panic. What in God's name was happening? The questions came too fast. His world seemed to be closing again, a hot black hell hole, just like Matera. He swallowed the puke which rose, forced it down because he didn't want to make a sound. He was shaking. He gripped his fists to make it stop. Somewhere on the other side of the room he now saw a third body, another butler or a guard. How many servants stayed at the mansion? Was it just these guys and the nurse? He tried to recall the faces he'd seen during his stroll in the gardens and when taking dinner. Christ and hell. It didn't matter. Survival did. Drago crossed back to the French doors, squinting into the black night. Silence. No crickets. Nothing.

He didn't know what made him move, but move he did and quickly. Drago dropped to the floor, chin smacking against the skirting. The bullets exploded through the windows before he'd even seen the lightning flash from the gun barrel. The glass doors disintegrated into confetti. Drago rolled tight to the wall, his body flung long and flat resting on his right arm. The bullets came in bursts, but not with any method, an echoing cacophony of snapping bangs reverberating and shimmering with deadly metallic glee. Furniture splintered. Walls shattered. The windows had disappeared. Slivers of glass and masonry flew around the room. A few seconds elapsed between each salvo. Drago counted the time. He heard more shooting from outside, the same repetitive zing and bang, other windows, other walls blasted into oblivion. Once more the wasp sting of bullets zipped around Drago's form. Fourth salvo. Stop. Reload. Count.

He jerked to his feet, ignored his screeching skin, and catapulted across the room, rolling in the blood and gunk that formed a carpet on the pine boards. He ended up on his front, the chaos continuing around him, getting more and more urgent, kicking closer and closer. Bullets thudded into the back wall, tearing the pine from its moorings. Wood splinters from the panels dug into the air around him. A big sofa had collapsed, upholstery forming a billowing cloud, whipped up by the stream of bullets that pounded the salon. A breather. Fifth salvo. Drago yanked at the door handle just before the next burst of gunfire engulfed the room. He was in the passageway, sprinting along it, determined to escape this savage little wing-ding. Thankfully, the bullets didn't penetrate the second shield. He tore into one of the front rooms, flung open a window and clambered out, rolling on the lawn. He was in the Garden of the Gods. The line of marble statues, representations of the eternal, seemed to mock his current predicament. From the side of the mansion, he saw more shooters. Coming at pace up the driveway were two black garbed security men.

    Drago scrambled through the undergrowth as the battle took place around him. The hedgerows rustled, bent, snapped. Mercury's head was blown to pieces. Someone yelled. A despairing sound as a bullet found its target. Drago kept moving, kept to the ground, elbows and knees pumping, scraping the dead burnt skin away. Fear propelled him. He crouched next to one of the larger plinths, his hand resting on the cool foot. It was Neptune and his naiads, watching over the huge centrepiece fountain. The nurse had walked him this way. The main drive was on the other side of the next stretch of lawn, if he could cross it.

    The action was concentrated on the house. Drago couldn't tell who was attacking or defending. It didn't matter. Sada was dead. Any hope of getting to Ariana was gone. Any hope of getting out of this savage little wing-ding was looking as bleak as hell. The flashes and bangs steadied for a few seconds. More black figures came out of the mansion's main doors, taking up positions on the portico, using the big ionic columns as cover. Others vanished into the ghoulish garden of the dead.

    Drago took his chance and sprinted low and hard across the path, around the water feature and onto the lawn. He almost made it before the zip-bang of bullets rang out. He dived for the nearest shrubbery, careered through it, leaves and petals blown about him as hot lead sizzled past his head. He rolled over, three, four times and came to rest against the opposite statue, an imposing Bacchus, too cheerful by half.

It was impossible to tell who had the upper hand in the firefight. Drago didn't want to wait to find out. He squirmed over the lawn like some huge, fat, blood-splattered adder, all the while heading away from the house and the gun battle. His body ached. His roasted skin screamed. Tall stone pines marked the perimeter of the driveway. The extra shade provided welcoming darkness. Drago propped himself upright against one big trunk, gasping. He delved deeper into the tree line following the drive until he reached a car port. A fleet of Mercedes Benz V Class cars sat beside a small wooden cabin. A dead man lay beside the vehicles. Drago crossed to the body. The man's chest had taken a bullet and the sickening hole seemed to wheeze open and shut. The man's eyes were fixed dead straight, the lids popped open in shock. Antonio. The carbuncle on his neck gave him away. So, it was the men from Tarantella. Ferrara was exercising a coup. The Unione Sacre Croce was being dismantled in the most bloodthirsty manner.

Drago went into the cabin. Relieved, he saw car keys placed on cheap hooks nailed to the wall. He grabbed one, pressed the key fob to deactivate the lock and saw which car's lights flashed. Thirty metres down the driveway he could make out the gate. There was a series of push buttons on the desk, a colour TV monitor at its centre which afforded the only light in the little hut. Nothing was labelled. Speculatively, Drago pressed one or two buttons. The first one activated cat's eyes along both kerbs of the drive. The second had no effect on anything that he could tell. The third button saw the big wrought iron gates separate and start to swing slowly open. He made for the car, jumped in and inserted the key. The engine rumbled into life. There was no time to familiarise himself with the controls. He just found first gear and depressed the hand brake. A glance in the rear mirror showed men of one side or the other running down the drive.

"Arrestare!"

Drago ignored the order, slammed his foot on the accelerator and the Mercedes jumped forward, wheels biting, tyres seeking traction. The shooters took aim. Drago heard the whip crack of gunfire, saw sharp white sparks as the car shot down the drive, felt the impact. Pockmarks appeared on the rear windshield. Thank God for bullet proof glass. The gate was already starting to swing shut. More bullets slammed into the bodywork. Drago gunned the accelerator, went from first to third, squeezing through the ever-closing gap, metal tearing against metal. The car came to a shuddering stop. It was caught three-quarters through the opening. The bullets kept coming. The screech of collapsing metal assaulted his ears. The car was rocking onto the passenger side, lifted from the road by the pressing iron pincers. Desperate, he hit first again, foot to the floor. With a final, frightening crunch, the Mercedes tore itself through the iron jaws and onto freedom, angry gunshots swirling through the air. Drago swung the wheel and headed down the road. He had no idea where it led. His only thought was to get away from the killing ground as fast as possible.

Twenty Three

Sudden Fury

He drove for half an hour with no clear idea of where he was heading. He just wanted to get away and fast. When he finally slowed and pulled into a deserted service station, Drago realised he was trembling.

He got out of the car and walked to the side of the road where he was violently sick. The image of Sada's severed head rolling across the floor recurred again and again. He moved away from the mess and breathed deeply, tasting the night air. A car approached, its headlamps invading his thoughts as if they were twin drills boring into his skull. The bright light stung. As he squinted, the cracked skin creased on his brow. As the car passed at speed, he rubbed a palm over his forehead. Dead skin fell away, the flakes caught in the slipstream.

Drago sat on a crash barrier trying to control his breathing, ignoring the aches and pains which shot like tiny needles across his body, trying to think. Atilla Ferrara had pre-empted his own downfall and launched an attack on the leadership of the Unione Sacre Croce. This put a new complexion on everything. Drago was uncertain if his life was in more or less danger than before, or Ariana's for that matter. Sada's had been taken. She was the Capo, the general of the Unione, but she wasn't the Godfather, that was the Comte d'Orsi. Even old, blind and under Ferrara's influence, the Comte was still held in high regard. Others would take his side. A civil war was about to ensue. Drago pondered the events of the night. Had it been Ferrara's voice shouting?

"Arrestare!"

Yes. He recognised the rough tones even at distance. So, Ferrara wasn't at Tarantella. He wasn't hiding. He was at Sada's estate. Drago had no means of contacting the Comte. If he was still alive, the Comte had to be warned his life was in danger. Perhaps he knew people who could assist them both. Drago straightened himself.

His mind was made up. He must make Il Padrino understand what was happening to his Unione.

***

Tarantella. It looked even worse at night.

Drago had driven vaguely at first. The Mercedes did have a sat nav installed, but it was code controlled. A chance finger pointer to Brindisi put him on the right track. He drove at dangerous speeds, intent on beating Ferrara back to Tarantella. His progress wasn't helped by a sweeping rainstorm which seemed to appear as if from nowhere and gathered strength pursuing him down the SS16. Eventually, he outran it, or its course altered, and the final miles were accompanied by nothing more than sticky air.

As the Mercedes swung around the coast road to Santa Cesarea Therme, Drago's attention was pulled to the seaward side. He slowed to a halt and stared across the bay at the big yacht stationed securely a mile off shore. *Diamantin*'s lights were on. She bestrode the sea like some luminous floating White House. Sabatini had beaten him here, but what did he aim to do? Maybe he was already warning the Comte. And what lies would he be spinning? Drago's mind drifted to a place called panic. His enemies were mounting to trap him.

Tarantella's gates stood open. The chain had been sliced through with bolt cutters, the two halves thrown to the ground. By whom, he wondered. Sabatini's men? Drago turned in and made a slow approach, dousing the headlights and travelling by moonlight. He saw one wild boar shuffling at the kerbside. If it had been disturbed, the animal didn't hold any malice. The boar lazily glanced at the interloper and dived back into the woods. Drago parked near the main entrance. He got out and listened.

It was just like I Campi di Mielle. Silent. The strange Arabic structure looked taller than its two storeys. The dome towered over everything. The climbing plants were alive, rustling in the heavy breeze. The tang from the manure heaps was hot and fetid. It hit him, passed on, then hit again. The place was in total darkness. He had nothing to guide him. Even the moon had vanished behind the rolling blackness of night. He trod carefully around the building, looking for a way in, considering his first course of action. He'd almost made a complete circuit, when a figure soared out of the shadows. A snout-nosed automatic jabbed directly on his breastbone and Drago collapsed, wheezing.

"What are you doing here?" whispered the man in broken English.

Drago looked at the tough face. It was one of Sabatini's top enforcers, one of the men who formed his close entourage, a bodyguard, a cigar lighter and a companion when no woman could be trusted. Where the hell he had sprung from, Drago couldn't tell.

"I came to warn the Comte."

"What for?"

"Atilla Ferrara is on a killing spree."

The man chuckled and pulled Drago to his feet.

"We rather hoped he would be," he said. "Less for us to deal with."

"He has machine guns."

"We have bombs."

The man retreated to the stone eaves of the surrounding terrace. There was a door set back in an alcove. The man flipped back the lock and motioned that Drago should enter first. A short flight of steps led to a huge cellar, separated into various sections by brick archways which also served as foundation stones. Drago saw rack upon rack of expensive wines which would sell for thousands on the open market. There was another section for fresh food stuffs; a third for tinned provisions; a fourth for game, the carcasses of rabbits and birds hung up to drain. Another alcove contained paintings removed from the house's walls. Yet another was crammed with old, cracked and dated crockery, some of it silver and gold plates from centuries back. It was a treasure house, a pantry and a rubbish tip put together. It was also a death trap. Against every supporting arch, every wall and ceiling dome was strapped an explosive charge, primed for detonation.

"What's happening?" asked Drago.

"A little fire to help them on their way," replied the bodyguard.

"What about the Comte?"

"The Krye has been very swift to rectify that situation."

"He's dead then."

"He will be. When Ferrara returns from the Honey Fields, we intend to kill them all. There was never any point in continuing the charade. It was good of Ferrara to still believe the Krye was on his side."

"He's never quite gotten the whole picture."

"Nor did Sada."

"And now no picture at all."

"No."

Drago scanned the basement. The bombs looked like small moulded bricks of clay fixed onto the cellar walls with thick black tape. He lightly pressed an index finger against one. It was malleable.

"Careful," said the man. "C4 mixed with black powder." He made a dumb-show with his hands to represent an explosion. "Big bangs."

Drago saw the detonators jammed into the clay, two electrodes, timed to deliver an electric charge, a shockwave which would set off the plastic explosives. These guys were experts, probably ex-army. They even had their own machine pistols strapped to their backs, M12s by the look of it. Drago had seen them in action at the gun club back home. Bloody lethal. He wondered where all this equipment had been stored on the yacht. A compartment in the hull do doubt. *Diamantin* clearly still had secrets to reveal.

There were three more men in the cellar. Two were fixing cables to the detonators. The third was standing with his eyes up to a pillbox slot which looked out of the cellar towards the main driveway. That must have been how they knew he'd arrived. The third man made a sharp gesture.

"Grigori!" he whispered. "It's them."

***

Atilla Ferrara saw the Mercedes and smiled thinly. This was an unexpected entrance from an unexpected quarter, although given Drago's ability to be a nuisance, it shouldn't have surprised him. It had been Drago's appearance in Sada's suite which had prompted the shooting at I Campi de Mielle. Alessandro had fought back intelligently and the assault had become more bloody than anticipated. Ferrara returned with eight men. He'd lost five good lieutenants, including Antonio. It was only the general complacency of Sada's guards that had finally turned the devil's luck his way.

Now, his sense of triumph was cut short. Seeing the V-Class made him doubt his own certainties. He'd left the youngest member of his team at Tarantella with specific orders to ensure the pharmacist administered the heroin. David ought to be here to greet him. Ferrara stepped out of the car. This had to be Drago's doing.

He gave orders to the men to enter the house slowly. It was difficult not to be hasty. The exhilaration of victory still pumped through his veins and that of his men, but the scene at Matera haunted him: Vito clinging to existence and Drago gone. He knew it was Sada even before Vito's last garbled words. Her intervention angered him. The Englishman had been his responsibility. It was the deal he made with Sabatini. Get Drago. Find out where he hid the diamond. Drago was nothing to do with the Capo. What was she doing interfering in affairs which didn't concern her? Sometimes Sada acted like the woman she was, like a mother admonishing her children. Women had no place in the Unione's business. They should be the supporters, the backbone of their men, keeping the family happy and fed, keeping the bed warm. That this Capo believed a woman could rule the great family of the Sacre Croce was as alien to Ferrara as it would be to venture from his own beloved Salentine. The heart of the Unione lay in the heads and bones and souls of men. Men who fought and killed. Men who loved and died. There was no place for a woman's compassion, her bargaining, her compromises. The welfare of the people was secondary to power. When they feared you, then you could improve their status, little by little, for a price. It never happened the other way around. What power had the Capo obtained with her good works? It was the same with Sabatini and his ridiculous charity; all those orphanages, such a waste of money and resources.

The first thing Ferrara was going to do was use the buildings for storing contraband. They all had attic space and some had basements. Ferrara himself had recommended the contractors involved because they were receptive to his demands as much as the architects. Another little project Sada knew nothing of. Sabatini too, he vouched. These imperial types needed to be taken down a rung or two, thrown off their marble pedestals and brought into the real world, the one Ferrara inhabited.

He was inside Tarantella now. His men fanned out through the building and the surrounding gardens. He wanted a quick clean kill. Drago's presence could work in his favour. The Englishman could be framed for the murder of the Comte d'Orsi. After all, it was Drago who stole the diamond, wasn't it? He had been caught casing the mansion. Inspector Gigli had even arrested him. Ferrara's teeth glinted in the last of the moonlight. The sky seemed to be getting darker by the second. He loosened his collar and went upstairs, one of his cohorts a pace behind. A hand seized his elbow. The man pointed. There was a splatter of blood on the floorboards. Breathing hard, Ferrara flipped on the lights. The entrance hall was suddenly bathed in white. It was a boot print. They could follow them all the way to the front door, lacking definition with each pace. A boot print, not a shoe. Whose? Where was David? Where was Drago?

Upstairs, the door to the Comte's bedroom was ajar. Ferrara stiffened as he approached. Everything was too quiet. Only the tap of leather soles of oak boards. He pushed open the door and it swung back to reveal the beautiful 19th Century room, a relic of the Kingdom of Sicily, a four-poster bed, cedar wood furniture enveloped with padded upholstery, heavy embroidered curtains, tapestries from ages past and the Comte, almost a relic himself, lying sideways on, breathing deeply. He was outside of the covers. The sheets were ruffled. Beside the bed, unseen until they'd walked in, was David's body, stretched out, the back of his head blown in, the front disintegrated.

"Drago!" hissed Ferrara. "Find him! Kill him!"

His companion disappeared to spread the order. Ferrara moved quickly to the bed. He grasped the Comte by the shoulder and shook the old man vigorously. The eyelids flipped up. The eyes stared at nothing.

"Atilla?" whispered the Comte. "Is that you? You've been shooting guns. I can smell it."

"Yes. A family affair."

"Whose family?"

"Yours."

There was a moment of delicious peace. It was like every other morning of the thousands of mornings Ferrara had spent in the Comte's bedroom. With sudden fury, the Comte's body whipped around and Ferrara felt the sharp stabbing thrust of the gun in his belly. He moved too late. The bang was louder than he expected. The bullet wrenched like a red hot poker. Ferrara jerked backwards, grabbing at one of the bedposts. The gun fired again and again, this time at nothing. The Comte reached forward trying to locate his target. Ferrara grabbed the wrist, hauled the old man off the bed and twirled him onto the floor. Ferrara stamped on the gun hand and kicked the weapon from the frail body.

"You bastard!" he cried. "Look what you've done!"

"Thief!" shouted the Comte. "Murderer!"

"As are many, old man! Why should I be different?"

"Your family were bastards," wailed the Comte. "Ambitious. Cunning. Self-serving. Devils for devils. How dare you betray the Unione! You are as much a bastard as your father. More so."

The Comte desperately sought the gun, his hands scratching on the floorboards, seeking something he had no hope to retrieve. Ferrara took great pleasure in watching the old man try. He winced at the injury, one hand staunching blood. With the other, he released the combat switch on his Tanfoglio pistol: ready to kill, but there was no rush.

***

Grigori, the leader, was urging his men to finish the work quickly. His lookout had seen nothing more which meant either the men were in the house or they were searching outside it. Someone would check the cellar soon. It was inevitable.

Drago watched them with tortured fascination. He didn't have much sympathy for the Comte, after all the old man had levelled accusations of theft at him; even so, killing him so cold bloodedly wasn't the answer either.

"You're not just going to let the old fucker burn are you?" he whispered to Grigori when the leader passed by.

"No. Sabatini's had us watching Ferrara for days. He doesn't trust him as far as he can smell him. When we saw him preparing to attack the Unione, well, we came calling here, told the Comte what was what. Sada's that man's niece remember. He's full of revenge now. Blood is blood. We shot the nightwatchman and gave the old man his gun. He wants to die –" Grigori paused and smiled as if he'd just understood the joke "– in a blaze of glory."

Drago nodded. Suicide, death and glory, just like those Roman heroes back at Sada's estate or maybe the fearless warriors of the Arabian nights whose strange palace Tarantella represented. Or perhaps it was all a kind of madness brought on by the spider's bite, the sound of fury and thunder, pumping blood, making it boil and steam, driving its body to the point of insanity until the music, the songs and the descants, the beautiful soothing wild words, until the blissful swirl of sanity purged the evil. Taranta. Tarantella.

The silent work was interrupted by gunfire. Immediately, Grigori issued orders and the other men abruptly curtailed the cat's cradle of a detonation sequence. They set the final timer, shovelled the remaining equipment into backpacks and made their way to the exit, unhooking the M12s from their shoulders.

"How do we get past whoever's out there?" asked Drago.

Grigori breathed deeply. He inspected Drago's outfit with one cursory glance. His men were kitted in black sweaters and trousers. Even their faces were wiped with black makeup.

"At least you've got shit on your clothes," he said. "We'll help you the best we can. We have to. The Krye will want to talk with you. If I brought him a corpse, he'd be most upset."

"Me too."

"Good boy." Grigori tapped Drago's cheek. "Watch. Learn."

The lead man eased the door open and stepped into the night.

He ran directly for the tree line, without a glance left or right. The second man followed. Drago was next up, Grigori hot on his tail. As he set off, Drago saw the second man stumble and fall. He made a single stubborn howl, forced out through clenched teeth. The sound alerted someone: a silhouetted figure far to the left. The third man both took hold of Drago and bundled him to the ground. Grigori kept running, scanning the mansion's rear and taking an angled route to the sanctuary of the pines. Drago saw a trio of attackers, moving across the wide path. On the half-turn, Grigori unleashed a volley of shots. Drago kept to the grass and gravel, head ducked into the grit. The third Albanian was half risen, shooting over the Drago's body. The death rattle of the M12s pierced the wooded arena. The Albanian wasn't moving. It was fatal. As his clip emptied, he was exposed and one of the attackers cut him down. He crumpled where he stood. Drago crawled on, charged by fear and urgency. He was almost in the forest. Among the gunfire and the shouting, he detected new dreadful, bellowing screams. The wild boar! They were loose. They were angry.

Drago didn't have time to worry about wildlife. Bullets pinged into the earth beside him and he jack-knifed into a sideways roll, got covered in dirt and bracken, buried by the foliage. More shells ripped the air, scything down those huge thistles, sending sharp leaves spiralling in all directions. He was back at Honey Fields. Back in the fucking shit.

It came not with a single bang, but with a series of ear splitting rumbles as the explosions cannoned through the walls of Tarantella. Almost simultaneously a series of billowing black and orange clouds spewed from the basement. Masonry, wood, bricks and mosaic tiles spun out of the inferno and landed dozens of metres away. Flames gushed as if from a volcano, lighting earth and sky, burning whatever they touched. The noise deafened. The result uncertain.

There was no sign of Grigori. Drago couldn't see any Albanians. Through the fire and brimstone, Drago made out the standing frame of the once magical villa, two and a half walls, the central dome partially collapsed. The inferno had ripped inside the carcass as if it was paper. Rubble was strewn everywhere. On the outskirts, Drago could make out severed limbs. Several boars were running amok in crazed alarm. One of them was ablaze, its back a mass of flame and smoke. The debris ignited the sun-dry grass. A huge chunk of one wall had been blown clear over the drive and buried the Mercedes. As he watched the blue flames suddenly turned white and the car disintegrated into a fireball of magnificent gold and grey. A superheated balloon of oil lashed out across the drive. The two Lancias were directly in its path. They too ignited. Seconds later they blew in spectacular fashion, one after another.

Drago could make out figures still engrossed in chaotic battle and there in among the shattered, burning remains of his home knelt the ailing Comte d'Orsi, one hand outstretched, half his body alight. Blind, angry, mad, all three. Agonisingly, engulfed in a monumental recreation of hell, the wilting pitiful figure collapsed and Ferdinand, 13th Comte d'Orsi, Il Padrino of the Unione Sacre Croce faded into the ashes.

The heat was pulverising. Drago moved into the forest. As he did, another silhouette made a haphazard, staggering try for the wooded sanctuary. The man was obviously in pain. He clung to his stomach, his clothes and face blackened, but the tall stride, even at a stumble, was unmistakeable. It was Atilla Ferrara. The usurper made it to the pines, paused and with a final look at the fiery building, disappeared into the tall shadows.

Drago set off at a run to catch him. Big thorns tore at his shirt, at his still coarse skin. His shoes slipped on sour ground, all that manure and crap and shit. The fire shed a dragon's glow across the forest, branches filtering orange light and grey smoke. Ferrara was just ahead. The bastard moved in short bursts, heading downhill and Drago knew where. He kept a fair distance and a minute or so later entered the little enclosure with the interlocking fallen tree trunks. Ferrara was on his knees, half inside the hollow, hooking out as many parcels as he could from the stash buried within. Drago calmly approached and gave Ferrara's backside a shove with his foot.

Ferrara was thrust into the cavity. Furious, he tried to wheel around. Drago was already pulling on his ankles. Angry at the Comte's death, angry at Sada's death, angry plain and simple, Drago wasn't thinking. As Ferrara's torso came free, so did his gun hand and the dead eye of the Tanfoglio stared at him once more.

Drago stepped away. The blooded figure struggled upright, leaning his backside against the trunk for support. Ferrara spoke in big uncomfortable pants.

"You really are an idiot, Drago."

"I'm not the one who's dying."

"You are about to."

"You won't get far with that heroin, Ferrara. The police will have you for sure this time."

"Money talks very loud. Somewhere in here I have hidden a few extra packages of the Unione's cash. I'll pay Madriano. I'll stay alive."

"Madriano?"

"The mayor."

"You think he'll help you now?"

Ferrara wheezed.

"Of course he will. I am the future. Not Sada or these fucking Albanians – me! I'll tell the story how I want the world to hear it. Madriano will believe me. I will be Capo. Padrino. I will lead the Unione, just how I always imagined it."

"Dreams never turn out how you imagine them."

"I have lived too long under the yolk to be denied power." Ferrara turned his eyes heavenwards. They rolled. His head lolled. He made a big effort to straighten. "Power, what all men crave. The power of gods. The power of life over death."

The Tanfoglio's gaze straightened. Drago felt his heart flutter as if the gun had whispered words of love, not death. The gunshot never came. Scared, fleeing from the fire and noise, the wild boars came trampling on mass through the forest, kicking and gouging anything in their way. A dozen of them, large and small, thundered into the copse and headed straight for the centre, straight for the fallen trees. If they knew Ferrara was standing there, they gave no indication. They didn't pause. They didn't swerve to avoid him. The monsters bulldozed their way into his legs. He fired two wild shots, screaming as he went down on broken limbs. He was at their mercy. The jutted hooves stamped on him. A tusk stabbed at his neck. Blood spurted. Screams echoed. Another final gunshot. The noise of the stampede didn't stop and neither did the screams.

Drago retreated back into the forest as the beasts poured past, steam hissing from their terrified flanks, their mouths and snouts making unearthly harrowing sounds. He stood, back pressed against a pine tree, chest catching shallow breaths, hoping the boars didn't spy him. When he was satisfied the charge was over, Drago edged out and followed the path the brutes had battered down for him. Soon he'd returned to what remained of the house. It resembled a huge fiery bird cage, just a skeleton outlined against the rolling orange flames. Slowly, wearily, Drago started along the driveway. He got no further than the exploded cars before Grigori appeared, his gun held steady.

"Did you kill him?" asked the Albanian.

"No. The boars got him first."

This seemed to amuse Grigori. A big grin split his features. It didn't distract him from the task in hand.

"Good. Now, you come with us."

He motioned with his hand that Drago should keep walking. The other two Albanians joined him. One of them was smoking, as if the battle was long gone, part of history already. Drago asked for a cigarette and one was lit and passed to him. God, he needed it. As they walked down the drive, there came a rolling shattering crash. Tarantella's dome had finally surrendered. The shell was nothing but a vast funeral pyre, the flames licking ever upwards. Nobody gave it anything more than a cursory glance.

The local population had begun to rouse themselves to what was happening on the hill outside town. There was no fire service in Santa Cesarea Therme, so they stood, worried, but immobile. The Albanians led Drago through the front gates and walked him down the avenues and alleys without holstering their weapons or paying any attention to the gathering which huddled the roadsides. The people knew life was about to change for them. The Unione Sacre Croce was no more.

The Albanians made it to a small jetty where one of the speed boats from *Diamantin* was tied. Finally, the guns were put away. The boat was untethered, the motor fired and the three men with their prisoner began a steady journey around the promontory, the town lit by the burnt butter glow of an inferno, ashes falling. A mile into the bay lay the yacht, all her lights on, a beacon beckoning them onwards.

Drago sat in the rear. The men didn't bother to restrain him. There was nowhere he could go, nothing he could do.

The launch nestled into the rear pontoon and the men started to disembark. One of them gestured for Drago to ascend the ladder. He did so, noting the hinged doors were being swung open from inside. The speedboat and the pontoon were going to be pulled into the stern. *Diamantin* was preparing for sail.

The deck was illuminated by the brilliant incandescent haze which poured from the huge stateroom. Once again, Drago ran his hand over the porphyry. It cooled him. The sweat and grime that trickled and clung to his broken skin seemed to evaporate at its touch as if an ancient incantation calmed him.

Standing in the centre of the room, a big tumbler packed full of ice and brandy in one hand and a fat Cohiba in the other, was Sabatini. He was dressed in a dinner suit, but the tie was loosened and the jacket discarded. Only the dramatic cummerbund hinted at formality. He took a long pull on the cigar and inspected the captive with his one good eye. Grigori spoke in Albanian, explaining quickly what had happened at Tarantella. Sabatini said nothing during the report, nodded and dismissed all the men except for Grigori who waited at the right side of Drago, his hands folded neatly in front of him. He'd handed over the M12 to a colleague, but there was still the pistol, tucked in his rear waist band.

Sabatini turned back to the cocktail bar and made a second brandy on the rocks, pouring from a bottle of Camus cognac. He returned and held out the glass to his prisoner.

"Welcome aboard *Diamantin*, Mr Drago," he said, but there was no smile. His eyes, one good, one dead, stared blank and dispassionate. The light caught the black opal and as it flashed, the jewel resembled the gates of hell itself, a pit of demonic frenzy buried among a countenance of hate.

Twenty Four

The Sweet Taste of Death

Sabatini held out the cognac to his guest. "Welcome, Mr Drago, and I suppose, a welcome surprise."

"That depends."

"A surprise only for me then."

Sabatini shook the glass and the liquor clung to the sides like Ligurian honey. The whiff of walnut and toffee apple was too good to resist. Drago took the offering and tasted. It was delicious, but stung his dry throat.

"This is very welcome."

"Eau-de-Vie." Sabatini swigged his own drink. "The water of life, Mr Drago. If nothing else, the French do have a beautiful term of phrase. There's nothing you can't solve over a cognac."

"That was Hemingway."

"Was it? I don't really care. I am not a scholar, but you, you are a writer, journalist, dancer, fist-fighter and, I dare say it, a killer. You seem to be a man with more hidden talents than a hundred Hemingway's. I feel I ought to make an impression. I feel you need to be intimidated."

"I respond better to a little cajoling."

The comment was lost on the big man, whose only reply was to suck loudly on the cigar. The cloud burst from his mouth and enveloped the space between them. Drago tasted coffee and dark chocolates. It mixed rather well with the cognac. He began to salivate.

"Nonetheless, I would like to parlay." Sabatini nodded to the row of leather sofas. "Do you have a moment to sit and talk?"

Drago felt the yacht shudder as the motors rumbled into life. He took another sip of brandy and felt *Diamantin* make the first small movement forward from her mooring.

"I don't appear to be going anywhere," he replied. "What do you want to talk about?"

Sabatini grinned. The opal eye blazed. He took a seat and balanced the cigar on an empty glass ashtray big enough to cope with its size. Drago placed his glass on the porphyry tabletop and sat on the same sofa, but as far from his antagonist as he could. Sabatini made a blunt gesture with his tumbler. The brandy slopped, spilt, but he made no attempt to clean it.

"I want to talk about power, Mr Drago, because that, more than any trinket, more than any amount of millions, more than any woman, is what I desire."

"I'm not an expert. It corrupts."

"It does. I am an example of it. Lust, greed, envy, all the great sins; all manifest themselves in power. I am a powerful man. I exert great power over my clan, the Banda Family. The family trust me. They do so from a strange mixture of choice and necessity and fear. That is subjugation. That is when true power has been discovered, not when a man bests another. When man triumphs in sport or battle, when he is financially successful, when he has attained a position of authority, these are trifling matters. No. It is when the people beneath you, the underlings, the insects, the vermin that chases the insects, it is when they recognise your status and autocracy, when you are to them a demigod, a breathing example of Solomon's wisdom and the Pharoah's menace, that is when power takes form. That is when all the sins you have accumulated, all the foul deeds and thoughts, the maleficence reveal themselves. That is the corruption you speak of, Mr Drago, the bile that creeps, erodes your soul, until there is nothing left, only control and fear. So now, despite the riches, authority and influence I wield, I still suffer lust and envy. I live with avarice, pride and anger, gluttony." He waved the cognac extravagantly and spilt it again. "Perhaps only sloth escapes me. Yes, it is power. That is what I crave because power ultimately gives a man control. If a man has control, he can do anything."

"But he isn't beyond the law."

"Whose law: Man's or God's?"

"That depends on whether you believe in God."

"Or whether you believe in power."

Sabatini's expression had grown vivid. His teeth bared when he spoke. He leant forward urgently every now and then, a rush of blood seeming to affect his every movement and thought.

"Think of it," he continued, "being master of others is the cradle I inhabit. I have them at my fingertips. They wait on my word. It is as if I am a general of an army and they are waiting for the signal to march. There is nothing which can be done within my world without my knowledge. There is nothing outside of it which I cannot have access. I will buy it. I will conquer it. I will steal it. Common people misunderstand power. They believe it resides in presidents and kings. It is that simple belief which denies them what they seek. My father understood that. He taught me how to master myself, to not stay beholden to fear, to strike not from cowardice, but from strength, to assert what I wanted above everything else.

"At this moment in time I am asserting exactly what I want. It is a route I should have taken a year ago when I recognised how fertile the Salentine was for selling heroin. I have thousands of tons of it, packed in warehouses in Durres. I decided to forge an alliance. My choice was not worthwhile. When a man decides he has many more masters, it is time to dissolve that relationship. Atilla Ferrara wanted power, but he misunderstood it. To him power meant money, not control, and hence he was out of control. He sought to steal from me in the same way he stole from the unfortunate Comte d'Orsi. He was lucky, of course, that Sada was too interested in the legitimate expansion of the Unione Sacre Corse to notice the problems of her estate.

"It does well to follow every avenue your conspirators take. I discovered how Ferrara obtained the money to pay me. He was not clever enough at covering tracks. I had my men follow his. A long trail which led from Tarantella to Melpignano to Bari and Via Roberto, where a tiny little man called Nrupal Patel extorts money from poor people and makes fake jewellery for people who cannot afford the real thing. He is in fact a very fine jewel-smith who once worked for a flourishing business in Madhya Pradesh. I'm not entirely clear why he chose to live in Italy, perhaps he was persecuted for being an untouchable. His life story doesn't interest me. What does is that he maintains good contacts with people who will pay great sums quickly for uncut Namibian diamonds. Nrupal Patel is a very simple man. He doesn't want trouble. He told me everything I needed to know about Ferrara and his people, that they are not professionals, that they are drug pushers, users, thieves, corruptible every-days. I, of course, only deal with the elite."

"Which is why you entered into an agreement with Sada," said Drago. The information seemed to take Sabatini by surprise. The big shoulders straightened. "Your problem now is there's no longer a Unione to work with. Atilla Ferrara's wiped them out."

"And my men have killed him and his phalange. I promised Sada I would do so in return for offering exclusive distribution of my heroin. I never renege on an agreement and that was two thirds of the agreement I made with the Capo."

"What was the other third?"

"That is where you come in, Mr Drago. There is a certain diamond I understand you have in your possession. It is a large red diamond, the rarest of stones. To Albanians it is known as the Blood Stone Poppy or Il Papavero. Sada allowed my men to steal it. I want to return it to Tirana. It would be a great gesture on the part of a future President of Albania, to discover the lost jewel of Skanderbeg, one of our greatest treasures. So, tell me where it is."

For the first time in a while, Drago took a sip of cognac. He replaced the glass carefully on the tabletop. It was very quiet in the lounge. He couldn't hear the engines, but he knew they were underway because the sky moved outside the windows. The shoreline, which he'd seen earlier, had vanished from the window scenes. The cigar sizzled. Drago studied the big man, his rough features, one dull eye, one blazing, a broad frame, muscle-tight, tense, eager, pernicious, those vulture features constricted.

"I think I'm the least of your troubles, Sabatini. Sada's dead. The old count is dead. Ferrara's dead. You can distribute as much heroin as you want, but every other Mafia family in the south is going to think you're responsible."

"A resolvable matter," smiled Sabatini. "The whereabouts of the diamond is not – unless you decide to tell me."

"Why should I do that? There'll be a reward for its return."

"There will: one which your friend might appreciate. What's her name? Madeleine is it? Think of it as a little compensation for her unfortunate accident."

"That's tempting, but no, there's something else."

Sabatini flinched. The big paw raised the cigar and his teeth clasped tight over the end. He tried to grin, but it was only the grin of a lion. Drago took another very slow sip of his drink. Lions don't smile. They only bare their teeth in anticipation of the hunt, the kill, the feed.

"I too made an agreement with Sada," Drago said. "She told me if I revealed the location of the diamond, she'd give me something very precious."

"Precious?"

"Ariana."

The cigar smoke hissed out like a snort from a bull's nostrils. Sabatini was all animal, from the piercing one-eyed hawk's stare to the coiled snakelike movements, the predator's grin to the arrogant horned toro. His brute body flexed. The muscles tightened under the suit. After a few seconds, he laughed. All his teeth shone. He stood up, downed his brandy and continued to laugh. Finally, Sabatini poured himself another drink and stabbed at the intercom.

"Novak?" he said. "Bring me the woman."

Drago sighed with relief, tried not to let Sabatini hear, but like one of those beasts the big man impersonated, he caught the release of tension, maybe in the ruffle of Drago's shirt or the stretch of his crinkled skin as he exhaled the one shallow breath.

"When I first met Ariana it was pure lust," said Sabatini. "She was a fresh, excitable beauty. It was an easy seduction. Keeping her was harder. She was not the easiest to control. For a time it was thrilling how she resisted. It was a great struggle to tame her. I even had to kill our child to ensure she never abandoned me. For a few years she was compliant. Then this wretched orphanage business reared its head. It was as if she'd forgotten what I made her. Those children," he paused and stubbed out the cigar angrily, "I never understood why she wanted children."

The rear doors opened and one of the crewmen entered. It was a woman, the cook Ariana had spoken about. Drago had seen Novak at the charity event, but not realised she was a woman. Novak was as rough and grim as the men. Behind her, tied by her wrists with a leash that also circled her waist was Ariana. She was naked. Her body was covered in ripe red blisters, fat ones the circumference of a cigar, some scabbed, raw and bleeding. She looked physically weak and stumbled over the threshold. Yet Ariana's eyes told another story.

"Jesus Christ."

Alarmed, Drago made a move to rise. Grigori quickly restrained him with a single hand. Drago winced as his burnished skin buckled. Sabatini ignored his guest. Instead, he looked viciously at Ariana.

"It appears, my dear, your saviour has arrived. Mr Drago wishes to buy you for a few simple lines of information. Cheaper than a rhumba, I venture."

"Get her some water, for God's sake," said Drago.

Sabatini gave a nonchalant wave. He swilled the cognac. Drago sensed the gangster's triumph. It made him queasy. He didn't want the bastard to win so easily, but he had nothing to bargain with, only an address. He could fake it, he thought, but to what purpose? Whatever fight he had was evaporating. The assassination of Sada, the funeral ashes of Tarantella, the mutilation of Ariana's beautiful skin, Madeleine's ruptured shoulder, his own baked epidermis, every injury was too much and the pain was piling up in waves against him. He felt the yacht gently rock for the first time.

Novak had poured water into a crystal tumbler. She loosened the ties and handed it to Ariana, allowing the captive to raise the glass. Ariana gripped it tight and took a single slow sip. She gave no indication of having noticed Drago. Her eyes were focussed entirely on Sabatini's back. Drago took the napkin from his trouser pocket and dropped it on the table.

"There."

Sabatini stepped over and reached to pick it up. Behind him, Ariana collapsed. The tumbler shattered against the edge of the table, its jagged remains still in her hand. Sabatini whirled. So did she. Drago saw the madness in her face. The glass ripped its way into the gangster's ankle, tore at the Achilles tendon. Blood spurted. Sabatini yelled. Both guards leapt to grab her. Drago jumped too. He intercepted Grigori before the bodyguard drew his gun. Drago struck out with a nihon, the balled fist crunching directly under the chin, lifting Grigori off his feet. A second blow collided with his temple. He spiralled to a heap on the floor. The woman had Ariana's hair and neck, but hadn't prevented a second attack. Sabatini screamed. He'd fallen to his knees, propped by the sofa. His legs gushed blood. Ariana attempted a third assault. Novak yanked her back. Drago swept up Grigori's gun and went straight to the screaming gangster. Releasing the safety button, he shoved the barrel straight in Sabatini's mouth and firmly ordered: "Stop it!"

Novak paused in her fight, uncertain what to do. Drago had a similar problem. He'd not reckoned on this. Ariana seemed as animal as Sabatini. On all fours, she wrestled free of the crewwoman and prowled towards her prey.

"Kill him!" she snarled.

"No!"

Sabatini's one good eye was alert to the twin danger. It fizzed between Drago and Ariana. Sweat bunched on his brow. His body jerked with the shock of having both ankles severed.

"Untie her," Drago ordered the crewwoman, who started to unpick the leash. As she did so, he pulled the gun from Sabatini's mouth, reversed it and cracked it hard on the base of the big man's skull. There was a thud as loud as a hammer and Sabatini lolled onto his side, his body still jerking, but unconscious. Once free, Ariana lunged for her tormentor. Drago, gun now pointing at Novak, caught her easily with his free arm. She was already sapping. Only her words remained defiant.

"We should kill him!"

"No!"

"Kill him!"

"Ariana, stop it."

She struggled, feebly.

"Stop it! Listen to me." Drago felt her weaken again and placed her backside on the marble table. She sank her head into her hands. Without taking his eyes off the crewwoman, without relaxing the weapon, he spoke urgently and forcefully: "Ariana, listen. Killing isn't going to solve anything. We've got work to do. Tie this woman up. I can't watch her and tie the others. Did you hear me?"

His bark broke through the suffering. Breathing hard, Ariana stared at Sabatini, her eyes like water. Then, propelled by Drago's words, she took up the rope.

Drago was impressed. Ariana must have watched the gangsters at work because she only used one end of the strap to tie the woman's wrists high up on her back, reducing leverage. When finished, Ariana pushed the woman to the floor and used the other end to secure the ankles.

While he watched, Drago had been calculating. Ariana had said there were nine crew including the woman and excluding Sabatini. Two of them were dead and he had two more trapped here. Captain Belzac must be on the bridge, probably with another. That meant there were three others unaccounted for.

"I can't see land," he said to Novak, crouching beside her. "Where are we heading?"

"Albania."

Drago frowned. He didn't have any use for this woman. If anybody could command authority, it'd be Grigori. He picked the napkin off the table and stuffed it roughly into her mouth. Next, he crossed to Grigori, stripped off the man's skin tight sweater and tossed it to Ariana.

"Put that on. Tell me, is there anywhere with rope or something so we can tie these bastards up?"

"We should be killing them."

"Maybe later. I want to get off this boat. We'll be safer on shore."

Ariana sniffed, wiped her eyes with the corner of a sleeve. The sweater dropped almost to her knees. "There's a utility cupboard on deck."

"Go and have a look, won't you? I'll wait here. Be as quick as you can, sweetheart."

If the endearment helped, Ariana didn't show it. She went back to the central lobby and Drago lost sight of her. He retreated to the rear of the lounge. No one was on the sun deck or the gangways. If there had been a moon, it had vanished behind ominous billowing thunder clouds. It was beginning to get choppy. The waves were rolling heavily against the hull and the yacht seemed to dip less elegantly through the wash. It hardly noticed in the main structure, where the size of the yacht obscured the movements, but outside he could see the weather lugging in. The black sky could have been an oil slick. He wondered if this was the same storm he'd encountered on the drive to Santa Cesare Therme, the rain clouds curling off the coast and following him into the Adriatic Sea.

Ariana returned with several metres of thin rope. Drago bundled Sabatini's hands and feet, fingers slipping on the still seeping wounded ankles. Now the blood red carpet was soaked in the real stuff. Ariana tied Grigori in the same fashion she'd secured the cook. There were some dish cloths behind the bar and they used them to plug the prisoners' mouths.

"What are we going to do?" she asked.

"How many men stay on the bridge when you're under sail?"

"I don't know. Two, usually."

"Good. I'm amazed we haven't been disturbed already. Where are the other crew – in the canteen?"

"I expect so."

"Does the door lock?"

"There's a master key." Ariana frowned. "Belzac has it."

"Not great."

Drago hefted the gun. He was vaguely familiar with it. A Beretta M9, the 'World Defender' of the U.S. military. A combat pistol with a semi-automatic mechanism and a short recoil, an ambidextrous safety, and a three dot sightline. The butt loaded magazine felt heavy, full. It would do the job.

"Let's get it anyway."

The boat rocked. Ariana clutched at his arm. The sea was getting rough. Together they went through to the lobby and went cautiously, silently up the spiral staircase. Drago heard voices. Poking his head above the perimeter he saw the bridge was in semi darkness. Most of the light came from the control stations, which blinked and winked and glowed with colour. Only the thin, oily haze of the night lamps provided brightness. Belzac stood to port, studying the weather system on the satellite scope, seeking clarification by staring out the forward windows. A helmsman was stationed at the main controls. There was no wheel. Steering was completed using a joystick. It had started to rain. Big clomping drops of it pounded the windshield and obscured the view. Two huge wipers were activated. Beyond the arc of the forward lights, the sea was pitch black. The bow lifted then crashed down. Bracing himself against the swell, Drago stepped forward.

"Stop!" he said loudly.

Belzac and the helmsman both turned. The Captain's eyebrows raised half an inch in surprise.

"You," said Drago, indicating the helmsman with a jerk of the M9. "Keep your eyes front."

The man didn't turn back. Ariana repeated the instruction and reluctantly the swarthy man returned fully to his post.

"Tell him what we've done," he instructed.

Ariana spoke quickly. Belzac nodded slowly.

"You speak English, Captain?" asked Drago.

"Yes. A little."

"A little is enough. Where are the other crew?"

"I can't tell. When the men came back from Tarantella, I expect they went to drink. It's normal."

"They'll be in the crew quarters then. Where's the master key?"

"You can't lock them in. It's against regulations."

"Fuck regulations. They're all killers. They'll understand."

Ariana was already walking towards a latched box on the wall. She flipped the catch and removed a bolt lock key.

"This is it, Jonathon. You stay here. I won't be long."

"Be careful."

Belzac sneered at him after she left. "Who is in charge, Drago: you or the woman?"

"Does it matter?"

The helmsman said something. Belzac replied with a chuckle. Drago told them to be quiet, but they kept talking. It was a test, Drago knew it. He ignored them. It didn't matter what they discussed. He needed to concentrate, keep the gun firm and keep them apart.

The ship took another roll. The outside entrance to the bridge was still open. Rain started to swirl under the canopy. Drago took up a position to one side of the stairs and the elevator, able to cover all three approaches and the two sailors. He tensed as the seconds crept by into long minutes. Eventually, his fingers sweating, Drago heard Ariana's feet padding on the stairs. He tensed, just in case surprise lurked. It didn't. The first thing she did was close the external door.

"I threw the key overboard," she said. "They were happy drinking. They didn't even notice."

"Good. Now, Captain, tell me our current location."

"We head for Durres. We are in the Otranto Strait."

"Okay. Turn the yacht around. Take us back to Italy."

"What if I refuse?" sneered Belzac. "You can't kill us. Who'll sail the ship?"

Drago squeezed the trigger once and the top of Belzac's shoulder exploded in a burst of blood. The bullet winged off across the cabin. Belzac collapsed against the instrument panel. The helmsman left his post to assist. Drago stopped him with one word and a wave of the Beretta.

"Eyes-front."

"He needs medics!"

"He's a big man. He'll do alright."

Nonetheless, Drago told Ariana to pull out the first aid kit. She kicked it across the floor and it bumped against Belzac's feet.

"Next time it's your head," said Drago. "Do what you can."

Secretly he was rather pleased as it gave the Captain something to worry about other than seamanship. Gingerly, Belzac opened the box and extracted gauze patches which he opened with his teeth.

"What's the other guy's name?" Drago asked Ariana.

"Petr."

"Petr, it's good to hear you speak English as well. Now, turn this yacht around."

There was a moment's hesitation before Petr slowly manipulated the throttle and the joystick to enact a shallow curve through the foul waters. There were digital displays on the forward panel representing the weather systems, sea charts and course navigation, all provided by GPS. The ocean ordnance survey which had shown the green coast of Italy at the bottom of the screen, rotated as they altered direction and reappeared at the top of the map. The compass revolved from south-south-east to north-north-west. The Strait of Otranto was the only avenue in or out of the Adriatic. Approximately forty-five miles wide, it was a busy stretch of water occupied by over a hundred transports at any time, most of them container ships, the rest were cruise liners heading for Venice or

Croatia, or pleasure yachts like this one.

"We were outrunning the storm," complained Belzac through gritted teeth. The bullet had torn clear through his shoulder muscle, but miraculously hadn't hit anything vital. He had scrunched up a handful of gauze padding, crammed it onto the wound and held it in place with a hand. "Now, you head us back into it."

"How long before we reach a safe haven?"

"Not long if the weather was good. In this, maybe an hour."

Drago thought he was stalling. The squall rattled the front windshield. They were heading directly into the storm. The light beams were half-blinded. The sea swirled in violent pools. Breakers cut across the bows and blew up fountains of inky sea water. A fork of lightning stretched across the sky, illuminating the whirling wreaking morass. He kept his forearm taut, the Beretta steady. Ariana stayed a pace away from him.

"We don't need a port," said Drago. "Just somewhere close enough to disembark. We'll take one of the speedboats." He glanced at one of the satellite maps. "What's that peninsula?"

"Costa a Sud di Otranto," replied Belzac. "A beauty spot near Ponta Palascia. Nobody lives there."

"That'll do then."

Belzac nodded. Ignoring the pain, he gave the order to Petr. He was still master of the ship and he had a responsibility to everyone on board even if one of them was holding him at gunpoint. The bullet wound had made up his mind. Sabatini was a good employer, but no employer was worth injury. His decision was based primarily on preservation.

Drago watched both men closely. He kept the Beretta trained between them, kept himself braced into the corner, maintaining balance as the yacht rose and fell. He glanced briefly at Ariana. She looked cold. The brief exaltation of the fight with Sabatini had worn off and now she was left with only her thoughts. He couldn't comprehend what they were. Maybe, he hoped, she thought about him.

Ariana was indeed thinking of Jon Drago. Jonathon. He wasn't like Sabatini. She knew that. Given reversed circumstances, Sabatini would have killed Drago without question. He was a threat and he had to be eliminated. Jonathon, for all his steeliness, didn't want to kill people. He had a fire in his belly, but it was ruled by his conscience not his fury. She liked that. He was determined. She liked that also. He did exude a certain roughness, as if some part of his life had always been that way, but he had also been gentle and fair. The combination was completely different to Sabatini who always projected malice and injected fear. Jonathon was not unlike Leo, her dance partner of old: firm, reliable, authoritative, maybe a little more aggressive. For a moment, she recalled the last time she'd seen Leo, how they had stood in the hotel foyer and embraced each other for minutes. He'd given up his dance career. He knew he would never find a better partner. If she wanted to travel the world with a rich benefactor, so be it. If it dragged her out of the mire of endless repetitive dances and endless obscene propositions, so be it. If Sabatini took care of her, so be it. She wondered if Leo understood what she had done in order to maintain such a life. She wondered if he would reject her, even as a friend. One day, soon, she might visit him, but she would never tell her story, not unless he asked. If he asked, she'd have to be honest. She could never lie to Leo. He knew her too well. And so, Ariana thought, did Jonathon. She could never lie to him, even if her life depended on it. He didn't deserve to be deceived. She'd tried already and failed. She stole a glance his way. The agile figure, almost elegant when it walked, like a panther; now coiled like a spring waiting to unfurl, waiting to release unbridled energy. The stern face, fixed on its task and targets, a scar here or there, even with the horrid black burnt blemishes on his skin, another series of scars he didn't comment on. They had to be from some awful torture, she supposed. She rubbed her arms, remembering her own injuries, the blooded burns. She hoped all their skins would heal. Perhaps then, she might see Jonathon smile again, that amused, delicate grin. It suited his demeanour. Why had she seen it so rarely? Even on the dancefloor, he'd stayed serious, reserved. When he smiled, it lit his face, banished the world which weighed heavily on his shoulders so his Atlas frame could straighten and steady. She saw the certainties that lay behind the off-centre, cheeky adult twinkle. Jonathon. Jon Drago. He liked to be called Jon. Maybe she should try to call him that: Jon. No, she couldn't. It didn't suit him; not when she was with him. Jonathon

– yes, much better – Jonathon was definitely not Sabatini.

"Jonathon," she whispered.

"Yes."

"Thank you."

It was the first thing either of them had said for some time. It distracted Belzac who was propped in a pilot's chair watching the GPS navigation systems as well as using his own eyes to assist the helmsman. Another wave threw over the bow. This was madness. The windspeeds had to be tipping thirty-five or forty knots. It was a tropical type of storm, unusual in the Adriatic, but not unheard of. The tightness of the channel and the steep shores on both sides meant occasionally bad weather systems got caught in the strait as they slid off the high surrounding hills. This was one such occasion. Thunder and lightning erupted every few seconds, inching closer.

Drago could tell from the changes in the satellite images that *Diamantin* was nearing their destination. Now, much depended on Belzac and how close he could come to shore. It would be an almost impossible journey in the speedboat. A hard ask for any seaman. Drago squinted into the blackness. Conditions were getting worse. The water was cascading in bigger and bigger waves, almost as if the sea wanted to bury the yacht for having the temerity to be at sail. As he watched, a huge wave suddenly appeared at close quarters. It rose higher than the yacht. Neptune must have risen from the depths and cast it. Instinctively, Drago shrunk into the corner. The wall of water crashed onto the starboard side, bombarded the battered bridge and swamped the windows. *Diamantin* tipped alarmingly to port. Everyone was tossed off-balance. Petr lost his footing, the controls went untended. Ariana made a grab for Drago. The two of them tangled, all legs and limbs. Belzac launched himself for the abandoned steering column. Petr, on a knee, took in the situation with a single glance. Drago's gun arm was dropped.

Petr leapt across the bridge in a bound. He crashed into his jailors, his long arms trying to encircle them both. The M9 was stuck under Petr's arm. Drago tried to pull if free. Petr grabbed the gun barrel. Ariana was on the man's back, fingers gouging. Drago's wrist twisted as Petr tried to yank the gun out of his hand. Desperate, he kicked out, focussed on holding the trigger guard. He missed it and yanked the lever down. The Beretta fired. Ariana screamed. There was a bang like an axe chopping wood. The windshield snapped. The crack fanned out erratically, a spider's web of jumbled lines accompanied by sharp, smacking sizzles, the snarling, spitting echo of a forest fire. Tiny splinters of glass burst out of the curved pane.

Diamantin tipped again. The window offered a long agonised groan. Out of the blackness, on a direct collision course, came another massive tidal wave. The onslaught was like an explosion. The sound penetrated Drago's whole body. It was a living, booming thing, a sepulchral resonance that burned and punched and screamed and obliterated the windshield. The sea crashed over the little stage in a second, a tumult of foam and slime and salt water. It came like a massive boulder, thrusting forward, smashing everything in its path. Glass, wood and air exploded. The pilot seat buckled, crushed by the ferocity of the onslaught. Belzac was flung aside as if hit by a cannonball. Drago felt the tsunami boil over him in one solid mass. It stung a thousand times. His skin was hot with the pain. His head was buffeted. He hit something. A shard of glass scythed angrily at his chest. The skin tore. Blood spiralled. Everything hurt. Everything bruised.

They'd all been lifted up and deposited on the far side of the cabin. Water rushed down the stairwell. The yacht was listing. Everyone was slipping and skating and rolling in seawater. The lights flickered. Died. Recognising the danger, Petr tried to return to the helm, one arm hooked around the pilot's seat. The yacht tipped the opposite way. Everything slid. Belzac seemed out cold, his head skewed angrily sideways. Drago tried to find the Beretta. There it was, skidding in a corner, swimming with the sea. He launched his body across the cabin, slithered to a stop and scooped up the M9. He was on one knee, his eyes suddenly taking in the two sea drenched figures climbing the last steps, machine pistols raised.

Grigori and Novak.

God knows how they'd untied themselves. Without a pause, the guns blazed. Bullets whipped through the chaos. The sea still thundered in the cockpit. Instinctively, Drago flattened himself, spreadeagled on the floor and fired blindly. Ariana screamed again. She was huddled like a baby. Pain. Screams. Rain. Thunder.

Lightning. Hell on bloody earth. Bullets. Snapping, whacking, whip-bang, crunch and crack. Petr toppled. The yacht's control desk was a mess of broken metal. Drago kept shooting until the chamber rang empty and the machine pistols dropped.

Suddenly, with a tremendous heave, *Diamantin* tipped up at the bow. There was an enormous wrench accompanied by a metallic howl. The hull was being ripped to shreds. For a few seconds, the yacht kept moving forward, unstoppable under her own momentum, then almost with a sigh, *Diamantin* came to a shuddering halt. The whole structure creaked. Drago groaned and got to his knees. He scrambled over to Ariana, seized an arm and shook her for attention. She was sobbing.

"We've run aground," he shouted. "It must be the Sud. Come on!"

He pulled her to her feet, caught her anxiously staring at the destruction. Uninterested in her cries, Drago sloshed Ariana through a brine laced with blood and bone and bodies.

They struggled down the stairs. *Diamantin* had pitched at an alarming angle. They almost had to climb across the foyer to exit on deck. They used the rail to stay upright. Shattered by the monsoon, charred by biting cold, doused by waves, they fought a path to the stern. Out in the pitch black, he could make out the other crew, life vests on, beacons flashing. Somehow they'd already escaped only to be assaulted by the storm. The stateroom lights buzzed and fizzed, extra crackles to add to the bolts and forks that struck the devil's sky. The sea battered remorselessly against the once magical yacht. *Diamantin* was wedged on an underwater reef, one which struck out unseen from the peninsula. Given daylight or good weather and without distractions, Belzac would never have collided with it.

"Where are the life belts?" he asked.

"The guardrail."

Drago started across the exposed rear deck. With no warning, two huge hands gripped him like a vice. A stiletto blade, thin as a rapier, sharp as a needle, stabbed at his chest and stuck.

Sabatini roared in his ears. Ariana screamed. She lost balance and slid down the deck coming to halt bunched against the barrier, swilling in the livid surf.

Only the devil knew where Sabatini's strength came from. His ankles had to be busted for life. He must have hauled his way across the stateroom, hand over hand, onto the deck, determined to get his quarry. The last reserves of his fury came mounting an attack of wicked, concentrated frenzy. The two men grappled. The big hands wrapped themselves on Drago's throat. There was a rope between Sabatini's fingers, the same one he'd been tied with. He was trying to tighten a noose. The two men staggered and scurried on the angled floor, wrapped in each other like angry lovers. Drago clawed at the remaining eye. With a curse, Sabatini broke his hold, fought him, tried to punch. Drago wriggled free and attempted to get behind Sabatini, hand on his neck, knee in his spine. Among the sounds of fighting and thunder and water, Drago heard another crack. The hull gave again. Sabatini thrust elbow after elbow into Drago's midriff until, bruised, winded, sucking in salt air, face littered with rain, Drago pushed the bastard away. Sabatini staggered on the uneven surface. His ankles couldn't take his weight. Drago landed one vicious uppercut and sent the body sprawling.

Diamantin lurched once more. Drago grasped a rail. Sabatini was on his knees, legs finally beaten. Behind the hulking figure, Drago saw Ariana. She was lifting a big metal cylinder. Fascinated, unable to move, Drago watched as she released the pin and jammed her hands on the plunger.

Ice cold CO_2 shot out of the fire extinguisher in a vicious cloud. Sabatini switched madly left and right. His face and head and shoulders became a crackled, frozen mess. He was suddenly totally blind. Ariana took aim again and unleashed a second volley of gas directly into Sabatini's face. The huge figure bellowed. He tried to wipe the acid away. He failed. Instead, he veered onto his side and came to rest by one of his own porphyry tables.

Drago dragged himself over. He grabbed Sabatini's wrists and used the rope to bind the gangster again, this time to the table legs. Fixed to the deck, the man was immobile, but even weak, blind and insane, Sabatini still tore at his bonds.

"Come on," Drago said urgently. He went to retrieve the life belts. "We need to get off this wreck before she breaks."

Ariana couldn't move.

She stood staring at the big screaming body lashed to its tombstone. Horrified, she felt pain and pleasure and petrifying fear, but her heart, however poisoned, beat strong and fast, a rhythm created by the madness and frenzy of a violent stampede, a sound which could purge the body of evil. It was not the beat of the taranta. It was one of worldly spirits, of good angels who watched over you: Drago's blooded hand took her arm and drew her away from the sweet taste of death.

Twenty Five

The Right Moment

While Drago embarked on his final confrontation with Marcelo Sabatini, across the other side of Europe a package was being prepared for delivery. The Italian postal service did occasionally get things right. The package Jon Drago had wrapped and addressed in Bari was now in North London, loaded on a delivery van and awaiting its final destination.

It was the courier's lucky day. Abbey Scott had been feeling under the weather and had phoned the office to inform them she was ill. The double ring on the bell annoyed her. Nonetheless, she pulled on a dressing gown large enough to contain two of her and waddled downstairs. She opened the front door just as the young man decided he'd have to write out a collection slip. Abbey signed for the package. It was surprisingly light and the weight seemed to shift inside the box depending on how she held it. Abbey went to the kitchen, picked up the pearl handled letter opener, a family heirloom bequeathed by her late grandmother, and sliced into the tape which bound the brown paper.

Inside she discovered the cardboard box and the long essay from Jon Drago. She immediately recognised the handwriting. You didn't live in the same student digs, read each other's essays and exchange Christmas cards forever without knowing your best plutonic male friend's calligraphy. It was messy. The 'f's looked like 't's and the 's's like 'r's.

"Oh, God, Jonathon," she murmured. "What have you gone and done now?"

The letter explained it. At the end, Drago requested Abbey took the contents of the box to Professor Paul Gainsborough, Head of Antiquities at the British Museum, a mutual friend. It wasn't the Professor's era of expertise, but he was the best placed person Drago knew to look after it. Only then did Abbey remove the crinkled newspaper pages.

At the very moment Drago and Ariana were urgently being treated by paramedics, the beach awash with his blood and her tears, Abbey Scott was staring into the deep crimson haze of a perfect red diamond: Il Papavero.

***

The ice cool edge of the tumbler touched his forehead. Jon Drago sighed. It was three weeks later.

Drago and Ariana were airlifted to the Il Citta Hospital. They were in a terrible state. The doctors informed Drago his battered body would be as good as new once his muscles decided to reform. The knife wound had not been deep. There wasn't much to be done about the sun burn. Time would heal that. Everything certainly looked unhealthy when they finally took off the bandages. Meanwhile, Ariana was being treated for the cigar burns, ugly sores which plagued her once flawless skin. She also suffered from post-traumatic stress, or so the doctors claimed. Paulo Vicino had other notions. He told Drago the girl was simply in love.

"And we all know with who," he said with a wink. "I'll see if I can get you two some private nursing."

The architect was back from his vacation. Once he'd heard Drago's story, tactfully embellished by Paulo, he offered them a new build further along the coast, a bungalow perched above a quiet secluded bay. Paulo supplied a junior chef from the restaurant. People came and went for days; Paulo, his mother, journalists, Reverendo Lampedusa, lastly and most worryingly Inspector Gigli. The Inspector was conducting the investigation with the coastguard. Drago and Ariana refused to discuss anything until representatives from their respective embassies were present.

The Albanian was a small, pale pinched man. Most of the talking was done by the British representative, a bureaucratic, tedious official named Toby Roberts. He wore the Inspector down with his officious behaviour and constant diplomatic legal jargon.

"It's obvious Signor Drago knows something of what has

occurred," blustered the frustrated Inspector. "I suggest, when he decides to tell me, that we make an appointment, an unofficial appointment. I have been instructed to construct a plausible story for the insurance companies, the judge, the newspapers." He paused dramatically and ran his finger down his cheek. "Even the Unione."

"Signor Drago will offer any assistance through this office," stated Roberts, "as I am certain my counterpart from Tirana agrees."

The Albanian nodded. There seemed to be an unwritten agreement between them that Roberts would do all the talking.

"I'd welcome some co-operation," sighed the Inspector. His mobile phone rang and he looked at it with a grimace. "You are making my life extremely awkward and my wife doesn't like it."

Gigli left with a resigned shrug. After a week, the visits ceased. Finally, protected on three sides by hills and forests, Drago and Ariana found something of solace.

The house only had five rooms, two bedrooms on either side of a massive lounge, the kitchen and bathroom to the front. The back of the property was bordered by a wooden terrace which faced the sea. Steps led to a winding path and a secluded beach. It was cool most of the day. The big overhanging carobs formed canopies of shade and bright cheerful birds paid regular visits, humming and cooing in the branches.

Drago spent most of the time on the terrace. He read, slept and ate. Twice a day, he swam. The battles had worn him. Exhausted, his body gave itself to apathy. The freshness of the place brought him painfully to life. His state of mind was not helped by Ariana, who stayed nervously pensive, yet talkative, constantly gabbling about something or anything, worrying what the chef was going to cook and why they even needed a chef at all. At first, Drago found it irritating, but as his mind was shot through, he resigned himself to her fussy nature. It felt good not to make decisions and let somebody else take the strain of living. The only choices he took were two discreet phone calls. One to Madeline during which he tried to explain as much as he could without horrifying her, and another to Abbey Scott asking her to visit Maddie with the long letter of explanation.

After a few days, Drago found Ariana's presence homely, as if she'd always been there, watching out for him. He noticed, with some curiosity and a lot of pleasure, that she didn't ask questions. To her, everything just was. She'd sunbathe all morning and swim with him in the afternoon. They were happiest snorkelling in the bay, spiralling in the clear warm waters, two silent human fish among hundreds of tiny amphibians.

In addition to the chef, Paulo had organised a middle-aged, chubby, fat-fingered nurse to fuss over them. She loved her charges from the first and couldn't understand why such a handsome couple slept in separate beds. Every evening for the first week, the nurse tutted and tittered her disapproval, but said nothing, as mannered women do in the Salentine. The sleeping arrangements bothered Ariana too. This evening, she'd dismissed both the nurse and the chef.

Drago sighed at the chill and opened his eyes. The sun was setting fast and the last vestige of pink sky was turning to black. Ariana stood over him. The glass in her hand contained something which smelled like a Scotch and American. Ice cubes rattled. She was dressed in an ivory white, knee-length sarong, dark hair tumbling over naked shoulders, a nervous smile on her lips.

"Our angels have deserted us at last."

"Good," said Drago. "What's this?"

"You haven't had a drink since we've been here. The doctors didn't ban it. Anyway, there's nothing to say you can't drink on antibiotics. That is a medical myth."

"Is that so?"

Drago smiled, took the glass and sipped. He noticed the tiny crease on her forehead, where the eyebrows met above her pretty nose. Ariana was brooding again; he'd come to recognise the expression. She took his free hand in hers.

"I'm glad we're here together," she said. "The doctors have told me I don't need to be looked after anymore. I need counselling, they said. I told them I didn't want that. I told them you'd give me all the counselling I need. I said, even if I didn't need looking after, you did, and I'm more than happy to do it, Jonathon. We can heal each other."

"That would be wonderful, Ariana."

Drago's fingers curled tighter around her hand. Slowly, deliberately, she took his hand and placed it on her breast. Drago felt the point harden under his palm.

"You haven't made love to me, Jonathon."

"I've been waiting for the right moment."

Ariana took the hand away from her bosom and kissed it. She unhooked the sarong. She was nude, shining with anticipation. The darkening light cast shadows across her skin and disguised the burn marks on her body. Drago put down the glass and pulled her towards him.

"Keep the lights off," she whispered. "I'm still sensitive about the scars."

"I understand."

"Now, my darling, is this the right moment?"

Drago kissed her beautiful, flat belly. It fluttered beneath his touch. Her wide mouth broke into a gorgeous broad smile.

"Yes," he said. "I think it might be."

Printed in Great Britain
by Amazon